Praise for

BELLA AND THE BEAST

"Once more, Drake proves the right pair of shoes can change your life—especially if they're red and belong to the Cinderella Sisterhood. This story is both charming with its light, fairy tale–based plotline, and intriguing with the dark, underlying Gothic twists. This is the perfect quick, pick-me-up read." —*RT Book Reviews*

"An intriguing and passionate story full of history and tingling romance . . . another winner by author Olivia Drake." —*Romance Reviews Today*

"Lush historical romance, complete with all the sprinklings of a fairy tale. Olivia Drake is an excellent writer, and this story knows how to submerge readers completely." —*Fresh Fiction*

ABDUCTED BY A PRINCE

"Drake will have readers believing in the magic of not only a pair of shoes, but also love and the joy of finding your soul mate." —*RT Book Reviews* (4½ stars)

"I am a huge fan of the 'Cinderella Sisterhood.' This novel is the enchanting third book in the series, and author Olivia Drake has kept the series very much alive with lots of heartwarming romance, and enough spice to warm even the coldest nights." —*Night Owl Reviews*, Top Pick

STROKE OF MIDNIGHT

"Drake's flair for mystery blended with humor and passion will delight readers . . . utterly enchanting."

—*RT Book Reviews*

"A compelling romance filled with intrigue."

—*Affaire de Coeur*

"Another wonderfully written novel by Olivia Drake."

—*My Book Addiction*

IF THE SLIPPER FITS

"Filled with romance, breathtaking passion, and a dash of mystery that will leave you wanting more."

—*Night Owl Reviews*

"A dash of danger and a dash of fairy tale in the form of a very special pair of shoes add to the romance plot, filling out *If the Slipper Fits* nicely." —*Romance Junkies*

"Cinderella knew it was all about the shoes, and so does master storyteller Drake as she kicks off The Cinderella Sisterhood with a tale filled with gothic overtones, sensuality, sprightly dialogue, emotion, an engaging cast, and a beautiful pair of perfectly fitting slippers."

—*RT Book Reviews* (4 stars)

"I was enchanted with this story as Olivia Drake took the residents of Castle Kevern *and* this reader on an emotional, delightful journey. A magical fairy tale deserving to be read and read again!" —*Once Upon a Romance*

THE
Scandalous
FLIRT

OLIVIA DRAKE

St. Martin's Paperbacks

This is a work of fiction. All of the characters, organizations, and events portrayed in this novel are either products of the author's imagination or are used fictitiously.

THE SCANDALOUS FLIRT

Copyright © 2017 by Barbara Dawson Smith.

All rights reserved.

For information address St. Martin's Press, 175 Fifth Avenue, New York, NY 10010.

ISBN: 978-1-250-06031-0

Our books may be purchased in bulk for promotional, educational, or business use. Please contact your local bookseller or the Macmillan Corporate and Premium Sales Department at 1-800-221-7945, ext. 5442, or by e-mail at MacmillanSpecialMarkets@macmillan.com.

Printed in the United States of America

St. Martin's Paperbacks edition / November 2017

St. Martin's Paperbacks are published by St. Martin's Press, 175 Fifth Avenue, New York, NY 10010.

10   9   8   7   6   5   4   3   2   1

Chapter 1

The merest breath of scandal can ruin a lady.

—MISS CELLANY

If Lady Milford hadn't received a last-minute invitation to dine with a member of the royal family, she might never have gone to the bank so late in the day. And she would never have found the next young lady who deserved to wear the enchanted slippers.

As she entered the bank, Clarissa shivered from a blast of chilly April wind. Heavy clouds darkened the skies and hastened the onset of dusk. It would be a good night to remain at home in front of a fire. But she was not yet so ancient as to huddle in a rocking chair with a rug over her knees. Besides, one did not ignore a summons to St. James's Palace. Nor did one wear ordinary jewels like those she kept in a strongbox at home. This grand occasion called for her most prized tiara.

Gas lamps had been lit inside the bank. The light cast a warm glow over the polished oak counters along the walls, and the caged stations where tellers served the last few customers. It was nearly closing time.

A middle-aged bank manager in a black suit swooped toward Clarissa. A set of keys jangled at his stout waist. He bowed, revealing sparse brown hair combed over a balding pate. "My dear Lady Milford. How may I assist you?"

"Good afternoon, Mr. Talbot. I should like to access my deposit box."

He ushered her toward a door where she paused to sign the register before entering the vault with its walls of iron drawers. Selecting a key from his ring, Talbot unlocked a numbered strongbox, carried it to a small private chamber, and set it on a table. Then he left Clarissa alone with her valuables.

The box contained various legal documents along with a selection of her costliest jewels. Picking up a black velvet pouch, she opened the drawstring to gaze down at a magnificent tiara. Diamonds in a honeycomb pattern winked in the golden light of the lamp. The centerpiece was a large teardrop diamond in a rare violet hue. It was a perfect match for her eyes . . . or so her dear prince had proclaimed upon giving her the tiara all those years ago.

A wistful smile played upon her lips. How she missed him. He had been her ardent lover for too brief a time . . .

She tucked the tiara into her reticule. Her mind occupied with nostalgic memories, she stepped back into the main vault to inform the manager that she was done. All of a sudden, the door to an adjoining private chamber burst open. Someone rushed out at her.

Clarissa had only half a second to brace herself before the stranger collided with her. She managed to maintain her balance, but her assailant was not so fortunate.

The woman stumbled backward into the door frame. A little box slipped from her kid-gloved fingers and fell with a crash. The golden casket sprang open and a strand of diamonds spilled onto the black marble floor.

"Oh, gracious!" she squeaked.

She bent down to snatch up the casket, stuffing the necklace back into its velvet-lined container. She was a rather buxom woman draped in the latest stare of fashion: a hip-length mantle in claret cashmere over an apple-green gown with several rows of ruffles circling the hem. The gauzy veil of her bonnet partially obscured her features, but as the woman stood up, Clarissa could see sausage-curled fair hair, wide blue eyes, and mature features.

There was something familiar about that face . . .

The woman dipped a quick curtsy. "My lady! I—I do beg your pardon." With that, she hurried out of the vault and into the lobby of the bank.

My lady. Clarissa could only presume the woman had recognized her. Who was she?

Clarissa followed at a more measured pace, her gaze fixed on the stranger ahead of her. The swift clicking of the woman's heels echoed in the high-ceilinged chamber. She appeared agitated, almost nervous. A guard opened the door and she vanished from the bank.

Mrs. Kitty Paxton. Yes, that was her name.

Although Clarissa knew everyone in society, she had only a nodding acquaintance with Mrs. Paxton. They moved in different circles, not merely because of Clarissa's elevated stature as the widow of an earl, but because she preferred to converse about weighty topics like politics and literature. Mrs. Paxton was a shallow gossipmonger who could speak only of fashion and the latest tittle-tattle. Her daughter recently had become engaged to the Duke of Whittingham. Clarissa had seen the betrothal announcement a few days ago in the newspaper.

Heading across the bank lobby, she frowned. There

had been an older daughter, too, hadn't there? A step-daughter who had made her debut some seven or eight years ago . . . Miss Aurora Paxton.

Clarissa recalled a lively debutante with glossy black hair and sparkling brown eyes, one of those rare girls blessed with both beauty and wit. In spite of her modest dowry, she'd possessed a vivacity and charm that had attracted a bevy of gentlemen admirers. She had exhibited a generosity of spirit, too. Clarissa recalled an incident at a ball when another girl had tripped and fallen on the dance floor, and Miss Paxton had been the first to rush to her aid, offering friendly chatter to allay the girl's obvious embarrassment.

Miss Paxton should have received numerous marriage proposals. Yet something had happened in the middle of the season. She had become entangled in a scandal with a foreign diplomat and had been banished for her indiscretion. Clarissa had never again glimpsed the girl in London society.

Where had Miss Paxton gone? What was her situation now? Had she been consigned to the dreary life of a disgraced spinster?

A spark of interest energized Clarissa. Given her own experience with a stepmother, she had a natural empathy for the girl. She knew what it was like to be unloved, unwanted, abandoned. Long ago, upon the death of her well-to-do father, Clarissa had been exiled by her stepmother to the kitchen to work as a servant. One night, a gypsy beggar had come to the back door. Clarissa had taken pity on the poor woman and fed her a hot meal, and in return had been given a pair of enchanted slippers that would lead the wearer to her true love. The shoes had certainly worked well for Clarissa and her prince. Ever since, she had made it her mission to help deserving girls in difficult situations.

Miss Aurora Paxton was the perfect prospect. Now would be a good time to have a word with Mrs. Paxton about the fate of her missing stepdaughter.

Clarissa hastened out of the bank. The dark clouds spat out a few icy raindrops as she glanced up and down the road. At this late hour, traffic had slowed to a trickle. Only a few hackney cabs rumbled over the cobblestones. Workmen headed home after a long day's labor, and the local shops were closing for the night. A lamp man trudged along the pavement, lighting the occasional gas lamp, the golden orbs shining through the fine mist.

Only a minute or two had elapsed. Yet Kitty Paxton was nowhere in sight.

Clarissa proceeded to the carriage parked at the curbstone. The coachman sat on the high seat, hunched in his greatcoat. Another servant stood by the carriage door, his shoulders squared, his husky form ramrod stiff. A thatch of salty cropped hair topped his weathered face.

Clarissa stopped in front of him. "Hargrove, did you see a veiled woman depart the bank just now?"

"Indeed, my lady."

"Where did she go so quickly? I don't see any other carriages, only hackneys."

"She was on foot."

"Walking? In this neighborhood? Why, Mrs. Paxton had a valuable necklace in her possession!"

"She went around that corner." He inclined his head toward the left. "Shall I follow her?"

"I'll accompany you."

They started down the street. Clarissa was glad for Hargrove's presence. He was more than a butler; he was her most trusted servant. She always brought him along whenever she visited the bank. With his military background, he served as her bodyguard and even her spy from time to time. He could be depended upon to use the utmost discretion.

Disquiet coiled in the pit of her stomach. Mrs. Paxton ought to know better than to proceed on foot in a business district at this hour. Ruffians abounded in the city. Something wasn't right, and Clarissa felt an obligation to assure herself of the woman's safety.

They turned the corner. Shadows cloaked the deserted side street. At the far end, a carriage and coachman waited. Perhaps the vehicle belonged to Mrs. Paxton since she was nowhere in sight.

"We must have missed her," Clarissa said, disappointed. She would have welcomed the chance to inquire about the woman's disgraced stepdaughter.

"There," Hargrove muttered. "By those bushes."

Stopping beside him, she peered down the street. A buxom figure lurked in the gloom underneath a tree. Clarissa would never have noticed without Hargrove's sharp eyes.

As they watched, Mrs. Paxton bent down to slip an object underneath the shrubbery. The dull glint of gold revealed it to be a small box. Then she scurried away down the street and stepped into the waiting carriage, which departed to a clattering of wheels.

"What on earth?" Clarissa said. "That must be her diamond necklace. I recognize the box."

How very peculiar. Why would Mrs. Paxton leave a costly piece of jewelry under a bush? And behave in such a clandestine manner? Was that the reason she had seemed so agitated inside the bank?

No sooner had those thoughts flitted through Clarissa's mind than the cloaked figure of a man emerged from a nearby building. At once, Hargrove drew her into the shadows of a doorway. The fellow snatched up the gold box and slipped it into his pocket, then hurried away.

"He's stealing it!" she exclaimed as he vanished from sight.

"No," Hargrove said. "It was left for him. A payment, possibly."

"Do you mean blackmail?"

"Perhaps. Shall I go after him, my lady?"

Clarissa thought for a moment. Into what manner of intrigue had they stumbled? "No. We shan't interfere. Better I should call on Mrs. Paxton tomorrow and find out what I can."

And hopefully she could use the incident as leverage to bring Miss Aurora Paxton back to London.

Chapter 2

*Gossips gleefully whisper their tittle-tattle
with little care for the lives they ruin.*

—MISS CELLANY

"Aurora Anne Paxton, wait! You mustn't toss that out!"

The raspy voice came from behind Rory. She had just lugged an old spinning wheel down from the attic. Setting the heavy burden at the head of the staircase, she turned to see Aunt Bernice hurrying out of her bedchamber.

Bernice must be truly distressed. She only called Rory by her full name when she meant business.

They had spent the morning engaged in a spring cleaning of the garret. Their purpose was to find items to donate to the upcoming jumble sale at the village church. Despite the work of several hours, however, the pile of castoffs in the foyer below remained pitifully small.

Bernice had trouble discarding anything. Threadbare petticoats were cut up for handkerchiefs and dust rags. Candle stubs were melted to create new tapers. Broken chairs and shelves were chopped up for firewood. Bernice's thrifty nature was as much a part of her as the robust figure clad in cheap black bombazine. A tall woman, she wore her thinning salt-and-pepper hair scraped back into a knob beneath a white widow's cap. Despite her fifty-eight years, she was as strong as an ox and just as stubborn.

Rory recognized the determined look on Bernice's craggy face. She loved her aunt, but as always, she swore herself to patience.

"There's no point in keeping it, Auntie." She pointed to the base of the spinning wheel, where the foot pedal had come loose from the bar that ran the length of the machine. "The treadle is broken. See?"

"Surely it can be mended!"

"Only think of the expense. It would be a pity to pay for repairs. I can't begin to guess what that would cost."

"Cost? I shan't lay out so much as a ha'penny. I shall ask Murdock to take a look at it. I'm sure he can have it shipshape in no time."

Murdock was their handyman, gardener, and sometime butler. Alas, Bernice had a more optimistic view of his skills than did Rory. The doddering old fellow had a habit of nipping at a jug of rum. Most afternoons, he could be found snoozing in the pantry or the garden shed. If they didn't dispose of the spinning wheel right now, it would end up in a stash of other damaged items that awaited repair in the cellar.

Rory had no wish to move broken items from one spot to another. It was a constant battle to prevent her aunt from accumulating more junk. That task often took a bit of diplomacy.

"The church is in dire need of contributions for the sale. You *would* like for us to do our part for the roof repair fund, wouldn't you?" Rory said, playing to Bernice's frugal nature. "Unless, of course, you'd prefer to make a monetary donation."

The mention of hard cash did the trick.

Bernice blew out a sigh. "I daresay we can spare this one item. It grieves me, though, to think we might have been spinning our own yarn all these years." She glanced hopefully toward the steep steps to the attic. "Perhaps there's a loom up there."

"No, there isn't." Thank goodness, too. Though Rory had been forced to practice economies since leaving London, she drew the line at weaving her own cloth. To distract her aunt from that direction of thought, she added, "Will you help me take this downstairs, please? It's rather heavy."

She grabbed one end of the spinning wheel, while her aunt took the other. Together they carried the awkward burden down the staircase, being careful not to bump the paneled wall or the ancient oak railing.

It would be nice to have new gowns, Rory reflected, though not made of rough homespun. She recently had embarked on a scheme to earn some pocket money, but it would be necessary to make do with her tattered wardrobe for a little while longer. Nevertheless, she missed the joy of shopping for silks and muslins, feathered bonnets and satin slippers.

She quashed a pang of regret. That life was over now. There was no need to follow fashion when one had been banished to the desolate coast of Norfolk to live in a stone cottage overlooking the sea. Her gowns had been mended and hemmed and patched, remnants of her debut season, when she had been caught in an indecent embrace with a dashing Italian diplomat. She still cringed to recall her naïveté in believing his ardent professions of love . . .

A loud rapping on the front door snapped Rory out of her reverie. The sound resonated through the foyer, rattling the old paintings on the walls.

Bernice fumbled her end of the spinning wheel. "Bilge and scurvy, who's that?"

Rory made haste to help her aunt. As she reached out

to grab the spindle, a sharp pinch assailed her fore-finger. The sting made her wince, but she grasped tightly to the spinning wheel, helping her aunt navigate down the last few steps so they could set the machine beside the small pile of their contributions to the rummage sale.

Bernice frowned at the wood panel of the door. "Fathom that, a visitor, all the way out here! Who could it be—" Her brown eyes focused on her niece. "Why, have you hurt yourself?"

Rory was examining her forefinger. A drop of blood beaded on the tip, and she used a corner of her apron to blot the throbbing spot. "I pricked myself on the spin-dle, that's all."

"Just like Sleeping Beauty, eh?" Despite her crusty exterior, Bernice had a soft spot for fairy-tale romance. "Well, perhaps that explains it, then."

"Explains what?"

"Your Prince Charming has arrived to give you true love's kiss."

"If you're referring to Mr. Nesbitt, I should certainly hope not!"

"Hmm. I can't think of anyone else who would drive three miles from the village to call on us."

The expectant stare she cast at her niece was suffi-cient to lure Rory's attention from her injured digit. "It can't be him. I hinted rather broadly last Sunday after church that I'm not interested in his courtship. He's far too young for me."

"Only by four years. Mr. Nesbitt might be a mere two-and-twenty, but he's not hard on the eyes and he owns three hundred acres of prime farmland. One of the other girls will snatch him up if you don't."

Mr. Nesbitt was indeed agreeable, handsome, and the most eligible bachelor in this little corner of England. But Rory had had enough of fine gentlemen to last a lifetime. "He still has peach fuzz on his face, for pity's sake. Besides, I'm perfectly happy living here with you, Auntie."

Bernice clucked her tongue. "I can't deny you've been my boon companion these past eight years. But every woman needs a loving husband to be her port in a storm. You'd realize that if only you were to meet a man as wonderful as my dear Ollie."

Bernice had spent much of her adult life aboard a ship, traveling the globe with her merchant husband. They'd shared many happy years, collecting the hodge-podge of exotic souvenirs that scattered the house, primitive statues from Brazil, native baskets from Canada, tribal masks from Africa. When Uncle Oliver had died a decade ago, she had settled here on the coast overlooking her beloved sea.

Bernice couldn't accept that her niece had rejected romance in favor of writing pithy commentary on modern society. "A husband would put a stop to my essays," Rory said. "I am quite content to be the anonymous Miss Cellany."

"If the fellow loves you, he'll allow you your own pursuits. Why, a woman as clever as you can wind him around her little finger if only she puts a bit of effort into it."

Rory had once been adept at flirtation, but those games were behind her now. She would rather expound on topics such as the injustice of confining a lady's education to sewing, dancing, and etiquette, while gentlemen expanded their minds through the study of Latin and Greek, algebra and geography. A London newspaper, *The Weekly Verdict,* recently had picked up several of her articles. The pay was a mere pittance, but she had been thrilled to see her *nom de plume,* Miss Cellany, beneath the headline.

The rapping sounded again, louder this time.

"It's surely Mr. Nesbitt, for that's a man's knock," Bernice said, reaching out to straighten Rory's collar. "And here you are looking like a scullery maid. What will he think?"

"He'll think I was cleaning out the attic. And that he ought to have warned us before coming to call."

"Foolish girl! Run upstairs and change into your rose-pink gown."

"No. He'll have to accept me as I am. With luck, the sight shall suffice to frighten him away for good."

Marching forward, she flung open the door. A brisk sea breeze whipped several strands of black hair around her face. But Rory was too busy gawking to take notice. An impeccably garbed footman stood on the stoop. From his white-wigged head to his leaf-green livery, the servant might have been transported here straight from a ducal palace.

"Miss Paxton?"

"Yes. Who—"

Before she could say more, he bowed to her and then retreated to reveal the elegant lady standing behind him.

She glided forward, a slim woman in a fur-trimmed mantle over a rich plum silk gown that rustled faintly with her every step. A bonnet decorated with egret feathers framed a face of lustrous beauty. Though clearly a mature woman, she had coal-black hair and smooth skin that made her precise age difficult to determine. With her long-lashed violet eyes and flawless features, she exuded a loveliness that was timeless as well as mesmerizing.

A sense of unreality gripped Rory. Her mind dredged up a name from the past. Though it was wildly improbable, she recognized this visitor.

"Lady Milford?"

A smile lent warmth to that fine face. "You are Miss Aurora Paxton, I believe. I remember you from your London season."

She did?

Lady Milford was a doyenne of high society. They'd never before met since Rory's family was mere gentry and lower on the social scale. Rory had only glimpsed her from afar at balls and parties in the company of titled gentlemen or government officials. Then she flushed to realize it must be the infamous scandal that had made her memorable to this woman.

Lady Milford was eyeing her with keen interest. She would be remembering Rory's terrible disgrace. But what could have brought her to this secluded house so far off the beaten path?

Just then, Rory noticed the splendid coach parked beside the scrubby grasses along the drive. Painted a rich cream hue, it looked like something out of a fairy tale, with oversized gilt wheels and gold appointments. A coachman stood by the team of white horses, and the footman had gone to join him.

"Has your coach broken down? Did you require help from us?" Rory bit back a gurgle of hysterical laughter at the image of old Murdock attempting to repair such a fancy vehicle.

"Certainly not. My coach is in perfect working order. Rather, I've come from London to call on *you*, Miss Paxton."

"Me?" Rory was floored. What interest could this woman possibly have in her? And to travel such a distance! Aware of gawking like a fool, she recalled her manners. "Oh, do pardon me. Please come inside."

She hastily stepped back to allow Lady Milford to enter the house. The woman brought to mind a fine jewel cast into a pile of junk. Thankfully, she was too polite to stare at the primitive pottery, religious statues, and other bric-a-brac that cluttered the small foyer.

Bernice watched, her eyebrows hiked in frank curiosity. "Who have we here?"

Rory performed the introductions. "Lady Milford, this is my aunt, Mrs. Bernice Culpepper. Auntie, this is Lady Milford. She's . . . an acquaintance from London."

"Welcome to Halcyon Cottage," Bernice said. "If I may be blunt, we don't often have visitors from London. Or any visitors at all, for that matter."

With dainty kid-gloved fingers, Lady Milford shook Bernice's chapped hand. "Pray forgive me for intruding without notice. I came to speak to Miss Paxton on a matter of some urgency."

The prospect of an accident or illness alarmed Rory. "Celeste—"

"Rest assured, your sister is in excellent health, as is your stepmother. Rather, I've come for another reason entirely. A private matter."

Rory released a breath. Thank goodness her sister was well. Celeste had been only ten years old when Rory had been banished. They had not seen each other since then, although they occasionally exchanged letters.

Just then, Murdock came shuffling along the corridor that led from the kitchen. A wrinkled black suit hung from his stooped shoulders, and he listed to one side as if tipsy. His white hair stood in wild disarray as if he'd been jolted out of an inebriated nap. "Blimey!" he grumbled. "I heard a knock loud enough to wake the dead!"

"Lady Milford has come to call," Rory said, aiming a severe stare at him. He was apt to blurt out salty opinions, and she had no wish to offend their exalted guest if there might be news of Rory's family. "Will you kindly fetch us tea and bring it to the parlor?"

"Tea?" He squinted at their visitor, looking her up and

down. "Rum's what ye'll want, milady. A bracing nip will take the damp chill from yer bones."

"Tea," Rory repeated firmly. "And a plate of Cook's gingerbread. Straightaway, if you will."

"Aye, aye, cap'n." Murdock saluted her, then made a wide circle and stumbled off in the direction from whence he'd come.

"Such a dear man," Bernice said fondly. "He was my husband's first mate for many years. A bit eccentric, but a great help around the house. I don't know what we would do without him."

"When one finds an excellent servant, one must endeavor to keep him," Lady Milford said with masterful diplomacy.

As Bernice led their guest into the parlor, Rory caught sight of herself in the age-speckled mirror on the wall. Her hair resembled a rat's nest. Numerous black strands had escaped the coil at the back of her head. She plucked out several sticky bits of cobweb, repositioned a few pins, then untied her apron and stuffed it into an over-sized Chinese vase. But she still looked like a servant in the faded blue gown.

Should she run upstairs and change, after all?

No. Honest work was nothing for which to be ashamed. She was no longer a member of society, anyway, so why should it matter what their guest thought of her? This was hardly a social call in a Mayfair drawing room.

She headed into the cramped parlor to find Lady Milford removing her bonnet and cloak. Rory took the items and laid them over one of the African drums that flanked the doorway. As the woman seated herself on a sagging brown chaise, her every movement was a study in grace and refinement. She gave no indication of noticing the lumpiness of the horsehair cushions or the sadly frayed arms.

Bernice was using the fire iron to stir the embers on the hearth. The small blaze they'd lit to ward off the morning chill had died while they were up in the attic. Her aunt tossed another log onto the grate and poked a few more times until the flames began to dance.

"There," she said, propping the tool against the mantel and turning her attention to Lady Milford. "May I say, I'm pleased to see one of Rory's London acquaintances come to call at last. Although she was banished for good cause, she need not be cut off forever."

"I quite agree," Lady Milford murmured. "You are to be commended for opening your home to her. That was most generous of you."

Bernice took measure of their guest, then nodded as if satisfied. "I'll just run along, then, whilst you two have yourselves a nice chat."

Chapter 3

*If a lady allows a gentleman liberties, she alone
will bear the brunt of shame.*

—MISS CELLANY

As her aunt cruised out of the parlor like a ship at full
sail, Rory swallowed an objection. She had hoped Bernice would help alleviate the awkwardness of conversing
with someone from Rory's old life in London.

Someone who clearly knew about her fall from grace.

Discomfited, she seated herself by the fire and arranged her skirts to conceal the holes where the stuffing
protruded from the chair's upholstery. Lady Milford was
engaged in taking off her kid gloves. The snapping of
the logs and the distant crashing of waves filled the
silence.

Rory lifted her chin. How foolish to care what this
grande dame of society thought of her! "You've come a
long way," she said, making polite conversation. "I trust
you had a pleasant journey."

"Yes, though I find myself more intrigued by *your*
situation, Miss Paxton." Lady Milford neatly placed the
gloves in her lap. "All this time, no one knew where you
had gone. I found out only yesterday upon visiting your
stepmother. Mrs. Paxton said it was your late father's
wish that you live here with his sister."

Rory's heart squeezed. It hurt to be reminded of

Papa's disappointment in her. She could still see his sad brown eyes, so full of censure. He had died of a fever the year after her banishment, and she'd never even had the chance to say good-bye to him.

"I've been very content with Aunt Bernice," she stated. "I much prefer the country, anyway."

"Do you? From what I recall of your debut season, you seemed to thrive upon the entertainments of society and the company of friends."

"People change. I'm a different person now."

"Indeed, it is the experiences in life that shape us. However, I cannot imagine you would relish being cut off from your acquaintances. Especially in so abrupt a manner."

Lady Milford's expression was kind, though Rory bristled nevertheless. Was that why the woman had come here? To dredge up old gossip? Was her purpose to ferret out all the sordid details of that long-ago disgrace?

"I'm glad to have witnessed the foibles of high society," Rory declared. "It is a place where gentlemen are allowed discreet affairs. They are even admired for their conquests. Yet young ladies are vilified if they so much as . . ."

She pressed her lips shut. It wasn't necessary to explain herself to this woman. Besides, she had made her peace with what had happened. She was no longer the reckless, gullible girl craving excitement, bowled over by the courtship of the most handsome, charming man she'd ever met.

How was she to have known that Stefano had a wife back in Italy?

"The rules a young lady must follow may seem unfair," Lady Milford said mildly. "Yet surely you can see that a gentleman only wishes to ensure that the firstborn son of the marriage is indeed *his* child. But enough about the past. That is not my reason for seeking you out."

"Oh?"

"Allow me to go straight to the point. Your stepmother is entangled in a matter of grave concern. You see, a packet of letters was stolen from her recently. And she is being blackmailed for their return."

"Blackmailed!" Rory gripped the arms of the chair. Nothing could have startled her more. Kitty had always been a stickler for propriety, overly conscious of protecting the Paxton family's modest rank in society. To imagine her guilty of some scandalous intrigue boggled the mind. "But . . . by whom?"

"Mrs. Paxton has a suspicion, though she lacks proof. She already has relinquished a diamond necklace, but the villain has yet to return the letters."

"I—I hardly know what to think. What on earth was in those letters? A secret of some sort?"

"I'm not at liberty to reveal your stepmother's confidences. If you wish to know, you'll have to ask her yourself."

Rory gave a sharp, cynical shake of her head. "When would I have such an opportunity? She wants nothing to do with me. She made that perfectly clear eight years ago."

Ever since, Kitty Paxton had refused all communication with her stepdaughter. Even when Papa had died, it had been Celeste who'd relayed the wretched news in a letter. By the time Rory had received word, it had been too late to attend the funeral.

Lady Milford wore a consoling look. "I think you'll find that time has tempered her animosity. She no longer holds you in contempt. In fact, she admitted to me that she greatly misses your company."

Rory released an unladylike snort. Kitty must have

been making polite conversation with Lady Milford, nothing more. "I very much doubt that."

"I am merely repeating what she voiced to me. According to her, you are cleverer than she is, and far more resourceful. Considering the delicate nature of the situation, you're the only one she dares to trust with this problem."

"Me?"

"Yes, she believes that you alone have the wit to solve this mystery and recover those letters. It must be done swiftly to avert a scandal. That is why I offered to stop here. To relay that she begs you come back home at once."

A disbelieving laugh choked Rory's throat. "Return to London? To help *her*? Absolutely not!"

Despite her resolve to remain calm, she sprang up from the chair and stalked to one of the windows overlooking the sea. Through the wavy glass, whitecaps spun long strips of lace against the greenish-blue satin of the water. Gulls screeched amid the muted hiss of the waves. The sight and sound of the sea usually soothed her, but not today.

Today she was too agitated to appreciate the view. How dare Kitty request her assistance after shunning her all these years! It was typical of her stepmother to wheedle other people to do her bidding. She was a clingy, self-centered woman who cared only for her position in society. Rory couldn't imagine what was in those letters, but if they caused trouble for Kitty, then it was her own fault.

Nevertheless, a longing as powerful as the tide tugged at Rory. She missed the hustle and bustle of London, the delight of having friends her own age, the pleasure of visiting a variety of posh stores instead of just one tiny shop in the village. Of course, even if she were to accept this unexpected request—and she had no intention of doing so—that didn't mean she'd be permitted to rejoin society. Kitty would never allow it.

Nevertheless, her stepmother had been so distraught that she'd blurted out the story to Lady Milford. And had prevailed upon her to come here . . .

Rory spun around. "How is it that you know about this blackmail scheme? My stepmother was never one of your confidantes."

An enigmatic smile touched Lady Milford's lips. "I happened across certain evidence that she was in trouble. When I questioned her, she admitted the sordid story. I offered my services at once. Since I am on my way to visit a friend, stopping here was no hardship."

Rory couldn't shake the suspicion that the woman wasn't telling her everything. But what did it matter? Rory had no intention of going anywhere. "Kitty will have to find her own way out of this mess. I shall write to her at once of my refusal."

"Please do reconsider. The scandal will affect your half sister, Celeste, too. That is why your stepmother is so desperate to retrieve the letters. If they are exposed to the public, she fears the wedding may be called off."

"Wedding?"

"Celeste's nuptials to the Duke of Whittingham. The ceremony is set for St. George's Church four weeks from now." Her violet eyes alight with concern, Lady Milford leaned forward. "Oh, my dear girl. Didn't you know? Did no one write to inform you?"

Rory mutely shook her head and braced her hands on the windowsill. Celeste, betrothed? Sweet little Celeste, who until last year had sewed doll gowns as a hobby and sketched silly pictures in her letters? When she hadn't written in the past few months, Rory had presumed her to be busy with her debut, the dress fittings and the dance lessons, the balls and the parties.

Yet it was only late April, and already Celeste had accepted a proposal of marriage. She would be a wife in a scant few weeks. And to such a high-ranking nobleman! From her own debut, Rory recalled the Duke of Whittingham as a haughty fellow who had regarded lesser beings with disdain.

He was not the gentle, loving husband she had envisioned for her sister.

Her stomach lurched. Never had she felt more isolated from her family. She should have been there to counsel Celeste. Such a grand alliance had to be Kitty's work. Her stepmother had long schemed to elevate herself in the social hierarchy through the marriage of one of the Paxton girls, first by throwing Rory at various titled gentlemen, and when that had failed, by focusing her ambitions on Celeste.

The sound of shuffling feet came from the foyer. Murdock hobbled into the parlor, his knobby form hunched over a silver tray. It tilted slightly, making the cups slide and rattle, putting them in danger of crashing to the floor. "Yer tea, milady."

Rory sprang forward to rescue the tray. She placed it on a table in front of the chaise, relieved to see that he'd remembered to use the only remaining pair of porcelain cups without chips or cracks.

He shuffled closer, his rheumy eyes fixed on Lady Milford. "I took the liberty of includin' a pitcher of rum on the tray. Nothing better than a wee dram in yer tea to fortify yerself."

"How very kind of you," Lady Milford said with perfect civility. "I confess, it's something I've never tried."

"O' course, I recommend takin' yer rum straight

up," he rambled on. "Aboard ship, we had daily rations with every meal, even breakfast. Why, I recall one voyage when our stores ran out and the crew near mutinied—"

"Thank you, Murdock," Rory broke in. "That will be all."

"Ye ought to take a thimbleful, too," he said, eyeing her critically. "Ye look too pale today. It'll put some color back in them cheeks." Upon uttering that unsolicited advice, he made a creaky bow and ambled out of the parlor.

Rory busied herself pouring the tea. It was a relief to have something to do to alleviate her anxiety over Celeste. "Sugar or cream?"

"A drop or two of rum should suffice," Lady Milford said.

"Oh, you needn't feel obliged . . ."

"Nonsense. Everything ought to be tried at least once."

Rory added a trickle from the little pewter pitcher, then handed the cup to Lady Milford. In her present state, she was half tempted to fill her own cup with straight rum. But liquor would not drown her worry over her sister.

Resuming her seat, she stirred a morsel of sugar into her steaming tea. "The Duke of Whittingham must be more than twice Celeste's age. I remember him as being rather stodgy—and that was eight years ago. He'll be even more set in his ways by now."

"He is forty, I believe." Lady Milford took a sip of rum-laced tea. "Mm. This is curiously delicious."

Rory paid no heed. "She's only eighteen! I can't believe she would agree to such a mismatch!"

"Few girls would turn down the chance to become a duchess. As to her age, it is customary for men of distinction to take a younger wife. They must consider the need to ensure an heir."

"But why Celeste? Her portion is hardly large enough to tempt a duke!"

"Whittingham is a man of great wealth, so he is free to marry where he pleases. And your half sister is exceptionally pretty. Quiet and shy, too, just as such noblemen prefer. She will make him an obedient wife."

Rory set down her teacup so abruptly that it clattered in the saucer. "Obedient, bah! He is *far* too old and snooty for her! He will crush her spirit!"

"Then perhaps, Miss Paxton, you ought to rethink your decision about not returning to London."

Realizing that she'd been masterfully manipulated, Rory huffed out a breath. "A better solution is to allow the stolen letters to be published. If they are as sensational as you suggest, it will put an immediate end to this misbegotten betrothal!"

Over the rim of her cup, Lady Milford regarded Rory benignly. "Alas, such a scandal will taint your sister, too. Is that what you wish? Do you truly want *her* to be made an outcast as you have been?"

The very thought withered Rory's objections. It had taken years to stop missing her life in London, and although she had found contentment at last, she had no right to condemn Celeste to spinsterhood, too. In her letters, Celeste had expressed a yearning to fall in love and become a wife and mother. Rory could not ruin that dream for her gentle, tenderhearted sister. Especially if there was the slightest chance that Celeste truly *did* want to wed the duke.

There was only one way to find out.

"All right, then," Rory snapped. "I'll go to London to see what can be done. But I cannot promise that I'll help my stepmother."

"Fair enough. It will be up to Mrs. Paxton to convince you." Lady Milford reached for her reticule and untied the silken drawstring. "Now, since you've been gone for so long, your wardrobe will need replenishing. If you should attend a ball or party—"

"I won't be rejoining society. My stepmother would never allow it."

"Yet your sister is betrothed to a duke. You must be prepared to accompany her to various events. Perhaps these will come in handy."

To Rory's astonishment, the woman drew a pair of shoes out of her velvet reticule. The elegant dancing slippers were fashioned of rich garnet silk and covered in tiny crystal beads that sparkled in the daylight. The sight stirred an instant covetousness in her. Even in her days as a debutante, she had never seen anything so exquisite, not even in the finest London shops.

She tore her gaze away to look at Lady Milford. Why would the woman offer such a peculiar, personal gift? It wasn't as if they were friends.

"I don't need charity," Rory said stiffly.

"Oh, the shoes aren't yours to keep, merely to borrow for a short time. You must return them to me when you no longer need them." Lady Milford leaned down to place the pair on the rug. "Go on now, do try them on."

Rory wrestled with her pride. If they were indeed only a loan, it would be churlish to refuse. "They aren't likely to fit," she warned. "I'm taller than you and no doubt wear a larger size."

Nevertheless, she removed her own sadly scuffed leather shoes. Then she wiggled her stockinged toes into the fine slippers. Softness enveloped her feet as if the shoes had been stitched by a master cobbler expressly for her.

Buoyed by an irresistible sense of lightness, Rory

arose from the chair and turned around in a pirouette, admiring the shoes that peeked out from beneath her faded blue skirt. Foolish or not, they made her long to dance again. How wonderful it would be to twirl around a ballroom in the arms of a handsome gentleman . . .

Lady Milford regarded her with a mysterious smile. "I see the slippers do fit you, after all."

"Amazingly so! But I don't know where I'll wear them."

"Why, anywhere you please, my dear. Perhaps even tomorrow on your journey to London."

Chapter 4

*It is a disgrace that naïve girls are so often maneuvered
into loveless matches with older gentlemen.*

—MISS CELLANY

As Rory stepped into the entrance hall of the house that
she'd once called home, a bittersweet sense of home-
coming enveloped her. How well she knew these pale
green walls, the black-and-white marble floor, the staircase with its wrought-iron rail. The tasteful decorations
included several landscape paintings, a pair of gilt chairs,
and an urn of white roses on a stone pedestal. The
fragrance of the flowers blended with the clean aroma
of beeswax. Yet perhaps she had grown accustomed to
Bernice's clutter, for this place looked almost austere in
its perfection.

"Shall I take your wrap, Miss Paxton?"

She turned to the black-clad butler who stood waiting, his lips thinned in his narrow face, his brown hair
neatly combed. Grimshaw had always been able to make
a simple question resonate with disapproval. Judging by
his disdainful expression, he believed the prodigal
daughter ought to have come to the tradesmen's entrance
instead of the front door.

Rory handed her cloak and bonnet to him. As a debutante, she'd despised him for his unforgivable interfer-
ence in her life. But now it tickled her fancy to find a

chink in that stiff façade. "There are bags under your eyes, Grimshaw. Is my stepmother running you ragged?"

On cue, he bristled. "I am perfectly hale. Now, you must not linger here where anyone might see you. Follow me."

Grimshaw led the way along a corridor toward the rear of the house. Falling into step behind him, she glanced up as they passed the stairway. The muted sound of voices floated down to her.

"Wait," she called. "I wish to see my sister at once."

He fixed her with a gloating stare. "Miss Celeste departed ten minutes ago to take tea with the Duke of Whittingham and his mother in Berkeley Square."

Blast! It would be an hour or more before she returned, perhaps longer if they were discussing wedding plans. Rory itched to find out if Celeste was being forced into the marriage. After today's long journey, it seemed a fickle turn of fate that her half sister wasn't even here.

Lady Milford had made all the travel arrangements. The previous day, after relaying her shocking news of blackmail and betrothal, the dowager countess had gone to visit a friend some ten miles distant. Her coachman had returned to Halcyon Cottage late in the evening. He and the footman had spent the night in the stables, and then at the crack of dawn this morning, with Rory ensconced alone in the coach, they had departed for London.

Bernice had stood waving in the doorway. Rory had invited her along, but Bernice couldn't abide big cities. Perhaps it was best for her aunt to remain in Norfolk, anyway. She was blissfully unaware of the secret blackmail scheme since Rory had let her believe the visit concerned Celeste's engagement.

Grimshaw proceeded down the long corridor. His steps were as clipped as those of a soldier on parade, the sound echoed by the tapping of her borrowed shoes. Ever since Lady Milford had loaned the fancy slippers to her, Rory had been beset by butterflies in her stomach, as if something of great importance were about to happen.

"Where are you taking me?" she asked.

"Mrs. Paxton is entertaining guests. She instructed me to have you wait in the library."

Rory didn't know whether to be more irked that her return to London was taken for granted, or by the fact that the disgraced stepdaughter was not permitted to mingle with fine company. But what did it matter, really? She had not come to rejoin society, only to assure herself of her sister's happiness.

Grimshaw ushered her into the cozy room that had doubled as her father's study. "I shall inform Mrs. Paxton of your arrival," he intoned.

The butler gave a curt nod and vanished out the door.

As Rory surveyed the surroundings, a tide of memories inundated her. The same bottle-green curtains framed the windows that overlooked a tiny walled garden. Oak shelves stretched to the ceiling, the many books filling the air with the rich scent of leather. And there, lying with Stefano on the russet chaise by the hearth, she had committed the worst mistake of her life.

That particular memory was best consigned to the dustbin of history.

Blotting it out, she turned toward the mahogany desk that dominated one end of the room. In her mind, she pictured Papa sitting there, a pair of gold-rimmed spectacles perched on his nose, his quill pen scratching across the paper.

The leather chair was empty now. Papa had died less than a year after her banishment. She hadn't even had the chance to say good-bye.

Rory blinked away the tears that blurred her eyes. As a little girl, she'd often visited her father here in the afternoon. It had been their special time together. He would push aside his ledger books or his letter writing and give her his full attention. They had played cards for amusement or read stories together. On several occasions in the misty past, he'd taken tea with her and her favorite doll.

That had been before he'd remarried.

Rory had no memory of her real mother, who had passed away shortly after giving birth. It had been Papa who had tucked her in at night. Papa who had taken her for walks in the park. She had been nearly eight when Kitty Paxton had come into their lives. Celeste had been born soon thereafter and everything had changed . . .

Rory walked to the desk and sat down in her father's chair. She fancied the faint aroma of his sandalwood cologne still lingered in the air. All of his papers and books had been cleared away, leaving only a barren, polished surface. Had Kitty purged everything of his from this room?

Hoping to find some forgotten token, Rory opened the top drawer and rummaged through the contents. A wistful smile touched her lips. His favorite goose-feather quills were still here, along with his silver inkpot and the stationery imprinted with his initials. She picked up a small dish of sand and sifted the grains through her fingers, remembering how he'd sometimes allowed her to sprinkle the sand over a letter to blot the fresh ink.

What would Papa have thought of her essay writing? Would he have been proud to learn that her modern opinions had been published in *The Weekly Verdict* under the pen name Miss Cellany? She yearned to believe he would have applauded her efforts.

"Aurora! Why are you poking through those drawers?"

Startled, Rory spilled the pot of sand on the pristine

desk. She looked up to see Kitty Paxton standing in the doorway. Her stepmother had not changed much with the exception of a few fine wrinkles around her eyes and a slight graying of her fair hair, worn in sausage curls around her face. She had the stout look of a matron now, too, her waist thick beneath a striped yellow silk gown with lace ruffles along the cuffs and neckline.

Rory used the edge of her hand to brush the sand back into the dish. "I was only wondering what had happened to Papa's things," she said coolly as she rose to her feet. "Pray forgive me for prying. I forgot for a moment that this is no longer my home."

Kitty pursed her lips for an instant. Then a contrite smile eased her expression. She closed the door and swooped toward Rory. "My dear girl, it is *you* who must forgive *me*. What must you think of me for failing to welcome you after all these years?"

Rory found herself enveloped in a rose-perfumed embrace. She returned the hug in a perfunctory manner. Though half of her wanted to believe Kitty felt a genuine affection, the other half acknowledged that her stepmother was likely scheming to cajole Rory into helping her.

Drawing back, she decided to skip straight to the point. "I came the moment I heard the news about Celeste's wedding. You cannot really mean to allow her to wed the Duke of Whittingham."

Kitty blinked. "Of course I do! Why would I object to such a splendid match?"

"For one, he's old enough to be her father."

"Bah. His maturity only ensures that he has sown his wild oats and is ready to settle down and devote himself to her happiness." A beatific look on her face, Kitty clasped her hands to her ample bosom. "Whittingham is madly in love with dear Celeste. You should see the many gifts he has showered on her, bracelets and flowers and shawls—and an heirloom diamond ring that would rival the Queen's jewels."

"The question that concerns me is not whether *he* is in love, but whether *she* is. Did you force her into this engagement?"

"Certainly not! Celeste was delighted to accept his offer. What girl would *not* be thrilled at the prospect of becoming a duchess? Only think of how it will elevate her status in society!"

And Kitty's status, as well. To be the mother of a high-ranking noblewoman was the summit of her ambitions; she had made that clear during Rory's debut, too. She would never admit to coercing her daughter. Realizing the futility of the discussion, Rory decided to abandon the topic of her half sister's betrothal for now. Only a private, heart-to-heart chat with Celeste would reveal the truth.

"I daresay the wedding may never take place, anyway," Rory observed. "I understand there is the threat of an imminent scandal."

A shadow dimmed Kitty's china-blue eyes. With the melodrama of a stage actress, she pressed a trembling hand to her brow. "Indeed! You cannot imagine how terribly distraught I have been . . ." She gave Rory a sidelong glance. "Just how much did Lady Milford tell you?"

"She said you're being blackmailed over a stolen packet of letters. And that I would have to ask you to explain the rest."

"It's so horrid, I can scarcely bring myself to speak of it. This past week, I've not slept a wink." Her abundant bosom heaving, Kitty swayed on her feet. "The very thought of what could happen makes me feel about to swoon."

"Then do sit down, for pity's sake."

Familiar with her stepmother's histrionics, Rory helped her over to the chaise by the fireplace. Kitty wilted against the russet cushions and drew a handkerchief from her sleeve, using the scrap of lace to fan herself. Rory went to the cabinet behind the desk and poured a generous measure of sherry into a glass, delivering it into Kitty's dimpled hand.

"Bless you, my dear," she said, taking a large swallow. "I can't tell you how grateful I am that you're here. You were always so much more capable than I at handling difficult situations. Why, you didn't even weep when your papa and I were forced to send you away."

Rory had wept, all right. In the privacy of her bedchamber during the dark of night, she had shed tears of anger and misery, reliving the memory of her humiliation and aghast that she had wounded Papa with her reckless actions. But she had indulged her self-pity only that one time. Ever since, she'd been determined to use the experience to reshape her life.

She sat down beside her stepmother on the chaise. "It's time you told me the entire story. I want to know every detail of what happened."

Kitty eyed her warily over the rim of the glass. "*Every* detail?"

"Yes. Let us start with the disappearance of the letters. When was it?"

"Over a week ago. I was in the morning room, rereading some old correspondence, when a visitor arrived. I tied up the packet with a ribbon and stuffed it under the cards of thread in my sewing basket. I was so busy with the arrangements for Celeste's engagement party that I quite forgot about the letters. It wasn't until two days after the ball that I realized they'd gone missing. And then only because . . . because I received that awful note in the post."

"The blackmail demand?"

"Yes, it was written in a gentleman's hand, and he directed me to surrender my diamond necklace—the one your father gave me as a wedding gift. If I failed to do so, he said, my private matters would be smeared all over the scandal sheets. Oh, you cannot imagine what a tizzy I was in!"

"I've a fair notion of it," Rory said dryly. "Which leads me to ask, what exactly was in those letters?"

Kitty thrust out her lower lip in a pout, while her fingers twisted the handkerchief. "That doesn't signify. There is no point in revealing it."

Rory resisted even the slightest pang of sympathy. Her stepmother was no child to be indulged or protected. "You will tell me at once. Or I shall walk out of here and leave you to your own devices."

"All right, then." Kitty released a shuddery breath. "They were private letters of . . . of affection. *Billets-doux* written to me by . . . a former lover."

Rory sat very still. The possibility of a love affair had crossed her mind on the journey here, though she hadn't wanted to believe it. The letters also could have contained government secrets from her father's work at the Admiralty, or perhaps just catty commentary about members of society that would have embarrassed her stepmother if it was made public.

How ironic that Kitty was guilty of the very sin that had resulted in Rory being banished.

"I see," she said coldly. "When exactly did this affair occur? After all, widows are allowed to enjoy a discreet liaison. Unlike debutantes."

Kitty squirmed beneath Rory's direct gaze. "Actually, it happened . . . a little while before your father's death."

She had cheated on Papa.

A hard knot clenched inside Rory. She burned with fury for her father's sake. This vain, foolish woman had broken her marriage vows in order to indulge her selfish desires. "Did Papa know about this affair?"

Biting her lip, Kitty looked down at her lap. "Yes, I did confess it to him. And he forgave me. I hope that you can, too."

Rory scrutinized her stepmother. She sensed the woman was holding something back. "Since you kept them, these love letters must have meant a great deal to you. If you were truly repentant, you'd have burned them."

"I wish I had. You can't imagine how much." Kitty sniffled, dabbing at her moist eyes. "Oh, I simply *must* get those letters back. If they're published, I will be subject to the most vicious gossip. I'll be ruined!"

"Retire to the country, then, as I was forced to do. It will all blow over eventually."

"You don't understand. The Duke of Whittingham will not abide any scandal in his fiancée's family. Last season, he cried off an engagement to Lady Mary Hastings when her sister eloped with a dancing master."

"Apparently, the duke is unaware of *me,* then."

"Eight years have passed. I managed to convince him that everyone has forgotten your little indiscretion, and you don't live in London, anyway. That is why he mustn't know you're back."

"I see. I'm to be hidden away like a madwoman in Bedlam."

Kitty held out her hands in supplication. "Pray don't take it ill, Aurora. It's only necessary for you to lie low until after the wedding. And please, you *must* help. If not for my sake, then for Celeste's."

She had struck upon the only argument that held any

weight. Rory could not subject her sister to the shame
of a scandal. Taking a deep breath to ease her tension,
she said, "The letters may have been stolen during Celeste's ball. There must have been a great many people
here. Do you have any idea who the culprit might be?"

"Indeed, I do! The villain is Lord Dashell."

"The Marquess of Dashell? That old rogue?" Rory recalled him as a ruddy-faced lecher who'd had a bad
habit of pinching the ladies and making them squeal.

"No. It wasn't William. He died in a coaching accident last year." She sniffled a little more, her mouth
drawing downward. "Rather, I'm referring to his eldest
son, Lucas. The present marquess."

Rory lifted an eyebrow. Lucas Vale? Impossible.

The man was a stone-faced prig. A few times during
her debut season, she'd caught him glowering at her
when she'd been surrounded by a bevy of suitors. Only
once had he solicited her hand for a dance, and although
his darkly attractive looks and powerful form had caused
her heart to flutter, it had been difficult to make conversation with such an aloof sourpuss. He'd scarcely uttered a
word in response to her chatty comments. Afterward,
he had walked away with nary a good-bye. Too cold and
straitlaced to be deemed handsome, he was the opposite of his happy-go-lucky sire.

"What nonsense," she scoffed. "He's even stuffier
than Whittingham. What possible motive could he have
for stealing your old *billets-doux*?"

"There *is* a reason, actually." Kitty squirmed in her
seat. "You see . . ."

"Whatever it is, say it."

"All right, then! My affair was with his father. It was
William who wrote those love letters to me. So, of
course, his son has a vested interest in them."

Rory pinched her lips tightly. Kitty had betrayed Papa

for that old roué? A man so dissipated, he'd been known to fall down drunk in the middle of a crowded ballroom? A man who'd driven his carriage through Hyde Park with a garishly painted lightskirt at his side? "Good heavens! What did you ever see in *him*?"

Kitty lowered her gaze. "You wouldn't understand."

"No, I suppose I wouldn't." Controlling her disgust, Rory forced herself to focus on the current problem. "None of this makes any sense. Why would Dashell threaten to publish his father's correspondence? It would bring scandal on his family as well as ours."

"Oh, but I daren't risk it, for he is a cold, vindictive man! And on the night of the ball, I saw him in the morning room, lecturing his brother. That must have been when he found the letters and recognized his father's penmanship. He put them into his pocket right then and there, you may be sure of it!"

"I still say he would be more likely to dispose of the letters than to blackmail you."

"Not if he is in dire need of funds." Kitty leaned forward in the manner of a gossip with a juicy tidbit to relate. "Rumor has it that he's squandered his entire inheritance by making a string of bad investments. His estates are mortgaged to the hilt."

Rory frowned. "He never struck me as the reckless sort. Are you certain he didn't inherit his debts?"

Kitty nodded her head vigorously. "Absolutely certain! I have it on the very best authority from Lady Milford. He lost everything on the Exchange—along with a fleet of merchant ships that sank in a storm. Now, he's said to be in the market for a rich bride, but even that may not be enough to save him from utter ruin."

"I see. Well, I daresay it is *possible,* then."

"It's more than possible. It's the truth. Anyway, everyone knows what a grouch he is, so unlike his charming, fun-loving papa. Why, the man is so heartless he wouldn't blink an eye while robbing me blind. Even Lady Milford agreed he is the likely culprit."

Rory considered the matter. A destitute man, even a rigidly proper one, might stoop to desperate measures. And she was inclined to believe Lady Milford's testimonial. Her ladyship was a highly respected, intelligent woman who would never accuse a fellow aristocrat of thievery without just cause. If she said Lord Dashell had taken the letters, then it must be so.

"Do you have the blackmail note?" Rory asked. "I should like to see it."

"It is in the bottom drawer of the desk. That's why I snapped at you for sitting there. I feared you might stumble across it before I had the chance to explain matters." Dabbing at her eyes, Kitty slumped weakly against the cushions. "Will you be a dear and fetch the note—both of them?"

"There's more than one?"

"Yes, another arrived this very morning. I surrendered my diamond necklace to the villain several days ago, but he is still refusing to return the letters. And he is demanding another payment by week's end!"

Going to the desk, Rory opened the bottom drawer. She found the two folded notes and examined them on the desk. Each bore a broken red wax seal without any identifying mark. The paper was standard vellum, the sort that could be purchased at any stationer's store.

As she scanned the brief messages, a chill feathered down her spine. There was something vaguely familiar about the masculine script, but it was an elusive impression, nothing more. Had she ever seen Lord Dashell's handwriting? She couldn't recall. In her brief debut season, she'd been inundated with poems and flowers from a myriad of suitors. Eight years had passed since then, and perhaps she'd forgotten about receiving a scribbled card from the marquess.

"May I take these two notes?" she asked. "I should like to compare them to a sample of Lord Dashell's penmanship."

Kitty made a remarkable recovery from her weepy malaise. She sat up straight, her face brightening with a smile. "Then you'll find the letters for me? Oh, bless you, dear girl!"

Rory despised helping the woman who'd betrayed Papa. Kitty ought to be forced to reap the rotten fruits of her wickedness. Yet there was Celeste to consider. Her sister didn't deserve to suffer the stigma of her mother's sins.

"I shall require a fee for my services," Rory said, rising to her feet to aim a steely-eyed look at Kitty. "Papa set aside a dowry for me. Since I'm unlikely to marry, you will grant those funds to me as payment."

"But . . . that's three thousand pounds! Between the expense of your sister's wedding and the blackmailer demanding a thousand by the end of the week, why, I could never manage it!"

"Half the amount, then. Fifteen hundred."

Kitty narrowed her eyes in a calculating glare. "A thousand pounds, for I should rather pay it to you than to that villain. And if you fail, you shall receive nothing."

"I won't fail."

Rory could hardly contain her delight. It was only a third of what she'd asked, but she'd never expected Kitty to part with more than a measly hundred or so. She wanted to dance around the room. It would be a windfall to have a thousand pounds at her disposal. With the funds, she could provide for her aunt, so that Bernice wouldn't feel obliged to count every penny.

"I must call on Lord Dashell," she said. "Do you suppose he will refuse to receive a fallen woman? Never mind, I won't allow him to turn me away. I will devise an excuse to make him write a few lines so that I might check his script against the blackmail notes."

Kitty levered herself up from the chaise and came toward Rory. "It will take more than a brief visit to find the letters. Why, they could be anywhere! You'll have to comb through his entire house—and such an enormous one it is!"

"I'll think of a way. Though I doubt he'll be inviting me to dinner anytime soon."

"I know the very thing. Dashell has an invalid mother. She's quite the harridan, and he's had terrible trouble keeping companions employed. However, if *you* were to secure the post, you'd have ample opportunity to conduct a search."

Rory's attention perked. The situation would be perfect, giving her access to private areas of his palatial home in Grosvenor Square. "How do you know the position is open at the moment?"

"Lady Milford assured me of it! I declare, no one knows the goings-on of society better than her. You could have knocked me over with a feather when she offered to help." Kitty took Rory by the arm and steered her to the door of the library. "Come quickly now, there's no time to waste. You must go at once and apply for the post."

Chapter 5

Lucas Vale, the fifth Marquess of Dashell, was about to take a bride. That is, when he decided upon the right time to ask her.

His soon-to-be fiancée, Miss Alice Kipling, poured tea in his drawing room for a small group of family and guests. He watched her graceful movements as she handed cups to her mother and to Lucas, then to his brother, Lord Henry, and Henry's closest friend, Perry Davenport.

Alice Kipling might not be a blue blood, but she embodied the perfect English lady: golden hair arranged in smooth ringlets, a flawless complexion the color of peaches and cream, and a slender figure outlined by a pale rose silk gown. In addition to her physical assets, she had a modest demeanor and an impeccable reputation. She was neither a flirt nor a chatterbox. Whenever he caught her eye, she smiled shyly and blushed.

Having dealt all his life with a petulant mother, Lucas appreciated docility in a woman. More importantly, though, he appreciated the fact that Miss Kipling's father was enormously rich, the owner of a number of textile mills in Manchester. Her marriage portion was rumored to be an astronomical fifty thousand.

He needed those funds. Desperately. He would marry a horse-faced harpy for that amount of cash. It would go a long way toward alleviating his dire financial situation. So why hadn't he made his offer already?

Lucas analyzed his vague reluctance. It had nothing to do with her common blood, for Miss Alice Kipling had been well trained for the role of nobleman's wife. Her fortune and manners ensured she would be accepted by society. Perhaps his feet-dragging had to do with the prospect of ending his bachelorhood. He was loath to upset the well-oiled routine of Dashell House. Females tended to change things, to make demands, to redecorate and run up bills. Yet the deed had to be done. At thirty-two, he had a duty to ensure an heir to the title.

He also had a duty to safeguard his estates, which at present lay in rack and ruin. He and Miss Kipling would make a fair trade: the title of marchioness in exchange for a pile of gold. The match would be equally advantageous to them both.

As Alice took her own cup and seated herself beside him on the chaise, her mother smiled approvingly from her chair by the hearth. A broad-featured woman with mousy brown hair and a well-fed figure, Mrs. Kipling had been none too subtle in pushing her daughter at him for the past month.

"Perfectly done, my dear," she said to Alice. "His lordship must be most impressed by your effort."

"Please, Mama," Alice said, her cheeks turning pink. "I'm sure he can find nothing to admire in such a simple task."

"Well, then, let us ask him. What do you think, Lord Dashell?"

Lucas blanked on her meaning. What had been said while he'd been woolgathering? Had he missed some vital element in the conversation?

Lounging in his chair, Henry caught Lucas's eye. The enjoyment that lit his brother's face made him look like a younger version of their late sire, with the same startling blue eyes and roguish smile. Henry's tousled hair might be brown rather than gray, yet he shared their father's penchant for debonair garb and, regrettably, his devil-may-care manner, as well.

His lips twitched in a grin, Henry slyly pointed his forefinger at his cup.

Tea. The women were talking about Alice pouring the tea.

"I can find no fault in your performance, Miss Kipling." Lucas fumbled for a better compliment. He'd never cared for small talk. It seemed a waste of time and effort. Lifting the cup, he took a sip. "May I say, you've added the perfect amount of cream."

Miss Kipling glanced at her mother, who gave her daughter a slight nod. A silent message seemed to pass between them. Then the girl looked back at Lucas and ducked her chin, her eyes very large and very blue.

"Please do call me Alice," she murmured in a melodious tone. "Surely we are well enough acquainted to dispense with formalities. That is, if you agree, my lord."

"Thank you, Alice. You may address me as Lucas, of course."

"Better yet, call him Dash," Henry interjected. "That's what *I* prefer. My brother is considered quite the dashing fellow now that he's the marquess."

"Dash," she repeated with a girlish smile. "Oh, I see, that is short for Dashell. I do like it, my lord. May I use it?"

He cast an irritated glare at Henry, who knew full

well that Lucas despised being addressed by the same nickname as their profligate sire. "I'd rather you did not," he said in a clipped tone. "My brother is jesting. You must always take whatever he says with a grain of salt."

Henry clapped his hand over the lapel of his burgundy coat. "Such an insult. What will Miss Kipling think of you branding me a prankster? She'll believe my word is not to be trusted."

Perry Davenport shifted his long, lanky form in his chair. He was a fair-haired fellow, not as dissolute as Henry and more a follower than a leader. "Do give her some credit, Henry. She's more well-mannered than that."

"Traitor," Henry accused, reaching out to jab Perry in the arm. "You should be defending your old chum, namely *me*. Isn't that right, Miss Kipling?"

Alice parted her rosy lips. She appeared confused by the banter and gazed appealingly at Lucas. "I . . . I . . ."

"Stop badgering her," Lucas ordered his brother. "I've had enough of your foolishness."

"Aw, Dash, you oughtn't interrupt her," Henry said. "According to an article I read recently, ladies should be encouraged to state their opinions. And they should study algebra and geography instead of etiquette."

"How very shocking!" Mrs. Kipling exclaimed, setting down her teacup so that it rattled in the saucer. "I would never allow my Alice to speak out of turn. Nor to fill her pretty head with such inappropriate masculine topics! Where did you read such a thing, Lord Henry?"

"In *The Weekly Verdict*," he said. "It's a thought-provoking newspaper dedicated to the betterment of mankind . . . and womankind, too."

Mrs. Kipling harrumphed. "Such radical notions surely cannot be acceptable in polite society. Who would write such nonsense?"

"Someone by the name of Miss Cellany. Miscellany, do you see? It's quite the clever pen name. That's why I remembered it." Henry grinned at Lucas. "*You* must have read it, too, Dash. After all, I found the news sheet on the breakfast table last week."

Lucas controlled the urge to grind his teeth. He had picked up the paper from a newsstand outside Parliament after overhearing several other MPs discussing it. He had found the article in question to be well written, though largely preposterous in its assertions. "*The Weekly Verdict* is a tabloid full of sensationalist drivel. Nevertheless, it's important for one in my position to keep abreast of what these extremists are proposing."

"I applaud you, my lord, for your foresight," Mrs. Kipling gushed. "Why, without leaders like you, the rabble might revolt against their betters. The next thing you know they'll be calling for a guillotine in Hyde Park!"

Alice made a squeak of distress. "Oh, Mama, don't say such a frightful thing! Lucas, you *will* keep us safe, won't you?"

Long lashes fringed her blue eyes as she regarded him imploringly. He felt a stirring that was more protectiveness than passion. Despite her beauty, Alice Kipling really was quite young and naïve. At times like this, he felt as if he were robbing the cradle. "Of course," he said.

A girl just out of the schoolroom was the ideal age to marry, he told himself. She could be easily molded into the perfect wife. More importantly, Alice's dowry would ease the crushing burden of his debts. He could consolidate the mortgages on his several estates and make many critical improvements. The leaky roof on his ancestral home in West Sussex needed replacement, the addition of drainage would increase the revenue from his pastureland, and the ramshackle cottages of his tenants could be repaired.

The prospect of improving his properties filled Lucas with firm resolve. No minor qualms must be allowed to interfere with his plans. He would call on her father tomorrow and ask his permission for the marriage. The request would be a mere formality; it was clear that his offer would be eagerly accepted by Alice and her social-climbing mama.

Jarvis entered the drawing room. The short, balding butler approached at a dignified pace and bowed to Lucas. "Pardon the intrusion, milord. If I might have a word in private."

Lucas arose at once. "Excuse me, ladies."

He followed the servant into the corridor. When they were out of earshot, he said stoically, "Is it Mama? Has she driven off yet another servant?"

The last one had departed only the previous day. He'd had high hopes for that no-nonsense, middle-aged matron. She'd stayed a month—longer than most. But even *she* had declared the Marchioness of Dashell to be impossible.

"No, milord," Jarvis intoned. "Rest assured, Mrs. Jarvis is sitting with her ladyship for the moment, though to the neglect of her housekeeping duties. Rather, I need to inform your lordship of a visitor. A Miss Paxton."

The name struck Lucas like a blow, emptying his lungs of breath. *Rory Paxton?* She was here?

Impossible!

From out of the mists of the past came the image of her laughing brown eyes, the jet-black hair that framed a face so lovely he could have gazed at her forever. Yet it had been more than mere looks that had fascinated him. It was the life radiating from her, the sheer exuberance and *joie de vivre*. Her vitality had drawn him like a magnet, though he had disciplined the urge to act upon his imprudent attraction. She had been far too rash and reckless for his tastes, not at all the well-behaved lady that he preferred. Back then, he had expected Rory to disgrace herself, and that was precisely what had happened.

"The footman bade her wait in your study," the butler went on. "I apologize for the interruption, but Miss Paxton was most insistent on speaking to you immediately, milord."

Nothing about this made any sense. Why the devil would Rory Paxton call on him? He'd scarcely known her. There had been only that one moment of weakness when he'd succumbed to temptation and asked her to dance. It had been a waltz, and he would never forget the pleasure of holding her delectably curvy body in his arms. At the end of the set, she had gone back to her flock of suitors with nary a backward glance at him.

Eight years had passed since then. After that ghastly scandal, she had been disowned by her parents and banished to the country. Why would she now be back in London? And desiring to speak to *him* of all people?

She wouldn't.

All of a sudden, the fog cleared from his brain. He almost laughed out loud at his foolish assumption. *Miss Paxton* didn't necessarily mean Rory. His caller must be her younger sister, Celeste, whose betrothal to Whittingham had recently been announced.

The band of tension around his rib cage eased. Yes, that explanation made far more sense. Since they belonged to the same club, Lucas considered the duke a friend. Perhaps Whittingham wanted him to perform some service in his upcoming nuptials, such as offering a toast at the wedding breakfast. Or perhaps Miss Celeste

Paxton merely wanted advice on a gift for her fiancé. He was only slightly acquainted with the girl, but such a request could explain why she had come here in person rather than write a letter.

"I'll speak to her in a moment," he told Jarvis.

He returned to the drawing room. Henry was leaning in his chair to whisper something to Perry, and they shared a smothered chuckle. Lucas peered sharply at them. What was it that amused them now? At twenty, Henry really ought to act more grown-up.

"I must excuse myself for a moment," Lucas announced. "Henry, I will depend upon you to converse with our guests until my return."

His brother waved a desultory hand. "Run along, Dash. Never fear, you can trust Perry and me to keep the ladies entertained."

Lucas subdued any qualms over leaving his brother with the Kiplings. Doubtless, Henry would flirt shamelessly and tell outrageous tales, but it would not put off Alice and her eager mama. Alice was smiling adoringly at Lucas right now. His bride-to-be was already hooked, and it was only a matter of reeling her in.

Leaving them, he descended the grand staircase to the ground floor and proceeded past the cavernous library. This great old pile of a house had been built by a more prosperous ancestor and was now in sad need of repair, from the cracked marble floor tiles to the shabby furnishings in the reception rooms. It was a constant reminder of the pressing need to settle his future. Whatever this visit with Miss Celeste Paxton entailed, it shouldn't require more than a few minutes of his time. He would go back to his guests then. And he would inform Mrs. Kipling of his intention to call on her husband in the morning. Once permission was given, Lucas could present his offer to Alice.

By this time tomorrow, he would be affianced to his heiress.

Satisfied with the plan, Lucas approached his study. The door was partly closed, and he pushed it open without knocking. He stepped inside and came to an abrupt halt.

Every particle of his body froze. He could not move or speak. It wasn't Miss Celeste Paxton, after all.

It was *her*.

Like a nymph from his dreams, Rory Paxton stood behind his desk, gazing down at an open ledger book. Her ebony hair was gathered up in a simple coil at the back of her neck, exposing the pale elegance of her throat. A soft green gown skimmed her womanly form, and the lace fichu tucked into her neckline did little to hide the full curves of her bosom. The passage of time had only made her more sinfully enticing than ever.

His mouth went dry. His pulse pounded. He could not fathom her purpose in being here. He could not think at all, for that matter.

Lifting her head, Rory Paxton spotted him and straightened to her willowy height. Her sherry-brown eyes had a bold directness that lacked proper modesty. Healthy color glowed on her creamy skin as if she'd spent a good deal of time outdoors without bonnet or parasol.

For one long moment, they stared at each other. Only as she stepped out from behind the desk did he notice that her gown appeared rather outdated, the lace frayed, the fabric faded. With a hint of naughtiness, a pair of garnet-red slippers peeked out from beneath her hem.

They advertised her status as a fallen woman.

Maybe Rory had come here with an immoral proposition. Maybe she was so desperate for money she would do the unthinkable. Maybe she intended to offer her services as his mistress.

Lust seared his veins in a hot, unwelcome wave. He'd be a fool to succumb to fleshly urges when he was as good as engaged. He wanted nothing whatsoever to do with Rory Paxton. She was trouble with a capital *T.*

She dipped a curtsy, imbuing even that proper ladylike act with carnal undertones. Her soft rose lips curved in a smile as she extended her gloved hand. "Lord Dashell, what a pleasure to see you again. I'm Miss Aurora Paxton, though my family calls me Rory. We met some years ago."

"I remember."

The hostile growl of his voice daunted Rory. He ignored her hand, and after a moment she withdrew it. Inheriting the title of marquess had only enhanced Lucas Vale's chilly manner. His features were chiseled from granite.

Nevertheless, he might be deemed handsome by those who favored haughty aristocrats. The navy blue coat had been tailored to fit his broad shoulders, and a starched white cravat contrasted with his swarthy skin. The penetrating gaze beneath his coffee-brown hair made a shiver tickle down her spine. Those iron-gray eyes regarded her with cold, unwelcoming hauteur.

What was he thinking? Was he remembering her fall from grace? Or worse, had he guessed her visit had to do with the packet of letters that he'd stolen? The latter seemed likely. She was, after all, the stepdaughter of the woman he was blackmailing.

Rory regretted peeking at that ledger without first closing the study door. It only served to make her look guilty. But she'd been hoping to compare a sample of his writing to the blackmail note. The effort had been in vain, for the page had contained mostly figures.

Now, she must allay his suspicions or he would know for certain that she had come to investigate him. It would take charm and finesse to convince him to hire a woman of her ruined reputation.

She dipped her chin in a coquettish pose. "I hope you'll pardon the intrusion, my lord. You must be a very busy man."

"State your business, then, and begone."

It was not an auspicious beginning. Perhaps a more direct manner would work better. "As you wish. I've come to inquire about Lady Dashell. I understand that she is bedridden."

His eyes widened slightly as if he'd expected her to utter something else. "My mother? I can't see how her health should concern you. The two of you were never acquainted."

"Yes, that's true. However, I have reason to believe that I can be of service to her—"

"She isn't receiving callers," he rudely cut in. "Especially not from someone who has been tainted by scandal. Good day, Miss Paxton."

As he turned to go, Rory sprang past him and into the doorway to block his departure. "Please, my lord, I only require a moment of your time. I've heard that you're seeking a companion for Lady Dashell. I would very much like to apply for the post."

Lord Dashell cocked an eyebrow. His lips thinned, he looked her up and down. The scorn in his gaze could not have been more obvious. "No."

"Has the position already been filled, then?"

"I meant that it is not open to *you*, Miss Paxton. I'll have one of the footmen see you out."

Rory seethed inside. Really, the man was insufferable. He didn't care how rude he was. She wanted to whip back her arm and slap his cheek just to rattle that disdainful arrogance of his.

Determined to win the job, however, she clasped her folded hands at her waist. "Perhaps you shouldn't be so swift to dismiss me. You don't even know my qualifications."

He glowered down at her from his superior height. "I know that your character has been blackened by your own misdeeds. For that reason alone, you are unsuited to the role of companion to a marchioness. I won't have my family subjected to tawdry gossip."

"If Lady Dashell is confined to her bed, then we shan't be going out into society. No one of consequence need know that I'm even here."

"Nevertheless, my answer remains the same. Move aside now."

He took a menacing step toward her, but Rory refused to budge from the doorway. "I've heard she's a rather difficult woman," she persisted. "And that she's driven away scores of companions."

"Then I will save her the trouble of driving *you* away."

"I am not so easily intimidated as all the others. That is precisely why you need me, my lord."

Even as the words left her lips, Rory realized the double meaning of her statement. Something hot flashed in Dashell's eyes, and it had to be anger, for he was too cold a man to feel anything so human as desire. Nevertheless, her heart galloped within the confines of her corset. She could detect his alluring scent of pine and leather, and it had a powerful effect on her senses, making her feel soft and languid when she needed to be strong.

How long had it been since she'd stood so close to a

man who wasn't an old drunkard or a peach-fuzzed youngster?

The answer didn't signify. She had no interest in men anymore, except as subjects for her essay writing. Her only purpose here was to locate the packet of love letters that Lucas Vale had stolen from Kitty.

She hastened to clarify, "I've developed quite the knack for dealing with irascible older ladies. You see, I've been living with my aunt in Norfolk for the past eight years. Aunt Bernice was peevish and cross when I first arrived, but we've since become the best of companions. All it took was patience and fortitude."

His lips twisted in a humorless parody of a smile. "You would need an endless supply of stamina to deal with my mother. For one, she throws things."

"Then I shall become adept at catching those things— or at least ducking out of the way. You'll find me to be a resilient, hardworking employee, and more than capable of handling Lady Dashell. I vow, you'll wonder how you ever survived without me."

As she uttered that audacious statement, he subjected her to a sharp, reassessing stare. Rory held her breath, hoping that she'd broken through his stony resistance. If Lady Dashell was as petulant as he'd implied, he must be eager to find someone strong enough to tolerate her, thus allowing him the freedom to spin his spiderweb of blackmail.

She'd been dubious at first when Kitty had claimed he was deeply in debt and in desperate need of funds. But now she could believe this man capable of any nefarious deeds. His callous manner would befit the most hardened criminal in Newgate Prison.

Lord Dashell walked away a few steps, then swung to face her. "You were banished. Why have you been allowed to return to London?"

He must be wondering if she was conspiring with Kitty. It was best to quash that notion once and for all by convincing him she was here of her own accord.

Rory adopted a woeful expression, lowering her chin and gazing up at him through the screen of her lashes. "If you must know, I wasn't precisely *allowed* to return. My stepmother was most unhappy when I showed up on her doorstep. Yet I had no choice but to come to the city, for I was facing impossible circumstances."

"Explain yourself."

"There are very few opportunities for genteel work in Norfolk," she improvised glibly. "My aunt is destitute, you see, and I need to find gainful employment so that I might send my earnings back to her."

"You've no funds of your own, then?"

"None whatsoever. I was cut off without a penny." It was the truth, for she hadn't yet earned the reward that Kitty had promised her.

Scowling, Lord Dashell paced back and forth on the threadbare oriental rug. "Your sister is soon to wed Whittingham. I cannot imagine your family would want it known that her ruined sister is seeking to go into service."

"My father passed away seven years ago, and my stepmother will be glad to be rid of me. In fact, she ordered me to stay out of sight during the wedding preparations."

"For good reason. You don't appear to have lost your propensity for rash behavior."

"I beg your pardon?"

He stepped closer, his gaze intent. "You were snooping in my ledger just now. Why?"

Her heart fluttered as he stopped directly in front of her. Though taller than the average lady, Rory had to tilt her head to meet his gaze. Even so, it was impossible to read the thoughts behind those flinty features.

He mustn't guess that she'd been seeking a sample of his penmanship.

She shaped her lips into a contrite smile. "I confess I was tempted by the desire to learn how much the position pays, my lord. My pockets are quite to let, you see. I pray that you can find it in your heart to forgive me."

His eyes were granite chips that lacked human warmth. How foolish of her to hope that a plea might soften him. He did not have a sympathetic bone in his diabolically masculine body. He was a blackmailer who had extorted a valuable diamond necklace from her step-mother and had demanded a thousand pounds as the next payment.

What more could she say to win over such a villain? None of her wiles had worked. He was oblivious to persuasion and immune to flirtation.

"The salary is sixty pounds per annum," he said abruptly. "You will be expected to attend to the marchioness day and night, including sleeping on a cot in her dressing room. You must pacify her quarrelsome nature and humor her demands. I will not have the rest of the household disrupted in any way."

Her heart commenced a wild knocking. "You'll hire me, then?"

"If you're willing to meet those conditions, be here tomorrow morning at seven. Good day, Miss Paxton."

With that, Lord Dashell thrust past her and left the study.

Stunned by her success, Rory felt the urge to twirl around in the cavernous corridor, to laugh out loud with delight. Instead, she scurried after her new employer as he stalked down the passageway toward the front of the house, his shoes clicking on the marble tiles.

What had made him decide in her favor? Did he suspect her true purpose here? Perhaps he thought it best to keep her under close observation.

No matter. This was her golden opportunity to earn a portion of her dowry. Half of her itched to begin the investigation at once; the other half wanted to return home and see if Celeste had returned . . .

As Lord Dashell reached the newel post and pivoted to ascend the grand staircase, he spied her. His face hardened into an iron mask so that he appeared even more inhospitable than ever. "Why are you following me?"

"I'm on my way out. You *did* say that I wasn't to start today."

"The servants' door is at the rear of the house."

Of course, she was now a member of the staff. The entrance hall in which they stood was reserved for the family and aristocratic guests. The realization might have been galling had she not been so elated over her victory.

She bobbed a breezy curtsy. "Do pardon me, Lord Dashell. For a moment, I had quite forgotten how far I've fallen in the world."

As he eyed her impish expression, a muscle tightened in his jaw. His gaze was so intent that it kindled an unsettling warmth inside her. His eyes fascinated her, the irises steel-gray rimmed by charcoal. He looked fit and strong, and again she felt that tug of unwanted attraction to him.

If he would just smile, he'd be an extraordinarily handsome man. And if he would thaw his heart, he might even tempt *her* from her self-imposed moratorium on romance. What would it be like to bury her face in the crook of his shoulder and breathe in his masculine scent? To feel his hands clasping her close, his lips tasting hers? To learn if she had the power to delve past his wall of reserve and make him wild with passion?

The trill of genteel voices penetrated the spell on her senses. The intrusive sound lured her attention upward. She blinked in surprise to see a party of two gentlemen and two ladies descending the grand staircase.

Chapter 6

*A woman should derive contentment from her own life
rather than requiring a man to assure her happiness.*

—MISS CELLANY

Lucas clamped his teeth around a curse. He had been
so focused on Rory's kissable mouth that he'd failed to
notice his brother and their guests until they were halfway down the stairs. Blast Henry! He'd been ordered to
remain in the drawing room with the ladies until Lucas's
return.

He pressed his palm to the back of her slim waist,
giving her a little push toward the rear of the house. "Go.
Now."

Curiosity glinted in her dark eyes. "As you wish."

Even as she took a step to depart, it was already too
late.

Henry galloped down the marble stairs ahead of the
others. "Well, well, Dash! So, it wasn't a crisis in Parliament that lured you away from us. It was this mysterious beauty. Won't you introduce me?"

Lucas had hoped to delay revealing his hiring of a
disgraced woman. Especially since he couldn't explain
it himself, aside from suffering a momentary fit of madness when Rory had looked at him with those soft doe
eyes and admitted she was desperate for employment.
He knew all too well the anxiety of needing money.

"I've engaged a new companion for Mama," he said curtly. "You can meet her tomorrow when she begins her assignment."

Henry seized Rory's hand and kissed the back. "Never mind my brother's rudeness. Dash was born a tyrant. I'm Lord Henry Vale. And you are . . . ?"

As she drew back her hand, she cast an oblique glance at Lucas. "It's Lord Dashell's prerogative to make me known as he sees fit."

"Then he must do so at once! Else I shall be forced to sniff along at your heels like a lost puppy until I discover your identity."

Lucas despised being backed into a corner. But the family would discover her name soon enough, and better it should come from him than spiteful gossips. "This is Miss Paxton. She was just about to depart."

"Paxton, you say?" Perry asked as he reached the bottom of the stairs, Alice on one arm and Mrs. Kipling on the other. Abandoning them, he hastened closer, his youthful features bright with interest beneath a thatch of fair hair. "Are you kin to Miss Celeste Paxton?"

"She's my half sister."

Perry and Henry exchanged a surprised glance. Lucas had witnessed them behaving like besotted idiots around this year's crop of debutantes, in particular, Celeste Paxton. Luckily, they were both too low in the pocket to entertain a serious courtship of a girl with so modest a dowry. And at least now she was off the market and no temptation to his brother. Unlike her elder sister, she'd had the sense to accept Whittingham's offer of marriage rather than ruin herself by cavorting with the wrong man.

"I see that beauty is a family trait," Henry said with an echo of their father's lavish charm. "You're as dark as she is fair, two sides of the same lovely coin."

"Odd, Ce-Ce never let on that she had a sister," Perry said.

"You used her pet name," Rory said, turning eagerly to him. "Do you know her well, sir?"

Perry flushed, his freckles becoming more prominent, as often happened when the attention turned on him. "Just—just a little," he stammered.

"No need to address this scamp as *sir*," Henry said, clapping his friend on the back. "He's Peregrine Davenport, though you may call him Perry if you like. Oh, and this is Miss Alice Kipling and her mama, Mrs. Kipling."

Lucas wanted to drag Henry out by his ear and ream him over the coals for that introduction. Mrs. Kipling and her daughter had been politely standing back, but now they were gazing askance at Rory, as if unsure what to make of a nubile spinster in his employ.

Especially one who was clearly a lady.

The only saving grace was that none of them could possibly know about Rory's scandalous past. Henry and Perry were too young to have heard the eight-year-old gossip, and the Kiplings had only recently been accepted in society due to their rich, eligible daughter.

"Miss Paxton needn't meet our guests," he told his brother. "She will remain upstairs with the marchioness at all times."

"But what if Miss Kipling wishes to visit Mama in her chambers? It would be nice for her to know that she has an ally present." In an aside to Rory, Henry added in a loud whisper, "She is Dash's romantic interest, you see, and she'll have to meet Mama sooner or later—"

"Henry," Lucas snapped. "That is quite enough."

But Rory's attentive gaze had already shifted from him to Alice, and he felt exposed and raw, his private plans laid out for her—for everyone—to scrutinize. He despised having his intentions bandied about before he'd even made his official offer.

Mrs. Kipling's pudgy face glowed. "It would be a great honor to meet the marchioness. I'm sure it must be tremendously dull for such a venerable lady to be confined to her chambers, and we would be happy to do our part in keeping her entertained." She cast a speaking glance at her daughter. "Wouldn't we, darling?"

"Oh, yes, indeed," Alice piped up, while batting her lashes at Lucas. "It would be our pleasure."

Good God, the last thing he needed was to frighten off his heiress by introducing her to his peevish mother. Better to wait until the last possible moment, just before the knot was tied. "Perhaps another time," he said vaguely.

"We hope it shall be very soon," Mrs. Kipling said. She cast another dubious glance at Rory, then turned a toadying smile at Lucas. "My lord, I should not wish to gainsay you, but are you quite certain that such a *young* female as Miss Paxton will be suitable company for her ladyship?"

"Yes. She comes highly recommended."

By herself, Lucas amended silently. He was annoyed at having to defend his choice. But if Rory could tame his mother's temper as she'd boasted, then hiring her would be well worth the trouble.

"I'm curious as to why you would seek employment here, Miss Paxton," Henry said. "With your sister marrying Whittingham, one would think you'd be required at home."

"Oh, but London isn't my home," Rory said. "I hail from Norfolk—"

"Henry," Lucas broke in, "we're heard enough of your impertinent commentary. Miss Paxton was just on her way out."

If Henry questioned her need to earn a living, he'd learn that she'd been cut off without a penny. And then he'd find out about the scandal.

Thankfully, Rory took the hint and curtsied, before gliding down the corridor toward the rear of the house. The sight of her sinuous walk sparked a fantasy of encountering her upstairs in her nightgown, her hair unbound and her feet bare. Heat bedeviled Lucas, and he had to quash the untimely reaction. He was a damned fool for letting her live under his roof. Even if she *had* gazed at him with those soulful eyes.

He dragged his attention from the sway of her hips and forced a smile at Alice as her mother blathered something about seeing him at the Earl of Copley's ball the following evening. Henry and Perry vanished into the library, no doubt seeking the decanter of brandy and a private chat about Celeste Paxton's sister.

As Mrs. Kipling and her daughter took their leave, a footman sprang to open the door and Lucas escorted his guests out onto the columned portico that faced the greenery of Grosvenor Square. Alice set her dainty gloved hand in his and graced him with a winsome smile while murmuring a shy farewell. It was only as mother and daughter were entering their luxurious black carriage that he realized he had forgotten to request permission to call on Mr. Kipling the following morning.

Lucas could have rectified the oversight by hurrying down the granite steps. But he didn't.

As the carriage rolled away, he subdued a guilty twinge of reprieve. What did it matter, really? There was no immediate rush. The marriage proposal could be postponed for another day or two. The bailiffs were not beating down his door.

At least not yet.

* * *

Stepping into the bedchamber with its French white furniture and the frilly rose draperies, Rory found herself gazing upon a scene straight out of the past.

Her half sister lay prone on the canopied bed, her back to the door and her arms straddling a feather pillow. She'd kicked up her lower legs and idly swung them back and forth, revealing silk stockings and a fluff of white petticoats beneath a pale-yellow gown. With her golden head bent over a sketchpad, she glided a pencil over the paper in quick strokes. She was so intent on her drawing that she hadn't even noticed the soft click of the opening door or the muffled patter of Rory's footsteps on the plush carpet.

Celeste's favorite occupation at age ten had been to sprawl on the bed and sketch fantastical pictures of dragons and princesses and castles. But she was not a little girl anymore. She was a woman of eighteen. A woman who would soon be a wife.

A flood of emotion inundated Rory . . . joy at seeing her sister again . . . regret for the lost years of separation . . . and anxiety that Celeste might have made the worst mistake of her young life in betrothing herself to the Duke of Whittingham. According to Kitty, the couple were madly in love. But it remained to be seen if that was really the truth.

Rory cleared her throat.

Without pausing the movement of her pencil, Celeste spoke over her shoulder, "You're far too early, Foster. I've nearly two hours yet before it's time to leave, and I do want to finish this. Can't you *please* help Mama dress first?"

"Ce-Ce." Rory used the pet name that Celeste had invented for herself, back when she was a toddler just learning to talk, just as Rory had done with her own name, Aurora. "It's me."

Celeste whipped her head around. A pair of startled blue eyes widened on Rory. The ormolu clock on the mantel ticked into the silence as the sisters stared at each other. Rory drank in the sight of that pert nose, the delicate chin, the arched eyebrows. Her sister looked hauntingly familiar, yet her youthful features had gained maturity, radiant now with womanly beauty.

Rory stepped forward. "I've come home. Aren't you happy to see me?"

The sketchbook and pencil went flying as Celeste scrambled off the bed and hurled herself into her sister's arms. "Rory!" she squealed. "It's really you! I can't believe it! Why, I must be dreaming!"

Rory caught her close in a hug. Tears blurred her eyes and tightened her throat. Inhaling the fragrance of lilac, she reveled in the warmth of the embrace before drawing back to fondly regard Celeste. "You're not dreaming, silly. And my, look at you! You were a little girl when I left. Now, you're all grown up."

"It's been eight years, after all. But why didn't you write and tell me that you were coming to London? Does Mama know you're here?"

A lurch assailed Rory's stomach. So, Kitty hadn't mentioned her arrival. She must have hoped that Rory would secure the post at Dashell House and remain there. Because, of course, Kitty would never have told Celeste about the blackmail scheme, or the plan to have her disgraced stepdaughter retrieve the stolen letters from Lord Dashell.

Rory hid her resentment behind a smile. "I wanted my arrival to be a surprise," she hedged. "I'm only here for a short time. Come, sit with me, and I'll tell you all about it."

She guided her sister over to a rose-and-white-striped chaise by the hearth. Celeste plopped down and clutched at Rory's hands. "What do you mean, only a short time?" she asked. "How long?"

"I'm departing in the morning for Dashell House in Grosvenor Square. You see, I've taken a position as companion to the Marchioness of Dashell. I'll be living there henceforth."

At least until she accomplished her mission and found the pilfered packet of *billets-doux*. She would relish seeing the coldhearted Lord Dashell receive his just due when his crimes were exposed. Then she would quit the post and return here for a nice long visit, no matter how much Kitty protested.

Celeste's lips parted in astonishment. "A companion! *You?* And to Lady Dashell!"

"Do you know her?"

She glanced away for a moment. "I know her son Lord Henry Vale. And his friend Mr. Perry Davenport. They've both been very kind to me, asking me to dance so that I wouldn't be a wallflower."

Rory wondered at her sister's blush. Could there have been a flirtation in the works before she had accepted His Grace's offer? "You, a wallflower? The gentlemen of the ton would have to be blind not to see your beauty."

Celeste shrugged off the compliment. "I don't understand why you must labor for a living. What about Aunt Bernice?"

"I'll be sending my wages back to her. She hasn't much to her name, and I have resolved to help out with the household expenses." It was only a small fib, for Rory had every intention of donating her reward money toward improving their living standards.

"Why don't you apply to Mama for funds? I'm sure she can spare enough to cover the amount of your salary. She never hesitated to purchase whatever was necessary for my come-out."

Her earnest manner touched Rory's heart. Celeste was too naïve to see that if Kitty had wanted to be generous, she would have done so already, instead of allowing her stepdaughter to languish in the country wearing eight-year-old gowns. But Celeste had always been the favored one on whom Kitty lavished gifts and affection. After Rory's disgrace, everyone had believed the worst of her, even her dear Papa, who had sided with his wife in banishing Rory for fear that her soiled reputation would eventually taint her half sister.

Yet none of that was Celeste's fault. She was as innocent of intrigue as a newborn babe.

Rory patted her sister's soft hand. "I shan't ask any such favors of Kitty, especially as she's already incurred the expense of your debut. Anyway, I am determined to do this on my own. The decision has already been made. I'm sorry to depart so soon, but at least we have today to catch up on things."

A shadow flitted over Celeste's face, chasing the sparkle from her eyes. "Oh, but I can't spend the evening with you. Mama and I have a dinner to attend."

"Can you make an excuse? Pretend you're ill as we used to do when we were children?"

"*You* did so, not I. *I* was never so brave! And I dare not, anyway. I must accompany the Duke of Whittingham to his aunt's house." Celeste dipped her chin slightly, her teeth worrying her lower lip. "Perhaps you don't know . . . I'm engaged to wed His Grace next month. I intended to write to you, Rory, truly I did. But Mama thought it was best that I wait."

"Because the presence of a disgraced half sister might make the duke withdraw his offer?" Seeing Celeste's shamefaced expression, Rory softened her tone. "Don't fret, Ce-Ce. Kitty only means to protect you, I'm sure. And she already told me the news when I saw her a short while ago."

"You must come to the wedding now that you're in town." Celeste leaned forward, her gaze earnest. "Oh, *can* you be there? Will you ask Lady Dashell to spare you for the day? I don't think I could bear it if you weren't present."

The urgency in her manner only increased Rory's suspicions. Gazing at Celeste's angelic face and smooth skin, the golden hair and big blue eyes, she could understand why that stuffy old duke had selected her as his bride. But what did Celeste see in a man more than twice her age? It was hard to imagine that she'd choose ambition over the desires of her tender heart. "Of course I'll attend. But darling, do tell me. Do you love Whittingham? Are you truly happy to be marrying him?"

Celeste hesitated the barest instant. "Why, certainly! His Grace is the premier catch of the season! All the other girls are pea-green with envy that I'm to be a duchess."

Her gushing testimony sounded like something Kitty would utter. Was Celeste merely echoing her mother? Had she subdued her own hopes and dreams in order to please Kitty? "I do hope you'll confide in me if you're suffering any doubts. It isn't too late to call the whole thing off."

"Oh, but I could *never* do that. His Grace has chosen me above all others. And Mama would be heartbroken."

"Better *she* is heartbroken than you," Rory stated. "Marriage is a lifelong commitment. You must be very sure of yourself—and of him."

"His Grace has been most attentive, sending me gifts and flowers nearly every day. He is kind and generous to a fault, a true gentleman."

Rory couldn't shake a nagging sense that Ce-Ce was playing a role in order to avoid conflict with Kitty. Even as a child, she had been too agreeable and malleable for her own good, and it was clear that she'd committed herself to the May–December union. Having just arrived, Rory didn't want to push too hard too soon; there would still be time after she found the letters to return here and coax the truth out of Celeste.

At the moment, Celeste's fingers were entwined tightly in her lap, indicative of an inner tension that she refused to voice. "Your mama mentioned an heirloom betrothal ring," Rory said. "Why aren't you wearing it?"

"Oh, my ring!" Pink heightened the cream of her cheeks. "It's rather heavy, so I sometimes take it off while I'm at home. I'll put it back on at once."

Rising, Celeste darted to the bedside table, opened an enameled box, and slid the ring onto her finger. She returned to the chaise and held out her hand rather shyly. "See? Isn't it magnificent?"

An enormous square-cut diamond winked in a thick, old-fashioned gold setting. It looked far too large and ornate for Celeste's dainty hand. "It's most impressive," Rory said tactfully. "I don't believe I've ever seen a diamond quite so large."

"The ring belonged to His Grace's mother. I must be very careful not to lose it." Celeste sank her teeth into her lower lip again. "I'm thankful you reminded me. The duchess will be at dinner tonight, and she would be very displeased if I appear in public without it."

Rory was about to reply when footsteps approached from the doorway. In a rustle of blue silk skirts, Kitty swept into the bedchamber, her wary gaze flitting from her daughter to Rory. Her tight smile held a note of displeasure.

"Grimshaw informed me that you'd returned, Rory.

I'm afraid that I must interrupt your little chat now. It's time for you to dress for dinner, Celeste. Foster is here to assist you."

A plain-faced maidservant with mousy brown hair hung back behind her. Clad in drab gray, she scuttled toward the dressing room, her eyes downcast. She must be relatively new, for Rory had never before seen the woman.

"But Mama," Celeste protested, "Rory has only just arrived. Can't she stay and keep me company while I dress? Perhaps if I send a note she could even accompany us to dinner—"

"That is out of the question. His Grace would be aghast at such a request. Pray recall that your sister is no longer accepted in society. And through no fault but her own."

Though irked by Kitty's manner, Rory knew that a quarrel would only upset her sister. She arose from the chaise and gave her sister a quick hug. "It's all right, Ce-Ce. I'll wait up and see you later when you return home."

She headed for the doorway with Kitty close at her heels. "I should like a word with you, Aurora."

"Of course."

They proceeded out into the corridor and Kitty closed the door behind them. Then she caught Rory by the arm and half dragged her down the passageway and into her own bedchamber, a sumptuous room decorated in gold and green. The air smelled of the cloying rose scent that she favored.

"I never thought to see you back here today," Kitty hissed. "Did you fail to secure the position?"

Rory considered making her stepmother squirm, then decided against it. Petty games wouldn't earn her that reward. "Never fear, I haven't failed. I was hired as Lady Dashell's companion. I'm to start in the morning."

Kitty withdrew a lacy handkerchief from her sleeve and fanned her plump face. "Thank heavens. I was so afraid Lord Dashell might refuse to employ a ruined woman. Or has he forgotten your notoriety? Oh, what a blessing *that* would be!"

The flinty contempt on Lucas Vale's face flashed into Rory's memory. As if he stood right in front of her, she could see his eyes, granite-gray irises rimmed by dark iron, staring at her. A strange shiver prickled her skin. He had gazed at her lips, as well. As if he'd contemplated having his wicked way with her . . .

"He remembered me, all right. He refused my application at first, but I managed to overcome his reservations. He seemed rather anxious to find someone to care for his mother. Especially as he appears to be courting a Miss Kipling. I met her as I was leaving."

"That little baggage! Whittingham was sniffing after her at the start of the season, before I made sure to put Celeste squarely in his path."

"Oh?"

"Yes, and I'm not at all surprised Lord Dashell is pursuing Miss Kipling. She's as common as dirt, but her father made a fortune with his textile mills in Manchester. It only confirms that Lady Milford was right, the marquess is desperate for funds."

Rory raised an eyebrow. No wonder he'd appeared angry at Lord Henry for introducing her to the Kiplings. If Lord Dashell had marriage on his mind, he wouldn't want anyone to think he was dallying with a disgraced lady under his own roof. "I only hope Lord Dashell hasn't guessed my true purpose. It must seem peculiar to him that the stepdaughter of the woman he's black-mailing wishes to work in his house."

"Quite so," Kitty said, clutching the handkerchief to her ample bosom. "You must take care not to tip him off to my plan. He might release those letters to the newspapers out of spite, and then I would be embroiled in sordid scandal. Whittingham might call off the wedding!"

How typical of Kitty to be more concerned for the success of her schemes than her stepdaughter being in danger from a blackmailer.

Annoyed, Rory strolled to the window and glanced down at the pedestrians hurrying along the street. She turned back around and crossed her arms. "Lord Dashell may be extorting money from you, but I'm not convinced he'd actually publish the letters. After all, they were written by his father. A scandal might threaten his own marital plans, too."

"Bah. The nouveau riche care little about dishonor so long as they can worm their way into the aristocracy. Besides, no one ever blames the man for the affair. *I* would bear the brunt of it—and your sister, as well."

Rory conceded the point. Society *was* unfair to women. "Speaking of Ce-Ce, I must again question the wisdom of this betrothal. After talking to her, I'm not entirely certain that she wants the marriage."

"Don't be absurd. Of course she wishes to wed Whittingham. It is the summit of every girl's dreams to marry a duke!"

"I rather think it is the summit of *your* dreams," Rory countered dryly. "You wouldn't wish for her to be unhappy, would you?"

"What nonsense. How could any woman be unhappy as a duchess?" Kitty stepped to the dressing table and preened in the mirror. "Why, my daughter will consort with royalty. She will lead the cream of society. And someday her eldest son—*my* grandson—will be a duke!"

Rory could see the futility of trying to dissuade her stepmother from that glorious vision. "Can you not at least delay the wedding? To give the two of them a chance to become better acquainted?"

"Delay? Why, the sooner they speak their vows, the better." Kitty turned to shake her finger at Rory. "And don't you dare try to talk your sister out of it!"

"I should like to meet His Grace. To observe them together and determine for myself if their love is true."

"Absolutely not! Whittingham would be furious to learn that you're in London. You cannot be so cruel as to spoil such a brilliant match for Celeste."

"But—"

"No ifs, ands, or buts, Aurora. When His Grace arrives this evening to fetch Celeste and me, *you* will stay out of sight."

Rory positioned herself in a shadowed alcove near the head of the staircase. From this vantage point, she had a clear view of the entry hall. As a child, she'd often crouched here during parties to peer through the wrought-iron posts of the balustrade. She'd loved to observe the comings and goings of the noble guests, the ladies in their colorful gowns, the gentlemen in formal black attire.

Tonight, only four people gathered in the foyer. Celeste looked angelic in a cream silk gown, her fair hair arranged in curls with a cluster of rosebuds tucked behind one ear. Grimshaw was helping her don her cloak. A short distance away, Kitty was fawning over the Duke of Whittingham.

Rory frowned. His Grace ought to be the one lending assistance to his bride-to-be, not the butler. If Whittingham was as madly in love as Kitty claimed, he would seize every opportunity to be near Celeste. He would brush her cheek with his fingers and bend close to whisper sweet nothings in her ear. He would gaze adoringly at her and have eyes for no one else.

But more than just his manner troubled Rory.

The duke had aged a great deal in eight years. He was even more portly than she recalled, and his hairline had receded rather drastically, leaving him with a bald pate that glistened in the candlelight from the wall sconces. His face had developed heavy jowls, and the spidery redness across his large nose betrayed a tendency to overimbibe in drink. As he turned to offer his arm to Celeste, he looked more like her father than her fiancé.

His smile was patronizing rather than affectionate. "How lovely you look, my dear. Shall we go?"

"Yes, Your Grace."

Their voices floated up the staircase, his booming and haughty, hers small and submissive. Celeste placed her gloved hand on the sleeve of his black coat. As the couple started across the foyer, followed by Kitty, Grimshaw scurried to open the front door.

Rory itched to march down the steps and grill the duke regarding his attachment to her sister. She wanted to order him to treat Celeste with the love and respect she deserved.

As she moved slightly, taking a step out of the alcove, Kitty turned and looked up the stairs. Her gaze was sharp and watchful, as if sensing her stepdaughter's presence.

Rory melted back into the shadows. Now was not the time for another clash with her stepmother. It wouldn't do to raise a ruckus about her sister just yet. Not until after she'd found the stolen letters and earned that reward money.

Chapter 7

The grandes dames of society rule with an iron fist.
—MISS CELLANY

Early the next morning, Rory stepped into the busy kitchen in the cellars at Dashell House. The air held the delicious aromas of baking bread and frying gammon. A maidservant directed her to the housekeeper, Mrs. Jarvis, a spry, birdlike woman in black bombazine who looked as if the slightest gust of wind might blow her away. Rory was introduced to a host of servants who paused their breakfast preparations to bob a curtsy to her. She also met Mr. Jarvis, the short, balding butler who was married to the housekeeper.

As Mrs. Jarvis flitted back and forth, arranging silverware and china on a tray, she gave a quick overview of the marchioness's schedule. "Her ladyship is to be awakened at half past seven on the dot. Coddled eggs and hot chocolate are to be brought up at the same time. Then luncheon at noon, a nap at two, and dinner at six." The housekeeper's plain features held a wary look as she regarded Rory. "You *have* been informed that she is bedridden, I presume?"

"Yes, but I was never told why."

"She was hurt in the coaching accident a year ago that

killed the late marquess, God rest his soul. Her lady-ship's spine was injured. May I add that she can be a mite . . . testy. I do hope his lordship warned you."

"He did, indeed."

"The other companions sent by the agency were quite a bit older than you. None of them lasted very long, I fear. Most stayed for a fortnight or so, though one left after only half a day."

"I've taken care of my aunt for the past eight years. Grumpy older ladies are nothing new to me."

"Perhaps you'll do fine, then."

Yet Mrs. Jarvis still looked anxious as they marched up the dimly lit shaft of the servants' staircase. A foot-man carrying her ladyship's breakfast tray followed them. After three steep flights, they entered a quiet cor-ridor, their footsteps muffled by a long carpet runner. Age-darkened landscape paintings decorated the peeling wallpaper; like the rest of the mansion, the place had a forlorn look of neglect. The doors on either side were closed, and Rory wondered which one of these bed-chambers belonged to Lord Dashell.

Was he still asleep? Most aristocrats kept late hours, going to balls and parties and the theater, then slumber-ing until noon. Her wayward mind conjured an image of him lying in bed, his dark hair mussed, the sheets rid-ing down to his waist and exposing his bare muscled form . . .

She banished the disturbing fantasy. Lucas Vale was a callous blackmailer, unworthy of being the subject of feminine desire. It was irrational to think of him in such a manner, anyway, after she had learned the hard way never to make a fool of herself over any man. She pitied Miss Alice Kipling who was being courted for her rich dowry. The girl had looked as young and naïve as Celeste.

Mrs. Jarvis paused in front of a door at the end of the long passageway. "Pray allow me to do the talking, Miss Paxton," she whispered. "It would be best for you to observe how to mollify her ladyship."

She turned the handle and tiptoed into a shadowed bedchamber. Then she pantomimed that Rory was to stand near a dainty writing desk in the corner. The footman went ahead to quietly place the tray on a table. He made a swift exit, closing the door behind him.

Loud snores emanated from the massive canopied bed. The darkness, along with a lump of covers, hid Lady Dashell from view. A small gilt clock ticked softly on the bedside table. The air smelled stale and musty as if the windows had not been opened in years.

Mrs. Jarvis scurried across the room and drew back the blue velvet curtains on one of the windows. "Good morning, milady," she chirped. "'Tis seven-thirty and time to awaken."

As the dull light of a drizzly day spilled over the fine furnishings, the snoring stopped and the marchioness stirred in the bed. A skeletal arm snaked out from beneath the embroidered white counterpane and groped on the nightstand. Clawlike fingers grasped the clock. She brought the timepiece close to her wrinkled face. "It's seven thirty-two," she accused. "Why are you late?"

"I humbly beg your pardon, for I was delayed in the kitchen." Mrs. Jarvis ventured closer to the bed and bobbed a curtsy. "Shall I plump your pillows now, milady?"

"Keep your distance until I tell you otherwise."

"Yes, milady, of course. I do hope you're feeling better today than yesterday."

"Better?" With sudden vigor, Lady Dashell hurled the little clock. It crashed to the floor and forced the housekeeper to take a backward hop to avoid being struck. "How am I to feel better? My joints ache so much that I didn't sleep a wink last night!"

The woman had been snoring as loudly as a drum-beat, Rory noted. And it was clear that the housekeeper's method of toadying to the marchioness was only making her more tyrannical.

Rory stepped out of the shadows and picked up the clock. Mrs. Jarvis gasped and made a motion to shoo her away, but Rory paid no heed. She walked straight to the side of the bed. "I suspect you slept a bit more than you think, Lady Dashell. And if you are indeed still weary, then there is no need for you to awaken quite so early."

Lady Dashell squinted her eyes. A white nightcap sat cockeyed atop a shaggy fall of gray hair. She donned a pair of pince-nez from the bedside table and peered through the narrow glasses. "Who are you? I won't have strangers in here. Leave this bedchamber at once!"

"I won't be a stranger for long. I've been engaged as your new companion. Surely your son informed you that I would be here today."

"Impertinent baggage! You're too young to be a suitable companion. What is your name?"

"Miss Aurora Paxton. My friends and family call me Rory."

"Paxton?" Lady Dashell stared for a long moment; then her upper lip curled into a sneer. "I remember the gossip about you. You're the reckless girl who cavorted with that foreign Romeo. The married diplomat."

Rory blanched. To hide her discomfiture, she inspected the clock, noted that it was still ticking, and replaced it on the bedside table. She knew from dealing with her aunt that it was best to stand her ground. Her situation would be far more difficult if she showed any sign of weakness. "Yes. I'm that girl. So, you see, the worst has already happened to me. There is little you can say or do to frighten me."

Lady Dashell glowered. She had iron-gray eyes like the marquess, and a manner that was just as coldly unforgiving. In fact, mother and son seemed very much alike. Rory refused to be the first one to look away. She would not let this sour woman get the best of her.

"Well?" The marchioness plucked at the tangled counterpane. "Why are you standing there, gaping like a fool? I wish to sit up and eat my breakfast."

While Mrs. Jarvis ran to the table to remove the domed cover from the plate, Rory slid her arm behind her ladyship's back and helped her scoot up against a nest of feather pillows. The woman felt frail and bony, yet seemed to possess a wiry strength.

Or perhaps that was just her mean streak.

The housekeeper brought the tray to the bed and set it across her mistress's lap. Lady Dashell slurped greedily at the chocolate and then grimaced. "Cold again. I fail to see why a hot drink cannot be procured in this house. Are you and the rest of the staff so incompetent?"

"I'm terribly sorry, milady," Mrs. Jarvis said, twisting her knobby fingers in her apron. "I did bring the tray up straightaway. I'll speak to Cook about the matter. I'm sure the problem can be rectified—"

"Enough of your gibbering!"

The instant Lady Dashell started to draw back her arm, Rory caught her by the scrawny wrist and extracted the half-empty cup before it could be hurled. She handed it to Mrs. Jarvis. "Please fetch a fresh pot. And bring an additional cup for me."

"Aye, miss." Looking grateful for the chance to escape, the housekeeper flitted out and closed the door.

"A cup for *you*?" the marchioness repeated scathingly. "Do not put on false airs, Miss Paxton. I don't share meals with servants."

"Shall I prepare your toast?" Without awaiting permission, Rory slathered orange marmalade on a slice. "As for my situation, I was raised a lady, so it would be polite of you to ask me to join you. And far more pleasant to treat me as a friend rather than an underling."

"Friend! What egalitarian nonsense." Lady Dashell snatched the toast that Rory held out to her. "You're as bossy as Bernice."

Rory blinked in surprise. "Bernice? Are you referring to my aunt?"

"Who else would I mean? She was a Paxton, too." Glowering, Lady Dashell bit into the toast and crumbs sprinkled the bodice of her nightdress. "We made our bows in the same season. I believed her to be a decent sort until she allowed herself to be duped into marrying that dreadful sea captain."

"Uncle Oliver didn't dupe her. And he wasn't dreadful, he was a former naval officer. She loved him dearly and they sailed all over the globe together."

"Love, bah! Marriages are meant to be grand alliances."

"Not everyone adheres to society's insular views. Anyway, if Aunt Bernice was as bossy as you claim, how would it have been possible for Uncle Oliver to dupe her?"

"With flowers and kisses and romantic drivel, that's how. The same way *you* were duped, Miss Paxton." Lady Dashell let loose a nasty cackle. "Except that *you* did not end up with a ring on your finger."

Rory refused to show any reaction to the gibe. How could she when it was the truth? And she had scolded herself enough over the years to be immune to criticism—at least mostly.

Leaning forward, she draped a linen serviette over the marchioness's bony bosom to catch the shower of crumbs. She wondered if Lady Dashell's bitterness sprang from more than the accident that had disabled her. Perhaps she'd also endured an unhappy marriage, for surely no woman could be content with a husband who was as notorious a philanderer as the previous Lord Dashell.

"I agree that starry-eyed girls are too often maneuvered into unsuitable matches," Rory said. "In particular, by gentlemen who covet a beauty or an heiress—or both. Only look at Miss Kipling."

Miss Kipling's situation held a disturbing similarity to Celeste's. Both girls were being pushed into marrying a haughty older nobleman when they ought to wed someone closer to their own age. Rory decided that it would make an excellent topic for an essay on the plight of women in society.

"Miss Kipling? Who the devil is she?"

The sharp query in Lady Dashell's voice startled Rory. She had presumed the marchioness knew about her eldest son's marital plans, especially since he needed to marry wealth after squandering his fortune through poor investments. But judging by the surprise on that bitter, lined face, it appeared that his mother had been kept in the dark.

A little devil made Rory say, "I'm sure Lord Dashell will tell you about her in due course."

"My son? *He* is the one courting this female?" The marchioness jabbed her fork in Rory's direction. "You will tell me about her at once. Everything you know. And don't leave out even a snippet."

"I believe that privilege belongs to his lordship."

"Do as I say. Or I shall sack you!"

Keeping an eye on that yolk-stained fork, Rory laced her fingers at her waist. Lady Dashell would find out sooner or later. In the meantime, Rory couldn't risk being turned out of the house before finding the purloined letters. "I know very little, I'm afraid. Only that Miss Alice Kipling is an heiress."

"You implied earlier that my son intends to marry her."

"That I cannot say for certain. I did, however, hear a rumor that she is Lord Dashell's romantic interest." Lord Henry had revealed that tidbit, but Rory deemed it best not to bring her ladyship's younger son into the discussion, for it might stir up trouble between the brothers.

The marchioness grimaced. "Well! The chit must be common, for I know all the best families and I've never heard of her."

"I'm told her father made his fortune in the textile mills of Manchester. But I can assure you, she is quite lovely and ladylike. I happened to meet her and her mother yesterday when they came to call. Had you come downstairs, you could have met them, too."

"Fool! Haven't you been told? I am unable to walk. My aches and pains have confined me to this bed for the past year."

The marchioness had survived the coach crash that had taken the life of her husband, Rory recalled. The woman ruled her bedchamber like a little fiefdom, snapping orders to the servants and haranguing her companions. A change of scenery might improve her disposition.

"Someone could have carried you downstairs to the drawing room. I'm sure Lord Dashell or one of the footmen would have been happy to oblige."

"Bah! What little you know of my suffering. You might at least pretend a smidgeon of compassion!"

"I *am* showing compassion in looking out for your happiness. It would be a pleasant distraction if you were to go elsewhere in the house for a portion of each day— or even outside in the garden. For that matter, you could go on drives in the park, as well."

"You're just like Lucas, always nagging. When I wish to hear your opinion, I will ask for it!" She pointed her fork at a corner of the bedchamber. "Now, go and sit down at that desk."

"Why?"

"Cheeky girl! Do as I say. I've had quite enough of your impertinence."

Rory went to the dainty desk, drew out the chair, and seated herself. "Here I am. Now what?"

"Now you shall write a note to Miss Kipling and instruct her and her mother to come here at once. If the chit is plotting to displace me as marchioness, I will judge her suitability for myself."

It was mid-afternoon when the visitors arrived.

Rory had been reading to Lady Dashell from a book of dull sermons. The marchioness had dozed off halfway through a homily on temperance, and Rory had decided to risk sneaking downstairs to search Dashell's study. He had gone to Parliament that morning, she'd learned from the footman who had delivered her ladyship's luncheon. He wasn't expected to return for hours.

She might never have a better opportunity.

Rory tiptoed to the door. Just as she was reaching for the handle, however, a knock rattled the wood panel and Lady Dashell's eyes snapped open. The marchioness fumbled for the pince-nez that had fallen onto the bedclothes and replaced it on the bridge of her nose. "Where do you think you're going?"

"To answer the door, of course."

"It had best be the Kiplings! I can't imagine why they haven't arrived yet. Did you send the note? Or did you tell the footman to toss it into the dustbin?"

Rory clenched her teeth. No wonder her ladyship's other companions had departed so swiftly. The querulous woman had been carping all morning and throughout the noontime meal, complaining that the chicken was dry, the potatoes too greasy. Her bed was lumpy, the pillows improperly arranged. The fire was too low, then it burned too hot. On and on, until Rory was ready to march out of the house and forget about finding those letters.

She opened the door to see Jarvis standing there. The stocky butler motioned her out into the corridor. "The Kiplings are waiting below," he said in an undertone, his brow furrowed. "They claim that her ladyship asked them to come upstairs to her chamber. Is this true?"

"Yes, she had me write the invitation this morning."

"I fear his lordship will not be pleased."

"Why? Has he ordered you to bar them from seeing her?"

"No, Miss Paxton. I merely think he would wish to be here to supervise the visit."

"I will do so in his stead, then. Pray send them up."

Ignoring his worried expression, Rory returned to the bedside. If she embroiled herself in trouble over the incident, then so be it. Yet surely all would be well so long as she kept a close watch on the marchioness. "Your guests are here, my lady. Allow me to straighten your collar. And you lost a few hairpins when you fell asleep."

While Rory made the repairs, Lady Dashell grumbled, "I wasn't asleep, I was merely resting my eyes. And stop your fussing! These visitors are mere commoners, not royalty."

But her gray eyes glittered and her fingers plucked at the bedclothes as if she relished a break from the monotony of the day. Rory felt a twist of sympathy. Did no one ever call on the woman, not even old friends? That wouldn't be surprising. She wasn't the sort to endear herself to others.

Jarvis stepped into the bedchamber. "Mrs. Kipling and Miss Kipling."

He bowed out while mother and daughter sashayed into the room. Clad in a gown of burnt-orange plaid, Mrs. Kipling led the way. A cluster of dyed brown egret feathers wagged atop her hat. Miss Kipling followed, a vision in pale green silk with a straw bonnet framing her dainty features and blond curls.

Lady Dashell surveyed them through the narrow pince-nez. A haughty expression pinched her face. "Where have you been? You ought to have come hours ago. Did you not heed my note?"

Despite the rude criticism, Mrs. Kipling dipped a curtsy with fawning humility. "Pray forgive us, my lady. I didn't think it suitable to call until after luncheon."

"When I say *at once,* I mean just that. You have kept me waiting for the better part of the day."

"What her ladyship means," Rory said, "is that she has been most anxious to meet you and your daughter." When the marchioness parted her lips, no doubt to utter another acid remark, Rory added, "My lady, if I may present Miss Alice Kipling."

Alice stepped forward, aided by a subtle push from her doting mama. Her nose nearly touched the floor as she made a deep curtsy worthy of presentation to the Queen. "It is a great honor to make your acquaintance, Lady Dashell."

"Come closer, gal. Don't hang back like a ninny."

Beckoned by that skeletal hand, Alice sidled closer to the bedside. "I am truly sorry for your illness. I do hope you're up and about again very soon."

"I'm crippled, you fool. I will never arise from this bed. If my son had any real interest in you, he would have told you so."

Alice cringed, glancing at her mother, both clearly nonplussed by the implication that they might have mistaken his interest in her. "Pray forgive me," the girl murmured. "I—I meant no insult . . ."

"Of course you didn't, my darling," Mrs. Kipling said with a nervous laugh. "It was a simple mistake, your ladyship."

"Simpleminded, that's what. As I've always said, it's better to look silly than to open your mouth and remove all doubt."

Mrs. Kipling's lips parted, but no sound emerged. She appeared too befuddled to know how to respond to such blatant discourtesy.

To ease the tension, Rory hastily brought over two straight-backed chairs. "Won't you please sit? Perhaps I could ring for tea."

"It isn't teatime yet," Lady Dashell snapped, overruling the suggestion. "And there is no purpose in them sitting since they shan't be here long."

The Kiplings dutifully remained standing side by side. Mrs. Kipling clutched her beaded brown reticule and inquired, "Is Lord Dashell at home? It would be a pleasure to see him again."

Lady Dashell gave her a shrewd stare. "No doubt, since you've an eye toward foisting your daughter on him. Tell me, how large is her portion?"

"It wouldn't be polite to say, my lady. I leave such matters to Mr. Kipling."

"Don't be coy. It must be enormous, else my son would not show any interest in a commoner." The old woman turned her spiteful gaze on Alice. "But if she won't say, then you tell me, girl."

Alice edged back, looking to her mother for guidance. "I—I . . ."

"Speak up! I've no use for shrinking violets."

Rory took a step forward. "Lady Dashell, it might be wise to save your questions for his lordship."

"Bah! They will tell me or depart, never to return."

"Alice has a dot of fifty thousand," Mrs. Kipling blurted out. "As our only child, she also will inherit a fortune someday. So, you see, she is quite well endowed."

Lady Dashell arched a graying eyebrow. Even she looked impressed by the astronomical sum. "I knew it," she crowed, slapping her hand onto the coverlet. "Dashell is sniffing after your money. You think to purchase the marchioness's tiara. *My* tiara."

"His lordship is deeply in debt, or so I've heard," Mrs. Kipling said, rallying enough to lift her chin. "I should think it is a fair bargain on both sides."

"Harrumph. Gold is nothing compared to a venerable title and blue blood." Her ladyship turned her malevolent gaze on Alice. "And you. What do you think of all this? You intend to make me the dowager, do you? You believe that a fine wardrobe and a plump purse makes you grand enough to rule a nobleman's household!"

Alice's blue eyes widened. Her gloved fingers were twisting the delicate lace on her bodice. "Only if—if his lordship thinks so . . ."

Rory had tolerated quite enough of the bullying. "She's right, Lord Dashell will have the final say in this matter. Until then, it is best that your visitors return later. When *he* is here."

Mrs. Kipling seized the hint and dipped another curtsy. "It has been good to meet you at last, your ladyship. Come, Alice, we mustn't overstay our welcome."

As the Kiplings scuttled toward the door, Rory followed, intending to see them out. A small scraping sound made her glance back over her shoulder. Just in time. Lady Dashell snatched a pewter candlestick from the bedside table and hurled it at the departing guests.

Rory acted on instinct. She leaped into the path of the projectile to prevent it from striking the women. In the same split second, she raised her arms in an attempt to catch it . . .

A hand flashed out from behind her. Masculine fingers deftly plucked the candlestick from the air. She whirled around to see her rescuer.

"Lord Henry!"

He grinned, his blue eyes twinkling beneath a thatch of brown hair. The coffee-colored coat and yellow-striped waistcoat lent him the look of a dandified gentleman. "You're brave to take a bullet for Miss Kipling. Though I don't believe the frightened fawn is even aware of your sacrifice."

The Kiplings had vanished out the door.

Rory released a breath. "Thank you. Though I'd have managed myself."

"Don't be so certain. Mama has quite the throwing arm."

He sauntered toward the bed, where Lady Dashell sat with her arms crossed. In an almost guilty expression, she lowered her chin and watched the approach of her younger son.

"I will not tolerate any rebuke from you," she stated. "The chit is dim-witted and cowardly. Only look at how she scurried out of here like a terrified mouse."

"You terrify even me, Mama." He placed the candlestick back on the table, then bent down and planted a smacking kiss on her gaunt cheek. "I'll wager she was running because you raked her over the coals."

"Only to test her mettle. And she failed miserably. She isn't worthy to fill my shoes—or my tiara."

"Oh, give the girl a chance. At least she's easy on the eyes. And Dash would be a fool not to take her as his bride. Her papa is as rich as Croesus."

"Has Lucas told you his intentions, then?"

"Of course not. You should know by now that he always plays his cards close to the chest."

"Well! I suppose her wealth *is* a mark in her favor." She petulantly grasped at the bedclothes. "Not that it shall do *me* the slightest bit of good as I am confined to this bed."

He chucked her under the chin. "Cheer up, Mama. At least it'll keep us out of the poorhouse."

To Rory's surprise, Lord Henry coaxed a smile out of his mother. He perched on the side of the bed and entertained her with the latest gossip. It was clear that Lady Dashell adored her second son. If she was of an age with Aunt Bernice, she must be no more than fifty-eight. Rory had presumed her to be older. When her face lost that sourness, however, she looked almost girlish again.

Rory went into the dressing room to give them some privacy. Surely Lord Henry had been jesting when he'd mentioned the poorhouse. It made her feel sorry for him and his mother, for they were victims of Lord Dashell's mismanagement of his financial affairs. She herself knew how dreadful it was to be penniless.

Nevertheless, it was wrong of Lord Dashell to blackmail Kitty. And Rory intended to make certain he paid for his crime.

Chapter 8

A nobleman often weds a girl half his age so that
he can mold her into the perfect wife.

—MISS CELLANY

Lucas wended his way through the crowded ballroom. The lilt of a waltz and the buzz of conversation filled the vast room. The air was stuffy from the crush of people and overheated from the blaze of candles in the crystal chandeliers. Ladies simpered at him, gentlemen spoke greetings, but he didn't grace anyone with more than a terse few words.

He was on a mission to find Miss Alice Kipling. To determine the extent of the damage that had been done.

While dressing for the ball, he'd heard the alarming news from his valet that the Kiplings had come to call on his mother and, shortly thereafter, had fled the house in a hurry. Both women had appeared frightened and distraught. It didn't take a genius to guess how maliciously the marchioness must have grilled them. She'd likely even thrown something at them.

Anger dogged his every step through the ballroom. This should never have happened. He'd planned to introduce his mother to the Kiplings himself—*after* he'd put a betrothal ring on Alice's finger.

Rory Paxton had orchestrated the entire mess. According to the servants' grapevine, she had sent a note to the Kiplings that morning. Which meant she must have gossiped with Mama about his interest in Alice. Blast Rory, she should have known better than to permit such a visit without his permission. He would have gone to confront her about the blunder right then and there, but he'd been running late for the ball already, having been delayed by a prolonged meeting at Parliament.

Now, he needed to find Alice. The last thing he wanted was for her to be so offended that she'd divert her attention—and her money—to another suitor.

Lucas made a complete circuit of the ballroom before spotting his quarry. Clad in virginal white with blond curls framing her dainty features, Alice was leaving the dance floor at the end of a set. She smiled demurely at her partner as he bent his dark head close to murmur in her ear.

Lucas couldn't identify the man. Too many milling guests blocked his line of sight. He stalked forward, intending to assert his claim on her. Half the bachelors present were on the prowl for an heiress to pay off their gambling debts. Hell, there were even a few of his father's old cronies who'd jump at the chance to ensnare a rich young commoner.

The throng parted and he spied Alice's partner. He had brown hair, debonair attire, and a devil-may-care grin on his boyish features.

Henry.

Lucas felt a wave of relief. His brother wouldn't poach Alice. And it was encouraging to see that she appeared at ease conversing with him. He hoped to God it meant that no permanent harm had been done.

He made his bow to her. "Good evening, Alice. I trust that my brother has been behaving himself."

Her smile dimmed. "Yes, my lord. He's been excellent company."

The formal mode of address indicated a distance in her manner. Her blue eyes held a hint of wariness. Damn! If he were better at small talk, he'd come up with a glib comment to charm her. "You look very fine tonight."

She allowed him to kiss her hand. "Thank you."

"It's a miracle she can bear the sight of us," Henry said, mischief dancing in his eyes. "The poor girl was traumatized by our mother today. You did hear about that, didn't you, Dash?"

"I'm aware of it."

"Miss Alice took quite a fright. Just now, I was assuring her that Mama's bark is worse than her bite." Henry chuckled. "That is, when she isn't playing cricket with the candlesticks."

Alarmed, Lucas scrutinized Alice's perfect complexion. "She didn't do you a harm, I hope."

"N-no. But . . . I don't think she liked me very much."

With her lower lip pushed out, she resembled a forlorn child who'd been scolded and sent to stand in the corner. He patted her hand. "You mustn't draw the wrong conclusion. The marchioness has her bad days, that's all."

"Yes, every day," Henry added unhelpfully. "Next time, Miss Alice, let me know when you come to call on her. I can always coax a smile out of the old harridan."

Alice looked distressed at the notion of facing Lady Dashell again. Her eyes were wide and her face pale. She glanced over her shoulder as if seeking an excuse to slip away.

Lucas had no intention of letting her go. Though, if truth be told, he felt a trifle impatient with her lack of pluck. The prospective wife of a marquess should be made of sterner stuff. But she was very young. Perhaps she just needed time to mature into the role—and he could mold her, as well.

Taking hold of her arm, he subjected his brother to a pointed stare that conveyed the message to make himself scarce. "Thank you for watching over her, Henry. I'll partner Alice in the next set. With her permission, of course."

The orchestra began playing a sprightly reel, and Alice allowed Lucas to guide her onto the dance floor. Yet she still looked a trifle nervous of him. Did she fear he might rebuke her for visiting his mother? Little did she know he didn't hold her at fault.

He blamed Rory Paxton.

The thought of Rory fed fuel to the fire of his discontent. His mind served up the memory of her fine features, those sparkling dark eyes, the bold tilt of her chin. It had been a mistake to hire her. One day in his house and already she had wreaked havoc in his ordered life. Once he had smoothed Alice's ruffled feathers, he'd stay at the ball only long enough to escort her for the midnight supper.

Then he would return home and dismiss Rory from his employ at once—even if he had to drag her out of bed to do so.

Rory tiptoed through the dark entrance hall. Gloom cloaked the chambers on either side of the front door, and the eerie stillness amplified her every footfall. The candle in her hand cast shaky shadows over the classical busts set into niches in the walls. Her skin prickled beneath her night robe. The marble eyes of those statues seemed to follow her progress as she made her way toward the grand staircase.

The sudden bonging of the casement clock from inside the library made her jump. Twelve sonorous booms echoed through the vaulted foyer. Midnight. She would have to hurry.

Rory had just finished searching Lord Dashell's study. In addition to seeking the stolen letters, she'd wanted to view a sample of his handwriting. But the drawers of his desk held mostly official documents from Parliament, and it was unclear who had written them. The bottom drawer had revealed a collection of unpaid bills, giving credence to his state of penury.

Then she'd chanced to look in the dustbin. She'd found a crumpled, half-finished memo to his banker regarding an extension on a loan. It was penned in a terse, efficient hand that lacked the curlicues in the blackmail notes. The problem was, she couldn't be certain the discarded memo had been written by Lucas Vale. He employed a male secretary who took dictation and copied out letters for his lordship's signature.

Frustrated, she'd hunted high and low for the packet of letters, but had been unable to locate a safe or a strongbox. Nevertheless, she would not accept defeat. His study wasn't the only hiding place in this vast house. She intended to have a look through his bedchamber, as well.

Grateful that no footman stood on duty by the front door, she hurried up the marble steps of the grand staircase. The rest of the staff had retired to bed since they were obliged to arise before dawn. According to kitchen gossip, Lord Dashell had gone out to a ball and wasn't expected to return until the wee hours. That meant two or three at the very earliest. During Rory's debut, the younger set had often danced until dawn.

She ought to have ample time to conduct a search.

After that disastrous visit today, Dashell would have to devote himself to making peace with Miss Alice Kipling. He would do everything in his power to charm the girl—if such a skill was even possible for so humorless a man. She only wondered why he hadn't yet popped the question. Marrying an heiress would be far more lucrative than demanding payments from Kitty.

Perhaps he needed funds to purchase a betrothal ring. He might not own one if he'd been forced to sell off the family jewels in order to hold his creditors at bay. Yes, that made sense. He must be so far in debt that no jeweler would extend him credit.

Upstairs, she made a detour to peek into Lady Dashell's darkened chamber. Steady snores emanated from the four-poster bed. Heaven forbid the bad-tempered woman should awaken to find her companion missing. Until Rory had those letters in hand, she couldn't afford trouble.

She quietly shut the door. Earlier, when Mrs. Jarvis had delivered dinner, Rory had queried the housekeeper about the many bedchambers. Most were empty, save for the ones occupied by Lady Dashell and her two sons. Lord Henry's room was situated halfway along the passage; thankfully, he too was out for the evening.

As she hastened through the shadows, the only light came from the candle in her hand. The threadbare carpet muffled her footsteps. At the end of the baroque corridor lay the marquess's suite.

Rory stopped in front of his door. Her heart thumped as she glanced up and down the deserted passageway. Just to be safe, she rapped lightly on the painted wood panel and then waited. All lay silent.

Emboldened, she turned the handle and stepped inside, closing the door behind her. She proceeded through an antechamber furnished with gilt chairs and fancy vases on tables. An arched doorway led into his bedchamber.

She lifted her candle to survey the spacious room. The décor was elegant yet masculine with dark mahogany furniture against the walls: a writing desk, a chest of drawers, a glass-fronted bookcase. A pair of green damask chairs flanked an elaborately carved marble mantel, where banked embers glowed on the hearth. An enormous four-poster bed with brocaded gold and green hangings dominated the chamber. Fluffy pillows and bolsters created an inviting sanctuary.

Rory envisioned Lucas Vale lying on the linen sheets in a state of undress, his lips curved up in a smirk. He crooked his forefinger and beckoned to her to join him.

She banished the naughty image at once, along with a troubling warmth that bedeviled her insides. How absurd! Not only did she despise the villain, she doubted that he'd ever cracked a smile in his life. Like his mother, he'd been born arrogant and aloof.

The clock on the bedside table ticked into the silence, reminding her that time was wasting.

She hurried to the desk. It was smaller than the one downstairs in his study and had a front panel designed to be folded down and used as a writing surface. The interior had several rows of cubbyholes that contained rolled papers and quill pens and other paraphernalia.

Ignoring the inkpots and pencils, she unrolled one of the papers. The light of the candle illuminated a heading: *Westvale Abbey*. Below it, there was a list of abbreviated notations along with scribbled numbers:

17 ac. oak: 350
126 ac. to L. N.: 1100
Cull flock: 275

Several additional items proved just as cryptic. What did it all mean?

Upon studying the ciphers, she realized this must be the inventory of an estate named Westvale Abbey. *Ac* could mean acres. Was Dashell calculating what could be sold to raise revenue? Did he mean to cut down a large stand of oak trees, sell off acreage to a neighbor, and cull a flock of sheep for income?

It certainly appeared so.

She found similar lists in the cubbyholes for three additional estates. Adding the figures in her head, she determined that he could scrape together some four thousand pounds. Had he done so? Perhaps he'd decided it would be better to preserve his holdings and instead procure the necessary funds through extortion.

Delving into the pocket of her peach silk robe, Rory withdrew the two blackmail notes. She laid them on the desk and compared them to the notations on the various lists. Just as in his study, she identified distinct differences in the handwriting. The estate listings were penned in bold, economical strokes unlike the flourishes in the blackmail notes.

She suffered a moment of doubt. What if Kitty had sent her on a wild-goose chase? What if Lord Dashell was not the villain, after all? What if the letters had been stolen by someone else entirely?

No. She must not allow misgivings to dilute her sense of purpose. He could very well have disguised his penmanship in order to avoid detection. After all, he wouldn't want the notes to tie him to his crime.

Better to focus her attention on locating the letters. When she found them in his possession, that would prove his guilt once and for all.

After returning the papers to their cubbyholes, Rory arose from the desk. She peeked behind several landscape paintings to see if there might be a wall safe, to no avail. Undaunted, she picked up the candlestick and scanned the bedchamber.

Perhaps he'd concealed the letters in his dressing room. His valet would be the only person to venture there. No well-trained servant would dare to question the presence of a packet of *billets-doux* in his master's possession.

Not even if they'd been written by Dashell's father to Mrs. Kitty Paxton.

She headed through an open doorway half hidden in the shadows. Here, a spacious oblong room held all the trappings of a well-groomed gentleman. The antique furnishings included several clothespresses and cabinets, a bootjack, and a dressing table. On the washstand, beside a white china basin, lay a silver tray with a shaving brush, soap, and long razor.

On impulse, she picked up the bar of soap and lifted it to her nose. The enticing scent of pine made her toes curl inside her slippers. She recalled that subtle aroma from her interview with him. The bar was still damp, and she could see him standing here, shaving, perhaps stripped to his waist . . .

As if scalded, Rory dropped the soap back onto the tray. Enough of that nonsense. He was a villain, not a prospective suitor.

She began a systematic search of the cabinetry, opening the drawers one by one. Inside lay neat stacks of folded cravats, handkerchiefs, and stockings. Though it felt shockingly intimate to handle his personal items, she forced herself to reach into the back of each drawer to see if the letters might be stashed there.

Then she turned her attention to the trio of clothespresses against the wall. Opening the top of each one in turn, she found more articles of clothing: breeches and shirts and waistcoats. Ten coats hung in the wardrobe. That was hardly an overabundance of apparel for a nobleman who was expected to attend a wide variety of functions throughout the season. Nor was he a dandy. His attire consisted of sober hues, mostly dark blues and charcoal grays, with no yellow-striped waistcoats like the one his brother had been wearing earlier.

A row of footwear lined the bottom of the wardrobe. On the off chance that Dashell might have tucked the packet into a boot or shoe, she knelt down on the carpet to shake out each one. Her effort yielded nothing.

Stymied, Rory sat back on her heels. She had poked through every nook and cranny in the dressing room. What now? What if the stolen letters weren't even in the house? It was entirely possible he'd stored them in a bank vault. Was there some way to trick him into retrieving them?

It was difficult to think here in his private domain while inhaling his distinctive masculine scent. Her gaze strayed to the copper bathtub in the corner as her wayward mind conjured the fantasy of him immersed in steamy water, his damp hair slicked back, his upper body exposed to her view . . .

Heaven help her. Was she so starved for male companionship that even a black-hearted scoundrel could tempt her?

No. She was an intelligent woman, armed with common sense and wise to the ways of the nobility. It was just that her nerves were on edge tonight. The sooner she found those letters, the sooner she could leave here.

With renewed determination, Rory carried the lighted taper back into his bedchamber and set it on the bedside table. The small clock there showed the hour to be a quarter past one, giving her sufficient time to complete her quest before Dashell returned home from the ball. She pulled out the single drawer to examine the contents. There was nothing unusual, only a few spare candles, a starched handkerchief, a tinderbox.

She picked up a small, leather-bound volume. Flipping through it, she realized it was a prayer book. The pages of the missal appeared to be well thumbed. How remarkable. Despite her overactive imagination, she could not picture Lucas Vale bowing his head in prayer. There wasn't an ounce of humility in the man. He likely thought of himself as the Almighty.

At that moment, a rattling sound broke the quiet. The door handle!

Rory's stomach took a dive. Surely it was only the valet come to wait for his master's return. Still, that was bad enough!

She shoved the drawer shut and whirled around, looking for somewhere to hide. The dressing room? Perhaps the wardrobe?

She hadn't taken more than a few steps in that direction when the outer door swung open. The large, black silhouette of a man came inside.

Chapter 9

Never trust a gentleman who is bent on seduction.
—MISS CELLANY

The newcomer strode into the darkened antechamber. In the blink of an eye, he passed through the arched doorway of the bedroom. His swift tread came to an abrupt halt.

So did Rory's.

Her heart hammering, she stopped halfway across the open space between the four-poster bed and the dressing room. Her fingers pressed against the small leather-bound missal that she'd neglected to return to the drawer. She felt as trapped as a butterfly pinned to a corkboard. It was too late to conceal herself. Worse, the intruder wasn't the valet at all.

It was Lord Dashell.

The candle burning on the bedside table illuminated his look of astonishment. His dark brows lifted and his iron-gray eyes fixed her with a disbelieving stare. An unbearable silence stretched out, disturbed only by the soft ticking of the clock.

Rory tried not to quail beneath that forceful gaze. She had to *say* something. To invent a plausible excuse for her presence in his bedchamber. Yet her mind remained stubbornly blank to all but the sight of him standing a short distance from her.

He looked exceptionally handsome tonight in a formal black coat with a gray watered-silk waistcoat. He had removed his cravat; the long strip of white linen dangled from one hand. His shirt was open at the top, displaying a wedge of bare chest. Catching herself gawking, she lifted her gaze back to his face in time to see his expression change.

A subtle seductiveness transformed those harsh features. His eyelids lowered slightly and one corner of his hard mouth quirked slightly in a suggestive manner. His scrutiny of her conveyed the alertness of a wolf eyeing his prey.

He dropped the cravat onto the nearest chair. Then he strolled forward and stopped directly in front of Rory. His gaze raked downward over her thin wrap, ogling the curve of her hips and bosom, where the tied sash at her waist defined her feminine shape. "Well, well, Miss Paxton. This is most unexpected. Though I cannot say it is unwelcome."

Rory blinked. She had braced herself for his cold fury. She had thought he might even accuse her outright of searching for the stolen letters. Instead, he had leaped to an outrageous conclusion. The knave thought she had come to his bedchamber to seduce him!

Seeing his attention linger on her breasts, she realized that her robe had gaped open to reveal the lacy bodice of her nightdress. She grabbed a handful of slippery peach silk to hold the lapels tightly closed. It had been foolish not to put on her day clothes, but when she'd crept out of bed she had feared to awaken Lady Dashell by making too much noise.

"I'm sorry, you've mistaken my purpose here," Rory

said. Much to her vexation, her voice came out breathy instead of firm.

"I rather doubt that. It's clear now why you were so eager to live under my roof. And it wasn't to take care of my mother."

"I beg to differ—"

"Don't deny it. Why else would you be in my bedchamber?" He let his forefinger lightly trace the outline of her face. "There really was no need for subterfuge, Rory. You could have come straight out and offered your services as my mistress."

His touch made her skin tingle and her breath catch. So did his scent, that enticing blend of pine and leather. His closeness befuddled her thoughts. It made her long to stand on tipoe and invite his kiss, though that would be the height of folly.

Her mouth dry, she stepped back out of his reach. "Your mistress?"

"Yes. The arrangement could be mutually beneficial. And quite satisfactory to us both."

His low regard for her character was a bitter pill to swallow. How galling it was to be treated so shabbily by a gentleman, as if she were a slattern in a house of ill repute. Yet in all fairness she could hardly fault Lucas Vale for his erroneous assumption. He'd come home in the middle of the night to find a scantily clad, ruined lady in his bedchamber.

What else was he to think?

Yet his unsavory offer wasn't what unnerved her the most. It was seeing cold, caustic Lord Dashell transform into a seductive rake. Fantasies aside, she had never believed him capable of being anything more than a toplofty prig. She felt far safer with that stuffy nobleman than this sensual stranger.

Calculating the distance to the door, she edged away from him. Perhaps it was best to let him go on believing his false supposition. Otherwise, he might guess her true purpose. "I—I had better go, my lord. I've changed my mind. It was a mistake to come here."

He stalked after her in pursuit. As she veered to avoid him, her spine bumped into the bedpost and his hands closed around her waist. Rory found herself trapped against him, her bosom pressed to the muscled expanse of his chest. His fingers languidly stroked her hips through the gossamer silk of her robe and nightdress, causing a heated disturbance inside her.

He bent his dark head to nuzzle the side of her neck. "You needn't play the shy damsel. We both know that you're experienced in such matters."

His warm breath tickled her skin. He dropped a series of spellbinding kisses along the line of her jaw. As his teeth nibbled her earlobe, a shivery sensation spread downward through her body and pooled in her belly. Her legs turned to jelly, and she twisted her head in an effort to escape his relentless assault. Her heart pounded so hard that she could scarcely think straight.

Dear God, what was she to do now? He'd refused to heed her protests. She had to find some way to stop him without sparking his suspicions.

"You can't afford me," she blurted out. "I come at a very high price."

The tip of his tongue laved the hollow of her throat as if to taste her essence. "I'm sure we can arrive at an agreeable arrangement. And I must say, as fetching as this negligee is, I find myself wanting to strip it from you."

Lord Dashell drew back to tug at the sash of her robe. She ached to feel his bare skin against hers, to lie with him in the bed and let the weight of his body cover hers.

The hunger was so enticing that it threatened to over-whelm her. It resurrected memories that had been buried for eight years, when she behaved so recklessly that she'd lost her family, her reputation.

And this time, there would be no *almost* to the act. She would be subjected to its full completion.

In a panic, Rory acted on instinct. She lifted her arm and whacked the prayer book hard against his wrists.

His hold on her loosened. He jumped back, cursing a blue streak. Rubbing his arm, he glared at her. "What the devil! Why did you do that?"

"To stop you from assaulting me."

"Assaulting? You were enjoying it! I felt you tremble."

"Out of fear. I was trying to get away, that's what."

"Why so prudish all of a sudden?" His lips tightened in a sneer. "Are you truly afraid I can't meet your price?"

"I only said that to dissuade you. But even then, you wouldn't listen."

His livid gaze flicked to the volume in her hand. "Why do you have my prayer book, anyway?"

She clutched the small missal like a shield against her bosom. "Because . . . because it's the real reason why I came to your bedchamber," she said on inspiration. "I needed to fetch it for your mother."

"My mother."

"Yes." Rory embellished the fib. "Lady Dashell couldn't sleep. There is a particular prayer in here that she asked me to read to her."

"How peculiar. A few minutes ago, I poked my head into her room and she was snoring like a top."

His iron-gray eyes held blatant disbelief. If only she'd thought of the prayer-book excuse earlier. Now she had to lay it on thick—or he might guess that she'd been searching for the stolen letters. "She must have fallen asleep while I was gone. You see, it took some time for

me to locate the book. She thought it was in your bookcase, when it was actually in your bedside table."

"Oh?" His voice dripped with sarcasm. "Exactly
which passage did she wish to hear?"

Rory nervously riffled the pages. Since she wasn't
standing beside the candle, the shadowed print was difficult to see. "I can't quite recall. I believe it had something to do with asking God's mercy for one's sins."

"I see. So why didn't you tell me this the moment I
walked in?"

His lips were compressed, his expression calculating.
He doubted her flimsy excuse, and she feared he would
continue to poke holes in the lie. Better to distract him
by going on the attack.

She lifted her chin. "You would never have believed
me—just as you don't believe me now. In fact, it might
do *you* well to pray for mercy, too, my lord. You're courting Miss Kipling and offering carte blanche to your
mother's companion all at the same time. Have you no
sense of honor?"

A muscle tensed in his jaw. The mention of Alice
Kipling seemed to have a sobering effect on Lucas Vale.
Or perhaps it was the attack on his character. Any gentleman would bristle to have his honor impugned. The last
trace of sensual warmth vanished, restoring his face to
that familiar harsh façade.

His glower spurred an uneasy tingle down her spine.
Had she pushed him too far? A man who would stoop
to extortion wouldn't hesitate to take whatever else he
wanted. He could force himself on her without fear of
reprisal. No one would believe she hadn't come here for
seduction, given her checkered past.

"I shan't disturb you any longer," Rory said with a
brashness that went only skin-deep. "I'll take this mis-

sal with me in case her ladyship awakens during the night."

She started briskly for the door. In two quick strides, he stepped ahead to block her path. His solid form posed a barrier that brought her to an enforced halt. "You aren't going anywhere, Miss Paxton."

Though her heart fluttered like a frightened rabbit's, she gave him a challenging stare. "I thought we'd settled the matter. I've no interest in your ungentlemanly offer."

"I want a word with you about Alice and what you did today—or rather, yesterday." He pointed to the pair of chairs by the fireplace. "Sit down."

"It isn't proper for us to be here alone."

"You should have considered that before setting foot in my bedchamber. Now do as I say."

As tyrannical as his mother, he closed his fingers around Rory's upper arm and marched her to the hearth, giving her a little push into one of the green armchairs. She sank down against the plump cushions, gripping the prayer book in her lap.

Lord Dashell looked furious enough to kill. When he picked up the fire iron, she half feared he meant to strike her, and she tensed her muscles to stop him. But he merely turned around and stirred the glowing embers on the hearth, then added more coal. Within moments, a welcome blaze warmed her. She hadn't realized how chilled she was or that goose bumps covered her skin.

He propped the fire iron against the mantel. Then he stood over her, his hands planted on his waist, pushing back his coat to reveal his lean waist. "Do you want to know the reason why I looked in on my mother? It was to see if *you* were still awake, Miss Paxton."

"Me?"

"Yes. But no sooner did I step into the room than my mother stirred. I decided that this confrontation could wait until morning."

"That sounds perfectly sensible. It would be wise to postpone any discussion for the light of day after we've both had some rest."

When Rory started to rise, he took a menacing step closer until she resumed her seat. "This isn't a *discussion*," he growled. "It is an interrogation. You will tell me everything I wish to know. Right now."

"Fine. Interrogate away, my lord."

"The staff had strict orders not to speak of Miss Kipling in front of my mother. So why were you gossiping about her?"

"I knew nothing of any such orders."

"Then you ought to have had the intelligence to work it out on your own. Once you mentioned Alice, you must have realized straightaway that the marchioness knew nothing about her. Even a simpleton could have comprehended that *I* wished to introduce Lady Dashell to Alice myself. So what idiocy made you invite the Kiplings to this house without my permission?"

He was shouting by the end of that speech. Unnecessarily, but at least he wasn't probing her reason for being in his bedchamber anymore.

Rory resented having to tilt back her head while he towered over her. She suspected he had remained standing in order to intimidate her. But if truth be told, she felt more comfortable with his icy manner than his seductiveness. "It wasn't idiocy," she said. "It was your mother's request. You know how demanding she can be. And you *did* say that I was to humor the marchioness and to keep her occupied."

"Not by discussing my personal life with her." He

jabbed his finger at Rory. "Nor by taking it upon your-self to invite guests into my home."

"It's her home, too. Anyway, it wasn't I who invited the Kiplings, it was your mother. I was merely the sec-retary taking her dictation. I could hardly gainsay my employer on my first day, could I?"

"*I* am your employer! You answer only to me. Is that clear? And I must say that you showed extremely poor judgment in failing to stop her scheme."

She watched him pace back and forth. As much as it pained her to admit, he had cause for anger. Once she'd realized the marchioness hadn't been told about the girl, she ought to have kept mum about Alice Kipling. The visit had been a disaster.

"I presume you saw Miss Kipling tonight at the ball," Rory ventured. "What did she say about meeting your mother?"

"She is convinced that Mama despises her. The poor girl was frightened out of her wits. I had to expend a good deal of effort to calm her." He pierced Rory with a sharp stare. "I understand my mother threw a candle-stick at her."

"Not very accurately," Rory said to minimize the in-cident. "The Kiplings were nearly out the door by that point. Anyway, I would never have allowed Miss Kipling to suffer harm."

"Yet you allowed a great deal of verbal harm," he snapped. "It must have been brutal, judging by Alice's reaction. Tell me, what exactly did my mother say to them?"

"She wanted to know the size of Miss Kipling's mar-riage portion. And she wished to meet your affianced bride. To see for herself if the girl is worthy of becom-ing marchioness."

"Alice and I are *not* affianced," Lord Dashell snarled.

He ran his fingers through his hair, mussing the coffee-brown strands. "And my mother has no say in whom I choose to marry, anyway."

"But her ladyship is bound to take an interest. You are her firstborn son, after all. And she must be bored spending her entire life in that dreary bedchamber. Have you ever looked into providing her with an invalid's chair? I believe she would benefit from going downstairs or even outdoors for a drive."

He glared balefully. "Don't you think I've already fought that battle with her? She's stubborn to a fault! And don't try to distract me. I've a good mind to send you packing for the trouble you've caused."

No. He mustn't do so. That would ruin everything.

Weary of craning her neck at him, Rory surged to her feet. "If you dismiss me, then who will care for your mother? She and I got on famously today. She's strong-willed, but so am I."

"I should rather think of you as *deceptive,* Miss Paxton. That prayer book was not the real reason you came in here. You've been lying to me."

His sudden shift in subject alarmed her, and she tightened her fingers around the missal. "Surely you cannot mean to accuse me again of plotting to seduce you. If you've only insults to say, I must bid you good night."

When she tried to walk away, he caught her by the arm. "I was referring to a different plot of yours." He plucked the book out of her hand and flung it onto the bed, where it landed against the pillows. "You are apparently unaware that my mother no longer prays. When she suffered her accident, she abandoned her faith and cursed the Almighty."

Rory felt a cold quiver. The pressure of his fingers on her upper arm prevented her escape. "People change. Perhaps she's regained her religion."

"She has that same prayer book on the shelf in her bedchamber. I saw it there only the other day. She would have no need to borrow mine."

"So she forgot where it was."

"No more excuses, Miss Paxton. You and I both know why you're here, why you've been telling me these tall tales."

"Oh? Why don't you enlighten me?"

His hands manacled her upper arms. "You're a common thief. You were looking for valuables to steal."

Her jaw dropped. His startling accusation made her want to both laugh with relief and spit in his face. Did he truly not realize that her interest was the letters? The letters that *he* had stolen?

Anger crowded out her surprise. How ironic that he of all people should brand *her* a criminal! "Don't be absurd. If that were the case, I'd have chosen a much wealthier man as my mark. Everyone knows you're destitute. I doubt you even have any jewels left to steal after all your investments went sour."

He frowned. "My investments— Where did you hear such a thing?"

"What does it matter?" She tugged at his hold on her. "Release me at once or I shall scream!"

"Go ahead. It will save me the trouble of ringing for a servant to send for the police."

"Yes, why *don't* you call in the law? I'd be more than happy to tell them all about . . ." A remnant of sanity made Rory clamp her lips shut.

"Tell them about what?" His face harsh, Lucas Vale gave her a little shake. "Talk to me! And this time, you had best speak the truth. I'm heartily sick of your lies and fabrications."

"I've nothing to say to you!"

"Yes you do, by God. You came into my house under

false pretenses. You're a blasted thief and I'll see you swing for it!"

He yanked her toward the door. She tried to dig in her heels, but his grip was too powerful. Fear and fury raged within her. He intended to have her hauled off to Bow Street Station. She'd land behind bars in Newgate, for the magistrate would certainly believe a nobleman's word over a mere female's—and a ruined one at that. She could not hope for any help from Kitty, either; her stepmother would deny sending her on this mission.

Lord Dashell would go scot-free. He would send her to the gallows when *he* was the criminal, not her!

With all her might, she wrenched herself away from him. Her silk sleeve ripped, but she paid no heed. "Stay away from me! *You're* the thief! *You* stole those letters from Kitty. And you will give them back to me!"

"Letters?"

"Now who's pretending? You know perfectly well I'm referring to the letters you took from my stepmother."

"I know nothing about any letters. This is just another of your ploys."

His haughty scorn made her come unhinged. It was the last straw in a night of frustration. She launched herself at him, battering his hard chest with her fists. "Scoundrel! Villain!" *Whack! Whack!* "Don't you dare sneer at me like that!" *Whack! Whack!*

Lucas froze in disbelief as a feminine ball of fury attacked him. He knew how to fight. Like any gentleman, he'd learned the art of fisticuffs in the boxing ring for the purpose of exercise. But never in his life had he been assaulted by a woman.

He thrust up his hands to deflect the worst of the blows. "Calm down!"

"Don't give me orders!" *Whack!* "You're the one at fault here." *Whack!* "And I won't let you get away with it!" *Whack! Whack!*

When she tried to hit him again, he caught firm hold of her shoulders and held her away, only to have her foot flash out and kick him in the shin. It hurt like the very devil. "Ouch! Damn it, Rory. That's enough!"

"It isn't enough. I won't stop until you're locked in prison where you belong! And don't you dare address me by my given name!"

She tried to kick him again, but Lucas feinted to the side. Thank God for long skirts. They prevented her from maneuvering as fast as him. She wriggled against his hold, panting, glaring at him as if he were the devil incarnate. Her strenuous efforts loosened a lock of black hair and it dipped across her eye.

She brushed it away with an irritated flick of her hand. "I want those letters back! Or—or I'll tell Alice Kipling that you propositioned me. I'll see to it that she never marries you! Now let me go!"

Lucas had no interest in any other woman at the moment. Not when Rory stood before him, her dark eyes sparkling with fury. Her enchantingly pretty face revealed the ferocity of genuine anger. For the first time since he'd walked into the bedchamber, he felt certain she was speaking the truth.

But . . . letters? Why would she think *he* had taken them? He barely even knew her stepmother; they were merely nodding acquaintances.

Compelled to get to the bottom of this mystery, he soothingly rubbed her shoulders. "I promise, I've not stolen any letters. Not from your stepmother or anyone else." When she parted her rosy lips in protest, he added, "I presume that is why you were prowling here in the middle of the night. You were looking for those letters. I can guarantee that you did not find them."

"Only because you've hidden them very well!"

Lucas shook his head. "For pity's sake, use your common sense. If I had taken those letters, do you seriously believe I'd have hired you to work in my house? And don't you think I'd have guessed immediately what you were up to when I found you in my bedchamber tonight?"

He had assumed Rory came to seduce him. The blaze of that realization would be forever seared in his memory. She had stood near his bed, the light from the candle behind her revealing the womanly curves beneath her silky negligee. He'd desired Rory Paxton ever since he'd met her eight years ago, and there she was, a stunningly beautiful gift of fate.

It irked him now to recall how swiftly his body had responded to her presence. He'd gone half mad with desire, in a fever to get her into his bed, coaxing her though she had protested. From where had all those suggestive utterances come? He knew little of charming women—nor did he wish to know. It had always seemed a skill more suited to libertines.

Until Rory.

Have you no sense of honor?

Her insult had stopped him cold. It had snapped clarity back into his passion-fogged brain. He could not dally with a penniless, ruined lady. Not when he was about to propose marriage to an heiress. Duty required him to make a grand alliance. He had an obligation to provide for his family and to preserve his holdings. Once he wed, he intended to be faithful to his chosen bride. He could not have a mistress, too. He'd vowed never to be like his father, a lecher who'd carried on with hundreds of females.

Nevertheless, Lucas had propositioned Rory tonight. He had damn near made a fool of himself by betraying his principles. He couldn't imagine a woman more wrong for him than Rory Paxton.

She was still gazing at him with suspicion. "You locked the letters in a bank vault, didn't you?"

"No, I did not." He looked deeply into her large doe eyes. "Rory, I swear that I don't have your stepmother's letters—nor did I ever. You have my word on that."

Lucas willed her to believe him. He knew the instant she did. Her gaze wavered and he felt a slight shudder run through her body. She released a long sigh of frustration. "But I was told . . . oh, never mind!"

"Come and sit down again. You will confess everything to me." Now that his anger had passed, he allowed a hint of humor to enter his voice. "And pray do so willingly. You owe me that much for assaulting me."

He steered her back over to the fireplace, and this time she did not resist. Ignoring an acute urge to cuddle her in his lap, he guided her down in one of the armchairs while he took the seat opposite her. The softly hissing fire and the shadowy room created an intimate bower that strained his willpower.

During their tussle, her sleeve had separated from her collar, and a swath of peach-colored silk hung loose and exposed a glimpse of her shoulder. Ladies routinely wore low-cut gowns to parties, yet he could not think himself more affected by the sight of bare skin than he was now.

He trained his attention on her profile as she gazed with a woebegone expression at the fire. "Shall we start from the beginning?" he prodded gently. "Your stepmother is missing some correspondence. What are these letters? Why are they so important that someone would filch them?

Rory drew a shuddering breath. "They are *billets-doux*—a packet of letters written by . . . her former lover. Apparently, they are very damaging, and if published, they will land Kitty in a terrible scandal. The Duke of Whittingham will likely cry off from his betrothal to Celeste. My stepmother is being blackmailed, you see."

"Blackmailed!" Lucas could understand the urgency, then. At the same time, he was peeved that Rory could believe *him* capable of such a despicable deed. "And you thought I was the culprit. What led you to such an implausible conclusion?"

"You were spotted in the morning room at Celeste's bethrothal party at the time the packet of letters disappeared from there." She paused, eyeing him cautiously. "But more to the point, the letters were written by the previous Lord Dashell."

His jaw dropped. His father had had an affair with Mrs. Kitty Paxton?

The news rocked Lucas to the core. He oughtn't be astounded. His father had been an infamous rake, romping with widows and married ladies alike. Lucas had grown up hearing heated quarrels between his parents on the matter, and he couldn't entirely blame his mother for her bitterness.

Rory sat watching him. He didn't want to discuss his father with her. The subject was too painful. "Are you certain about all this?" he asked. "The blackmail?"

"Yes." Reaching into a pocket of her robe, she leaned forward and handed him two slips of paper. "You may read the notes for yourself."

There were two of them, both written on ordinary vellum. The first demanded a diamond necklace as payment, the second, one thousand pounds by the coming

Saturday. The heavy script suggested a masculine hand, yet was adorned with feminine curlicues.

He returned his gaze to Rory. "I do hope you realize this does not in the least way resemble my penmanship."

"Yes, I know," she said frankly. "I found some samples of your writing in your desk. But I thought you might have disguised your hand."

"You hold a dismal view of my character."

She had the good grace to blush. "I'm very sorry, my lord. I truly believed you had taken the letters. Kitty seemed so certain of it."

He wanted Rory to call him by his given name. He wanted to hear her say *Lucas* in that breathy voice she'd used when he'd taken her in his arms. How illogical. No lady's companion addressed her employer with such familiarity.

Though perhaps Rory would now quit her position here. It was no longer necessary since her purpose in seeking the post had been to search his house.

Lucas wasn't yet ready to face having her vanish from his life again, so he turned his mind to something else. "Was your stepmother also the one who told you that my investments had . . . how did you put it? Gone sour."

"Yes. Though she'd heard it from Lady Milford. Her ladyship came to Norfolk to fetch me, you see. To tell me that Kitty needed my help."

Lady Milford!

Frowning, Lucas sat back in his chair. The woman was a leader of society. She also could be meddlesome and had a reputation as a matchmaker. What the devil was she up to now?

"If these letters are published," he said, "they will bring shame onto my family, too. Did that not occur to you?"

"Of course. But . . . society will excuse a nobleman

of his peccadilloes far more easily than a lady. So Kitty thought . . ." Her voice trailed off and she gave him a contrite look. "It does sound rather flimsy now, doesn't it?"

He was glad that at least Rory recognized her folly. It still galled him to know that she'd considered him to be a soulless villain.

The last thing he wanted was for his father's bawdy letters to be smeared across the tittle-tattle newspapers. Alice Kipling already was suffering doubts about their courtship, and a scandal might prompt her family to decide she was better off seeking a husband elsewhere. He didn't dare take that risk.

He folded the notes and tapped them against his palm. "Well. The next payment is due in a few days. We haven't much time."

Rory raised a dark eyebrow. "We?"

"Yes, *we*. You cannot continue this quest alone. It's far too dangerous. Henceforth, I intend to assist you in finding the blackmailer."

Chapter 10

How like a lord to bark orders and expect obedience!

—MISS CELLANY

The next morning, Rory stepped into the entry of her childhood home and greeted the butler. In a glance, she took in the familiar black-and-white marble floor, the pale green walls, the staircase with its wrought-iron banister-rail. So much had happened since she'd arrived here from Norfolk two days ago. In particular, she had formed a reluctant alliance with Lucas Vale—the very man she had suspected of vile deeds.

Accordingly, she had come here on a mission.

Grimshaw's narrow face wore its usual superior expression. "It is too early for callers. I shall check if Mrs. Paxton is awake yet."

Untying her old straw bonnet, Rory dropped it onto a chair. "Of course she's awake. It's ten o'clock, so she'll be in the breakfast parlor. And there's no need to bother with formalities. I'll announce myself."

"It is my duty to escort you there."

As she started toward the staircase, Grimshaw made haste to lead the way. His resentful look spoke volumes. It was clear he thought her unworthy of being treated as a family member due to her fall from grace.

Clutching her blue skirts, Rory mounted the steps and

frowned at the butler's back. Grimshaw was a busybody who knew everything that went on under this roof. Was it conceivable that he had spied the letters stuffed into Kitty's sewing basket?

Could *he* be the blackmailer?

She wouldn't be surprised. Only look at what he'd done to *her* eight years ago. But she had more pressing things to consider than the past.

The previous night, she and Lord Dashell had discussed the possible suspects. He had stated his belief that the culprit was likely someone close to Kitty. Someone who had access to the house, perhaps a servant, a friend, a relative. There was no definite proof, after all, that the deed had been done by a guest at Celeste's ball. Since Kitty had secreted the letters in her sewing basket two days prior to the party, they might have been stolen earlier.

Rory saw the logic in his reasoning. Yet she'd balked at accepting his aid because it hadn't been an offer, it had been a command. Dashell had overridden her objections, insisting he had the right to help recover the letters since they'd been written by his late father. How like a lord to bark orders and expect obedience!

She pitied Miss Alice Kipling. The innocent girl had no notion of what lay in store for her, marrying such a tyrant. In fact, Rory been inspired to write a column about that very topic.

Too agitated to sleep after the encounter with him the previous evening, she'd sat at the desk in Lady Dashell's dimly lit bedchamber and composed a scathing denouncement of aristocratic marriages. On the way here, she had dropped it in the post to the office of her London publisher, *The Weekly Verdict*.

Not that Lord Dashell would ever read it. She doubted

he paid any heed to radical newspapers that disagreed with his stuffy beliefs.

Rory followed Grimshaw along the upper corridor. She had come here today because Dashell had peppered her with questions that she hadn't been able to answer. Odd that, for during their one dance in her debut season, she'd scarcely been able to drag a word out of him. But last night, he'd had plenty to say. And he'd whipped up a maelstrom of emotions in her—rage, resentment, need.

The bodily attraction disturbed her the most. Over the past eight years, she had learned to leash her natural passions. She had transformed herself from a headstrong girl into a disciplined woman. Yet in one encounter, Lucas Vale had resurrected all those dangerous desires.

Nevertheless, his assistance might prove useful. This morning, he was investigating the possibility that the culprit could be one of his father's old cronies, many of whom were gamblers in desperate need of funds. She would be foolish not to acknowledge that he had certain connections she lacked.

The one thing Rory hadn't told him about was the reward. With the deplorable state of his finances, he'd likely demand half of the thousand pounds as his share. But it was *her* dowry money, not his!

Grimshaw stepped through an open doorway. "Miss Paxton, madam. She insisted on seeing you."

Rory entered a cozy breakfast parlor to find Kitty seated at a table by the window. Clad in tangerine muslin, she was sipping tea from a porcelain cup. A dish containing pastry crumbs lay before her.

To Rory's surprise, another lady occupied the chair to Kitty's right. The visitor looked to be in her late thirties and wore a smart plum silk gown trimmed in cream lace.

An artful arrangement of chestnut ringlets framed her handsome features.

Kitty's blue eyes widened on Rory. Clearly anxious for news, she glanced in consternation at her companion, then gave a little wave, her gold rings glinting in the sunlight. "Aurora, my dear! Why, this is most unexpected. Do come in and sit down. Grimshaw will bring you a dish of tea."

Proceeding to the table, Rory took the seat opposite the other guest and set down her reticule. The butler placed a cup in front of Rory, rattling the china to indicate his displeasure at being obliged to serve her. Then he stalked out of the breakfast parlor.

Kitty gave Rory a warning stare and slid a look at her friend, as if to convey the message that the woman knew nothing of the blackmail scheme—or Rory's employment at Dashell House. "Nadine, do allow me to introduce my stepdaughter, Aurora. She is visiting from Norfolk. Aurora, this is Mrs. Edgerton."

Mrs. Edgerton appeared cognizant of the gossip about Rory, if that keen hazel scrutiny was any indication. "Ah, Miss Paxton. It's a pleasure to make your acquaintance." She extended an elegant, gloved hand for Rory to shake. "How long will you be in London?"

"For a short while," Rory said vaguely. "I'm sure my stepmama can tell you all about it."

"Oh, there's little to tell!" Kitty released an artificial laugh. "It's merely a quick visit to help me plan dear Celeste's wedding. Alas, Aurora has duties back home and shall be unable to attend the nuptials."

Rory would see about that. "Speaking of the bride, is Celeste still abed?" she asked, stirring a crumble of sugar into her tea.

"Yes, which means it's the perfect time for us to consult on the arrangements." Her stepmother nervously toyed with the gold button on her sleeve. "I fear the poor girl is overwhelmed by the many details. She has deferred all the decisions to me—and to her half sister, of course."

Taking the hint, Mrs. Edgerton rose gracefully to her feet. "I can see that you two have private matters to discuss. Kitty, I shall return this evening. Oh, and don't forget, I've decided to forgo Tinsley's ball tomorrow night in favor of Newcombe's card party."

"Will you see your new suitor? Oh, I do wish you'd tell me his name."

Mrs. Edgerton smiled like a cat licking cream from its whiskers. "All in due time. If you'll excuse me now, I must pick up that new bonnet from the milliner's."

Heading toward the door, the shapely woman walked with a sensual slither that surely made her popular with the gentlemen, Rory assessed. Was she a frequent visitor here? Could *she* be the blackmailer?

If so, she had gall to enter the house of her victim.

As Mrs. Edgerton disappeared from sight, Rory murmured, "She must be a particular friend since you received her so early in the day."

"Yes, we are both widows and she's quite lively company. But never mind her." Leaning across the breakfast table, Kitty hissed, "Tell me, do you have the letters already? Is that why you're here? My, that was fast work! Are they in your reticule?"

She reached for the small bag, but Rory pushed it aside. "I'm afraid I must disappoint you. I haven't been able to find the letters. I'm beginning to think Lord Dashell doesn't have them at all."

A frown wiped away Kitty's elation. "What do you mean? Of course he has them. He must! You did not search thoroughly enough."

"I had a close look through his study and also his

bedchamber last night while he was out at a ball. But the letters simply aren't there."

Rory said nothing about Dashell catching her in the act, or that she had accused him of being a thief. The moment of seeing the stark truth on his face resonated in her memory. His gray eyes had been penetrating and intense, his shock too genuine to be fabricated.

She'd known in her heart that he was not the blackmailer.

However, they'd agreed to keep that development from Kitty for the time being. Given her high regard for Lady Milford's judgment, Kitty would be loath to acquit Dashell of the deed. It was better to let her go on thinking he was the villain so that she didn't interfere with the investigation. Otherwise, Kitty might inadvertently tip off the real blackmailer through some chance remark.

Rory glanced at the open doorway. If the guilty party was someone in this household, perhaps he or she was out there right now, eavesdropping to find out if they were close to identifying the culprit.

Cup in hand, she quietly arose from her chair. "I've something to discuss with you," she murmured to her stepmother. "But first I'd like to freshen my tea."

Instead of going to the sideboard, Rory poked her head out into the corridor. Grimshaw stood there with his head cocked and his ears perked. Upon spying her, the butler made haste to straighten one of the paintings on the wall.

"Careless maidservants!" he blustered, redness creeping up his neck to darken his narrow face. "They leave the pictures crooked when they dust."

"Then perhaps you ought to go have a word with them. At once."

Muttering under his breath, the middle-aged man

turned on his heel and marched toward the staircase. She waited until his black-clad figure vanished before shutting the door. Then she poured her tea and returned to the breakfast table.

"What was all that about?" her stepmother asked in confusion.

"Grimshaw was lurking in the passageway. I'm sure you don't want him to overhear our conversation."

"Dear heavens, no! Though of course I trust the man implicitly. I'm sure he wouldn't listen in on purpose."

Rory doubted that. Grimshaw had always been a snoop. No one knew that better than her.

"Well?" Kitty prompted. "What is it you wish to discuss? I do hope you haven't come to inquire if you may quit your post. Not when my letters are still missing."

"Of course not. I intend to keep searching." She and Dashell had agreed she would stay on as his mother's companion for a few more days. The arrangement would make it easier for them to compare notes. "I was able to steal away this morning while the doctor visits Lady Dashell for her weekly therapy. There's something I must clarify with you."

"Clarify?"

In the wee hours of the morning, Dashell had grilled her about the illicit affair between Kitty and his father. But Rory knew little of the particulars. Her purpose today was to gather clues that might help them identify the criminal.

"Since time is short and the next payment is due on Saturday," she said, "I believe we should consider the possibility that the blackmailer may be someone other than Lord Dashell."

"Impossible. If Lady Milford believes he is guilty, then you may be certain it is true!"

"Regardless, I'm hoping you'll provide me with some

information. For one, did anyone else know of your affair with Dashell's father? Other than Papa, of course."

Kitty puffed up with indignation, her cheeks turning rosy. "Certainly not! We were extremely discreet."

"Perhaps Grimshaw saw you together. And what about your lady's maid?" Rory recalled meeting the plain, nondescript woman the other day. Nothing in her timid manner would suggest a criminal bent, but appearances could be deceiving.

"Foster? She knew nothing of the matter. Why would I confide such a thing to a mere servant?"

"How long has she been with you?"

"Nearly five years now. But if you're implying that Foster might have filched the letters, that is utter nonsense. She is perfectly loyal to me. And far too much the mouse to commit such an offense."

Rory wished she herself could be so certain. "When exactly did the affair take place?"

Scowling, Kitty turned her gaze to the pastry tray and nabbed an apple tartlet. "I fail to see how that can be of any consequence. It is all in the past. I would prefer to forget the entire matter."

"It *is* of consequence. The more information I know, the better." Rory couldn't resist adding, "And if you'd really wanted to forget the affair, you'd have burned the letters. As I burned all my correspondence from Stefano."

"Well!" her stepmother huffed. "I fancy you are comparing your own transgression to mine. Perhaps you think this puts us on equal footing. You couldn't be more wrong. At least I had the good sense to . . . Oh, never mind!"

"The good sense to do what?"

An obstinate look on her face, Kitty attacked the tartlet with her fork. "I've had quite enough of your impertinent questions. Why, it is plain as the nose on my face that Lord Dashell is the guilty one. Such a cold, sour man! He will stop at nothing to rob me blind."

Lucas Vale wasn't always cold and sour, Rory knew. He could be quite burningly attractive when wooing a woman. The mere memory of him nuzzling her throat made her heart race. "Regardless, I only wish to find out—"

A discreet knock interrupted her. The door opened and Grimshaw stepped into the breakfast parlor. He looked harried, glancing back over his shoulder. "A visitor, madam. Mrs. Culpepper."

No sooner had he spoken than a tall, sturdy woman with salt-and-pepper hair sailed past him. She wore a plain brown cape that had seen better days and a dull gray gown that made her resemble a servant instead of the wellborn lady that she was.

The conversation forgotten, Rory leaped to her feet. "Aunt Bernice!"

She flew across the room and threw herself at her aunt. Bernice's arms closed around Rory in a bear hug. "My dear, you are a sight for sore eyes. That journey was worse than any sea voyage, what with all that bumping and swaying over bad roads. The worst of it was when the dogcart broke an axle near St. John's Wood."

A disbelieving laugh caught in Rory's throat. "You drove all the way from Norfolk in the dogcart?"

"Yes, and such a nuisance it was! Especially as the accident forced us to stop overnight and bear the expense of an inn."

"Us?"

Just then, Murdock shuffled inside, his shoulders bowed and a large leather portmanteau tucked under each arm of his wrinkled black garb. "I fixed the axle myself," he bragged. "Leastways, I told the smithy how 'twas best to be done."

Grimshaw fairly trembled with indignation. He pointed to the door. "You! Depart this chamber at once. Proceed to the servants' staircase as I instructed you."

Murdock fixed his rheumy eyes on that pristine dignitary, looking the butler up and down. "I don't take orders from no fancy-pants. Only from the cap'n's widow."

The two servants sneered at each other, seeming on the verge of coming to blows, when Bernice said, "Do run along, Murdock. I'm sure someone down in the kitchen can give you directions where to take my cases."

"I'll fetch me a drop o' rum, that's what. A man needs t' fortify hisself after such a journey."

As he trudged out, Rory gazed at her aunt in happy perplexity. "But Auntie, why have you come to London? I thought you disliked the city excessively!"

Bernice removed her cape and thrust it at Grimshaw, whose upper lip curled as he bore the ancient garment away. "No sooner did your carriage drive out of sight than I decided that Halcyon Cottage was far too quiet. I deemed it high time I paid a visit to my sister-in-law."

Her mouth agape, Kitty sat staring in obvious consternation. She arose and came forward, a stiff smile plastered on her mouth as she gave her late husband's sister a perfunctory embrace. "Dear Bernice. What an unexpected pleasure. It's been quite a long time."

"Eight years, to be exact. Would have been only seven if you'd have notified me when my brother died so that Rory and I could have attended her papa's funeral."

Kitty blanched at the bald reprimand. "I'm terribly sorry. Roger fell ill . . . it happened so quickly . . . I was in such a dreadful state . . ." Drawing out her handkerchief, she sniffled.

If Rory didn't know better, she'd believe that display of heartfelt grief. But how could Kitty have loved Papa and then engaged in a sordid affair with a renowned lecher? If it weren't for the reward money and Celeste's happiness, Rory would be tempted to wash her hands of the whole matter.

Unaware of Kitty's lapse into depravity, Bernice patted her on the shoulder. "We'll let bygones be bygones. Now, let me drink a cup of tea and rest these old rattled bones while we catch up on the family news."

Rory fetched a cup and added a drop of cream the way her aunt liked, while the two older women sat down for a comfortable few minutes discussing Celeste's upcoming wedding. Then Rory was forced to broach the topic that pressed on her mind. She informed her aunt that she had taken a position as companion to Lady Dashell.

Kitty gave her a stare that shot daggers. But what else was there to do? Rory couldn't sit and chat the rest of the day. She added, "I'm afraid that I'm expected back at Dashell House very soon. And I mustn't be tardy. Her ladyship is quite cantankerous enough already."

Bernice looked stricken. "Is that the reason you came to London, dearie? To find another place to live? Why, I could have sworn you were content at Halcyon Cottage."

"It's only temporary. I'll be returning to Norfolk in a few weeks, I promise. I merely thought that so long as I was here in London to plan Celeste's wedding, I might earn a bit of pin money, that's all."

Her face fierce, Bernice set down her teacup with a clatter and rounded on Kitty. "Why, I never! Is this how you treat your stepdaughter? Sending her out to labor for her bread while you live in luxury! For shame! And all these years you've given her nothing! Are you so cruel that you could not crack open your purse enough to spare her a small allowance?"

Kitty's mouth flapped, though no sound emerged. Her cheeks were pale, her brow furrowed, her gaze flitting about as if seeking an escape route. She appeared in danger of needing her vial of hartshorn.

Rory took some satisfaction in seeing her stepmother at a loss for words, for Kitty deserved to be rebuked. At the same time, Rory disliked lying to her aunt. It wasn't fair to let Bernice go on thinking she'd been deserted for greener pastures. The best solution was to let her aunt in on the ruse. Kitty would object strenuously, but that was just too bad.

She addressed her stepmother. "Aunt Bernice has every right to be upset. And I believe it's time you told her the truth."

Having been announced by a hatchet-faced butler with the bearing of an ex-soldier, Lucas stepped into a morning room decorated in feminine hues of rose and yellow. A lady sat reading in a chair by one of the tall windows. Sunlight lent radiance to her raven-black hair and smooth features, though surely she was close to his mother in age.

She set aside her book and arose with a smile. "Ah, Dashell, what a surprise. How do you do? You're looking well on this fine morning."

He gave a terse bow. "Lady Milford. This is not a social call, as I'm sure you can guess."

"Oh? That sounds intriguing. Would you care for refreshment? A brandy, perhaps?"

"No." Anger simmered in him, and he had to remind himself to be polite. "Thank you."

She seated herself on a chaise by the unlit hearth, arranging her lilac skirts and then folding her hands in her lap. "Do sit down and join me."

Lucas ignored the request. Instead, he propped his elbow on the marble mantel. Never one to value the exchange of useless pleasantries, he got straight to the point. "I've discovered your latest scheme. And I want to know if *you* stole that packet of letters from Mrs. Kitty Paxton."

He succeeded in startling Lady Milford. Her long-lashed violet eyes widened and lent her a dewy beauty despite her mature years. Rumor had it that she had once been mistress to a prince. He could believe it, for she was still unduly handsome—and conniving enough to befuddle a man who wasn't on to her schemes.

She did not blink or look away. She answered him as frankly as he'd spoken. "No, I most certainly did not. Did you?"

"Of course not!" He slashed his hand downward for emphasis. "Would I be here otherwise? And if I'd taken the letters, I'd have burned them at once. It will be a disaster for me if they're published."

"You're referring to Miss Alice Kipling, I presume."

He glowered. Was everyone privy to his private marital plans?

He'd come here to confront Lady Milford because she had a penchant for matchmaking. She was the spider at the center of the web, spinning her intrigues, wrapping her sticky threads around him. Her maneuverings had induced Rory Paxton to come to his house in search of the *billets-doux*. Ever since learning of Lady Milford's involvement, he had wondered if this blackmail scheme was all an elaborate hoax designed to throw Rory back into his path.

He had no right to lust for her. No matter how drawn

he was to Rory Paxton, no matter how keenly he craved her, he was obliged to marry an heiress. That fact could never be changed.

He must provide his brother with an estate free of debt. He must hold on to the London house for his mother's sake. He must preserve the remaining family assets for future generations. The last thing he needed was for this busybody to try to match him with an impoverished outcast.

He directed a hard stare at Lady Milford. "I intend to take Miss Kipling as my bride. And I will not abide a scandal."

"I see. Have you set a wedding date?"

"No." He hadn't even sought permission from Alice's father yet. But he'd be damned if he confessed that to this schemer. Instead, he attacked from another angle. "You told Kitty Paxton that I'd squandered my inheritance through bad investments. Why did you lie to her?"

Lady Milford smiled rather guiltily. "I wanted Miss Paxton to investigate you. She was more likely to do so if she thought you a dastardly fellow rather than a sympathetic figure who'd merely inherited his father's gaming debts."

"Ah, so you admit you conspired to get her into my house!"

"Of course. Because I believed you to be a likely suspect. If you must know, I've glimpsed the perpetrator myself."

Nothing could have been better designed to distract Lucas. Leaving the fireplace, he strode forward to stand over her. "What the devil? Describe him."

Lady Milford proceeded to relate how she'd chanced to spy Kitty Paxton outside the bank several days earlier, placing a small box containing the diamond necklace underneath a bush. A few moments later, a cloaked figure had darted out to retrieve the jewels. "It was nearly dark and I wasn't able to get a good look at him, but he was about your size. When I called on Kitty the following morning, she confessed to having had an affair with your father and said that she was being blackmailed for the return of a packet of his letters to her."

"Flimsy evidence to convict *me* of the crime!"

"I never convicted you. I merely thought it wise that you be investigated, given your connection to the letters."

"And my obvious need for funds," he added bitterly. Too agitated to stand still, he prowled back and forth. "So you plotted to entrap me. You went to Norfolk to fetch Rory—Miss Paxton. I would venture to guess that you even paid off my mother's previous companion so the position would be open."

Lady Milford didn't deny it. "I have no regrets about making such arrangements. Or engaging Miss Paxton's assistance. She's a resourceful woman and I knew that *you* would not do her a harm, but—"

"But? You believe me capable of heinous deeds!"

"I humbly beg your pardon, my lord. However, I never thought Miss Paxton had real reason to fear you. That is why I had no compunction about sending her into your employ."

"Small comfort, that."

"Given her headstrong nature, I daresay she will continue her quest to find the blackmailer." Lady Milford rose to her feet and took his hand, urgently pressing it. "Please, Dashell, you must promise to watch over her. If the villain is desperate, he may be very dangerous."

Chapter 11

*Not all women are helpless creatures in need
of a man's protection.*

—MISS CELLANY

In light of the revelation about Kitty's secret, Aunt
Bernice decided to accompany Rory back to Dashell
House. She declared that she could not bear the sight of
her deceitful sister-in-law a moment longer and would
pass the afternoon by paying a call on her old acquaintance, Lady Dashell.

Walking briskly toward Grosvenor Square, Bernice
muttered under her breath. "An illicit affair—imagine!
I knew there was something improper about that saucy
female from the moment I met her. Who but a flibberti-
gibbet has a name like Kitty, anyway? I warned Roger
against marrying her, but he was besotted."

"Papa loved her, I'm sure. He certainly doted on
her."

As they crossed a busy cobbled street, pausing to allow a carriage to rattle past, Bernice gave her niece a
contrite look. "You're right, dearie, and I don't mean to
go on. It's just that she deserves to be keelhauled for involving *you* in a calamity of her own making."

"There's Celeste to consider, though. I don't wish a
scandal to taint her."

A pot of gold also waited at the end of the rainbow,

but Rory wanted that to be a surprise. Wouldn't Aunt Bernice be thrilled when they had an extra thousand pounds with which to spruce up Halcyon Cottage, refurbish their wardrobes, and create a nest egg as a cushion against penury?

"We'll weather this storm together," Bernice avowed. "His lordship daren't threaten you so long as I'm around."

"That's just it," Rory murmured as they turned a corner to the stables behind his mansion, the air laden with the odor of horses. "Despite what Kitty believes, I'm certain that Lord Dashell did *not* take those letters." Quickly she related how he'd caught her searching his bedchamber the previous night, though leaving out the more sensational aspects of the encounter. "He's offered to help me find the blackmailer."

"Well! Are you certain he wasn't just spinning a yarn?"

"Yes, I'm quite sure. I was mistaken about his character. He might be cold and despotic, but he isn't a thief."

The memory of his penetrating gray eyes made her insides clench. It was difficult to put into words exactly why she now trusted him—at least insofar as he wouldn't stoop to extortion.

Bernice cast a quizzical glance at her niece as they went through a gate and down a pebbled walk that skirted the large formal gardens. They entered the house by descending a short flight of stone steps to the tradesmen's door in the cellars. As they passed through the kitchen, the staff was busy with luncheon preparations and no one questioned the presence of a drably garbed older woman in Rory's company.

A moment later, they were climbing the steep wooden steps of the servants' staircase, their footfalls echoing in the narrow shaft. "This isn't right," Bernice muttered.

"A lady like you should be admitted to the entrance hall and shown into the drawing room."

"I expect I'll survive," Rory said with a hint of humor. "If nothing else, the experience has given me a better appreciation for the plight of the working class."

They said no more as they went down the corridor to Lady Dashell's bedchamber. The door stood partway open, and Rory slipped inside with her aunt bringing up the rear.

Like a little brown wren, Mrs. Jarvis flitted around the room, while the marchioness barked orders from her pillowed throne in the four-poster bed. "Adjust those draperies. The sun is hurting my eyes. And stir the coals before the fire goes out. Fetch me a glass of water, too. I am as parched as a desert."

The hapless housekeeper attempted to complete all the tasks in a hurry to her mistress's satisfaction. Rory removed her bonnet and glided to the bed. "You've a pitcher of water right beside you, my lady. You've only to lean over and refill the glass yourself."

Nevertheless, Rory reached for the crystal jug and poured the liquid.

Lady Dashell fixed her sharp gray eyes on her. "Where did you run off to, lazybones? Two hours you've been gone! Meeting a lover, perhaps? I won't abide such mischief in my house!"

Bernice stepped to the foot of the bed. "Nor will *I* abide such insults toward my niece. She was visiting with me, not a man."

"What? Who are you to speak to me thusly?" The marchioness fumbled for her pince-nez and jammed it onto the bridge of her nose. Her eyes widened behind the narrow spectacles. "Bernice? Bernice Paxton?"

"It's Bernice Culpepper, as well you know. I've had a different surname for nigh on forty years now."

"Why, you're old. Your face is weathered like a common sailor's. And you're dressed like a washerwoman. Have you lost all pride in yourself?"

Chuckling, Bernice drew a straight-backed chair over to the bed. "Have you peered in a mirror of late, Prudence? Your hair is gray and your skin is wrinkled. It happens to all of us as we age."

A smothered squeak came from the fireplace, where Mrs. Jarvis had just finished stoking the fire. She stood there, her fingers pleating her apron, as if fearing another outburst from the marchioness. "Er . . . will you be wishing your luncheon delayed, milady?"

"Of course not, you dolt. And bring an extra tray since my guest has been rude enough to show up at mealtime without an invitation!"

While the housekeeper scurried out of the bedchamber, Rory settled down in a chair by the hearth. She appreciated the fire since the vast stone house held a chill, and Lady Dashell would not permit the windows to be opened to let in the warm spring breeze. It was a treat to be spared the marchioness's ill humor for a few minutes. Besides, the argumentative interplay of the two older women was as entertaining as having a front-row seat at a play.

"If you'd had the good sense to marry well," Lady Dashell was griping, "you could be mistress of a splendid mansion like this one. Instead, you ran off with a common seaman."

"Ollie was both owner and captain of a fine merchant ship," Bernice said with pride. "And Halcyon Cottage is perfectly suited to my needs now. What would I want with such a great pile of stone as this?"

"One's home is a monument to one's rank. Especially here in London where polite society is the pinnacle of the civilized world."

"Society is full of gossiping hens and preening dandies. I met far more interesting people among the savages of Canada and Brazil."

"Such blather! You never did understand that a lady derives her status from her husband."

"And you never did understand that a lady derives her *happiness* from marrying a man whom she loves." Despite her pithy retort, Bernice had a kindly, almost pitying look on her lined face. "But neither of us has a husband, anymore, Prudence, so that's that."

Lady Dashell persisted doggedly in her one-upmanship. "Yet you will finish out your days as a plain missus, whereas I retain the title of marchioness. I shall always outrank you. It matters naught that I've been widowed for a year now."

"I've been widowed for ten. And I'd trade all my worldly possessions to have my Ollie back. My only regret in life is that he and I were never blessed with children. Be thankful you have two of your own, both fine young men, to my understanding."

Lady Dashell plucked at the counterpane. "Thankful! I am confined to this bed ever since the accident, plagued by every ache and pain imaginable."

"Not *every*. I doubt you've ever had scurvy. That made my hair fall out during one voyage. Ever since, it grew back in sparse."

"Hair! That is nothing compared to being crippled. Or suffering chronic dyspepsia and arthritic joints, too. Why, I can scarcely sleep a wink at night."

"I was seldom ill while sailing the high seas, breathing all that fresh air. It helps foster deep slumber, too. Speaking of which, the air is rather stuffy in here. I daresay that has a debilitating effect on your health."

Bernice sprang up and went to the wall of windows. Rory parted her lips in warning, then decided to bide her tongue and see what happened. As her aunt raised the sash on one window, the inevitable screech came from the bed.

"Close that at once! I'll catch my death!" Lady Dashell hurled one of the bolsters at Bernice, though the pillow fell harmlessly short of its target.

"'Twas my belief you hurt your legs, not your lungs," Bernice countered, as she went to open another window. A pleasant breeze stirred the draperies, carrying the scent of the outdoors. "It isn't the ocean, but it's nicer than that stale sickroom smell."

"Miss Paxton!" the marchioness barked. "Run over and shut those windows immediately."

"Rory, stay right where you are," Bernice countered, her arms crossed obstinately. "As for you, Prudence, I won't have you treating my niece like a lackey. She's as wellborn as you!"

Having arisen from her chair, Rory stood uncertainly. She felt caught between the dueling curmudgeons. Her duty was to obey Lady Dashell, yet she agreed with her aunt that fresh air could be beneficial.

While she was debating what to do, a masculine voice spoke from the doorway. "What is all this uproar?" Lucas Vale demanded. "I could hear shouting all the way down the corridor."

He walked into the bedchamber, planted his hands at his waist, and stared at the women. His dark blue coat brought out a trace of cobalt in the iron-gray of his eyes, and an austere white cravat emphasized the smooth-shaven angles of his face. He was not smiling.

Then again, he never smiled.

Nevertheless, Rory's heart did a little flip inside the confines of her corset. She hadn't seen him since they'd parted company in the middle of the night, and she had convinced herself that her attraction to him had been a product of candlelight and semidarkness. Yet now that keen awareness rekindled in her, adding a hitch to her breathing and a sparkle to her veins.

"It's about time you came to visit me," Lady Dashell carped. "I'm being harangued on all sides. It's enough to bring on one of my megrims."

He bent down and kissed her wrinkled cheek. "I'm sorry, Mama. I had business to attend to this morning."

When he straightened up and gave Bernice an inquiring look, Rory remembered her manners. "Lord Dashell, I'd like to introduce my aunt, Mrs. Bernice Culpepper. She arrived in town this morning to visit my stepmother and asked if she might call on the marchioness."

Bernice came forward to shake his hand. She examined him up and down and gave an approving nod. "So you're the marquess. How do you do? It's a pleasure to meet you."

"You're the aunt from Norfolk, I presume." A faint furrow to his brow, he glanced from her to Rory and then to the marchioness. "Am I to understand that you and my mother are old acquaintances?"

"We made our bows the same season," Bernice began.

"Then she married a lowly sea captain," Lady Dashell broke in. "You must forgive her any gaffes. She tossed away well-bred society in order to mingle with sailors and savages."

"Now, what gaffes have I committed?" Bernice said, humor tugging at her weathered face. "I vow I've been as polite as you deserve!"

"You opened the windows against my wishes! Lucas, I want them closed immediately, lest I develop a lung disorder on top of all my other afflictions."

Lord Dashell took a step in that direction, but Bernice was closer and beat him to it. "Oh, I'll shut them if you insist, Prudence," she said over her shoulder as she pulled down one sash with a bang. "Though you'll never be hale enough to leave that bed at the rate you're going."

"Hale?" the marchioness scoffed, her upper lip curled. "How cruel of you to suggest such a thing. The finest specialist in London said my case was hopeless."

"There's no sense wallowing in the doldrums about it, then. One must always make the best of things, as Ollie used to say."

Lady Dashell dug her fingers into the counterpane. "Oliver Culpepper! What could *he* have known of anything? If the fellow was forced to earn his living, he might at least have chosen a more respectable profession!"

Instead of being offended, Bernice clucked her tongue in commiseration. "You're bitter. I was that way for a time, too, after my husband's death. But when my niece came to live with me, she helped me to see that I was squandering my life by being unhappy. Isn't that true, Rory?"

All eyes turned to Rory. Bernice was smiling, Lady Dashell scowling, and Lord Dashell . . . well, Rory didn't quite know how to describe his look. It was forceful and penetrating as if he wished to peer into her soul.

Unwilling to let him do so, she gazed at her aunt. Bernice had a point. Her ladyship would never enjoy any contentment if she continued to let acrimony rule her life. "You *were* difficult at first, Auntie. But I suppose I was, too, being sent to rusticate so far from London. So, we helped each other, I'd say. And we've scraped along quite well together these past eight years."

At that moment, a small parade of footmen entered the bedchamber. Each bore a covered tray from which emanated delicious aromas. Lady Dashell snapped an order to one of the manservants to move a small table and chairs close to the bedside for Bernice and Rory.

Dashell strolled to Rory's side. The directness of his gaze caused an unwelcome fluttering in her bosom. He bent his head close, enveloping her in his alluring scent of pine and leather. "We need to talk," he murmured for her ears alone. "If you won't mind leaving your aunt here, you'll take luncheon with me downstairs."

Half an hour later, Rory sat at Dashell's right hand in the dining chamber while a pair of footmen served them spring lamb, braised endive, and roasted potatoes. She felt oddly at home in the formal setting, though a lifetime had passed since she had enjoyed a meal served on fine china. And in the company of a handsome gentleman.

Not that she cared a fig about handsome gentlemen anymore, except as a coconspirator. Lucas Vale might prove useful if he could help her nab the blackmailer and earn her reward money.

He made a discreet gesture to the servants, who bowed and departed, leaving them alone in the cavernous room with its baroque décor and the burgundy drapes fastened by tasseled gold cords. For a few moments, the only sounds were the clinking of heavy silver utensils against the plates. The marquess seemed content to eat without conversing. Perhaps he wished to finish his meal before broaching the topic of the mystery. Then again, she knew from their one silent dance together all those years ago that no one could ever accuse him of being a chatterbox.

The memory tickled Rory's sense of humor and made her want to tease him out of his stuffy manner.

"Are you not aware that dining with a scarlet woman could damage your reputation, Lord Dashell?" she said, cutting a slice of lamb. "What would Miss Kipling say if she knew?"

"My servants don't gossip and my brother has gone to Newmarket for the day, so there's no one to see us."

"Your mother might tell her. She seemed rather put out when you whisked me away from her bedchamber just now."

"My mother won't see Alice again until I say so." He flashed Rory a reproachful look over his wineglass. "Though it seems you haven't learned your lesson about extending invitations to this house without my permission."

Rory arched an eyebrow. "I didn't imagine you would object to Aunt Bernice paying a call. She is an old friend of your mother's, after all. And they seem to be getting on quite well."

"From the clamor I heard down the corridor, they were quarreling."

"The marchioness thrives on quarreling. I suspect that no one has pushed back before now, so she's become something of a tyrant." Rory thought the same thing was true of him, though she kept that observation to herself.

His eyes narrowed on her. "I see. So, you've solved all her problems even though you've been here little more than a day."

"Sometimes an outsider can view the situation more clearly. And I believe it would do the marchioness a great deal of good to renew old acquaintances. Does no one ever visit her?"

"There were quite a few callers directly after her accident. But when she refused to see anyone, they stopped coming."

Though his expression remained flinty, Rory noted a trace of worry in the furrowing of his brow. She set down her fork to give him her full attention. "The accident happened over a year ago, did it not? Will you tell me about it? If you don't mind, that is."

His gaze flicked to hers before he stared down into the ruby contents of his wineglass. For a moment, she thought he might refuse. Then he spoke in a monotone. "She and my father were traveling back to London from the family seat in West Sussex. He'd been drinking heavily and decided to climb up to the coachman's seat and take the reins. Mama tried to stop him, but he refused to listen. He drove too recklessly and veered off the road while passing another carriage. The coach overturned. He was thrown to the ground and broke his neck. Mama might have died, too, had she not been sitting inside."

Rory imagined the horror of that moment, the crazy tilt of the coach, the jarring crash, the agonizing pain. Sympathy for the marchioness stirred in her. And for her son, who'd had to take on the burden of her care.

It was also the longest speech she'd ever heard Dashell make, which indicated the incident still deeply disturbed him. "I'm so very sorry," she murmured. "It must have been a difficult time for you and your family."

He turned troubled eyes at her. "Do you really suppose my mother can ever find contentment again? I'm at my wit's end with her."

She was moved that he'd let her see a crack in his granite façade. On impulse, she reached across the white linen to touch his hand. It felt warm and solid, a testament to his masculine strength. "Yes, I do think she could be happy again. But she has to find that resolve within herself. Perhaps my aunt can help her see the way."

His stark gaze held hers for another moment. Then he withdrew his hand and picked up the crystal decanter to refill his wineglass and hers. The cool look returned to his face. "Handing your post over to someone else already, are you?"

"Only because Aunt Bernice is more qualified, given her own widowhood. If she's agreeable, it will be good for your mother. And it will allow me more time to find the blackmailer."

He frowned. "The man is a criminal and likely dangerous. I would rather you left this matter to me."

And give up her reward? Never!

"My stepmother asked me to find him, and I intend to do just that. Besides, it may be someone in her household, and you can't investigate there. I've identified several suspects already."

"Who?

"When I called this morning, a Mrs. Edgerton was present. Do you know her?"

"Only slightly. A widow and quite popular with the gentlemen."

Having witnessed the woman's sensual walk, Rory had no trouble imagining that. "She is a particular friend of my stepmother's, so she would have had the opportunity to steal the letters. There's something I don't quite trust about her. I'll need to find out if she's short of funds."

"Who else?"

"There are two servants of interest, one is Foster, my aunt's maid. She's a rather timid sort, but if she'd spotted Kitty with the letters, she might see it as her ticket out of service."

"And the other?"

"Grimshaw, the butler. He's always been a snoop. This morning, I caught him listening outside the breakfast parlor."

"Servants do eavesdrop," Dashell observed. "Is there another reason why you suspect him?"

Rory battled the rise of a blush. She had no intention of revealing that Grimshaw was the one who'd caught her *in flagrante delicto* with Stefano. Or that the butler had gleefully informed her father and brought him running.

"He's a busybody, that's all. He knows everything that goes on in the house, so it wouldn't surprise me to learn that he'd found the letters where Kitty left them in her sewing basket."

"There was no one else?"

She shook her head. "You were to check into your father's old cronies. Who did *you* find?"

A secretive look entered his eyes. "I had other things to do this morning, but I do have two suspects in mind. Colonel Hugo Flanders is an old lecher who likes to lavish expensive gifts on his mistresses. And Lord Ralph Newcombe is a hardened gamester who's up to his eyeballs in debt."

"Newcombe! Mrs. Edgerton mentioned going to a card party at his house tomorrow night."

"Indeed? I don't gamble so I wasn't invited. But I might just have to wangle an invitation."

Rory itched to go, too. She couldn't let Dashell be the one to catch the blackmailer, or Kitty might renege on the reward. But how could a woman of her reputation infiltrate society? She would have to ponder the matter.

In the meantime, something else weighed on her mind.

"I've been thinking about the necklace that Kitty gave to the blackmailer," she said. "If the culprit is in need of money, then he may have tried to sell it."

"I'd been considering that angle myself." Dashell pushed back his chair and came to draw back hers. "You don't mind skipping the dessert course, do you? We'll go to my study and fetch paper and pen. You can sketch the necklace for me."

"For you?"

"Yes, I'll take the likeness around to jewelers and pawnshops. The proprietor may be able to give me a description of the seller."

Rory sprang to her feet, her fists clenched at her sides. "You're not going without me."

He wore the indulgent look of a father mollifying a petulant daughter. "Don't be irrational. Ladies don't frequent pawnshops. I'll be venturing into the most treacherous parts of town."

"Not all women are helpless creatures in need of a man's protection. I am perfectly capable of taking care of myself."

"Oh?"

"It's true." When he gazed skeptically at her from his superior height, she added, "And for that matter, I'm terrible at drawing. I can't even do a credible stick figure." She didn't mention that Celeste could create a lifelike illustration of the necklace in a flash.

"Then describe it to me," he said. "Surely you can manage that much."

Rory contrived an innocent look. "I'm afraid description isn't my strong suit, either," she fibbed. "It seems you'll just have to take me along with you."

Chapter 12

*It is far more beneficial to the feminine mind to study
algebra and geography than to memorize rules of etiquette.*

——MISS CELLANY

Half an hour later, they sat side by side in a well-sprung
brougham driven by a coachman. The enclosed vehicle
was a new mode of carriage that had not been in use during her debut season. It resembled a coach cut in half,
leaving room for only two passengers.

The tufted blue satin on the walls and cushions created an intimate bower. The gently rocking motion of
the brougham should have had a soothing effect on the
senses, but Rory felt alive with excitement. She had to
force herself to sit still, for if she dared to move, her
skirts would brush Dashell's leg or her arm would touch
his sleeve.

Not that he seemed aware of her presence.

He gazed out the window, observing the busy traffic
and the many shops along Oxford Street. His classically
handsome profile might have been chiseled from marble. Yet maybe he wasn't so hard-hearted, after all. During their luncheon, he had showed deep concern for his
mother's well-being.

Feeling more charitable toward him, Rory refused to
attribute the exhilaration inside her to anything but the
adventure of tracking down a blackmailer. Allowing

herself to feel something deeper would only lead to trouble. It would be the height of folly to develop an affection for a nobleman who believed her to be suited only to the role of his mistress.

Besides, Dashell was wooing Alice Kipling. He needed the heiress's vast wealth to save him from financial ruin. It bothered Rory to recall his formal manner toward the girl the one time she'd seen them together. He had displayed not a trace of affection. What a pity he couldn't marry for love.

"I hope you're better at conversing with Miss Kipling than you are with me," Rory said.

Those dark gray eyes focused on her. "I beg your pardon?"

"You haven't spoken a word since we left your house. If you're as reticent with her, it could very well put a damper on your courtship."

"Useless chatter serves no purpose."

"Rather, conversation tells a lady that a gentleman cares for her," she advised. "That's how I knew you had no real interest in *me*. The one time we danced during my debut season, you scarcely uttered a word to me."

He glanced away for a moment, then returned his sardonic gaze to her. "*Did* we dance, Miss Paxton? I'm afraid I don't recall."

Rory had the distinct impression he was lying. But she could think of no reason why he would deny the memory, except perhaps to needle her. "Well!" she said with a laugh. "You certainly know how to shatter a woman's illusion that she is unforgettable. You ought to have made a polite excuse for your silence instead of claiming no recollection of the dance."

He looked a trifle shamefaced. "Forgive me. Just how much babble is necessary to meet your exacting standards?"

"More than you do now. If you wish to win Miss Kipling's heart, it would be wise to charm her. To engage her in a tête-à-tête whenever you meet."

"I've had many a tête-à-tête with Alice."

"Have you? What are her interests?"

The question seemed to startle him, and he rubbed his hand over his smooth-shaven jaw. "Shopping, I suppose. Visiting. Going for drives in the park. The usual sorts of things young ladies enjoy."

"Does she like reading?"

"We've never discussed books."

"What is her most vivid childhood memory?"

"The subject has never come up."

"That is why you should broach it. The more you know about her, the more likely she will be to form a strong attachment to you—and you to her." Unable to stop herself, Rory added, "I wonder how she feels about her father earning his wealth from child labor?"

Dashell's dark eyebrows descended in a glare. "Good God. You can't expect me to ask her *that*. I'm sure Alice knows very little about the operation of textile mills."

"Do *you* know, my lord?" Having read extensively on the topic herself, Rory welcomed the opportunity to expound on it. "Children as young as ten are employed in such factories, working long hours under frightful conditions. As a member of Parliament, you ought to sponsor laws to end such practices."

"How do you know that I haven't?"

She studied his face to see if he was serious. The trouble was, Dashell *always* looked serious. "Perhaps once you marry Miss Kipling you could use your influence to convince her papa to improve his mills."

"That is certain to endear me to him," he said on a dry note of irony. "Now, how did we venture onto such a weighty topic? Most women know nothing of such matters."

The glint in his eyes made her aware that he was indulging her. How like a man to dismiss feminine opinions! "*I* certainly keep informed of the news," she declared. "I believe that women should be encouraged to study politics, along with algebra and geography and other substantial subjects. It's far more beneficial to improve the mind than to memorize rules of etiquette."

"I recently read an essay that said precisely that. Dare I conclude that you derive your modern notions from the pages of *The Weekly Verdict*?"

Rory's heart gave a thump. That was the newspaper that had published one of her pieces! Had Dashell truly read her work? He was gazing curiously at her, and she burned to find out what he'd thought of it.

Very casually, she asked, "Would that be the essay by . . . what was her name? Ah, yes, Miss Cellany."

"An absurd *nom de plume,* given the content of the article. Better she should have chosen Miss Staken. Or Miss Judged."

Rory strove not to grind her teeth. "So you found it to be beneath your exalted standards, did you?"

"It was well written, I'll grant you. But I was referring to the radical ideas set forth in the essay. The author wishes to fundamentally alter the roles of men and women. In other words, to shake the very foundation of civilization. Does she mean that women should go off to war while men stay home to raise the children? Ridiculous!"

Well written. Rory latched on to that praise to keep from shaking her fist in his too handsome face. How she would love to debate the issue with him, to make him see her point of view. "You've misconstrued the basic premise. Why can men and women not have the freedom to fill either role—"

At that moment, the brougham slowed and came to a halt.

She glanced out to see that the fine houses and shops had given way to a dingier part of the city. Here, the streets were narrower, the pedestrians a motley assemblage of rough-clad laborers, tawdry women, and the occasional flashy gent. Men loitered on corners and in the doorways of gin shops, and she wondered if they were thieves or pickpockets looking for a victim.

Rory felt a craven relief that she didn't have to venture into such an area alone. "Where exactly are we?"

"Near Seven Dials. At a shop reputed to buy stolen goods with no questions asked. It's as good a place as any to start."

"How do you know about it?"

"Parliament is looking into ways to control crime in the city. I recently read a report that included the locations of certain criminal networks. This pawnshop is one of the more infamous ones."

As a footman opened the door, Dashell leaned closer to her and added, "You will allow me to do the talking, Miss Paxton. You are to speak only when I say so."

"But I—"

"But nothing. You will play along with the story that I tell. And you will bide your tongue. This is no time to chatter, or we might contradict each other. Is that clear?"

Rory could only nod, albeit unwillingly. He had a point. If he meant to spin a tale in order to obtain information about the necklace, then she wouldn't want to give away his game. "What story is that?"

"You'll find out soon enough."

They stepped out of the brougham. The neighborhood was nothing like the pristine cobbled streets of Mayfair. An empty gin bottle rested against a stoop. Torn circulars, trampled by a thousand feet, papered the dirty walkway. Mud puddles from the previous day's rain threatened to soak her hem.

Leaving the coachman and footman to guard the carriage, Dashell guided Rory past a row of soot-stained brick buildings. His hand rested at the small of her back and made her keenly aware of him at her side. The gesture had a masculine possessiveness that threatened her independent nature.

She didn't object, however, especially when they walked past a knot of crouching ruffians gathered around a long wooden box rather like a coffin. The fellows were cheering loudly and uttering raucous expletives. She tried to see what held their attention, but just then Dashell pushed open a door and whisked her into a dimly lit shop.

A bell tinkled overhead. The narrow, oblong room had rows of locked glass cases that displayed a clutter of items for sale, bracelets and candlesticks and pocket watches. An oil lamp cast a meager illumination at the rear of the shop. The proprietor must have stepped out for a moment, for there was no one on duty behind the counter.

"What were those men doing out there?" she asked Dashell.

"They appeared to be racing rats."

"Rats!"

"This area is infested with vermin. Surely you knew."

Shuddering in visceral disgust, Rory shook her head. She had been more concerned about rats of the human variety. But if one fact could have convinced her to stay in the carriage, that was it. She'd always had an acute revulsion of rodents.

"Speaking of rats, did you see that?" Dashell asked, peering toward a gloomy corner.

"See what?"

"Something scuttled through the shadows over there."

With a yelp, she launched herself at him. Fear wiped all rational thought from her mind. She was consumed by the dread of a rodent running underneath her skirts and scrabbling up her petticoats. As a child, she'd overheard a nursemaid relate such an incident to the governess, and for years afterward, she'd been plagued by nightmares.

Clinging to Dashell, she felt a tremor convulse her from head to toe. His arms came around to hold her close. The heat of his body made her feel marginally safer, and after a moment, she became acutely aware of his hard, muscled chest against her soft breasts, the alluring pine scent that clung to him, and the fact that she'd buried her face in the starchy folds of his cravat.

The impropriety of their embrace intruded on her apprehension. Yet she could not bring herself to release her death grip on him. "Is it . . . is it gone?"

"Yes. At least I can no longer see it. I'm sure the little fellow is more terrified of you than vice versa."

"Are you *quite* certain it didn't run toward me or . . . or under my skirts?"

"Very certain. But in such an event, you may rest assured that I shall slay it with my bare hands."

She shivered again, unsure if it was from residual horror or from the stroking of his fingers over her back. "Don't tease, Dashell. I can't abide rats. They're filthy and repulsive."

"It's rather a relief to find something that frightens you, Rory. Especially since you declared yourself not to be in need of a man's protection. And perfectly capable of taking care of yourself."

She relished the sound of her name on his lips. Then the thread of mirth in his tone galvanized her. How dare he mock her!

She lifted her chin to challenge him, but the rebuke died on her tongue. His features had softened with amusement, and a twinkle lightened the iron-gray of his eyes. Both corners of his mouth were tilted upward to give him a look of heart-melting handsomeness.

"You're smiling," she said, dazzled by the sight.

"I do on occasion."

"Well, it's something *I've* never seen before."

The smile transformed him from a cold granite statue to a warm-blooded man. If he were to turn that roguish look on Miss Alice Kipling, she would fall in love with him forever. Why was that thought so very unsettling?

Rory stepped back out of his arms and added crisply, "You should smile more often, Dashell. It quite humanizes you."

His smile subsided slightly, though still playing with the corners of his mouth. He maintained a loose hold on her wrists. "Call me Lucas. It seems foolish to be formal when we are working together."

"Lucas." Murmuring his given name created an aura of intimacy between them. His expression changed subtly from amusement to something warm and wicked. His gaze dipped to her lips and she realized with a thrill that he wanted to kiss her. Heaven help her, she ached to feel the heated pressure of his mouth on hers. The desire to engage in carnal acts with him burned in her very core.

He lifted his hand to touch the dainty fichu draped around her neck. She could scarcely contain a shiver as the pads of his fingers brushed the bare skin of her throat. He must surely feel the rapid thump of her pulse . . .

"Is this scrap of lace pinned to your gown?" he asked.

"Hmm? No, it's only tucked in place— Oh!"

He deftly snatched the fichu from her bodice and thrust it into an inner pocket of his coat. Shocked, Rory clapped a hand to her bosom. The rose silk gown was a relic of her debutante days, the neckline far too revealing for day wear. "What do you think you're *doing*?"

"You'll see."

Just then, the tap of hurrying footsteps came from the rear of the shop. A well-fed man emerged from the back room. He wore a shiny russet coat with a gold kerchief tied at his throat in lieu of a cravat. In the light of the lantern, his dark hair glistened with pomade.

He beckoned them forward. "Good day, milord and milady. How might I assist you?"

Dashell—Lucas—slipped his arm around her waist and propelled her forward, keeping her close as if they were lovers. "There's nothing ladylike about this pretty little piece," he said. "And I'm glad of that."

So that was his game. She was to be his lightskirt. When he flashed his gorgeous smile at her again, Rory wasn't taken in by it. Because this time it was as calculated as his removal of her fichu.

Standing on tiptoe, she landed a kiss on his smooth-shaven cheek. "Nor are you a gentleman, dearie. At least not in the bedchamber."

He raised a chiding eyebrow as if to remind her to stay silent. Despotic man. If he wished her to play the part of his doxy, she had no intention of doing so as a tongue-tied idiot.

The proprietor bowed. "Ned Scully, at your service. And you, sir, would be . . . ?"

"Lord Dashell. And this is . . . Jewel."

Jewel?

Rory had the mad urge to laugh. The impulse died a quick death when she realized the proprietor was ogling the mounded flesh revealed by her fichu-free bodice. She took a keen dislike to Scully. It wasn't just his crude manners, either. His beady black eyes, narrow face, and sharp nose made him resemble a rat. He even had a thin moustache that looked like whiskers.

"Word has it that you stock the best selection of jewelry in town," Lucas said. "And *my* lovely Jewel is demanding an expensive bauble for her services."

"I want more than a mere bauble, darling. Only a diamond necklace will do." Annoyed with his portrayal of her as greedy, Rory walked her fingers over his lapels, up his cravat, to trace the outline of his mouth. His lower lip had a sensual fullness, and she took perverse pleasure in seeing his gaze darken with hot interest. She cast a pouty look at the proprietor. "Dashell has been very stingy with his gifts, you see. He even refused to take me to a proper jeweler's shop."

"As well he should refuse!" Scully said, his moustache fairly quivering with eagerness. "I keep the finest quality goods right here in this establishment. And at a fraction of the cost of such hoity-toity places!"

No doubt, she thought dryly. *His* jewelry was stolen property.

"Show me what you have," Lucas said in a lordly tone. "And only your very best, mind."

"At once, milord!"

Scully scurried into the back room. Rory could have sworn she saw a tail twitch beneath the backside of his russet coat.

The instant he was gone, she whirled toward Lucas. Mindful of being overheard, she pressed close to his arm and whispered, "You might have warned me of your intentions."

"And have you argue against playing my mistress?" He, too, kept his voice to a low rumble. "No, it was best to spring it on you. Lest you subject me to a lecture on the exploitation of women or some such nonsense."

"*You're* speaking nonsense. You *know* I'd do anything to find the necklace. And to identify whoever extorted it from Kitty."

"Fine. Just try not to overplay your hand and attract Scully's attention. I don't care for the way he's been staring at you."

His gaze flicked to her bosom, and the notion that Lucas might be jealous pleased Rory inordinately. "Then you oughtn't have stolen my fichu. And you also oughtn't be staring at me yourself."

His attention snapped back to her face. In the light of the lamp, she glimpsed a dull red flush creep up his neck. He fell silent, but that was nothing new. She rather enjoyed seeing him at a loss for words.

"By the by, you shouldn't have told Scully to show us his very best," she murmured. "My papa gave the necklace to Kitty and he was hardly a nabob!"

"Then you should have described it to me when I asked . . . Jewel."

A hint of that playful smile had returned to his lips. Suddenly breathless, she said, "Where did you come up with such a ludicrous name?"

"Ludicrous? Your eyes are like two gorgeous, golden-brown topazes." He was leaning closer, gazing deeply at Rory, making her heart trip over a beat. Was he trying to court her? Did she want him to do so? Then he straightened up and added, "How's that for charming? Do you suppose it will work in a tête-à-tête with Miss Kipling? Though of course with her blue eyes I'll have to change the analogy to sapphires."

He might as well have thrown a bucket of cold water over Rory. It irked her to realize that he could fool her so completely—and that a dry wit could lurk behind his stern mask. He was supposed to be a humorless prig. She had only an instant to glare at him before the approach of footsteps alerted them to the proprietor's return.

Ned Scully hurried back into the showroom of the shop, followed by a hulking man with an ugly scar slashed across one cheek. The menacing guard took up a stance behind his superior. Apparently, Scully was taking no chances that his customers might be thieves themselves.

Scully set a leather case on the counter. He spread a swatch of rich blue velvet beside the lamp, then reached into the case and carefully laid out a necklace for their inspection. "There now, take a gander at this one. These are my finest sparklers."

Rory gawked in awe. The ornate piece appeared fit for a queen and must be worth a fortune. A stunning number of diamonds and pearls winked against the blue velvet, with a large teardrop pearl as the centerpiece pendant.

Regrettably, the necklace looked nothing like Kitty's dainty strand of diamonds.

Lucas fixed Rory with a keen stare. "What do you think, darling?"

She pretended to cringe. "Pearls! They're bad luck! Take them away!"

"But look at the size of them diamonds—" Scully began.

"She said no. Show us something else."

"Aye, milord. Never fear, I've plenty more where that came from."

The proprietor tucked the necklace back into the case, then drew out another, this one a bow fashioned of diamonds and dangling from a gem-studded gold chain. Rory shook her head. "It's gaudy. I don't like it."

She pretended to find fault with each necklace that

he presented to her. The stones were too garish or too simple, too baroque or too paltry, too ostentatious or too trifling. At the end of it, Scully looked harried, his moustache twitching as he strove to convince her to buy this one or that.

"Is that all you have, then?" Lucas inquired in his most disdainful tone.

"In diamonds, yes, milord. However, I've sapphires and emeralds aplenty. And others, as well. Only imagine Miss Jewel, her fair skin draped in a rope of fine rubies—"

"Never mind. We will try another shop. Good day."

He took Rory's arm and led her toward the door.

"If 'tis diamonds you want, I have brooches," Scully called after them. "Earbobs! Bracelets! Tiaras!"

The bell tinkled as Lucas opened the door and ushered her outside. Clouds had banished the sunlight and a chill now tinged the air. The rowdy men had taken their rats away, thank goodness. That was the only bright spot in the afternoon.

"None of those even resembled Kitty's necklace." Rory hadn't realized until now how much she'd expected to triumph in this quest. It was a letdown to know that they were no closer to finding the blackmailer. "What now?"

"We proceed to the next place on my list." Lucas tapped her under the chin to tilt her face up. He gave her that slight smile again, the one that made her legs weak and turned her heart to mush. "And pray don't look so glum, Jewel. I wouldn't want word to get out that Dashell can't keep his mistress happy."

Chapter 13

What does a nobleman seek in a wife? Modesty, obedience,
docility, and beauty, all traits that shun the intellect.

—MISS CELLANY

It was nearing dusk by the time Lucas stepped out of the
brougham in front of his house. Having spent all afternoon in Rory's company, it seemed perfectly natural for
him to escort her up the steps, past the tall columns of
the portico, and through the large door opened by a footman. It wasn't until they were standing in the entrance
hall and she was giving her bonnet to Jarvis that Lucas
realized his mistake.

And then only because Rory flashed a startled look
at him. "Oh! I completely forgot. I should have gone to
the mews with the coachman, then come in by way of
the kitchen."

"Never mind, Miss Paxton," he said, adopting a formal tone. "This is more convenient. Come, I want a word
with you and my mother before dinner."

As they started up the grand staircase together, he
was careful to keep a circumspect distance from her.
That had been a close call. He had almost treated Rory
as a respectable lady of the ton, rather than his temporary employee. It was damned lucky he hadn't addressed
her by her given name in front of the butler and footman.

Or worse, called her Jewel.

Remembering her scorn of the tawdry name, he subdued a chuckle. It was time to shed his roguish act and return to the real world with its rules of proper behavior. Yet he had grown perilously comfortable in Rory's company. A part of him regretted having to put their ruse aside until the morrow, when they would continue their hunt for the blackmailer.

In all, they had visited six establishments that dealt in pilfered jewelry. The task had been an exercise in futility. They had examined scores of diamond necklaces while failing to locate the one belonging to Kitty Paxton. Nevertheless, Lucas couldn't recall another day that he had enjoyed more.

It all had to do with Rory. She had adapted brilliantly to the role of his mistress. Even now, his insides felt twisted into a carnal knot. She had teased him and tempted him, caressed and cooed, until at times her playacting seemed unnervingly real. She knew exactly how to entice a man with sultry looks and suggestive touches. They were an exaggerated version of the same techniques she had used eight years ago, flirting with a bevy of ardent swains, making each one of them feel he was the only man on earth.

Lucas glanced at her. She apparently had no inkling at all that he, too, had felt an acute passion for her back then—as he did now. He had deemed her too fast for his fastidious tastes. He had resisted her allure except for that one time when he'd succumbed to temptation and asked her to dance.

His claim that he'd forgotten their waltz had been a bald-faced lie. Every detail of clasping her in his arms remained seared into his memory. He recalled the slim indentation of her waist, the feminine curve of her hips, the silken sweetness of her skin. He had not been tongue-tied, either, despite what she believed. Rather, he had been determined not to make a fool of himself by babbling poetic flattery like her other admirers. He had known even then that Rory Paxton was all wrong for him.

Just as he knew it now.

Reaching the top of the stairs, he stole another look at her. She was frowning down at the long carpet runner as they headed past the closed doors of the many bedchambers. The glow of her beauty caught his chest in a velvet vise. He felt obsessed by the wisps of ebony hair that curled around her delicate ears. The graceful line of her swanlike neck. The finely etched profile that belied the boldness of her spirit.

Eight years ago, maybe he should have behaved like her other beaus and actively pursued Rory, having intimate tête-à-têtes with her in an attempt to win her heart. Maybe she had needed someone steady and principled in her life. Maybe he could have saved her from ruining herself.

What foolishness. Had he married her back then, he wouldn't have the means now to fix the dire financial straits in which his father had left him. Rory Paxton didn't have a penny to her name. That fact alone put her as far out of his reach as the moon.

Yet something had changed between them today. It was more than mere lust, though that was an undeniable part of it. Over the course of playing their game, he had come to think of them as equals. Not as master and employee, nor as lord and commoner, but rather, as friends on even footing. Though he took issue with her modern opinions, he appreciated the fact that she wasn't a meek, mindless female who could speak only of fashion and gossip.

Like Alice Kipling.

He shut his mind to that disloyal thought. He was

playing with fire. Rory Paxton could never be anything to him other than a momentary diversion. Once they found the blackmailer, she would leave his house and he would marry Alice. He would never take a mistress— even if Rory was agreeable, which was highly doubtful. He had sworn long ago never to emulate his father, who'd changed women as often as he'd changed clothes.

Her brow furrowed, she slowed her steps and glanced back toward the stairs. Her velvety brown eyes lifted to his face. "Jarvis looked rather scandalized just now, don't you think?"

"He's seen women in low-cut gowns before."

She gave an impatient shake of her head. "I meant about our excursion today. It must seem suspicious for you and your mother's companion to go off alone together." She held out her hand. "Now give me back my fichu before Lady Dashell sees me looking like a doxy."

Lucas thought Rory looked stunning enough to attend a society party, despite the washed-out rose gown with its frayed cuffs. Nevertheless, he reached inside his coat and handed her the wadded lace. "I told Jarvis a version of the truth before we left. That I am assisting you in investigating a delicate problem involving your stepmother."

"*What?* But Kitty doesn't want anyone to know!"

"Jarvis is absolutely trustworthy. I did not give him the particulars, anyway. He's under orders to ensure that none of the servants gossip about our outing."

He watched her arrange the strip of white lace around her neck and then tuck the edges at strategic places along the edge of her bodice. The feminine grace of her movements captivated him, though he deeply regretted the need for her to conceal that delectable bosom. It was a damn shame he couldn't take her to any balls, where plunging necklines were permissible. Or better yet, take her to his bed with nothing on at all, so he could savor every silken inch of her.

Rory glanced up and intercepted his stare. Pursing her soft lips, she turned around and finished with the fichu, saying over her shoulder, "The servants likely know about my sordid background by now. I'm afraid they will assume the worst. Of course, *you* needn't worry. It is only the woman who is held to blame."

"We men rule the world. It is high time you accepted that fact and behaved accordingly."

She spun around in a huff. "I will accept nothing of the sort . . . !" Her indignant voice died as she spied the cunning grin that tugged at one corner of his mouth. "Oh! You're teasing me . . . aren't you?"

"Perhaps. Or perhaps not." She was so easy to rile, especially now that he knew her weakness. "Come, we've tarried long enough. I want to see how the marchioness has fared today."

As they resumed walking, Lucas turned his mind to his mother. He'd suffered misgivings over leaving her with Bernice Culpepper. Rory's aunt had a no-nonsense manner that must have caused friction during his absence. He himself had always found it best to humor Mama. Otherwise, she would carry a grudge for days on end, never letting him forget his error, complaining until he bowed to her wishes.

Rory stopped in front of the closed door to his mother's bedchamber. Her gaze studied him quizzically; then she laid a light hand on his sleeve. "Are you worried, Lucas? You needn't be. I'm sure Aunt Bernice took excellent care of Lady Dashell today."

"I won't have my mother bullied. It's my duty to see that she's happy."

"Your mother also has a duty to keep *herself* happy. After all, it isn't your fault she's crippled."

"Maybe it is."

The minute he said that, he was sorry. Because his deep-seated guilt was something he'd never admitted to another living soul.

"What?" Rory questioned, giving him a probing stare that sought to invade his private thoughts. "Why would you say that?"

"Never mind. You're only a servant here. It's none of your concern."

Instead of bristling at his jibe, as he'd intended, she took his hand between both of hers and rubbed it soothingly. Her fingers felt soft and delicate, and he wanted to feel them exploring every part of his body. "Tell me, Lucas. If it involves your mother, then I should know."

The warmth of her touch seeped into his cold core, unfreezing the memory of that accident. He found himself talking without making a conscious decision to do so. "I was visiting my parents at Westvale Abbey last spring. They asked me to travel back to London with them. But I had no desire to listen to them quarrel for hours, as they were wont to do. So I rode ahead on horseback and left them far behind. I didn't receive word of the accident until the following morning." Drowning in a sea of regrets, he added aggressively, "I should have been there. I should have stopped my father from taking the reins from the coachman."

Her grip squeezed his hand. "Oh, Lucas, no. You couldn't possibly have known he would decide to do that."

"I knew he was a daredevil. That he had a lifelong habit of reckless behavior."

"But you weren't his keeper, either. If anything, your mother should have been the one to stop him."

"She tried. But he wouldn't listen."

"Then he wouldn't have listened to you, either." Her

soft dark eyes held an intensity that willed him to believe her. "You oughtn't torture yourself over something that you never imagined would happen."

"Perhaps."

As she continued to study him with that unnerving zeal, he assumed his most glacial expression. He didn't know what madness had made him blurt out his innermost thoughts. She alone among women seemed to have the power to make him open his mouth and talk.

She must have decided it was useless to belabor the matter any further, for she released his hand and murmured, "Wait here, if you will. I'll see if your mother will receive us."

The moment she disappeared into the bedchamber, guilt dug its claws into Lucas. No matter what Rory said, it was still his fault. If only he had stayed with his parents. If only he had dissuaded his father from driving that coach. If only he had been there to protect his mother, she would not be confined to her bed now.

If. If. If. Too bad a man couldn't reinvent his past and erase those *ifs*.

The door opened again. Rory poked her head out and gave him a pert smile. Her eyes large and brilliant, she motioned him inside. "Hurry. You'll want to see this."

Lucas entered the large bedchamber that he'd come to think of as his mother's prison cell. She had all the trappings of luxury that he could muster, yet material possessions could never make up for her crippled legs. A branch of candles had been lit by the hearth to ward off the encroaching dusk. His gaze shot straight to the four-poster bed with its blue and white hangings. The pillows were plumped, the white counterpane folded down neatly to reveal a glimpse of linen sheets.

His insides lurched. Where was his mother?

In the next instant, a movement from the corner of

his eye drew his attention to the dressing room. He turned to see Mrs. Bernice Culpepper emerge from the doorway.

The sight made his jaw drop. She was pushing a wheeled chair in which Lady Dashell sat like a queen on her throne. It was the rattan chair that he'd purchased shortly after the accident. The same chair that he had pleaded with his mother to use. She had vetoed it in no uncertain terms, thundering that she never wished to be seen in public as a cripple and then punctuating her rejection by hurling a book at him.

Mrs. Culpepper must have found the invalid's chair where he'd had it stored in one of the nearby bedchambers. By what magical powers had she persuaded his mother to sit in the hated thing?

Even more astonishing, how had the woman convinced his mother to change out of her nightclothes and into an elegant green gown when she'd refused to do so for the past year?

His eyes burned and he blinked hard to clear them. His chest felt as tight as a drum. Who the devil cared how it had been accomplished? All that mattered was that Mama was out of that cursed bed.

In a joyful daze, Lucas walked forward, his eyes on the marchioness. Her gray hair had been arranged in neat curls. He could swear there was even a hint of rouge on her face. He bent down to kiss her wrinkled cheek. "Mama. You look . . . marvelous."

She scowled in her usual imperious manner. That much hadn't changed. "You're late. I wish to have dinner in the dining chamber tonight and you've kept me waiting."

"I'm sorry. If I had known . . ." He ran his fingers through his hair, mussing the dark strands. He felt caught in a trance. Her willingness to go downstairs again was such a novel prospect that he could scarcely string two thoughts together. "Have you notified the staff?"

"No, my lord," Mrs. Culpepper said. "I told the kitchen to hold her dinner, that's all. We thought it best to be a surprise. She wanted to see the look on your face first. It was well worth the wait, wasn't it, Prudence?"

Glancing up at the sturdy woman, his mother let loose a rusty chortle. "Quite a shock I gave the boy, eh? It's a wonder he didn't keel over in a swoon!"

Lucas couldn't take issue with his mother's portrayal of him as a weakling. He was too grateful to see her up and about. And laughing, for God's sake. He hadn't heard her do so in forever.

"Shall I ring to inform Jarvis of your dinner plans?" Rory asked Lady Dashell.

"Yes, make yourself useful, girl, now that you've taken the day off to go gallivanting around the city. I demand to know what exactly you've been doing with my son all this time."

"You'll have to ask Lord Dashell, my lady." Rory cast a mischievous look at him on her way to pull the bell rope by the bedside.

The minx was remembering how she had spent the afternoon pretending to be his mistress. Lucas would never reveal how much he'd enjoyed the subterfuge. Nor would he ever tell his mother that they were trying find a blackmailer who had stolen a packet of love letters written by her husband to his paramour.

He looked at the marchioness. "As I explained to you earlier, Miss Paxton and I have been assisting her step-mother in investigating a certain . . . misconduct against her. That is all I am at liberty to say."

"Misconduct, bah! You're as tightlipped as Bernice. Everyone knows what's going on but me. It is extremely unfair of you to exclude me."

"I'm sorry, Mama, but you cannot expect me to betray a confidence. It is a private matter that Mrs. Paxton wishes to be kept quiet."

"Then she should summon the police rather than involve my son in her sordid business!" Lady Dashell cast a crafty look at him. "Besides, what's the harm in telling me? I've no one to gossip with, anyway!"

Bernice stepped out from behind the wheeled chair to shake a stern finger at his mother. "You know very well that you'll have the chance to gossip very soon, Prudence. Unless you've changed your mind, that is."

The two older women exchanged a secretive smile. It was the sort of snickering look that one would expect from a pair of immature debutantes.

Watching them, Rory planted her hands on the curve of her hips. "Just what are you two planning?"

"Do you want to tell them, or shall I?" Bernice asked Lady Dashell.

"You go ahead. I wish to watch their faces when they hear this!"

"Hear what?" Lucas demanded.

Bernice glanced at him, then at Rory. "There's no need to beat around the bush, so I'll just say it. Lady Dashell has decided it's time that she rejoins society."

Lucas reeled from his second shock of the past five minutes. He had all but given up hope that his mother would resume her rightful place in the ton's exalted hierarchy. She had always thrived at balls and other society events. Basking in the warmth of friends and other hangers-on had seemed to compensate for the lack of love in her marriage.

He broke into a smile. "That is most excellent news, Mama. What in the world brought you to this decision?"

"Bernice told me I was a fool for hiding myself away. That people must be pitying me. That I was missing a great opportunity to make a grand entrance and show them all that I'm still one of the foremost leaders of society."

"Then I owe my gratitude to Mrs. Culpepper," he said.

"We both do," Rory added, gliding to Bernice to kiss her weathered cheek. "I declare, Auntie, you are quite the schemer!"

Bernice smiled modestly. "It's Prudence's decision, not mine. Why let those snoots write your obituary when you're not even dead? Better to show up at one of their parties and give them some real fodder for gossip!"

"Exactly," Lady Dashell agreed, her gray eyes alight with relish. "This afternoon, I had Jarvis bring me all your invitations, Lucas. Lord Tinsley is hosting his annual ball tomorrow night, and I intend for you to escort me there."

"So soon?" The swiftness of his mother's intention bowled Lucas over when he was still adjusting to the news of her recovery. And it would interfere with his plan to attend Newcombe's card party in order to investigate him as the possible blackmailer. "But what will you wear? How will you manage—"

"Oh, pooh! I've a dressing room jammed with gowns that I never wore last season. One of those will do perfectly well. Though Miss Paxton will likely have to borrow something appropriate from her sister."

"Miss Paxton?"

"You heard me. If I intend to make a splash, what better way than by bringing a notorious woman with me as my companion?"

Aghast, Lucas stared at his mother. This arrangement had mushroomed into an event far beyond his liking. It was one thing for her to reenter society after being injured in that terrible accident. But another entirely for Rory to accompany her.

His family would be tainted by scandal at a time when he hoped to wed Alice Kipling. No, not *hoped*. He *had* to secure that marriage, or financial ruin awaited him. He had put off his creditors with promises of a forthcoming windfall. And he could not squeeze any more capital out of his heavily mortgaged estates. Like it or not, his future—his family's future—depended upon him marrying an heiress.

He glanced at Rory, but she too was gazing at his mother in arrested shock. Her eyes were rounded and for once she appeared at a loss for words.

Lucas stepped forward. "I'm sorry, Mama, but that's impossible. Miss Paxton has been banished from society. Tinsley will bar her from entering his house."

"Nonsense." Lady Dashell tossed a quarrelsome look up at him from her invalid chair. "You are forgetting the power that I wield. I certainly have the ability to make the ton accept one slightly tarnished lady!"

"*Slightly* tarnished? I don't think you quite understand me. I cannot—I will not permit you to appear at a ball in the company of a scandalous flirt."

"Now, see here, my lord," Bernice objected. "My niece is a fine woman who made one mistake. It isn't right that she be forever shunned for it."

Lucas shifted his attention to Mrs. Culpepper. With that glower tightening her plain features, she looked like a mother bear defending her cub. It struck him that she was the one responsible for this mess, and his gratitude toward her took on a tinge of anger. Had she used his mother? Had she finagled this scheme solely as a means to relaunch Rory into society?

The two older women wore matching obstinate expressions. He would get no relief from either of them.

He swung toward Rory, hoping to find an ally in her. With all her modern notions, she surely would scorn playing the lady among aristocrats who had rejected her. But her dainty features looked as stubborn and determined as those of the other two women.

Lifting her willful chin, she aimed a challenging glare at him. "I may be a *scandalous flirt,* my lord, but I am perfectly capable of comporting myself in society. If Lady Dashell wishes my company, then so be it."

Chapter 14

*Aristocratic marriages are grand alliances
in which love is irrelevant.*

—MISS CELLANY

Rory hurried through the dark alley behind her step-mother's house. The sun had set, making it difficult for her to see her way through the gloom. The yellow glow of lamps in the windows of the neighboring town homes did little to penetrate the deep shadows.

Aunt Bernice had stayed for dinner at Lady Dashell's insistence, but Rory had begged off on the excuse that if she was to borrow a dress for tomorrow night's ball, it would be wise to do so immediately in order to allow time to make any necessary adjustments. In reality, she had been too angry to sit at the dining table with Lucas.

I will not permit you to appear at a ball in the company of a scandalous flirt.

In one fell swoop, his judgmental decree to his mother had banished all the warmth and camaraderie Rory had developed toward him during their afternoon together. It had even erased the compassion she'd felt after he'd confessed his guilt over his mother's accident.

Scandalous flirt, indeed!

He had relished her flirting today when it had been required for their ruse. She had seen the glint of desire intensify those iron-gray eyes. She had felt the heat of passion radiating from him. She had heard the caressing quality of his voice and witnessed the wicked warmth of his smile.

But in reality, Lucas Vale had not changed one whit. He was still the coldhearted despot who regarded her as less than a worm beneath his well-shod foot. How dare he condemn her as a scandalous flirt when eight years had passed since that mortifying incident! Didn't he realize she had grown up since then? That she'd paid a steep price for believing a man's lies?

"You are so beautiful," Stefano whispered in her ear. "You are a woman made for loving, carissima. The woman I will love forever."

His ardent declaration, spoken with his charming Italian inflection, thrilled her romantic heart. When his hands pushed up her skirts, she didn't resist. As he brazenly stroked her most intimate place, a tide of excited longing made Rory feel she might swoon. She disregarded all the warnings she'd heard about cads who took advantage of naïve girls. Stefano wasn't like that. He loved her. He would ask her to be his wife and they would live happily ever after.

In a haze of pleasure, she had not expected what had happened next. The slam of an opening door. The angry tread of feet. Papa's furious voice . . .

The darkness of the alley suited her own black mood. Lucas was wrong to condemn her for that one mistake. She had been young and gullible, ripe for an expert seducer. Yet he seemed to think she would make a spectacle of herself at Tinsley's ball. Blast him, couldn't he give her any credit for having learned her lesson about being indiscreet?

When Lady Dashell had proposed that she attend the ball, Rory's initial reaction had been alarm. She'd quailed at the thought of facing all the gossips who had scorned her. She had not seen any of them since the awful night when she had been caught with Stefano in her father's study in the middle of a party.

Papa had been livid. He'd demanded Stefano marry her at once. That was when she'd found out the horrifying truth: the handsome foreign diplomat already had a wife back in Italy.

Rory winced to recall her father's fury. Only by leaping between the two men had she kept them from blows. Stefano had scuttled off like a coward, never to be seen again. Far worse than her disillusionment, however, had been the profound sadness on Papa's face when he had banished her to Norfolk to live with her aunt. He had died a year later without her ever having had the chance to make amends.

But she refused to hang her head in shame any longer. It was time to face her demons. She intended to go to that ball, and if Lucas didn't like it, he could stuff it. If he couldn't abide a real woman, tarnish and all, then let him court his innocent, empty-headed Alice. He was welcome to her!

Rory reached the garden gate behind her stepmother's town house. She'd decided to enter by the back way in case the Duke of Whittingham was visiting this evening. Now wasn't the time to antagonize Kitty. Her stepmother would be irked enough when she learned that Rory would be rejoining society.

As she reached for the handle, the wooden gate abruptly opened. Someone dashed out and collided with her.

Rory uttered a startled gasp that merged with a squeaky cry from her accoster. The meager light from the house outlined a woman clad in a dark cape. As her hood slipped off to reveal her face, her plain features became recognizable through the shadows.

"Foster?" Rory asked. "Is that you?"

"Miss Paxton! Forgive me! I didn't expect to encounter anyone . . ." The woman's nervous voice petered off into an awkward silence.

"Never mind that. Where are you off to in such a rush?"

"I—I must visit my sick mother. Mr. Grimshaw gave me permission."

"I see." Rory was dismayed. Surely the woman wouldn't depart if her mistress was still here. "Have Mrs. Paxton and my sister already gone out for the evening? I was hoping to catch them before they left."

"Oh, they're still here, miss. I believe His Grace is expected at nine. If you'll excuse me, I'm late."

Foster sketched a curtsy and then scurried down the alley.

Rory watched the woman vanish into the darkness. This being the first time she'd exchanged words with Foster, she was surprised at how well-spoken the maid sounded. Had she been educated as a lady? And how odd that Kitty would allow her to go, even in the case of a sick mother. Servants were seldom given time off aside from their scheduled half-day once a month.

Pushing open the gate, Rory proceeded through the tiny garden. Now that she knew His Grace wouldn't arrive for over half an hour, she abandoned her plan to sneak in by way of the kitchen. Instead, she went to the glass door of the library. It was locked, but she knew just how to jiggle the handle and coax it to open. Thankfully, the bolt had not been fixed in all these years.

Stepping into the library, she wended her way past the dark lumps of furniture. The scent of leather book bindings stirred nostalgic memories of her father. This room had served as his study, and as a child she'd spent many a happy hour here in his presence. It pained her to recall that she had hurt him immeasurably when he'd found her here, lying on the chaise with Stefano.

As Rory proceeded to the foyer and up the stairs, she had the misfortune to meet Grimshaw coming out of the drawing room. He saw her, and his upper lip curled. He'd worn that same derisive look eight years ago, when she'd spied him eavesdropping in the corridor while her father had berated Stefano.

Grimshaw was the one who'd alerted Papa about her misbehavior, she'd found out later. He was always lurking and listening, which was why he'd landed at the top of her list of blackmail suspects.

"How did you enter this house?" he said in his snootiest tone. "I did not hear a knock on the door."

"I have my ways. Is Celeste in her bedchamber?"

"She and Mrs. Paxton have a guest in the drawing room. I would advise you not to disturb them. His Grace is expected to arrive at any moment."

The tall clock in the hall chimed the half hour. Eight-thirty. Foster had said Whittingham was due at nine. She handed the butler her fringed paisley shawl, a shabby relic of her debutante days. "I'll take my chances."

Brushing past him, Rory stepped into the drawing room. The dark green décor of her youth had been discarded for a rose-and-cream palette and dainty walnut furniture. Kitty had refurbished this chamber—perhaps using the funds that Papa had set aside for Rory's marriage settlement.

She headed toward the small party seated by the marble fireplace. The visitor was the same woman who'd been here that morning. All three ladies were arrayed in elegant evening gowns, Mrs. Edgerton in jade silk, Kitty in cerulean blue, and Celeste in pale yellow with a cluster of matching rosebuds nestled in her blond curls. While the older women chatted, the girl sat with her hands folded in her lap, looking like a pretty china doll on a nursery shelf.

The illusion vanished as her blue eyes widened on Rory. A warm smile blooming on her face, Celeste jumped up to embrace Rory. "What a wonderful surprise! Did Lady Dashell give you the evening off?"

A lump formed in Rory's throat. It was marvelous to have someone love her unconditionally. Someone who didn't scorn her for the mistakes of the past. "Actually, I can only stay for a few minutes. I'm expected back shortly."

"Lady Dashell?" Mrs. Edgerton inquired in an avid tone. "Kitty, you told me your stepdaughter was in London to assist with the wedding plans. Surely she isn't *employed* by the marchioness."

Kitty looked rattled. "I'm sorry, Nadine, did I neglect to mention it? Aurora has agreed to be her ladyship's companion for a brief time. I thought it best to keep quiet about it. You know how people can talk."

Celeste's smile died. "Forgive me, Mama. I didn't realize I wasn't to mention it."

"Never mind, dear. We can trust Mrs. Edgerton, I'm sure." Kitty arose from the chaise, her anxious attention turning to Rory. "Did you come to see me, Aurora? If you wish to speak in private, let us go to the morning room."

Her stepmother clearly had assumed this visit had to do with the stolen letters. Rory needed to correct her without mentioning Lady Dashell's plan to take her to the ball. That would only invite Kitty's wrath.

"Actually, I came on a rather pedestrian errand," Rory said. "Lady Dashell has been critical about the sad state of my wardrobe. She wondered if Ce-Ce would be so kind as to lend me a gown or two."

"Lend you gowns!" Kitty said. "Why, that is very bold of her ladyship!"

"An unusual request to be sure," Mrs. Edgerton concurred. "But the marchioness has become quite eccentric since her tragic accident, or so I've heard. Is that not true, Miss Paxton?"

The woman might be elegant with her upswept chestnut hair and emerald earbobs, but she had the keen eyes of an inveterate gossip, and Rory had no intention of supplying any tittle-tattle. "She merely wishes for me to look presentable. I cannot think that odd, considering that Dashell House is such a grand establishment."

"Perhaps you hope to attract Lord Dashell's eye, too?" Mrs. Edgerton said, her speculative gaze on Rory. "You may abandon any such aspirations, for he is courting an extremely wealthy commoner, a pretty little chit named Miss Kipling."

"I am aware of that, thank you."

Rory forced herself to smile, though inwardly she fumed. How rude of Mrs. Edgerton to imply Rory was a fortune hunter who would secure a position in a noble bachelor's household for the purpose of tricking him into marriage!

She wouldn't put it past the woman to spread such a sensational rumor. But was she unscrupulous enough to steal the packet of letters that Kitty had hidden in her sewing basket? Would Mrs. Edgerton blackmail her own friend?

At present, Rory had only her own instinctive dislike of the woman to go on. She needed to find proof to verify the possibility.

"I'd be happy to lend some gowns to Rory," Celeste said, beaming. "May I, Mama? There's time to run upstairs right now and choose them before His Grace arrives."

Kitty thinned her lips. Rory surmised she was reluctant to allow her stepdaughter to wear costly clothing intended for Celeste. But she also must be considering the need to placate Lady Dashell until the letters were found.

"All right, then," Kitty said grudgingly. "But do be quick about it, darling. And mind you don't select your prettiest ones. They wouldn't be appropriate for a mere companion. By the by, Aurora, where is Bernice? Did she return here with you?"

"She was kind enough to stay with Lady Dashell during my absence," Rory said. "They're old friends, and they got on famously today."

"I see. Well, do tell her that I shall expect her to return as soon as possible. She mustn't overstay her welcome."

Rory noted Kitty's worried expression. This morning, she'd been forced to confess to Bernice about the affair and the stolen letters. Kitty would want assurance that her sister-in-law had kept that secret. But Rory didn't care to enlighten her. Let her stepmother stew.

The sisters hastened upstairs to Celeste's dressing room. By the light of a candelabrum, Celeste threw open a wardrobe to reveal a dazzling array of gowns, most in the pastel hues suitable to a debutante. "Take whichever ones you like," she said magnanimously. "I can't imagine why Mama insisted on purchasing so many. How about this one?"

She drew out a morning dress in a delicate leaf-green muslin. The style and fabric were more suited to daywear than formal evening events. Rory could see that she'd have to let her sister in on the marchioness's scheme.

"It's beautiful, but . . . can you keep a secret?"

"Of course!"

"Lady Dashell has recovered enough from her injuries to rejoin society. She plans to attend Lord Tinsley's ball tomorrow night. And she wants me to accompany her."

A smile beamed across Celeste's lovely face. "Truly? You'll be at Lord Tinsley's ball, too? Oh, Rory, that's wonderful! It will be so nice to talk to you there. But why didn't you tell Mama?"

"I very much doubt that she will approve, that's why. I'm still persona non grata, you see."

Celeste hung the gown back on its hook in the wardrobe. "I always thought it was cruel of her and Papa to send you away."

"No, it wasn't, actually." It had taken years for Rory to face that truth. She had behaved recklessly, taking a risk that led to her own ruin. All because she'd fancied herself in love with a charming foreigner who'd turned out to be a cheating lothario. "You're too young to remember all the particulars, but I stirred up quite the nasty scandal eight years ago. I deserved to be ousted from society—at least for a time."

"Mama told me about it. She said that you . . . you allowed a man to have his wicked way with you." Celeste caught hold of her sister's hands and squeezed them. "But I don't care, Rory. I won't shun you because of something that happened so long ago. I'm sure that if Lady Dashell acts as your sponsor, then people will come to accept you again."

Rory hoped so. Not because she had any desire to regain the approval of the upper crust, but because she needed to find the blackmailer. Lucas had mentioned two of his father's former cronies as possible suspects, Colonel Hugo Flanders and Lord Ralph Newcombe. If she could move freely in society, she would be better able to investigate them, along with Mrs. Edgerton.

However, identifying the culprit wasn't her sole purpose. She also would relish the chance to thumb her nose at Lucas and prove him wrong to condemn her as a scandalous flirt. Devil take that starchy man!

"I've no wish to call attention to myself at the ball," Rory said. "That's why I wanted to keep quiet about it, to ward off the busybodies."

"Now it's my fault that Mrs. Edgerton knows you're Lady Dashell's companion." Celeste woefully dipped her chin. "How stupid of me not to have realized I wasn't supposed to tell. Can you ever forgive me?"

Rory gave her sister a quick hug. "There's nothing to forgive, darling. The woman would have found out soon enough. And anyway, she doesn't know that I'm about to reenter society. One can only imagine how her tongue would wag about that."

"She *is* a terrible gossip. I wonder what she says behind *my* back."

"She says you're a lovely girl, I'm sure. And remember, once you are the Duchess of Whittingham, you will enjoy seeing her curtsy to you."

The brightness suddenly fled Celeste's face. Her eyes turned tragic as if she'd put the betrothal out of her mind and regretted the reminder of it.

As she spun around to poke through the wardrobe, plucking at the gauzes and silks, the huge diamond engagement ring on her finger flashed in the candlelight. "It's odd to think of people bowing and scraping to me. I know nothing about being a duchess."

The quiver of distress in her sister's voice touched Rory's heart. She turned Celeste around to see that she was biting her lower lip. "You'd make a fine duchess. But are you sure about this marriage, Ce-Ce? Whittingham seems far too old and stodgy for you."

"He's very kind . . . and generous, too. He gives me lots of gifts."

"So does a father. But you need a husband whom you

love with all your heart and soul. Can you truly say the duke is that man?"

Celeste blinked as a rush of tears turned her blue eyes watery. She buried her face in her hands, and a choked little sob escaped her throat. "Oh, don't ask me that, Rory! Please don't. I—I daren't say!"

Rory gathered her sister close and let her weep. She was torn between concern for Celeste and anger at Kitty. Clearly, her stepmother was fulfilling her own selfish ambitions without a care for her daughter's happiness.

Rory pressed a folded handkerchief into her sister's hand. "Oh, Ce-Ce, you needn't feel obliged to marry Whittingham. You should have an honest talk with your mother and tell her your concerns about this wedding."

"I—I've already tried." Celeste dabbed at her wet face, her fair lashes sparkling with tears. "But she's so thrilled about my betrothal. She wants me to be a duchess. I couldn't bear to disappoint her!"

"You mustn't consign yourself to misery simply to please her. It isn't too late to stand up for yourself. Tell the duke that you were wrong to accept him. Apologize to him and beg his pardon. He will likely rant at you, but that's better than a lifetime of unhappiness."

"I wouldn't dare! I'm not as brave as you. I never was."

Rory brushed a warm tear from her sister's cheek. "You certainly can be. You just have to believe in yourself and stay firm. Don't let anyone force you into a marriage that you don't want. You're only eighteen, and you've plenty of time to meet a man you can love with all your heart."

Her sister glanced away. The candlelight shone on her damp cheeks and she lowered her lashes in a secretive look that caught Rory's attention. Had Celeste formed a romantic attachment to someone else? Who was he?

Rory remembered the enthusiastic manner in which Lord Henry and his friend Perry Davenport had spoken of Celeste. They had both seemed enamored of her, but at the time, she hadn't thought much of the matter.

She tilted her sister's face back toward her. "Look at me, Ce-Ce, and tell me the truth. Are you already in love with another man?"

Her eyes grew wide and guilty. "If you must know, yes," she uttered in a wretched tone. "He's so easy to talk to and *much* closer to me in age. But he's only a second son. He hasn't any funds and he can't afford a wife just now. Perhaps in a year or two, but by then it will be too late!"

Lord Henry was a second son. Was he the secret object of Celeste's affections? The rest of the description fit him, as well. Lucas was deeply in debt, so it stood to reason that his younger brother must be penniless as well. Also, Lord Henry would be better able to support a bride in a year or two, once Lucas secured Miss Kipling's substantial marriage portion.

"Will you tell me his name?" Rory asked. "Perhaps I can speak to him on your behalf and find out just how dire his financial situation is."

Celeste violently shook her head. "No! If he learns how unhappy I am, he'd feel obliged to call out the duke. I don't want him to do anything rash!"

He was a young hothead, then, who had cast himself in the role of her knight in shining armor. That image also pointed to Lord Henry. But if Celeste didn't want to reveal his identity, then Rory had to respect her wishes.

"All right, darling. I won't press you. Now dry your eyes and find a ball gown for me."

Celeste seemed relieved to put aside their conversation. She turned around to search through the wardrobe, sifting through an array of organdy skirts, figured white gauze, and soft pastel silks. She drew out a gown from deep inside the cabinet, a bronze watered silk with a cream ribbon cinching the waist. "This one would look stunning with your black hair. And Mama says it's a tad too dark for a debutante, anyway. What do you think?"

Rory held the gown up to herself in front of the pier glass. For a wistful moment, she saw herself as a young lady again, exuberant with hopes and dreams. But that girl was gone forever. "It's perfect. Thank you, Ce-Ce."

"You'll need a few day dresses, too. Take the leaf-green muslin. And this pink silk with the pearl buttons."

Rory laughed as Celeste piled up several more gowns. "Enough! I can't possibly carry all of these to Dashell House."

"Did you *walk* here?" Celeste looked appalled by the notion. "You mustn't do so on your return. It's night-time and there may be footpads."

"Grosvenor Square isn't too awfully distant. I'll be fine."

Just then, a rapping on the outer door made Celeste spin around. "His Grace must have arrived. I must go downstairs at once."

More cheerful now, she seemed to have overcome her despondent mood. Rory had the distinct impression that her sister had come to a decision. In fact, a strange excitement made her eyes shine as brilliant as sapphires.

"Have you decided to break off with Whittingham?" Rory asked.

"Not quite yet," Celeste said evasively. "But I shall give it serious consideration, you may be sure. Now, do pick out some bonnets and reticules to go with the gowns. Take whatever you like! And thank you ever so much. You've been a huge help!"

Blowing a kiss, she hastened to the door. Rory followed in time to see her murmur something to Grimshaw in the corridor. Then her sister headed down the passageway with a girlish spring to her steps.

What had Celeste decided? Would she listen to her heart and wait for her young gentleman? Was Lord Henry that mystery man? Oh, if only they'd had more time to discuss the matter!

Grimshaw gazed down his long nose at Rory. "Miss Celeste has requested that I summon the carriage for you. In the meantime, it would be obliging if you had a word with that drunken sailor in the kitchen."

"Murdock?" Rory swallowed a laugh, imagining the butler's disgust at seeing Aunt Bernice's manservant tippling a jug of rum. "If he's a bother, just send him off to bed."

"He is sprawled out snoring on the floor of the pantry. Cook is quite beside herself. I will not tolerate such debauchery in this house!"

"I'll have my aunt wake him later." As far as Rory was concerned, Grimshaw could suffer the problem himself. Meanwhile, seeing the butler reminded her of something more important. "By the way, I ran into Foster earlier in the garden. She said that *you* had granted her permission to leave."

To Rory's surprise, he shifted his gaze in a cagy manner before recovering his usual haughty aplomb. "Her mother has taken ill."

"Will she return tonight?"

"Yes. It is only a brief visit to deliver medications."

That was odd, for Rory hadn't noticed the maidservant carrying anything. "What ails her mother?"

"I wouldn't know, miss. If you will excuse me, I shall order the carriage."

Rory watched as Grimshaw vanished through the door to the servants' staircase. His eagerness to depart stirred her suspicions. It was almost as if he were trying to escape her questions. But why?

Why would he not want her to inquire about Foster's purpose? Was the woman's mother not really ill? Had the maidservant gone off on some other clandestine errand?

Rory pondered the mystery. If Grimshaw was covering for Foster, then that would indicate a close comradeship between the two. Was it possible they were in cahoots over the blackmail scheme?

Chapter 15

Gossip is the lifeblood of the upper crust.
—MISS CELLANY

Had Rory known the shock that awaited her at Lord Tinsley's ball, she might have considered staying away. That shock had nothing to do with her being snubbed by the ton, since Lady Dashell snared most of the attention.

From the moment Lucas wheeled his mother into the entrance hall with its marble columns and domed ceiling, the marchioness became the belle of the ball. The huge room hummed with excitement as many guests came forward to express their delight at her recovery.

Lord Tinsley, a bull-necked man with coarse gray brows, paid no heed to Rory in the receiving line. He had eyes only for Lady Dashell as he kissed her gloved hand. "My dear Prudence, I'm honored that you would make your reappearance here at my home. I trust you are feeling better?"

"I'm an invalid stuck in a chair, so what do you suppose? But at least you will not feel obliged to dance with me anymore!"

Lord Tinsley chuckled. "I see that the long convalescence hasn't dulled your wits in the least. You've still the same sharp tongue as ever."

As Lucas navigated the wheeled chair through the

crowd, Rory noticed that people seemed in awe of the marchioness despite her biting manner. They approached her with reverence as if being granted an audience by the Queen. Lady Dashell relished the attention, and with all the hubbub, it took quite a while to inch their way toward the grand staircase.

Lord Henry escorted Rory and Aunt Bernice, offering an arm to each lady. They walked directly behind Lucas and the marchioness. Lord Henry seemed in a high humor, and Rory wondered if Celeste had told him that she might cry off her betrothal. There was no chance to ask. Upon learning that Bernice had known his mother as a girl, Henry turned his full attention to the older woman, teasing her with playful questions and impertinent commentary.

Rory didn't mind. It suited her to be overlooked. Arrayed in the bronze silk gown with the cream sash, she felt pretty for the first time in years. The festive atmosphere stirred a glow of excitement beneath her skin. Her senses feasted on the sight of ladies in fashionable dresses, the buzz of conversation and the tinkle of laughter, the fragrance of expensive perfumes. She hadn't realized until this moment just how much she had missed being a part of society. She basked in the happy anticipation of dancing, conversing, flirting.

But of course, flirting was taboo. Lucas had made that abundantly clear. He didn't approve of his mother keeping company with a scandalous flirt.

She glowered at his back as he rolled the chair just ahead of her. The formal black coat fit his wide shoulders to perfection, nipping in slightly to skim the lean contour of his waist. She was close enough to see that his coffee-brown hair curled ever so slightly against his stark white collar. The mad urge to touch those thick strands consumed her.

How unwise of her to admire him. Had she learned nothing from her past mistakes? A woman should derive contentment from her own life rather than needing a man to make her happy. That was why she had devoted herself to essay writing.

If the editorial she'd mailed to *The Weekly Verdict* the previous day was accepted for publication, she hoped that Lucas would read her scathing denunciation of aristocratic marriages. Wouldn't he be appalled to learn she was the elusive Miss Cellany? Not that she cared a fig for his stuffy opinions.

Nevertheless, he had a commanding presence that held her attention. He must never know she had fantasies of him sweeping her to his bed where he would strip off her clothes and kiss her senseless. Those daydreams always ended with her feeling overheated and dissatisfied.

It served no purpose to desire him. Lucas could never be hers—nor did she wish him to be. She led a very fulfilling life already. And he had all but announced his betrothal to a lady who was everything that Rory was not: young, innocent, and most of all, fabulously wealthy.

Rory had nothing but the promise of that reward money from Kitty.

That was the real reason she was here tonight. To nose around for information about the two dissolute cronies of Lucas's father. Lord Ralph Newcombe was hosting a card party at his house tonight, but she hoped to run into Colonel Hugo Flanders here.

Reaching the base of the grand staircase, Lucas signaled to a pair of footmen. Then he stepped to the side of the chair to address his mother. "I'll need to carry you, Mama."

With easy masculine grace, he scooped his mother up into his arms while the footmen transported the wheeled invalid's chair up the staircase. The skirt of her claret satin gown lay draped over his sleeve and she grabbed at his neck for support.

"How pitiful I am," she groused. "I am reduced to being held like a baby."

"You cradled me like this as an infant, so now I'm more than happy to return the favor."

The frank way he smiled at his mother made Rory go soppy inside. His face revealed such affection that her heart melted into a puddle. Why couldn't he regard *her* with even a smidgen of such warmth? He hadn't smiled at her at all since his mother had announced her intention to bring Rory to this ball.

She and Lucas had spent the day much like the previous one in a futile search of pawnshops and jewelers. Once again she had played the role of his mistress. She had batted her eyelashes coquettishly and teased him with leading comments. But today he had reverted to his habitual reserved manner. She had not been able to goad him into speaking more than a few words. It was as if their brief camaraderie had never existed.

It was better this way, Rory told herself. They could never be friends. Once they identified the blackmailer and recovered the stolen letters, she would return to Norfolk with her aunt. Lucas would marry his heiress. Their paths weren't likely to cross ever again. So why did that prospect dispirit her?

At the top of the stairs, he settled his mother back into the chair. Their party headed toward the arched doorway of the ballroom, where a white-wigged majordomo in blue livery announced the arrival of each guest.

The marchioness craned her neck around and beckoned to Rory. "Don't hide back there, Miss Paxton. Stand beside me. I want everyone to take a gander at you. There's nothing I like more than a titillating scandal."

Lucas frowned. "A companion requires no introduction, Mama."

Rory flashed him a defiant look as she stepped forward. "This is your mother's night. We should allow her to make that decision."

He regarded Rory with that granite mask, his jaw firm, his lips taut. She couldn't tell if he scorned her, or if he was just worried Miss Alice Kipling was about to learn that he'd employed a ruined woman.

But he was not indifferent to her, Rory judged. The force of his gaze revealed a keen awareness of her. It made her tingle all over and stirred her feminine vanity. Did he like what he saw? Did he appreciate the care she'd taken with her upswept curls and the new gown?

It shouldn't matter. She was merely a servant to Lucas. And an impudent one, at that.

Lady Dashell made another imperious wave of her hand. "Bernice, you come forward, too. Henry, go and tell that fellow their names."

"Your wish is my command, Mama." With a devilish grin, Lord Henry stepped away to speak to the majordomo.

Lucas steered his mother into the ballroom as the manservant intoned, "Lord Dashell and Lady Dashell."

Rory and her aunt dutifully walked on either side of the marchioness. Her heart fluttered, and Rory flushed with dread at having the attention drawn to herself. She told herself not to feel nervous, but her body seemed to have a mind of its own.

The majordomo boomed their names. "Miss Aurora Paxton and Mrs. Bernice Culpepper."

A brief lull interrupted the hum of conversation. People craned their heads to stare. Then an animated hiss of voices arose as ladies whispered to one another behind their fans and gentlemen lifted their monocles to squint at her. One matron appeared to be lecturing a fresh-faced debutante who, along with a group of her friends, turned to gawk and giggle.

Despite her bravado, Rory felt like a pet monkey on display. These aristocrats must be warning their daughters not to behave like the infamous Miss Paxton. She had been one of those girls a long time ago. In fact, she had attended a party in this very ballroom. She remembered the decorative gilt woodwork on the white walls that made the place resemble an enchanted palace. Dark blue netting had been draped from the ceiling so that the candles in the crystal chandeliers twinkled like stars against the midnight sky.

The fairy tale had ended for her, though. She had thrown it all away for a silver-tongued seducer who'd wanted only to lift her skirts for his own pleasure.

Rory felt wretchedly alone now. A quiver of cowardice rippled through her. Yet she elevated her chin and surveyed the throngs as if she were the Queen herself. She would not quail before these judgmental snobs. She had already been tried and found guilty in the court of public opinion, and she had paid for her crime by serving eight years of exile. If that wasn't good enough to suit these small-minded gossips, then she wanted nothing to do with them.

A man's hand settled at the small of her back. It was large and firm and reassuring. As its heat radiated into her cold depths, she sucked in a shaky breath and glanced back over her shoulder.

Lucas stood just behind her. His cool gray irises surveyed her. Though he wasn't smiling, the warmth of his touch eased her tension. The heavy burden of isolation vanished like a wisp of fog under strong sunlight. In its stead, a sense of well-being uplifted her.

Out of sight of the crowd, his hand glided lightly over

the back of her silk gown and left a trail of sparks. She ached to lean against him and invite his embrace. That same desire flared in his eyes, too. Then it vanished in a trice. The imprint of his hand lifted from her spine as he turned back to his mother.

Lucas steered the invalid's chair toward the edge of the ballroom. Realizing that she blocked his path, Rory stepped aside. Without another glance at her, he guided his mother through the jam-packed ballroom to a place where the other matrons were gathered.

Aunt Bernice and Lord Henry followed, continuing to banter about his mother's debutante days. Rory lagged behind them all. She needed a moment to sort through what had just happened. That little interlude seemed almost like a dream. Had Lucas truly meant to offer her comfort? Or had she misread a simple, careless touch? Perhaps he had only intended to nudge her aside in order to clear the way for his mother's chair.

By the time he settled Lady Dashell beside a group of matrons, Rory had herself convinced that his brief touch had meant nothing. It had been an impromptu gesture, nothing more. She had ascribed too much meaning to it because at that moment she'd been in sore need of a friend.

She studiously ignored Lucas as he stood talking to a group of elderly gentlemen who had come to pay tribute to his mother. Once again, her ladyship was flooded by well-wishers. The marchioness took gleeful pleasure in introducing Rory to a number of the guests. Rory knew that Lady Dashell wanted to prove she still had the power to manipulate public opinion, and the project seemed to be something of a success. Though no one was warmly welcoming, they didn't dare cut Rory dead, either. Many exhibited a cool politeness, others gave her a critical stare, yet they were civil at least.

Rory recognized a few of the people, but many were unknown to her. Before that long-ago disgrace, she had been in society for only half a season. It had been too short a time to learn everyone's names and faces. Besides, the circle of her friends had been much younger than these codgers.

Then one of her former acquaintances arrived in the company of a stout matron. The older woman said in a rather gloating manner, "You remember my daughter, Marion, don't you, Miss Paxton? She is now Lady Bolton. Her husband is Sir Jerome Bolton."

Miss Marion Chesterton had been Rory's nemesis, a sharp-faced girl with brown sausage curls and a superior disposition who had always been jealous of Rory's many admirers. Back then, Rory had attempted to befriend the girl to no avail. "It's a pleasure to see you again, Marion."

She held out her gloved hand, but Marion pointedly ignored it. "What a pity that you have ended up on the shelf," she said with oily sympathy. "But I suppose that is what comes of flirting with married men."

Rory produced a sweet smile. "Is your husband here tonight? Jerome was a dear friend and I would love to renew our acquaintance."

Marion's eyes widened. Her mouth formed a nasty pucker. "Keep your distance from my Jerome. You will not go near him!"

Her strident voice attracted attention. People glanced over at them in curiosity. At once, Rory regretted needling Marion. Though she'd been incensed by that catty remark, it was unwise to cause trouble. She might hamper her ability to move freely in society.

Just then, a regal woman strolled to join them. She had the sort of timeless beauty that drew admiring looks. A diamond tiara glinted in the smooth coils of her coal-dark hair. The deep violet silk of her gown matched the color of her long-lashed eyes.

"Lady Milford!" Rory exclaimed. "I'm surprised you're already back from your visit to the country."

"I can never stay away from London for very long. I miss all the excitement here."

She embraced Rory as if they were longtime friends. It was a masterful move. Her ladyship clearly intended to convey her approval of Rory to Marion and her mother—and the rest of society. Nothing could be more guaranteed to boost her status, Rory knew.

The other two women were suitably chastened. Marion's mother dipped a curtsy and her daughter followed suit. They practically stuttered in their effort to please society's leading hostess.

Lady Milford smiled. "Ah, Lady Bolton. Were you and Miss Paxton sharing old memories just now? I'll never forget the awful mishap you suffered on the dance floor when she was kind enough to help you to your feet."

Marion blushed crimson. "You—you saw that? I—I was terribly grateful for Rory's assistance, I assure you!"

She and her mother stammered a few more pat phrases before making a swift retreat. Although grateful, Rory didn't quite understand why Lady Milford had taken her side so firmly. Perhaps she just didn't want Rory tossed out of society before finding those letters for Kitty.

"I'd forgotten all about that incident," Rory said. "I'm surprised you would remember."

"I never overlook a kindness. It is a great revealer of a person's character." Lady Milford's eyes held curiosity as she looked Rory up and down. "What a delightful surprise to find you here tonight, my dear. May I presume things are going well?"

It was a delicate way of inquiring about the search for the purloined letters. Like Kitty, Lady Milford believed that Lucas was the blackmailer. If only they knew the truth! "Yes, certain matters are shaping up quite nicely. I've taken a post as Lady Dashell's companion."

"Indeed. You've worked a miracle in convincing her to rejoin society."

"Oh, I cannot take credit for that. Aunt Bernice arrived yesterday and offered to help. She's an old friend of her ladyship's, you see."

"So am I. Perhaps you can understand, then, why I am concerned about her eldest son." Lady Milford glanced over at Lucas, who stood a short distance away, listening as a white-haired matriarch yammered about something that was inaudible in the noise of the ballroom. She added in a murmur, "I believe he aspires to higher office someday. In light of that, do you think he and Miss Kipling are a good match?"

The news startled Rory, as did the question. Her gaze lingered on his tall form as she mulled over the notion of him in a position more powerful than just another hereditary member of the House of Lords. With his serious demeanor, Lucas looked every inch the stately nobleman, and she could imagine him as a cabinet member or even prime minister someday.

If he did entertain such an ambition, he would require an intelligent, engaging wife with an interest in politics to be his hostess at dinners for high-ranking members of the government. Perhaps she would read his speeches and offer advice on policy. It all sounded fascinating to Rory, but she doubted Miss Kipling would agree. The girl seemed too young and silly for the role.

She returned her gaze to Lady Milford. "I hardly think it my place to say whom he should wed."

"Come now, you must have an opinion."

"She is rich and he is poor. That is the basis of many an aristocratic marriage. Or the reverse, in the case of Celeste."

Lady Milford arched a dainty eyebrow. "Speaking of your sister, I spied her and Mrs. Paxton standing near the string ensemble. Are they aware that you were coming here tonight?"

"Celeste is, since I borrowed this gown from her. But not Kitty."

"Ah. Well, you look quite stunning. May I add, I'm pleased you're wearing the slippers I lent you. They should bring you good fortune."

Rory glanced down at the tips of the garnet shoes that peeked out from beneath her bronze gown. The soft, supple feel of them made her want to twirl and dance. Yet Lady Milford's comment was puzzling. Bring her good fortune? What did that mean?

She wanted to ask. But Lady Milford already was gliding away on the arm of a distinguished older gentleman.

The stream of well-wishers began to thin out, leaving Lady Dashell with a gaggle of her closest friends. She was clearly enjoying the time of her life. "Well, Bernice, if you were worried that people might scorn you for marrying that common seaman, it was a waste of time. As you can see, only a very few even remembered you!"

Bernice chuckled as she sat down beside the marchioness. "At my age, I'm quite content to stay in the background. This is hardly my maiden voyage, after all."

"Nor is it your niece's maiden voyage," the marchioness said craftily, looking up at Rory. "She's a mite long in the tooth, but still handsome enough to nab a husband, especially one who isn't too particular about her past. Why don't you dance with her, Lucas? That will encourage the other gentlemen."

Rory stood paralyzed while the intensity of his gaze

focused on her. His eyes were like hot ice, heating and freezing her at the same time. They flicked downward to her plunging décolleté. Since Rory was more well-endowed than her sister, the bodice was a bit tight, pushing hills of creamy flesh above the edge of her gown. The force of his scrutiny sparked a tingling that spread from her nipples down to her privates. If not for the orchestra tuning their instruments and the cacophony of voices, she was sure that everyone would hear the wild thudding of her heart.

How she longed to dance with him, to whirl around the floor, to be clasped against his strong form. She held her breath in foolish hope.

He returned his gaze to his mother. "I'm afraid I promised the first dance to Miss Kipling."

"Miss Kipling, bah. Bring the chit over here when you're done, then. I want to see if she's still scared wit-less of me."

"We shall see. I shan't make any promises on her behalf."

With that, he strolled away, his broad-shouldered form disappearing into the sea of elegant guests. It was ridiculous to feel as if the party had lost a bit of its lus-ter, Rory thought. She wasn't a ninny whose happiness depended upon a man. Especially not one so irritating as the Marquess of Dashell.

Lord Henry bowed to Rory. "Since Dash has ab-sconded, will you do *me* the honor of this dance, Miss Paxton?"

"I had better not," she said, softening her refusal with a wry smile. "I don't believe you realize just how noto-rious a figure I am."

"Your notoriety will lend me a bit of cachet. All the other young bucks will be pea green with envy. Surely you won't deny me that."

His blue eyes twinkled with charm. He cut a devilishly handsome figure in his tailored black coat with a gold stickpin glinting in the folds of his cravat. A lock of brown hair had slipped onto his brow, adding to his rakish look. She could see how her sister might have fallen in love with him.

Rory glanced at Lady Dashell. She and Aunt Bernice were engaged in a cozy chat with several other middle-aged ladies. It didn't seem they would even notice if she slipped away.

"All right, then," she told Lord Henry. "I shall be happy to add a little tarnish to your good character."

Afterward, she would have to find Kitty. By now, word of Rory's presence would have reached her stepmother's ears. Better to have their confrontation in the open, where Kitty wouldn't dare make a scene.

They made their way through the hordes of guests to join the dancers. Lord Henry led her onto the parquet floor just as the orchestra launched into the strains of a waltz. Rory experienced a moment's trepidation. "It's been eight years. I hope I still remember the steps."

He winked at her. "Just follow my lead. I'll endeavor not to shriek when you tread on my toes."

Her worry was for naught. With effortless grace, Lord Henry spun her around the dance floor, and her feet recalled the movements even if her mind did not. Lady Milford's fine slippers created the illusion of skimming over a cloud. Lord Henry entertained her with light-hearted commentary about the other guests. He was so much more relaxed and talkative than his older brother that for the first time that evening she could simply enjoy herself. It felt wonderful to dance again, to trade witticisms, to feel the exuberance of youth. How had she lived without all this?

Her buoyant mood faltered only when she spied

Lucas squiring Miss Kipling a short distance away. As they danced, he bent his head to murmur something to her. They made a striking couple, he so tall and dark and she so dainty and blond. A hard kernel of envy burrowed into Rory. He'd scarcely spoken a word to her during their one dance all those years ago.

What if he had? What if he'd used that heart-stopping smile on her? Would she have been drawn to him instead of Stefano? Would she have been saved from ruin?

It was useless to wonder. She could not change the past.

Rory resolutely turned her gaze from them. While perusing the crowd along the edge of the dance floor, she caught sight of her sister standing with her hand tucked in the crook of the Duke of Whittingham's arm. He was chatting with another starchy old fellow and ignoring Celeste altogether.

Now there was a couple who *didn't* look as if they belonged together.

She noticed Lord Henry stealing glances in that direction, too. This might be her chance to discern the depth of his emotions. "Do you see my sister standing near the orchestra? That pale pink gown certainly becomes her. Wouldn't you agree?"

"Anything becomes Miss Celeste," he said gallantly. "She could wear sackcloth and ashes and still look pretty."

"High praise, indeed." She kept her voice light and teasing. "Tell me, are you sorry she's already spoken for?"

Lord Henry made a face, the mask of charm dropping for a moment to show a hint of disgruntlement. "I'm sorry she accepted that ancient codger. All the fellows are. He's old enough to be her grandfather."

"I don't believe he's quite *that* old. Only forty, I've heard."

"Old enough to be her father, then. Well, Whittingham *is* a duke, so that would make a girl overlook his other defects. But I wouldn't have thought Miss Celeste to be the title-hunting sort."

"She's not. My sister isn't covetous in the least. Although she *is* a bit too malleable for her own good."

His blue eyes sharpened on her. "Do you mean her mother pushed her to accept this match?"

"I wasn't here when it happened, but I believe that's a fair guess."

"I don't suppose there's any chance she might jilt Whittingham, is there?"

"Why, I don't know," Rory fibbed, thrilled that he would even ask such a question. "I've hardly had the chance to speak to her since I've been so busy with your mother."

Lord Henry fell silent, though she noted his air of interest. She toyed with the notion of asking him straight-out if he was in love with Celeste. Yet perhaps it was enough to plant the seeds of action in his mind. It would be up to him to decide whether or not to try to persuade Celeste to end the betrothal.

Rory couldn't do it for him.

The waltz came to an end, and he swept a courtly bow. "Thank you, Miss Paxton. Shall I escort you back to the old biddies?"

"Actually, I'm looking for someone. Do you remember a Colonel Hugo Flanders? He was a friend of your father's."

"Jolly fellow, but not your sort. Why do you ask?"

"Your mother mentioned him, that's all," Rory said vaguely. "I think she had something to tell him. Can you describe him for me?"

"He's as bald as a baby's behind and has a bushy ginger moustache to compensate. But do have a care. He preys upon beautiful women."

They parted company, and he sauntered off to join a cluster of young gentlemen by the punch bowl. She recognized Perry Davenport's fair features, but none of the other fellows. Of course, they had all been in grammar school when she'd been a debutante. It made her feel older and wiser by comparison.

At least her talk with Lord Henry had been encouraging. Maybe, just maybe, she'd nudged him into pursuing her sister. He would be able to provide for a wife once his brother married Miss Kipling.

Rory was sorry she'd thought of Lucas. She didn't see him anywhere and she imagined him kissing his chosen bride in some private corner. Well, let him. She didn't care what the almighty Marquess of Dashell did. While he romanced his heiress, Rory would track down Colonel Hugo Flanders.

Strolling through the ballroom, she scanned the throngs for a bald man with a ginger moustache. Some people met her eye and nodded coolly, though no one made any attempt to speak to her. Rory didn't mind. Her purpose here wasn't to make friends. Besides Flanders, she also needed to seek out her stepmother and smooth her ruffled feathers.

As if conjured by Rory's thoughts, Kitty appeared through a shifting of the crowd. She had joined Celeste and the duke as they chatted with several other noblemen. A tense smile on her plump face, the woman covertly glanced around as if seeking her irksome stepdaughter.

Rory veered toward the group. It was time to reacquaint herself with the Duke of Whittingham. If he detested scandal as much as Kitty had said, then he'd be appalled to be seen with his fiancée's ruined sister.

And he might be more amenable to releasing Celeste from the betrothal.

Just as Rory drew near, however, someone grasped her wrist from behind. A firm male hand pulled her backward behind a huge pot of ferns.

Her heart cavorted in her bosom. Lucas? In spite of all common sense, her lips curved upward as she swiveled around to face him.

Her smile died a swift death. The breath stuck in her throat. Her entire body felt paralyzed, her feet rooted to the floor.

Liquid brown eyes gleamed at her from beneath a cap of wavy, raven-black hair. Her abductor had the classically handsome features and chiseled physique of a Roman god. He was every young girl's dream of swoonworthy male perfection. His essence of exotic spice sent her hurtling back eight years.

He lifted her gloved fingers to his lips, the action concealed from the crowd by the potted greenery. *"Carissima,"* he said huskily. "I hope you have not forgotten me."

Dizziness swept Rory. Her mouth tasted as dry as dust. He was an illusion. He had to be. She blinked in the hope that he would vanish. Yet he stood in front of her, a flesh-and-blood phantom from her past.

Her lips formed his name. *"Stefano?"*

Chapter 16

Gentlemen are admired for their conquests, whilst young ladies are vilified for the slightest indiscretion.

—MISS CELLANY

"At last, fate has brought us together again," Stefano said, his voice vibrating with passion. He glanced furtively past the ferns to the throng of guests in the ballroom. "But we dare not talk here. Meet me in the garden in five minutes. You must come, Aurora, I beg of you. I have much, much to tell you."

Rory was left gawking as he slipped out from behind the urn and then strolled away in his jaunty manner. That confident style was what had drawn her to him in the beginning. She had been enthralled to be courted by a dashing Italian diplomat with a charming accent. Stefano had been the most wildly romantic man she'd ever met in her sheltered life.

At least until she'd learned the sordid truth about his marital status.

Hidden by the greenery, she sagged against the gilded woodwork of the wall. Her legs had all the substance of jelly. She drew in several deep breaths in an effort to restore her shattered senses.

Stefano! He was the last person in the world she'd ever thought to encounter again. She'd believed him to be gone from her life forever.

After ruining her, he had fled England in disgrace. The memory of that intimate encounter still made her sick with mortification. His whispered endearments, his smooth compliments, his alluring promises all had played on her naïve longing for love. She had fallen into his trap like a ripe plum, only to see him run like a cornered rat when confronted by her irate father.

How dare Stefano approach her here after the way he had bamboozled her! And he a married man with a wife back in Italy! A rising fury rioted inside her. Even someone with his overblown conceit couldn't possibly believe she was still gullible enough to be sweet-talked by him.

Let him rot out there in the garden. She had no intention of listening to any more of his lies. Nor would she trot after him like a trained mare at the snap of his fingers.

Yet this was her chance, she realized. Her opportunity to voice all the rebukes that she'd never had the chance to say to him back then. She had never given him the scolding that he richly deserved. Most importantly, the scoundrel mustn't be allowed to think that she had been pining for him all these years.

Rory stepped out from behind the grouping of ferns and started toward the row of glass doors at one end of the ballroom. She kept her head down, for she did not wish to catch anyone's eye. Nor did she want Kitty or Aunt Bernice or anyone else to inquire where she was heading.

The doors stood open to allow the evening air to cool the overheated ballroom. The orchestra was playing another tune and many of the guests were turned toward the dance floor. It was a simple matter for Rory to slip outside and walk across the shadowy stone veranda.

Lanterns had been suspended from the trees to illuminate the pebbled walkways. The lush scent of roses drifted to her. A crescent moon beamed like a benevolent smile against the starry blackness of the night sky.

It was a scene made for romance.

Which was probably why Stefano had chosen the garden as their meeting place. He was a master of seduction. Where was the devil?

Rory stepped down from the veranda and marched through the garden. The pebbles dug into the soles of her dancing slippers. At least no other guests roamed the paths. The April evening was chilly for ladies in low-cut gowns.

Rory scarcely noticed the cold. She was too scorched by anger to require a shawl. Now that she'd survived the shock of seeing him, she was looking forward with relish to this confrontation.

"Psst."

The hiss came from the gloom near the back wall of the garden. She headed in that direction. Stefano stood up from where he'd been lounging on a stone bench beneath the shadowy plumage of a flowering tree. Moonlight silvered his black form, as if he were a creature rising from the underworld.

"Carissima! I knew you would come to me. You cannot imagine how much I have missed you."

He swooped forward as if to embrace her. She adroitly stepped aside and held up her hand to forestall him.

"Keep your distance," she stated coldly. "You had no right to return here, let alone to approach me in a crowded ballroom."

Stefano hung his head in an uncharacteristically humble pose. "You are angry with me, Aurora. I cannot fault you for that. But you must understand how irresistible you are. Such beauty! Such passion!"

She ignored his tirade. "How are you back in England, anyway? My father worked for the Admiralty. He used his government contacts to ensure that you would never be allowed to return."

"I am assistant to the most excellent ambassador. I begged him to take pity on me. He yanked cords—how do you say? Pulled strings."

"He could not have pulled strings with society. So how is it that you're even at this party? No one told me that you were here." If Kitty had known of his presence in London, she would have said something. If not her, then someone here at the ball would have gleefully informed Rory. But there had been no inkling whatsoever from the gossips.

"I confess I was not invited. But it is not so difficult to find a way inside when one is determined. You see, I had to find you, *carissima,* from the moment I arrived in England a fortnight ago."

"Then you should have learned quickly that I'd been banished."

"I heard, but I could not give up." He clapped his hand over his heart in a dramatic pose. "For many days, I have searched everywhere for you."

She frowned at him through the shadows. It made no sense for him to keep looking once he knew she wasn't in London. Even she herself hadn't known until yesterday that she would be rejoining society. "Everywhere?"

"Yes, even in the house of your father. I pretended to be part of a group of guests who were entering a party there. No one questioned me."

"Wait. You sneaked into my stepmother's house? During Celeste's betrothal ball? And no one recognized you?"

"It was necessary to elude that nosy butler, of course. As to the guests, I talked to no one, only watched and listened. I changed my ways and pretended to be very shy. People do not notice a timid man."

Stefano was the least shy man she'd ever met. He was boisterous with his compliments, effusive with his lies, lavish with his kisses. So maybe behaving in a radically different manner, along with the passage of time, could explain why he had escaped detection.

Yet she couldn't shake the notion that he wasn't telling her the whole truth. "So you have been skulking around society parties these past two weeks. If you were truly eager to find me, it would have made more sense for you to go to Norfolk, where I was living until a few days ago."

"I could not leave London because of my duties to the ambassador. And I had faith that we would meet eventually." He took a step toward her. "You have haunted my dreams for many years, *carissima*. I tried to forget you, but it is no use. You are a fire in my blood. I had to come back. I could not help myself."

"Nor could you help yourself, I suppose, when you attempted to seduce a naïve girl."

He must have heard the chilly censure in her voice. "I beg your forgiveness most humbly. But we are both older and wiser now. I did not have the chance to finish what we started that night. We will have more passionate lovemaking this time."

He reached out to caress her cheek. Infuriated, Rory smacked his hand away. "Disgraceful cad! How can you think for even one moment that I'll fall for your mischief again? You have a wife back in Italy!"

"Please, that is what I must tell you. I am sad to say . . . Paola died of a fever. For two years now, I have been alone." His shoulders drooping, Stefano sank down on the stone bench and hung his head. "It was a punishment for my sins. I did not deserve her, and I do not deserve you."

Looking down at his dark head and his abject pose

of misery, Rory couldn't stop a smidgen of compassion from creeping into her heart. His regret, at least, bore the semblance of authenticity. Yet she had a sneaking suspicion she had not been the only woman he'd romanced.

His wife had probably died of a broken heart.

She sat down beside him, keeping a proper distance between them. "I'm sorry, Stefano. It can't be easy to lose your spouse. But that doesn't change the fact that you were cheating on her and deceiving me, as well."

"I am truly sorry. Yet it does change things between us. Now I am free to court you in the way that you deserve." His dark eyes gleamed in the moonlight. "*Carissima,* give me another chance. Let me show you heaven in my arms. Let me love you again."

In a sudden rush, he closed the gap between them. His arms clasped her close to his chest. His mouth fastened to hers, the tip of his tongue probing the seam of her lips. Startled, Rory kept her teeth clenched. It happened so fast that she couldn't move, anyway. His spicy scent and persuasive kiss overwhelmed her with memories. In her mind, she became a vulnerable girl again, desperate to win his heart, aching for someone to love her. He had made her feel beautiful and cherished . . .

His nimble hand slid downward over her gown and tugged at the hem of her skirt. His fingers stroked her stocking-clad ankle, then tracked upward over her calf. The invasive sensation jerked her out of the brief stupor.

Rory pulled away. Her palm met his cheek with a loud crack, and the slap sent him reeling backward on the bench. The sting of the blow radiated up her arm, but the trifling discomfort felt very satisfying.

He uttered a squawk of pain. A string of unintelligible foreign words spewed from him. She could only presume they were curses.

"Have you gone mad?" she snapped. "I told you, I want nothing to do with you anymore."

"I have frightened you, *carissima*. It is only because I love you so very much. I will be gentler this time. Please do not deny me."

He leaned closer. She tensed her muscles in preparation to strike him again if he dared to touch her. "Keep your hands to yourself," she hissed. "If you don't, I swear I'll—"

The sound of running footsteps distracted her. She looked toward the house to see the dark figure of a man barreling down the path straight at them.

Lucas should have been listening to Alice.

Instead, his attention was focused on the door to the garden where Rory had just vanished. Clad in a soft, shimmery bronze gown that enhanced her shapely charms, she had been walking with her head tilted downward. As if she didn't wish to attract notice.

What the devil was she doing?

"Would you like that, Lucas?"

He glanced down to see Alice's big blue eyes gazing coyly up at him through the fan of her lashes. He was standing with her by the punch bowl while she sipped from the cup that he'd just fetched for her. Taking refreshment had given him an excuse to delay his duty to escort her to his mother. But he had completely lost the gist of what Alice was saying.

"Pardon?" he inquired.

"Why, I was asking you to come to dinner tomorrow evening with my parents. It would make me very happy if you would accept."

"Dinner." Why had Rory gone outside? Had someone insulted her?

"Papa mentioned it in the carriage on the way here." Alice dipped her chin in a modest pose. "He hasn't seen you in days. He's hoping for a chance to speak with you."

Lucas's gaze sharpened as he honed in on the unspoken message. She was hinting that her father wanted to know Lucas's intentions. This dinner was a ploy to force his hand.

Force? Hell, he *needed* this betrothal.

But just not now, while he and Rory were trying to find those letters before the blackmailer decided to smear them all over the tittle-tattle newspapers. "I'm afraid I have a prior engagement. Perhaps next week."

Alice pushed out her lower lip in a pout. "You've been terribly busy these past few days, Lucas. I've scarcely seen you at all."

"You may blame it on my duties at Parliament," he hedged. "Listen, the orchestra is striking up another tune. It wouldn't be proper for us to dance again just yet, but I'm sure my brother will be happy to escort you."

Before she could object, he took her cup and set it down, then steered her toward Henry, who had his head together with his friend Perry. They looked deep in conversation, and Lucas presumed they were debating one of their favorite topics—which horses to bet on at Newmarket or who was the prettiest debutante.

He tapped his brother on the shoulder. Henry turned, an unexpected flash of irritation on his face. Perry frowned at the interruption, too, his green eyes serious beneath a thatch of sandy hair. He had a scattering of freckles that made him appear more boyish than his twenty years.

"I've a lady who needs a partner," Lucas said to his brother. "I'm hoping you'll oblige."

As Henry's blue gaze fell on Alice, his annoyance

vanished and his mouth eased into its usual rakish smile. That rascally expression made him look more like their father than Lucas cared to admit. "I'd be honored," he said.

Lucas bowed over her dainty hand. "Until later, Miss Kipling."

He turned on his heel and walked away, though not before noticing her wounded expression at his use of her formal name. Damn. He'd have to make amends for the slip at a future time. For now, though, he could think only of finding Rory.

There had been something decidedly peculiar about her departure from the ballroom. He sensed it in his gut. She either had been slighted by one of the guests, or she was up to something stealthy in regard to the blackmailer.

He was inclined to believe the latter. She wasn't one to quail at a rude comment. Only look at the fearless way she'd faced down the hostile crowd when her name had been announced by the majordomo. Lucas had been close enough to spy the slight quiver of her body. In that moment, he'd glimpsed the inner scars that she kept hidden from the world. Scars from being ruined by a scoundrel, from her estrangement with her family, and from the long years of exile. That was why he had placed his hand on her back. He'd wanted her to know she wasn't alone.

It had been a damn-fool risk to take. Anyone might have noticed him wearing his heart on his sleeve, including Alice. Yet he didn't regret it. He had been vehemently opposed to Rory's coming to this ball and opening herself to criticism. The guests had reacted to her with predictable scorn. Society considered itself the pinnacle of civilization, but it could be savage toward those who broke its strict rules.

He had remained near her and his mother for a time in order to indicate his approval of Rory. That was all he dared to do on her behalf.

At least this dangerous attraction he felt for her would end soon. Once they recovered the letters, Rory would return to Norfolk. She would leave his life forever. And if the prospect wrenched at his chest, well, he'd survive.

He had no other option. Duty required that he wed an heiress. His family would suffer penury otherwise.

He stepped outside and inhaled a lungful of chilly night air. From the shadows of the veranda, he scanned the garden. Lanterns lit the empty pathways. What the devil could she be doing out here? Had she come across a new clue? Was she meeting an informant—or worse, an actual suspect? He didn't trust her not to go haring off on her own to investigate a dangerous criminal. She was far too reckless for her own good.

A movement in the gloom at the rear of the property snared his attention. The sharp sound of a slap broke the silence. Raised voices carried to him, one male, one female. *Rory.*

Lucas plunged down the path, gravel spitting out from under his shoes. He spied the outline of two people seated in the darkness beneath a tree. The man was reaching for Rory, leaning closer to her, threatening her.

At his approach, they turned as one to peer at him. The shadows were too thick for him to discern their facial features.

Lucas seized her attacker by the scruff of his neck. He yanked the scoundrel to his feet, keeping an iron grip on the collar of his coat. "What the hell do you think you're doing?"

Rory sprang up from the bench. "Lucas!"

He turned his attention to her face, a pale oval in the darkness. "Are you all right? Did this bastard hurt you?"

"I'm perfectly fine. Now, do let him go!"

"Not until I find out what's going on here." He gave the man a hard shake. The weasel wasn't even fighting back. "Who the devil are you?"

"You cannot treat me this way," the man said in an aggrieved voice tinged by a foreign accent. "I am—"

"Keep quiet," Rory spat. "Lucas, I demand that you release him at once."

Her indignant tone caused a crack in the armor of his anger. Another possibility wormed into his mind. Had he completely misread the situation? Had this been a romantic assignation? Maybe she had met one of her old swains in the ballroom.

The notion made him see red. He wanted to pound her would-be lover into a pile of dust. But he had no right to do so. None whatsoever. Rory didn't belong to him. She never would.

He forced himself to loosen his fingers. The instant he did so, the man ducked under Lucas's arm and dashed away into the shadows. His feet chewed up the loose gravel. Running was the act of a guilty coward, and Lucas took a reflexive step after him, already regretting releasing him.

Rory leaped in front of Lucas to block his path. "Let him flee! It's what he does best. Maybe this time, he'll stay away from me."

The sound of footsteps faded into the distance, followed by the squeak and slam of a garden gate. Lucas scowled at her. She had stepped out from the murky depths of the tree and he could see her better now. In the faint light of the lanterns, her features appeared taut with distress. She folded her arms beneath the pale mounds of her bosom and hugged herself.

"This time?" he prodded.

She nodded shakily. "That was . . . Stefano."

The name plunged a spike into his chest. Stefano was the rogue who had seduced Rory. The married Italian diplomat who had stolen her virtue.

Fury so choked Lucas that he needed to punch something. He had to settle for striking his fist into the open palm of his other hand. "Dammit, Rory! Why didn't you say so? I would have laid him out flat for what he did to you!"

"What purpose would that serve? He's gone and that's all that matters."

"No, it isn't all. You slapped him. What did he do just now? If he tried to force himself on you again, by God, I'll hunt him down like a dog."

"He only kissed me. There was no harm done."

"No harm." The thought of that slick Romeo daring to lay a hand on her made Lucas clench his jaw. "Heed me well. If he comes near you again, I'll kill him."

"Truly, it was nothing. I wasn't in any danger."

"Stop defending him. What was he doing here, anyway? Tinsley wouldn't have invited him. And why did you come out here to meet him after the reprehensible way he treated you eight years ago?"

A shiver rippled through her body. She covered her face with her hands and drew a shuddering breath. "I just thought . . . Oh, never mind. You wouldn't understand."

Awareness of her anguish broke through the hot mist clouding his judgment. He immediately regretted having shouted at her. He had never seen Rory look so despondent. She was always pert, witty, bold. Never miserable and beaten. The sight stirred a mawkish softness inside him.

Closing the distance between them, Lucas enfolded her in his arms. It was both agony and ecstasy to feel her soft bosom pressed against his chest, to embrace her warm, womanly curves. She could never be his. Yet, in defiance of logic, his groin tightened with merciless hope.

That Rory snuggled so easily into his embrace was a testament to the distraught state of her emotions. She tucked her face into the crook of his neck and wrapped her arms around his waist. He bent his head close to hers, the better to breathe in her elusive flowery scent and to feel the silkiness of her hair against his cheek. The urge to kiss her bedeviled him. Hell, he wanted much more than kissing. He wanted her naked beneath him in bed.

But then he would be treating her as cavalierly as Stefano.

He could never do that. Yet it was frightening, this rush of emotion that surged through him. He had a fever for her that was far more intense than in their youth. These past few days with Rory had only strengthened his attachment to her. He would give his life to keep her from being hurt again.

"Come and sit down," he murmured.

She didn't resist when he guided her to the stone bench beneath the flowering tree. A cool breeze scattered white petals as if to celebrate a wedding. The lilt of a waltz drifted from inside the house. He recognized the danger of the romantic setting. He sat down beside her, anyway, keeping one arm firmly looped around her slender waist.

He nudged up her chin so that she would look at him. Her face was barely discernible in the darkness. Being so close to her made him dizzy, as if he'd imbibed too much wine.

"Tell me everything," he said, striving for normalcy.

"Did you just happen to run into Stefano tonight? Or had you made prior plans to meet him here?"

"Prior plans? Of course not! He was lurking behind a vase of ferns in the ballroom. He asked me to come out to the garden so we could talk. I didn't see any harm in it."

Lucas clenched his jaw. "Did it not occur to you that he might have forced himself on you out here? With the loud music and noise inside, no one would have heard you scream."

"I was never in any danger. I can assure you of that."

The defiance in her voice perversely pleased him. He hadn't liked seeing her look so defeated. But she was delusional if she thought such a sorry excuse for a man wouldn't try to overpower her. "How did he know you would be here?"

"He didn't. Apparently, he's been sneaking into balls and parties, looking for me for the past fortnight."

"The bastard is lucky I didn't spot him. I'd have sent him on the next ship back to Italy with his teeth in a bag."

Rory made a choked sound in her throat, and he feared he'd offended her with his language. With her, he didn't seem to have control over his tongue. He was no longer the deliberative speaker, carefully parsing his words.

Her laughter rang out like the tinkle of bells in the darkness. "What a dreadful image. Although he does deserve it, I suppose."

"There is no supposing about it. Only a knave would still pursue you after you found out he's married."

"Oh, Lucas, his wife died," she said in a sobered voice. "He's a widower now. That's why he came back to find me, to tell me."

Struck by the sympathy in her voice, he felt a vortex

of jealousy suck at him. Damn! Did she still harbor feelings for that cowardly Casanova? The possibility threatened to swallow him whole. Stefano had been her first love. Lucas himself had never been able to forget his first true love—Rory Paxton.

He caught her face in his hands. Her skin felt silken smooth to the touch. "You mustn't trust a single word out of his mouth, Rory. For all you know, his wife may still be alive. If the rogue lied to you before, he could be lying to you again."

"But he sounded so heartbroken."

"He doesn't have a heart. He's an accomplished actor, that's all. Promise me you'll steer clear of him from now on."

Sassy as ever, she tipped her chin up. "There's no need for you to fuss, Lucas. I'm perfectly capable of taking care of myself."

"Is that so?" He gave a harsh laugh. "Then you don't comprehend the darkness that lurks inside of men."

"Bah. What darkness do *you* hide, Lord Prig?"

Her taunt made him teeter on the verge of the abyss. The silvery moonlight, her womanly form, his burning desire, all conspired to snap the last threads of his resolve. The urge to indulge his craving for her swept him over the edge.

"This," he growled.

Putting his hand to the back of her head, he brought his mouth firmly down over hers.

Chapter 17

*Sheltered girls are thrust into society with little
knowledge of the vices of men.*

—MISS CELLANY

The kiss caught Rory by surprise. She had never expected her gibe to shatter his self-restraint. Or maybe
she'd secretly hoped that it would. It had become a game
to tease him, to watch those iron-gray eyes darken with
desire, to make him suffer the torment of unrequited
passion. From the moment he'd interviewed her three
days ago, she had sensed his attraction to her. But she'd
always felt safe with Lucas. He was too disciplined, too
aloof, to pose any real threat.

How wrong she had been. And how glad she was, too.

Any notion of resisting him melted away at the first
touch of his tongue. She had imagined this moment too
often not to indulge her fantasies. Whimpering, she gave
herself up to pleasure and parted her lips to invite him
inside. He obliged by tasting her thoroughly and completely. Lucas kissed as he did all things, with controlled
aggression and single-minded purpose.

As if she were the most important woman in the
world to him.

Longing flooded her. How glorious it would be to be
loved by him. The notion shook the foundation of her

beliefs, for she had made up her mind that a man wasn't necessary to her happiness. Her one brush with intimacy had ended abruptly, and afterward, it had seemed to be something she could be quite content to live without. Only now, in this moment, did she face the loneliness hidden within her own heart.

She needed to love and be loved. She needed Lucas.

With one hand, he cupped the back of her head, dislodging a few pins from her hair. His arms felt like bands of steel around her. Yet their bodies still were not close enough to satisfy her. She strained against him, gratifying the urge to move her hands over the muscled wall of his chest and then up into the silken thickness of his hair.

Lucas. He was not the cold, stuffy prude she'd believed him to be. He was the most fascinating man she had ever met, full of veiled depths and delicious surprises. And he could kiss with a tenderness and passion that touched her very soul.

Never before had she felt so vibrant, so aware of her sensual needs. It was as if she'd been asleep these past eight years. Like the prince in a fairy tale, he alone had the power to awaken her. He alone could restore her to life after a long hibernation.

He broke away to nuzzle her face and throat, laying a necklace of moist kisses along the edge of her bodice, his tongue tasting the sensitive skin of her bosom. A weakness swept through her body. He must surely feel the rapid drumbeat of her heart, she thought in a daze. No other man had ever made her feel so splendidly alive.

Not even Stefano. Especially not Stefano.

His name was a discordant note in the sweet melody of her desire. How was it that after such a long dry spell, she'd been kissed by two different men in a matter of minutes? Doubts encroached on her pleasure. Did Lucas think her fast? Maybe he expected her to succumb to him as she'd done to Stefano. Maybe he viewed her as a ruined woman ripe for plucking.

She drew back slightly, pressing her palms to the front of his coat. "Lucas . . ." His name emerged on a gasp as she struggled to catch her breath. "We shouldn't be doing this."

"Yes we should." His words low and throaty, he pressed kisses over her face, then nibbled her ear. "I want you, Rory. You can't imagine how much."

The torment in his voice called to her soul. She wanted him, too, with every fiber of her being. The craving coiled inside her, a twisted knot that ached for release. For the first time in many years, she felt needed, desired.

But he'd said nothing of love. Nothing of a future together.

She forced herself to speak. "You want Alice Kipling, not me."

He went still, his breath hot and harsh against her neck. His fingers flexed around her arms as if to deny her words. Slowly, he straightened up to gaze down at her through the darkness. "Not in the same way that I want you."

He might as well have dashed a bucket of ice water onto Rory. She froze, for his intentions were now clear. He wished to take Alice as his wife. And to keep Rory as his mistress.

She pressed backward against his grip. "I refuse your unsavory offer, my lord. There, I've saved you the trouble of making it."

"I didn't mean . . ." Lucas paused to run his fingers through his hair. He released a harsh breath. "Oh, hell. I don't know what I meant."

The growl of his voice held an undercurrent of frustrated confusion. A frustration she felt as keenly as he did. When he unlocked his arms, she scooted back on the bench. Instantly, she felt cold without him. Cold and incomplete.

He bent down to hunt for something on the ground beneath the stone bench. The strains of a lively country tune drifted from the house. It was peculiar to think that people were dancing inside the ballroom as if nothing had happened, when Rory's whole world had just been turned upside down.

"You lost these," he said.

Lucas dropped something into her palm, the pins that had fallen from her hair. Distractedly, she patted her coiffure to assess the damage, finding and securing several curls that had fallen loose.

Her throat felt painfully tight. "Go back to the ball," she said coolly. "We mustn't be seen walking in together."

"I'm only staying long enough to bid farewell to my mother. Then I'm leaving for Newcombe's house."

Rory dropped one of the pins. "What? Why didn't you warn me? I could have asked Aunt Bernice to take over my duties for the evening."

"I'm going alone. You're to stay here under my mother's protection. Newcombe's party will be a den of iniquity. It's no place for a lady."

She glowered at him through the darkness. "I suppose I should be glad that you consider me a lady. A minute ago, I'd have thought otherwise."

"I won't apologize for something we both enjoyed. But it's best that we forget this ever happened."

Forget? Did he think she'd run blabbing to Alice Kipling? How like a man to take his pleasure and absolve himself of all accountability! "Fine."

"Well, then. I'll let you know tomorrow what I find out from Newcombe."

Rising, he gave her one last piercing stare. Then he

started toward the house, his tall dark form holding her obsessive attention. She watched until he vanished through one of the open doors.

With the toe of her shoe, Rory kicked at the white petals that sprinkled the ground. Beastly man! If he thought she would be content to twiddle her thumbs while he did all the investigating, then he had a big surprise coming.

She was not about to let him steal the glory of nabbing the blackmailer.

An hour later, Rory mounted the steps to Lord Ralph Newcombe's town house and grasped the lion's head knocker to rap hard on the door. It opened almost at once. A manservant in crimson livery blocked her entry.

He was a shady-looking character with shifty black eyes who gave her a sharp stare. "Your invitation, miss."

"Invitation . . ." She pretended to search through her beaded reticule, then made a rueful face at him. "Why, I seem to have forgotten it."

"I'm sorry, you can't come in."

He started to close the door, but she stuck her foot in the gap. If Lady Milford's slippers had failed to bring her good fortune in love, at least they now had a practical use. "Lord Ralph will be terribly upset if I don't attend his party tonight. Do you truly wish to explain to him why you turned away his dear friend Jewel?"

Artfully letting her shawl drop to her elbows, Rory thrust out her bosom to give him a view of her mounded breasts. His lascivious gaze dipped to ogle her. That look made her skin crawl, but at least she achieved success. He opened the door wider.

She stepped into a dimly lit foyer with a checkered marble floor and a narrow staircase. A stench of tobacco smoke tainted the air. The rumble of male voices and a high-pitched female giggle came from upstairs.

She removed her bonnet and shawl and handed them to the manservant, gracing him with a sultry smile. "You needn't stir from your post here. I'm sure I can just follow the sounds of revelry."

Before he could object, she started up the stairs, her steps light and quick. She did not want the escort of a servant who would deliver her straight into the party. Not with Lucas present. Rather, she intended to skulk in the corridor and see what she could observe. Then she would find Newcombe's study and search for the pilfered letters.

It had been absurdly easy to obtain his address. She had simply asked Kitty after her stepmother had finished scolding Rory for attending the ball. She'd convinced Kitty that Lucas was up to no good, and that he might even be planning to show the letters to the unsavory group of ne'er-do-wells here. Another word of explanation in Aunt Bernice's ear, and Rory had been free to set out on foot to her destination, some three blocks distant.

As she reached the top of the stairs, a burst of hearty laughter drew her toward a room halfway down the corridor. The haze of tobacco smoke was thicker here, making her eyes sting. Stopping just outside the open doorway, she cautiously peered inside.

Aristocrats in fine garb gathered around a number of tables that had been set up in the drawing room. Some of the gentlemen sat and dealt cards, others cast dice in games of hazard. After each roll, roars of pleasure or groans of defeat rang out. Stacks of banknotes exchanged hands from losers to winners.

A few women mingled with the men, most appearing to be doxies, judging by their tawdry gowns and loose manners. One blond beauty had climbed onto a table to perform an erotic dance for a cluster of hooting fellows. A redhead in a peacock-green dress sat entwined with a portly man on a chaise, kissing him in full view of the other guests.

Rory stared in fascination at the party. Not even Grimshaw, with all his lurking and listening, could have ever witnessed such a debauched scene. As a debutante, she had heard whispers of such carousing among the racier set, although these events were strictly avoided by decent folk. But never before had she had occasion to see the lewd display.

Which one of these reprobates was Lord Ralph Newcombe?

She had no notion what the fellow looked like. She knew only that he'd been a crony of the previous Lord Dashell. Lucas's father must have frequented these sordid parties, too. How different from her own honorable papa, who had been devoted to his family and his position at the Admiralty.

Rory could only imagine what it had been like for Lucas, growing up with a rakehell as a father. When speaking of the accident that had crippled his mother, he had sounded bitter about the man's reckless nature. Perhaps that was why he himself had grown up to be so stern and starchy.

Yet there had been nothing prudish about his kiss. Not in the least! That too brief interlude in the garden had revealed the strong, sensual nature behind the cool façade he showed the world. A current of passion ran deep in him, and one kiss had not been enough to plumb those depths. She ached to discover more of him, to understand his innermost thoughts and feelings.

Nothing could ever come of her forbidden desire, Rory reminded herself. Lucas was as far out of her reach as the moon. She had no money to tempt him, and her reputation lay in tatters. She wasn't malleable or innocent or docile, all those qualities a nobleman sought in a wife. Better she should put him out of her mind and concentrate on finding those letters.

Was he already searching for them somewhere in the house? She didn't want him to beat her to them.

She inched closer to the open doorway and scanned the throngs of gamesters. To her relief, she spotted his tall form by a crimson-draped window. He was puffing on a cheroot while smiling at someone. With a jolt, she saw that his companion was female. A second jolt struck harder as she realized the woman's identity.

Mrs. Edgerton.

Kitty's friend wore a daring gown of grape-colored satin that accentuated her curves and enhanced the creamy paleness of her skin. Her chestnut hair had been arranged in loose curls to give her a slightly disheveled look, as if she'd just arisen from bed. The woman hung on to Lucas's arm, pressing her voluptuous bosom to his chest.

Rory clenched her fists as resentment spread like poison through her. Though the widow had to be more than five years older than him, Lucas appeared to enjoy her carnal attentions. He aimed that devastatingly attractive smile at her as she reached up to stroke his face, one of her fingertips tracing his lips. Instead of pushing her away, he took hold of her hand and kissed her knuckles while gazing deeply into her eyes.

What a rat, Rory fumed. She had been wrong to believe him upright and principled. Drop him into the right situation and he became a scoundrel like so many other men. He'd even warned her of that tonight.

You don't comprehend the darkness that lurks inside of men.

She had scoffed at him. Even though he'd bestowed on her the most thrilling kiss of her life, she wouldn't have categorized him as the sort to carry on with loose women. In her heart, Rory had wanted to believe that he was like her papa, faithful and steadfast, guided by a strong moral code. But Lucas had left her at Tinsley's ball so that he could come here and flirt with a racy widow.

No wonder he hadn't wanted Rory to accompany him. He'd intended to join in the nasty fun. How she longed to give him a piece of her mind!

Just then, a pair of male hands clamped onto her waist from behind. A voice roughened by years of dissipation sent a blast of sour brandy breath in her ear. "Hello, my pretty. Were you waiting for me?"

Rory twisted out of his grasp to find herself facing an older man with the florid complexion of a drunkard. In contrast to his shiny bald skull, he had a large ginger moustache to compensate for the lack of hair atop his head.

Her senses sprang to alertness. Lord Henry's description fit this man perfectly. "Are you by chance Colonel Hugo Flanders?"

"At your service." He waggled his bristly eyebrows. "I presume that my less-than-sterling reputation precedes me. And you are?"

"You may call me Jewel."

"Jewel. A pretty name for a pretty piece."

The leer he aimed at her bosom made Rory feel soiled. She would relish slapping his face almost as much as she had Stefano's. Flanders was precisely the sort of villain who might steal a packet of personal letters and hold them for ransom. Yet that was mere supposition. She needed proof.

"I've heard so much about you, Colonel," she said in

a breathy tone. "In particular, your appreciation of the fairer sex."

"Righto. And I'd love nothing better than to add a lovely Jewel to my list of conquests."

When he reached for her, she stepped adroitly out of his path. "I would venture to guess that your current mistress wouldn't be happy to learn you're flirting with another woman."

"Never mind Mabel. She needn't know about our little fling. Let's go upstairs, eh? Newcombe won't mind if we borrow one of his bedchambers."

Again, he lunged, and again she feinted to escape him. "Tell me, do you keep Mabel in a fine feathered nest? Because I shall require it for myself should I agree to this fling."

His avid brown eyes gleamed. "I'll toss her out tomorrow if you like. Now come here, little girl, and give papa a kiss."

This time, he caught her by the shoulders and his strong fingers bit into her flesh, drawing her relentlessly toward him. She averted her head so that his moustache tickled her cheek instead of her lips. "There'll be none of that just yet," she said, trying not to shudder. "First I must inspect this love nest and see if it's suitable. Where is it located?"

"It's a cozy brick house in Covent Garden."

"What is the address?"

"Corner of Shelton and Neil. Now, it's time you gave me a taste of what I'm buying."

One of his hands scrabbled over her gown, cupping her breasts while he attempted to wiggle his stubby finger inside her tight bodice. With his other arm, he circled the back of her waist and fondled her bottom. Rory squirmed against his grip, but it was like fighting an octopus. She was about to bring the heel of her slipper down hard onto his instep when he was abruptly lifted away from her.

She blinked in mingled surprise and wariness. Lucas stood glaring at the two of them.

Actually, he was glaring mostly at her.

Chapter 18

A noble rakehell takes his pleasure at will and absolves himself of all accountability.

——MISS CELLANY

"You're poaching my woman," Lucas said, his eyes flashing steel as he released Flanders. "I've a good mind to strangle you."

The colonel flapped his lips and blustered, "*Your* woman? Jewel was begging to be *my* mistress!"

Lucas's gaze flicked to Rory. His stern expression held nothing of the passionate man who'd kissed her senseless. "Begging, was she? It's a little game she likes to play to make me jealous. Isn't that so, Jewel?"

Rory decided it would be practical to cut her losses. Especially since she had succeeded in mining a vital nugget of information from Flanders. Pushing out her lower lip, she affected a shamefaced look. "I admit it was merely a silly ruse. Pray forgive me, Colonel. It was wrong of me to toy with you."

He smoothed his bushy ginger moustache while uttering a loud harrumph. "Best keep a tight rein on her, Dashell, if you intend to bring her back here. That is, if you've finally decided to fill your father's shoes at our little gatherings."

Casting one last covetous look at Rory, he sauntered away, disappearing into the drawing room to join the other revelers. She was relieved to see the back of him. That made the third time this evening that a man had attempted to kiss her. Thank heavens only Lucas had been successful.

He caught her by the arm and marched her down the dimly lit corridor toward the rear of the house. She had to scurry to keep up with his long strides. When they reached a private spot out of earshot of the party, he pressed her up against the wall and thrust his face close to hers.

Anger lowered his dark eyebrows and tightened his jaw. "I told you to stay at Tinsley's ball with my mother. What the devil are you doing here?"

She refused to quail at his growled question. Or to dwell on how handsome he looked in his formal black coat and white cravat. "Why, I have to preserve my reputation as a scandalous flirt, of course."

"This is no time for flippancy."

"All right, then. Like you, I'm investigating New-combe. Running into Colonel Flanders was merely a bonus. And a very profitable one at that."

"Profitable. That's an interesting choice of words considering you were about to sell yourself to that old lecher."

"Don't be ridiculous. I wasn't intending to go through with it. I was merely angling for the name of his current mistress. I intend to pay a call on her tomorrow."

"The devil you will! What possible purpose could that serve?"

"It occurred to me that if Flanders is the blackmailer, he may very well have given Kitty's diamond necklace to his mistress. If she has it, then we'll know he's our culprit."

Lucas stared at her. His lips were taut, his gaze steely. But when he spoke, a portion of the fury had left his voice. She fancied there was even a hint of admiration in his eyes. "I hadn't considered that," he said. "But you might have told me earlier. I could have found out the information myself."

"Told you when? You gave me no warning that you intended to come here tonight. You sprang it on me and then walked away." She folded her arms under her bosom and tilted up her chin at a mutinous angle. "And why should I cooperate, anyway? We're supposed to be partners, but you haven't exactly been forthcoming with me."

"You know perfectly well why I couldn't bring you here. This party is no place for a lady."

"Oh? Mrs. Edgerton is present. And you were flirting outrageously with her. In fact, that was the most disgusting display I've ever seen!"

His mouth quirked into a hint of that attractive smile. Reaching out, he ran a fingertip down her cheek. "Are you jealous, Jewel?"

The air suddenly felt charged with energy. The seductive murmur of his voice stirred excitement in her, as did his light caress on her face. A filament of fire raced downward from her breasts to her innermost depths, making every inch of her prickle with heat.

Not that she would admit it to him.

"I'm irked, that's what. You're supposed to be helping me find those letters, not trifling with wicked women at a party."

His cocky grin deepened. He braced his hands on the wall, one on either side of Rory, trapping her in place without quite touching her. "You didn't seem to mind when it was *you* I was trifling with."

He stood close enough for her to feel the warmth of his body. Weakness eddied through her, making it difficult to maintain a defiant expression. She tucked her hands behind her waist to keep from sliding them inside his coat. "I thought we'd agreed that kiss was a mistake and best forgotten. Anyway, I'm more concerned that your flirtation with Mrs. Edgerton will hurt Miss Kipling. She's too young and innocent to know about the darkness in men."

That softening of humor vanished. He dropped his arms to his sides. "Leave Miss Kipling out of this. And it would behoove you to consider that my interest in Mrs. Edgerton might have a legitimate purpose."

"Yes, it proves you're a tomcat like most men."

His scowl returned. "It proves nothing of the sort. As it happens, I was employing the same technique as you did."

"What is that supposed to mean?"

Lucas glanced up and down the passageway, then walked across it to open a door. He peered inside before closing it again. "I befriended Mrs. Edgerton in order to discover if she had a motive for stealing the letters. And I have to agree, there's something fishy about the woman."

"Fishy. Yes, she was fishing, all right. Trying to reel in the nearest available man to warm her bed."

"Actually, she already has a lover."

"How do you know that? Did you ask her to be your mistress?"

"I hinted at it. All in the interest of the investigation, of course."

Rory dogged his heels as he proceeded to another door. She seethed at the notion of him playing up to that hussy. "Who is he?"

"She rather coyly refused to divulge his name. But he's supposed to join her here tonight."

Rory watched as he looked into another room off the passage. "It couldn't be Flanders—could it? He was just arriving when he accosted me. But he told me he keeps his mistress in a love nest near Covent Garden."

"I can't imagine it's Mrs. Edgerton, then. Unless he's disloyal to her."

Rory had thought herself rather worldly. But she cringed nonetheless. "Do you mean to say that reprobate keeps more than one mistress at a time?"

He cast an amused glance at her. "It's possible. I was hoping to tie Mrs. Edgerton either to him or Newcombe since both men attended your sister's ball when the letters disappeared. Before I could get an answer out of her, though, I spotted you out in the corridor, flaunting your breasts at the colonel."

"I was *not* flaunting my—" Rory broke off, flustered by the turn of conversation, even though Lucas wasn't even looking at her anymore. He had poked his head into another room. "What *are* you doing, anyway?"

"Come." He grabbed a candle from a table in the corridor. Then he disappeared through the doorway without waiting to see if she followed.

Her heart thudded. Perhaps Lucas was seeking a private place where they could be alone. Maybe he meant to kiss her again, to clasp her to that strong body and arouse her passions. It was dangerous to crave his embrace when he intended to marry another woman, yet an irrepressible longing sent her darting after him.

She found herself in a small study with bookshelves and an untidy desk strewn with papers and bric-a-brac. The embers from a fire glowed orange on the grate. Instead of taking her into his arms, Lucas sat down in the desk chair and opened the center drawer.

"Close that door," he said. "Then you can help me hunt for the letters."

Her bubble of yearning burst. Staving off disappointment, Rory pushed the white-painted panel shut and then wandered around Newcombe's study with its hunting scenes on the walls and the two overstuffed chairs by the hearth. So much for romance. She felt foolish for not having guessed his purpose and annoyed with herself for letting her imagination run wild. How was it that he could distract her so much she had forgotten the real reason why she'd come to Newcombe's house?

To find those letters. To earn that reward money.

Nothing else mattered.

Not to be outdone by him, she picked up a candle and lit the wick from his, then crouched down in front of a rosewood credenza. When she opened a cabinet door, a clutch of miscellany came tumbling out. There was a magnifying glass, several snuffboxes, a collection of folded maps. None of it held any interest for her. Upon opening another door, however, she discovered a mishmash of letters. She began a methodical search through the old correspondence, making sure none were the *billets-doux* written to Kitty Paxton by old Lord Dashell.

"Your father's name was William, was it not?"

Lucas glanced up inquiringly from the drawer he was examining. "Yes. Did you find something?"

"A number of letters, but they seem to be mostly from Newcombe's estate manager. There are quite a few dun notices, too."

He grimaced without replying. She remembered seeing a pile of such notices when she'd searched Lucas's study a few nights ago. Something about his financial situation puzzled her. Now that she knew him better, she could see that he wasn't overly extravagant. He also struck her as too intelligent and careful a man to sink his entire inheritance into risky investments.

She sat back on her heels and watched him poke through the contents of a drawer. "Your father used to attend these parties, didn't he?"

Lucas grunted in reply. Though he clearly didn't wish to talk, she needed to get a certain matter settled in her mind.

"I don't mean to pry—" she began.

"Then don't."

"Yet I find myself curious. He must have been quite the avid gambler. Flanders even seemed to expect *you* to fill your father's shoes."

"Flanders is a drunkard," Lucas said, slamming a drawer shut. "Don't heed a word he says."

"He was a friend of your father's. That would suggest they shared the same vices—women and gambling and the like."

"My father is gone. It can serve no purpose to rehash his sins."

"I only wanted to clarify something. According to Kitty, Lady Milford said you'd squandered your inheritance on bad investments. But that isn't true, is it? It was your *father* who misspent the family fortune. It wasn't you at all. *He* gambled it away. And you inherited all of his debts."

He yanked open another drawer. "You're wasting time with all this babble. Just look for those letters."

The fact that he didn't deny it spoke volumes. His dire financial straits were not his fault. Rory felt better knowing that, yet sad for him, too. His father's reckless behavior had affected his whole family. It had crippled Lady Dashell, prevented Lord Henry from following his heart, and saddled Lucas with the duty to marry an heiress in order to stave off his creditors.

She poked through the credenza, finding little else of interest. All the while she felt disturbed by what a bad role model old Lord Dashell had been. She remembered him as a drunkard who'd liked to pinch the ladies. But he'd been so much worse. He had fit right in with the depraved throng in the drawing room here.

"I have to commend you," she said.

"Pardon?"

"Your father set a very poor example, but you turned out rather well in spite of it. Were you never tempted to gamble? Or to engage in other vices?"

Her nosy questions made Lucas feel like a caged bear being poked with a stick. The quill he'd just picked up broke in his fingers, and he dropped the pieces back into the drawer. He never discussed his sire with anyone. It was best to keep those memories locked in the vault of the past. But he couldn't think when Rory was gazing at him with those expressive brown eyes.

She was sitting on her heels on the floor in a puddle of bronze silk skirts. Tendrils of inky hair curled around her face and neck. The candle on the credenza cast a flickering golden light over her delicate features and bow-shaped mouth. He now knew just how velvety soft those lips were. And how very much he craved to enjoy them again.

"Of course I was tempted," he said. "My father made certain of that."

"You mean he *tried* to corrupt you?"

Damn, he had not meant to admit that. But the words had slithered out of a dark place deep inside of him. Maybe if he told her, she'd cease badgering him. "On my sixteenth birthday, he took me to a brothel. And he hired three whores to service me all night."

Her eyes grew larger. "Three! But . . . why so many?"

"He wanted me to learn the joys of sampling multiple women. So that I would never settle for just one. He found monogamy quite dull, you see."

"Oh, Lucas. I'm sorry."

"Don't be. I reveled in every moment of it. I learned quite a lot that night."

He had been as randy as any teenaged boy who had never been kissed by a girl, let alone bedded by a trio of skilled hussies. The hours had passed in a frenzy of enticement and ecstasy, soft flesh and hot kisses, decadence and debauchery. Even now the memory held a dark allure that tested the bounds of his self-control.

"I despised myself afterward," he added gruffly. "I knew then that I couldn't live like my father. I'd grown up seeing how his many affairs hurt my mother, and I swore never to emulate him."

Her cheeks pink, Rory sat watching him with her fingers entwined in her skirts. He could only imagine what she must think of him, springing from the loins of such a father. Her good opinion shouldn't matter to him. Yet it did.

Needing something to do, he opened a wooden box that lay on the desk. A row of cigars filled the interior, perfuming the air with their pungent aroma. He snapped the lid shut. "Those blasted letters don't appear to be anywhere."

Rory didn't respond. She rose to her feet and went to the bookcase behind the desk. Behind *him*. Her light flowery scent enticed him as did her nearby presence. From the corner of his eye he could see her soft bronze gown and the cream sash that defined her slender waist. If he turned slightly in his chair, he could wrap his fingers around her hips and tumble her down into his lap. He could kiss her again, bury his face in the valley of her breasts, slip his hand beneath her skirts and—

"What about Lord Henry?" she asked suddenly. "Did your father try to corrupt him, too?"

Lucas refocused his thoughts. "Of course. But I was old enough by then to put a stop to it."

Finding it too unsettling to sit so close to her, he sprang up from the chair and prowled the study. He checked behind the painting of a hunting scene on the wall, seeking a safe where the letters might be secreted. There was none.

Rory removed a leather-bound ledger from the shelf and took his seat at the desk. "The other day, you said that your brother went to Newmarket—to the horse races, I presume. Does he gamble?"

She had honed in on his darkest fear, that Henry possessed the same weak tendencies as their sire. Her sympathetic gaze enticed him to unburden himself. "Sometimes," he admitted. "He hasn't much money and I've given him strict limits on his spending. But I'm afraid . . ."

"Afraid?"

"That he might be tempted to play too deeply. He's more like our father than I am, you see. He's charming, sociable, flirtatious. Henry even bears a strong physical resemblance to him. The same blue eyes, the same devilish smile, the same jaunty mannerisms."

"He doesn't go around pinching ladies' bottoms, does he?"

Lucas swung toward her in horror. "Did my father do that to *you*?"

"No! I stayed clear of the older roués." She opened the ledger, though her gaze remained on Lucas. "But I shouldn't think you need to worry about your brother. It isn't his outward appearance that matters, it's his inner character. And he seems to be a very polite, agreeable young man."

Lucas looked behind another painting, this one of

hounds milling around several red-coated hunters on their mounts. "He's a daredevil, though. Never met a challenge he didn't accept with relish. He's especially fond of racing my tilbury."

"That isn't a sin. Though I imagine you're thinking about how your father caused that coach accident by taking the reins from the coachman."

The soft understanding on her face stirred a morass of emotions inside him. Guilt that he hadn't been able to prevent the accident. Grief at his mother's suffering. Anger at his father's stupidity. And most of all, an acute yearning to pull Rory into his arms and lose himself in her warmth.

He closed the lid on those sentiments. He was venturing into dangerous territory. It should be Alice who stirred such feelings in him, not Rory.

She was frowning slightly, as if pondering more questions to ask. But she'd probed quite enough into his life. It was time to turn the tables.

"For someone who's spent the past eight years in exile, you're full of opinions," he said. "What were you doing all that time?"

"Living in a cottage by the sea with my aunt Bernice."

"I know that. How did you occupy your days?"

"Household chores. Sewing. Reading. The usual sorts of things."

He had a hard time picturing her being content with domestic routines. While checking behind another painting, he couldn't help needling her a bit. "Given your eccentric notions about the role of women, it seems you'd have taken up blacksmithing or doctoring or some other male occupation."

Her chin tilted to a saucy angle. "I could have if I'd wanted to do so."

"The other day, you professed to be a fan of that tabloid *The Weekly Verdict.* I'm surprised that in so remote a locale, you were even aware that such a radical journal existed."

Her eyes widened and she quickly looked down at the open ledger on the desk. "I have a subscription. We do receive mail in Norfolk, you know."

Despite her sarcastic retort, there seemed to be something furtive in her manner. Lucas couldn't imagine what could be the cause of it. She was proud of her unconventional beliefs, so what would there be for her to hide?

He was about to ask when she uttered an exclamation. "Oh, look! Newcombe recorded a rather large bank deposit earlier this week."

Lucas crossed the room to the desk. Stopping beside her chair, he leaned over her, trying not to stare at the delectable mounds of her bosom. He dragged his attention to the open ledger. She was pointing to a figure listed near the bottom of the page.

"Eight hundred and fifty pounds," he read. "Is that the value of your stepmother's diamond necklace?"

She tilted her face up to look at him. "It's worth more, I'm sure. But if Newcombe pawned it, maybe he didn't receive the full amount."

"We checked all the major pawnshops, though. Unless he sold it to an individual."

"Perhaps. I just wish we could be certain this is the proceeds from the necklace."

"It should be simple enough to determine if he won a similar amount at the gaming tables recently. I'll check into it." He couldn't help smiling into her sparkling eyes. "Well done, Rory."

She smiled back and he experienced that peculiar catch in his chest that she always triggered in him. She really had the most fetching smile. It lit up her eyes and added vivacity to her beauty. That spirit and liveliness had attracted him to her from the very start—perhaps because it was missing from his own life. How unsettling to think he had become so burdened by duty that he had forgotten how to be happy.

Rory made him happy. The fire she ignited in his soul burned like an eternal flame. He craved her as much as he needed air to breathe. Yet she could never be his. For that reason, he must never kiss her again. He had no right to dally with her when he intended to wed another . . .

The muffled sound of voices came from out in the passageway.

Galvanized, he seized the ledger and shoved it back on the shelf behind the desk. "Someone's coming."

Her eyes wide with panic, Rory jumped to her feet. "Should we hide?"

"There's no time."

Lucas needed an excuse to explain their presence in Newcombe's study, and he realized there was only one thing to be done. And what an enticing thing it was. He pulled her against him and captured her mouth in a kiss. She tensed in surprise, but only for an instant. Then her lips softened and she looped her arms around his neck. She arched on tiptoe, her bosom cushioning his chest, and the eagerness of her response unleashed a wild need in him.

The dam of his self-control broke and a rushing river of desire swept through Lucas. He rubbed his lips over hers, drinking the sweetness of her mouth and enjoying her wholeheartedly, for it was the perfect pretext for their presence here. They were two lovers seeking a private place to be alone. The more passionate their kiss, the better their chances of allaying any suspicions.

Rory seemed to realize that too, for she melted against him, her fingers threading into his hair and her tongue tangling with his. When she moved her hips, he felt it as a flash of lightning that sent all the blood in his body searing down to his loins. Everywhere she was soft, he was hard, a perfect match of male and female. He cradled her bottom and pressed her closer, wanting her to know how desperately he desired her.

The allure of the forbidden beckoned to him. All the reasons why she was wrong for him slipped away into nothingness. There was only the here and now, the receptiveness of her feminine form and the insistent urge of his thirst to possess her. His entire body pulsated with the need to lay her down on the desk, to lift her skirts and sink into her velvet depths. He wanted so badly to hear her cry out in ecstasy that he was actually tilting her backward when a sound penetrated the fog of passion in his brain.

The door opened. The tramp of heavy footsteps approached. A nasty chuckle broke the romantic aura.

Lucas dragged his lips from hers. He looked over Rory's head to see a lardy man who resembled a ball of butter from his graying fair hair to the round belly that strained the buttons of his yellow-striped waistcoat. Talking around the stub of a cheroot clenched between his teeth, Lord Ralph Newcombe said, "Well, well, what have we here? Two lovebirds, eh?"

Lucas glanced down at Rory, who had a sweetly dazed look on her face. She tried to turn her head to see who had come in. But he put his hand at the nape of her neck and hid her face in the lee of his shoulder. It was bad enough that Flanders had had a good look at her. Better that Newcombe didn't recognize her, too, should she attend any future society events.

Lucas gave the man a casual nod. "I trust you don't mind that Jewel and I have borrowed your study."

"Be my guest." Newcombe waddled to the desk and

picked up the humidor of cigars. Tucking it into the crook of his arm, he flashed a grin that showed his yellowed teeth. "Old Dash would be proud. Indeed, he would. Like father, like son."

The reference was a sluice of icy water that snapped Lucas to his senses. Nevertheless, it took several deep breaths to chain the beast inside him. Even then, his senses clamored against his rationality. Only long years of practice helped him to keep a lock on his base instincts.

He held Rory close until Newcombe left the study. The moment the door closed, he regretfully released her and stepped back.

She still had that adorable expression of desire on her face. It glowed in her soft doe eyes and glistened on her damp rosy lips. Out in the garden, it had been too dark for him to see the aftereffects of his kiss. But now the image of her radiant features would be imprinted on his memory forever.

His fantasies would be the only time he saw that look on her face again. He must never let himself touch her again. He would not be like his father, betraying his wedding vows by bedding a woman who was not his wife. The prison of his situation barred him from doing it.

"We've found out all we need here," he stated. "Shall we go?"

As he'd intended, the coolness of his voice dimmed the passion in her eyes. She studied him quizzically as if pondering the abrupt change in his mood. "Yes. Of course."

He forced himself to walk away from her and open the door. As they went out into the corridor, the rowdy voices and noisy laughter of the drawing room repelled him. "We'll leave the back way."

She balked. "I left my bonnet and shawl with the footman at the front door. Besides, didn't you wish to find out the identity of Mrs. Edgerton's lover? She *is* one of our prime suspects, after all."

"I'm not allowing you to enter that pack of degenerates!"

"We'll just have a peek in the door, that's all. Now, don't you think you ought to at least put your arm around me? In case we run into anyone, I mean."

Feeling outmaneuvered, Lucas slid his arm around her waist and steered her down the corridor to the drawing room. At least he had an excuse to hold her close one last time. His hand rested on the womanly flare of her hip, and he breathed in the faint flowery aroma that belonged to her alone. Despite his iron resolve, he wanted to put his face to her bare skin, to see if that scent clung to her all over.

Rory came to an abrupt halt. She swiveled in his arms and looked up at him, her eyes large with shock. "Lucas, look," she hissed. "By the fireplace."

He hadn't even realized they'd reached the doorway of the drawing room. They stood to the side, half hidden from the guests. From this position, he had a partial view inside the chamber. Ignoring the raucous gamblers at the tables, he flicked his gaze to the marble mantelpiece.

Mrs. Edgerton stood there, giggling like a silly girl as a black-haired man strung kisses over her face. The sight stunned Lucas. He recognized the knave from Rory's entourage of suitors eight years ago. And more recently, from the encounter in the garden.

It was that swine Stefano.

Chapter 19

*In the highest echelons of society, gentlemen choose
their brides in much the same manner as they purchase
fillies at a Tattersall's auction.*

—MISS CELLANY

The following afternoon, Rory stepped into the
brougham with Lucas. The coachman set the vehicle at
a jaunty pace through the Covent Garden neighborhood, where the busy street was lined with narrow row
houses. They had just called on Colonel Hugo Flanders's
mistress, a frowsy actress who worked in one of the
nearby theaters.

"What a pity Mabel didn't have the diamond necklace," Rory said. "Do you think we should cross Flanders
off our list?"

"Not yet. Though he and Newcombe are certainly not
my top suspects any longer." Lucas gave her a pointed
stare. "I think you know who is."

He was referring to Stefano.

An inner quake shook her at the memory of seeing
her former beau kissing Mrs. Edgerton. Rory had
blinked, then blinked again, certain she was mistaken.
But that classic Roman profile was intimately familiar
to her. After all, she had once fancied herself in love with
the man.

He had to be the mystery lover that Mrs. Edgerton
had bragged about to Lucas. How had they met? Had it

been at a society party where he'd been skulking, hoping to find Rory?

Yet she doubted his declaration that he'd returned to London in the hopes of winning her back. If that were true, he'd have quit looking for her upon learning she'd been banished to the country. More likely, he had been scouting for Mrs. Edgerton at Tinsley's ball and had happened upon Rory utterly by chance. He'd decided on the spot to see if she was still as gullible as she'd been eight years ago.

The rat!

Nevertheless, Rory wasn't convinced that Stefano was in cahoots with Mrs. Edgerton in the blackmail scheme. She and Lucas had debated the issue at length. Stefano was an unprincipled man, but she questioned whether he'd risk his diplomatic career again. Lucas had been adamant, though, and Rory suspected he was swayed by his contempt for the man who'd ruined her.

Her heart softened as she glanced at him sitting beside her. Lucas was gazing out the window as the brougham turned onto the Strand. The mere sight of him sparked an unquenchable fire inside her. She loved the slight curl of his hair over his collar, the strength of his jaw, even the gravity of his expression. She no longer minded his silences, either. He wasn't a silver-tongued devil who spouted extravagant compliments in order to lure a woman into lifting her skirts. Lucas valued honor and integrity above all else.

Why couldn't she have been wise enough at eighteen to entice a man like him? She'd been headstrong and spoiled, craving romance, ready to believe the lies of a charming foreigner. She had scorned Lucas Vale as a prig. If only she'd had the sense to value substance over flash!

Now she found him far more fascinating than any

other man of her acquaintance. He had hidden depths that a woman could spend a lifetime exploring. A fever pulsed in her as she recalled his kisses the previous evening. The first one in the garden had been a revelation, unveiling the passion he concealed behind that stern mask. The second, in Newcombe's study, had won her heart and made her realize just how perfect Lucas was for her.

Old Dash would be proud. Indeed, he would. Like father, like son.

Newcombe's pronouncement had gone straight over her head at the time. She'd been too dizzy from Lucas's embrace to realize the impact of those words on him. It wasn't until later that she understood why he had turned cool. The last thing he wanted was to become a lecher like his father.

She gazed out the window at the hustle and bustle of the city. Pedestrians traversed the foot pavement in front of the various shops and businesses. There were stores selling used clothing, a tobacconist with an array of pipes in the window, a furniture shop with a painted chair on a sign. How she wished she could just be a carefree shopper and forget the heartache that twisted her insides.

Lucas had to marry Miss Kipling in order to pay off his father's debts. He would never take a mistress. Not that Rory would ever agree to such a role, anyway. She scolded herself even for being tempted by such a demeaning prospect. She had plans for her life. Plans that didn't involve a man. She would continue writing under the pen name Miss Cellany. Being here in London had filled her head with ideas for future articles. Perhaps someday she would even publish a collection of her essays in a book . . .

A sign on one of the business fronts caught her eye. A lightning shock sizzled through her. "Stop!" she cried out.

Lucas immediately rapped on the front panel, and the coachman angled the vehicle through the traffic to park by the curbstone. Concern etched his brow as he studied her, and he took her gloved hand in his, squeezing it gently. "What is it? What's wrong?"

Under his sharpened gaze, Rory realized the utter idiocy of her impulsive shout. "Never mind. I—I thought I saw someone I know."

Those penetrating gray eyes pierced through her fib. Lucas leaned over and gazed out her side of the brougham. In a moment, he turned back to her, a gleam in his eyes. "The offices of *The Weekly Verdict*. Did you wish to pay a call there?"

"No! Tell the coachman to drive on, please. Seeing it just . . . caught me by surprise, that's all."

To her consternation, he reached past her and opened the door on her side. "You want to go there. I can see that you do."

"We haven't the time to spare."

"Nonsense. We're only going to call on your stepmother. She isn't expecting us just yet."

The allure of visiting the newspaper that had published her essays proved impossible to resist. Rory wanted a glimpse of the offices, a peek at the printing presses, perhaps even an introduction to the staff members, so that she could have a fond memory to take back to Norfolk. For this opportunity to appear from out of nowhere was truly a gift of fate.

"Well, then. Perhaps I'll just see if the latest issue is available." Rory hopped out onto the street, then turned to realize that Lucas was about to follow. She held up her hand to forestall him. "Do wait here, please! You needn't bother coming with me. I shan't be long."

Turning her back on him, she darted a path through the throng of pedestrians and headed toward the printing office. A dilapidated sign hung over the doorway, the peeling letters painted in gold against a dark red backdrop. THE WEEKLY VERDICT. The sight sent a happy shiver dancing down her spine.

How many times had she yearned to travel to London to meet with her publisher? The expense to Aunt Bernice had always stopped Rory. She had been paid only a pittance for her first few essays, but had high hopes of earning more once she established a name for herself. That was why she must make the best possible impression today . . .

As she reached for the tarnished brass knob of the door, Lucas materialized at her side. Rory froze, glaring at him. "I told you I'd only be gone a minute. Why are you here?"

"In case there are any rats to chase away."

His smile ironic, he opened the door and motioned for her to precede him. She fumed inwardly at his high-handed manner. Rats, indeed! She should never have told him about her aversion to rodents. It provided him with a handy excuse to interfere.

She would have to be exceedingly careful not to give away her *nom de plume*. Lucas already scorned her modern opinions. She could only imagine his repugnance if he found out her secret identity as Miss Cellany.

A little bell over the door tinkled to announce their arrival. She stepped into a long, narrow room lit by a few scattered lamps. The rich scents of ink and paper perfumed the air. She had expected to see a bustling staff, all of them busy at the myriad tasks of producing a weekly newspaper. But no one occupied the single cluttered desk situated at the front of the office.

Midway down the hall, a gangly young fellow leaned over a large tray on a table, plucking out letters and putting them into another box in alphabetical order. He turned around and spied them, then came ambling forward with a loose-limbed gait, his face freckled beneath a thatch of untidy red hair.

A puzzled look in his brown eyes, he glanced at their fine clothing. "Can I help you folks?"

"I saw your sign as we were passing," Rory said. "I'm an avid reader of your journal. I was hoping to express my praise to the editor."

"I'm the editor. Jeremiah Chandler, at your service."

Rory's heart hammered. Chandler was the man who'd purchased her essays. But she had pictured someone older, more distinguished, an academic type with gold-rimmed spectacles and gray hair. Or alternatively, a wild-eyed anarchist with a revolutionary cockade pinned to his coat.

Not a freckled-faced youth who looked younger than she was.

Lucas held out his hand. "Dashell here. And this is—"

"Jewel," Rory said swiftly. "Miss Jewel."

The game would be up if Lucas uttered her real name. She had submitted her articles as Miss Aurora Paxton, requesting to be published under a pseudonym. The last thing she needed was for the editor to connect her to Miss Cellany in front of Lucas.

Chandler wiped his inky fingers on the apron tied around his waist before shaking hands with Lucas. "It's a pleasure to meet you, sir. And Miss Jewel."

"Likewise," Lucas said, his keen gaze on Rory.

He was far too astute not to sense something was up,

so she quickly babbled, "I expected there to be more em-
ployees here. Has everyone gone home for the day?"

Chandler's face wore a wry smile. "Actually, in addition to being the editor, I'm also the publisher, the
typesetter, even the reporter. There's just myself and a
few lads I hire to deliver the paper to the newsstands."

He glanced back at the worktable as if anxious to return to his duties.

"Might I purchase a copy of your latest issue?" Rory
said.

"You're in luck. I just finished printing this week's
edition." He reached to a stack of papers piled on the
desk and plucked one off the top. "Here it is, hot off the
press."

As she took the folded sheet, Lucas said, "Make that
two copies."

"That isn't necessary," she protested. "You may borrow mine later."

"Nonsense. I like to keep up with the latest radical
notions." Lucas tossed Chandler a coin which the editor
caught with deft, ink-stained fingers. "Keep the change."

"Much obliged," Chandler said, pocketing the coin
with a grin. "I'm operating on a shoestring and every bit
counts."

Rory could think of no other reason to dally. She
would have liked to have shooed Lucas out and remained
to talk business with Chandler. Perhaps she could return
before she was obliged to leave London.

Thrilled nonetheless, she clutched the news sheet like
a talisman as they returned to the carriage. A few days
ago, she had dashed off another editorial and mailed it
to the newspaper. But she'd been hesitant to divulge her
London address, so any response from Chandler would
have been delivered to her aunt's cottage in Norfolk.

Had he received it in time to include it in this week's edition?

She hoped not. The subject matter was bound to catch Lucas's attention. It might even tip him off to her as the author. She tried to remember the precise wording of the piece. Had she given herself away?

As the brougham set off again, the horses clip-clopping, Rory knew she ought to rein in her curiosity until she was alone. But she couldn't help herself. She stole a glance downward to scan the headlines in her lap: "Angry Citizens Protest Outside Parliament." "Chimney Sweeps Deserve Higher Pay." "A Housemaid's Tale of Horror."

Then Rory spotted the essay featured in a special box in the center of the paper: "Bartered Brides: An Exposé of Aristocratic Marriages by Miss Cellany."

Elation skittered over her skin and swelled in her bosom. It was all she could do not to burst out with prideful bragging. No matter what the consequences, she felt ecstatic to see her words in print.

Seeing Lucas's gaze on her, she hid her delight by lifting the news sheet to her nose. "Mm. I do love the smell of fresh ink, don't you?"

"Why did you give Chandler a false name?" he asked.

She affected a guileless look. "You did, too. After all, you didn't tell him you were the *Marquess* of Dashell."

"But you interrupted as I was about to introduce you as Miss Paxton."

"Of course. Chandler is a newsman and, heaven knows, he might take it into his mind to print in the next issue that I'd visited his office. That I would frequent such a place could be embarrassing when my sister is about to marry the Duke of Whittingham."

Lucas raised a quizzical eyebrow. It was clear he still found something peculiar in her explanation, though he couldn't put his finger on why. Rory felt overly warm under that scrutiny and hoped she wouldn't give herself away by blushing.

He studied her another moment and then glanced down at his copy of *The Weekly Verdict*. As he tilted it to the sunlight from the carriage window, his mouth quirked up at one corner. "Ah, here's a new one by your favorite author, Miss Fortune. It appears she's gunning for the aristocracy again."

"That's Miss *Cellany*." His automatic scorn for her work incensed Rory. Why, he hadn't even read the essay! She shifted uneasily on the plush velvet seat. What would he think when he did?

"Miss Begotten might suit her better," Lucas said. "Let's see what rubbish she has to say this time."

The hint of drollness in his tone only served to increase her ire. "If you intend to mock it sight unseen, then you oughtn't have purchased a copy."

She tried to snatch the paper from him. He deftly yanked it out of her reach and safeguarded it on the other side of him. In order to seize it, she would have to lean over him, pressing herself to his strong body and engaging in a wrestling match in full view of any passersby who looked in the carriage window.

Besides, it occurred to her that objecting too strenuously would only serve to increase his suspicions. Better to feign indifference.

Tilting her nose in the air, she said, "Think what you will, then. It matters naught to me."

He rattled the paper and cleared his throat, then began reading aloud, " 'In the highest echelons of society, gentlemen choose their brides in much the same manner as they purchase fillies at a Tattersall's auction.'" He glanced over at her. "Fancy that. I have not been tempted in the least to part Miss Kipling's lips and inspect her teeth. Nor to lift her skirts and check the soundness of her hocks—or rather, her knees."

Rory stiffened. "The comparison is not meant to be taken literally. And you must admit the author makes a sound point. Ladies are treated as objects to be acquired by the highest bidder."

He cocked an eyebrow, then glanced down at the newspaper again. "'Ladies are treated as objects to be acquired by the highest bidder.' Why, that is the very next sentence. You are quite attuned to Miss Cellany's thoughts, if I may say so."

She blanched, struggling to hide her dismay. "I happened to notice that sentence a moment ago. But I'm not interested in dissecting the essay with you, sentence by sentence. I prefer to read it myself later when there is no one around to irritate me."

He chuckled, a low sound that emanated from deep in his chest. It stimulated a fevered reaction in the pit of her stomach, and she was irked with her own body for its betrayal. If she was attuned to anything, it was him— much to her ill luck. She adored his scent, a mixture of pine and leather. Her pulse surged at the mere brush of his arm against hers. And like it or not, she cared about his opinion of her. When Lucas said nothing more, she turned her head stiffly to stare out the window on her side of the brougham.

She was only marginally aware of the neighborhood growing posher as the carriage neared Mayfair. With every jot of her being, she focused on the faint rattle of the paper as he turned the page. He was reading the rest of the editorial; she knew that without looking. It was agonizing to imagine him perusing words that she herself had penned.

She tightly clutched her own copy of *The Weekly Verdict* in her gloved fingers. Tension vibrated in her muscles. What else had she written? The memory was something of a blur. It had been very late on the night that Lucas had discovered her searching his bedchamber. Afterward, unable to sleep, she had sat at the dainty desk while Lady Dashell lay snoring in the canopied bed and had scribbled off her thoughts in a rush. She had been worried about her sister and thinking also about Miss Kipling after the girl's disastrous interview with the marchioness . . .

"What the devil—" Lucas muttered under his breath.

Rory swiveled toward him. "What is it?"

"Listen to this. 'Miss C.P. is a prime example, an innocent beauty just out of the schoolroom, sold to the Duke of W., a man old enough to be her father.'"

She struggled to appear surprised. "Why, that's Celeste! Imagine that. Though I suppose her betrothal is common knowledge. And it *is* one of the grandest matches of the season."

"That isn't the worst of it. 'Likewise, rumors abound that Lord D. will use his title to entice Miss A.K., the richest filly on the marriage mart, even though his intended fiancée is fourteen years his junior. When buying a bride, love matters naught to heartless noblemen.'" He threw aside the newspaper. His jaw was taut, his lips thinned, his expression thunderous. "Blast the woman! I'd like to know who the devil she is, hiding behind a pen name. I've a good mind to bring the law down on her for libel!"

Rory swallowed. The snippet *did* sound a bit over the top. "Surely it isn't libel if it's true, is it?" she asked cautiously.

"How would she know whether it's true or not? My feelings for Alice can only be pure speculation for this writer!"

"I don't think what she said is really all *that* damaging."

"Oh? My private life will be bandied all over London. Everyone will be gossiping about my intentions before I've even had the chance to make my offer to Alice. And my rivals will be trying to convince her that I'm heartless."

Rory wanted to slide down on the cushion and hide her face. At the time she'd dashed off that essay, she had believed him to be a cold, callous man devoid of human emotions. She had not realized that Lucas played his cards close to the chest for a reason. His reticence arose from a fierce desire for privacy to counteract his father's boisterous reputation. Unlike the gregarious crowd at Newcombe's party, Lucas was not one to expose his feelings and desires to the world at large. He was a man of deep emotions and impeccable honor, yet he reserved the sharing of his thoughts to a select few.

Including her, Rory realized with a tremor. To her he had confided his guilt over his mother's injuries, his father's attempt to corrupt him, his worry over his brother. And she had repaid him with betrayal.

"Miss Cellany must be a member of society," Lucas said, drumming his fingers on the newspaper in his lap. "Whittingham's betrothal may be common knowledge, but my intentions are not. I've danced with Alice at every ball, but so have many other gentlemen. Only someone very observant would realize that I'm on the verge of making her an offer. Or someone who knows me well."

Remorse threatened to choke Rory. A cowardly impulse told her to keep silent. He might never look at her the same way if he learned her *nom de plume*. Yet if she respected him, then she owed him the truth.

Reaching out, she placed her hand on his arm, drawing strength from the tautness of his muscles. "Lucas, I—I must tell you something . . ."

Her voice faltered as his gaze narrowed on her. Those steel-gray eyes seemed to bore into her very soul. He cocked his head in a calculating stare. "It's you," he said in a gravelly tone. "*You* are Miss Cellany."

His accusatory tone struck at her heart. She drew back her hand and curled her fingers into a fist at her bosom. It was difficult for her to meet his eyes. She drew a deep breath, but it did little to ease the ball of misery in her chest. "If you must know, yes. I am. I wrote that essay. But I did so before I knew you very well. And I vow, I never meant any harm by it."

Silence stretched between them. The rattle of the carriage wheels and the clopping of horse hooves competed with the drumming of her heartbeat. Lucas stared at her as if she'd sprouted horns. His eyes were steel mirrors that prevented her from reading his thoughts. He had never appeared sterner, not even on the day when she had faced him in his study to beg him for a job.

She clenched her teeth to keep her chin from quivering. Tears burned her eyes, but she blinked them away. She was proud of her work. It was just that she couldn't bear to think of him despising her. "I didn't mean to cause trouble for you, Lucas, truly I didn't. And yet . . . the essay *does* express my beliefs. Although I'm sorry that I involved you, I won't apologize for my views on aristocratic marriages. Too many of them are loveless, unhappy alliances."

"It's naïve to think that love is all that is necessary in a marriage," he said testily. "There are other important considerations, as well. Especially to a man with my responsibilities."

"Perhaps. But without love, how can one ever know true happiness?"

"What is mistaken for love is often mere lust. It burns out quickly."

"No! You mustn't be so cynical. Only look at Aunt Bernice. She left society to marry the man she loved, traveled all over the world on his merchant ship, and she was as happy as a clam!"

"Are clams happy? Perhaps you ought to address that issue in your next editorial. You may feel free to spout your opinions. I doubt that any clams will threaten you with a libel suit."

Rory watched him cautiously. Perhaps his mockery was a good sign that he didn't hate her. "You aren't really going to sue me, are you? I haven't any money to pay a settlement."

"Nor do I wish my private life waved like a flag in public any more than you've already done. So there is your answer."

Relief eddied through her. Not because she'd truly feared Lucas taking her to court, but because he seemed somewhat less angry now. His eyes had relaxed slightly, although his expression remained cool.

What she wouldn't give for one of his rare smiles right now!

The brougham slowed to a halt and she looked out in surprise to see that they'd arrived at her stepmother's house. She was reluctant to go inside just yet. She desperately wanted to patch things up with Lucas.

How foolish of her. She had driven a wedge between them, ruined their budding friendship. Once this mystery was solved, he would never willingly associate with a woman who penned inflammatory opinions that struck out at the very sort of marriage he had chosen for himself. Especially if he was planning a life in politics, as Lady Milford had suggested. He would wish to avoid all controversy for the sake of his career.

Rory drew a shaky breath. But at least her secret was out now. And it might be for the best, for it would serve to keep him from ever kissing her again.

Chapter 20

*When courting a lady, a gentleman should
heed his heart, not his bankbook.*

—MISS CELLANY

Lucas disliked Grimshaw on sight. Not because of his snooty expression or the vain way in which the butler combed his brown hair over his bald spot, but because of his condescending manner toward Rory. The man had looked down his long nose at her the instant they'd stepped into the foyer and he had gleefully informed them that Kitty Paxton was not at home.

"But I sent a message that I would call this afternoon after three," Rory said, untying her bonnet strings. "Did she not receive my note?"

"I took the mail up to her this morning," Grimshaw intoned, his eyes betraying pleasure at being the bearer of bad tidings. "She mentioned nothing of your visit."

"When will she return?"

"It is impossible to know. She was summoned by the Duke of Whittingham's mother to discuss the wedding preparations. I'm sure she found that to be more important."

Rory's disappointment showed on her expressive features. Lucas felt a stab of the same frustration. The second blackmail payment was due the following evening, and they needed to devise a plan to entrap the villain. From the moment he had seen Stefano with Mrs. Edgerton, Lucas had been certain the two were conspiring together. But he had yet to persuade Rory of that fact.

He had yet to forgive her, too, for inserting that loathsome reference to his marital plans in *The Weekly Verdict*. With his imminent betrothal, this was the worst possible time for him to be embroiled in a scandal. He would never forget the moment of realization when he'd put it all together, her modern notions, her expert knowledge of Miss Cellany's columns, her excitement on spotting the newspaper office.

Because of her careless disregard for his privacy, he would become the topic of titillating gossip. All of his life he'd taken pains to avoid controversy in order to overcome his father's tarnished legacy, and she had blithely dragged his name through the mud.

Nevertheless, he stepped to Rory's side, placed his hand at the small of her back, and fixed the butler with a cool stare. "I would like to write a note to Mrs. Paxton. You are to see that it is delivered immediately to Whittingham's house in Berkeley Square. Is that clear?"

Grimshaw's lips curled sourly as his gaze flicked downward to take in Lucas's protective gesture. "I shall be happy to oblige, my lord. However, you must not expect her to hasten back here. Her Grace's wishes surely must take precedence."

Lucas could see why Grimshaw rubbed Rory the wrong way. She'd said that he listened at keyholes and had a meddlesome manner. The man also had an irritating way of injecting his opinions into every response rather than merely obeying orders.

"That remains to be seen," Lucas snapped. "Now, fetch me pen and paper at once."

"There's a writing desk upstairs in the drawing room," Rory said. "I'll show you the way."

She started toward the staircase along one wall of the foyer. Grimshaw fairly leaped into her path, nimble for a man approaching his middle years. "Miss Celeste is entertaining a visitor in the drawing room. I very much doubt that she wishes to be disturbed."

Lucas had had quite enough of the butler's insolence. "*I* very much doubt you are paid to make such determinations for your betters. Now move aside."

Grimshaw complied with a pretense of subservience. "Only kindly remember it isn't my fault."

He lowered his gaze, though not before Lucas noted a strange excitement in his eyes. Fault? What mischief was the man contemplating now?

Then Lucas forgot about it as he started up the stairs after Rory. He told himself not to ogle her, yet her womanly form served as a siren's call. The gown of leaf-green muslin embraced her curves and accentuated the slenderness of her waist. As she lifted the skirt slightly to keep from tripping, he glimpsed her shapely ankles. His obsessive mind produced a fantasy of untying her garters, peeling down those white silk stockings, putting his lips to her soft bare skin . . .

He felt a light touch on his upper arm. "What do you suppose he's up to?" she whispered.

Lucas realized they'd reached the top of the stairs. Rory was leaning close to murmur in his ear, and with a searing jolt, he realized it wasn't her fingers resting on his sleeve. It was her bosom. A feast of creamy flesh swelled above the edge of her bodice, and his body reacted with irrepressible swiftness. Desire sizzled downward and brought him to throbbing readiness. The fierce urge to take her into his arms made him dizzy.

But she wasn't even gazing at him. Her attention was focused down the stairs. When she turned her head to look inquiringly at him, he realized she was commenting on the butler.

With effort, he broke the delightful contact of their bodies and guided her a few steps down a carpeted corridor to an alcove out of sight of the foyer. He kept his voice as low as hers. "I presume you mean Grimshaw."

"Yes. I had the distinct impression that he's hiding something. Do you suppose it has to do with the missing letters?"

"He did seem determined to keep us from talking to your stepmother. Yet it's a bit of a stretch to conclude that that makes him guilty of a crime. He is merely a servant, after all."

"Oh, but you can't begin to imagine his twisted ways. Why, just look at how he . . ." Rory compressed her lips into a firm line that he dearly wanted to soften with a kiss.

He tipped up her chin with his fingertip. "How he what? You cannot expect me to believe him a viable suspect unless you tell me everything."

She studied him another moment, then spoke in a low, resentful whisper. "If you must know, Grimshaw is the one who saw me with Stefano in my father's study. He's the one who reported me to Papa."

Lucas could see how that might seem horribly interfering to a young girl who fancied herself in love. Surely with the perspective of maturity, though, she ought to recognize it for a stroke of luck. "You deserved to be caught."

"But . . . it was underhanded! The snoop opened the door and peeked inside the study!"

"Suppose he had simply closed the door again. Suppose you'd carried on your affair with that knave. You might have ended up with child, Rory. It was best to put an end to it. So maybe Grimshaw did you a favor."

She uttered a harrumph. Brushing past him, she flounced down the corridor. It was clear she was miffed with him for not taking her side, and he found himself unexpectedly charmed by the willful tilt of her chin.

He went after her, catching up just as she sailed through an arched doorway and into a drawing room decorated in rose-and-cream hues. "Rory, if you'll just stop and think—"

She did stop. But her attention was not on him. He turned his head to see what had made her eyes suddenly widen.

And he cocked an eyebrow in surprise.

A young couple sat on a chaise by the window, their heads close together in conversation. Afternoon sunlight dappled Celeste Paxton's golden hair—and his brother's debonair handsomeness.

The pair glanced up and saw them. They sprang apart almost guiltily. Henry jumped to his feet. "Dash! Fancy meeting you here!"

Lucas didn't trust that suave smile. He walked closer. "I should say the same to you. Why are you here?"

"I only stopped for a moment to return a handkerchief that Miss Celeste dropped at the ball last night. There it was, lying on the street, after she and her mama departed in their carriage."

The girl waved a white scrap of lace. "I'm ever so grateful, Lord Henry. It was very kind of you."

The couple exchanged a smile, and Lucas was struck by how attractive they looked together. There was an air of conspiracy about them, too. Damn it, his brother couldn't be so reckless as to flirt with Celeste Paxton. She was betrothed to Whittingham.

A man old enough to be her father.

That phrase from Rory's column disturbed Lucas on a profound level. He didn't want to consider that she might have a point, that it was wrong to pair a dewy-eyed innocent with a man more than twice her age. He hesitated to face it because he, too, was intent on marrying a girl much younger than himself.

A girl he did not love.

"I'd best be on my way," Henry said, bowing to Celeste. "You'll be wanting to visit with your sister, I'm sure."

He walked jauntily toward Lucas, gave him a playful salute, and then headed out the door and down the corridor to the staircase. Lucas could swear his brother was whistling under his breath. He debated whether or not to go after Henry and read him a lecture, then decided it could wait until later.

Rory had gone to take the spot vacated by Henry on the chaise. She was talking to her sister in a low tone, and from Celeste's guilty expression, it was clear she was being chastised for receiving a gentleman without a chaperone present. Lucas deemed it prudent not to interrupt them.

Glancing around, he spied a dainty desk and sat down to write the note to Mrs. Paxton. He opened a silver inkpot and picked up a quill. He had a clear view of the sisters, and instead of composing the message on a sheet of cream vellum, he found himself watching Rory.

Rory with her sparkling brown eyes and lustrous black hair. Rory who was optimistic and opinionated, blushing and bold, witty and wise. Rory who still believed in love though it had led her to ruin. He wanted to explore every inch of her lush body. It wasn't just her physical attributes that fascinated him, either. He also wanted to discover all the complexities of her mind. He wanted to debate her views and tease her into a hotheaded response. No other woman had ever maddened him so much or made him feel more alive.

The truth caught him by the chest and squeezed hard. It was Rory he loved with all his heart. Rory, whom he could never, ever marry.

"I'm shocked that you would make such a horrid accusation," Kitty said as she paced back and forth in a huff. A rich gold gown adorned her plump figure and her graying fair hair had been arranged in an elaborate coiffure of curls. After returning home late from the duke's house, she had insisted upon dressing for the evening before meeting with Rory and Lucas. "Why, Nadine is my very dearest friend!"

Rory exchanged a glance with Lucas. He was standing with his arm propped on the mantelpiece in her father's old study. Dusk had fallen, the lamps had been lit, and shadows played across his solemn features. Nevertheless, she could see frustration in the set of his jaw.

"Lord Dashell and I saw Mrs. Edgerton with Stefano at Newcombe's party," Rory said. "She told you she has a new lover, didn't she?"

"She would never take up with *that* cad! You must be mistaken."

"There is no mistake about it. They were kissing openly—in full view of everyone there."

Kitty sniffed. "That doesn't mean she stole my letters. She would never do such a terrible thing!"

"She had the opportunity. So did Stefano. They may very well be working together. Did you know that he sneaked into Celeste's betrothal ball?"

Her stepmother stopped pacing to stare at her. "What? Here in this house? Why, that's impossible. I would have noticed the fellow. And Grimshaw would have stopped him for certain. He sees everything that goes on here."

Rory pursed her lips. It did seem odd. Was it possible the butler *had* seen Stefano but had kept quiet for some unknown reason? "Speaking of Grimshaw, are you aware that he allows Foster to leave the house in the evenings? I saw her departing the other night."

"Her mother is quite ill. Some sort of chronic condition. So long as she readies Celeste and me for the evening, she may go. I am not a harsh mistress, you know!"

Rory stepped to the glass door overlooking the shadowed garden. It was out there that she'd caught Foster leaving by the back gate. Remembering the maid's furtive manner, she couldn't shake the feeling that something peculiar was afoot. And that Grimshaw was in cahoots with the maid.

"We are wasting time speaking of servants," Lucas said, a note of impatience in his tone. "We should be focusing our attention on Stefano and Mrs. Edgerton."

"*Only* Stefano," Kitty said, turning toward him, her skirts rustling. "Why, he surely resents me for telling Mr. Paxton to banish him from England. The fellow might blackmail me just for the sake of revenge. But never Nadine! I would as soon believe the villain to be your brother, my lord."

"Henry?" Scowling, Lucas stepped away from the fireplace. "How ludicrous."

"Is it?" She flashed him a mistrustful look. "On the night of the ball, I saw the two of you quarreling in the morning room. The letters were hidden there in my sewing basket. With all due respect, my lord, y*ou* may proclaim your innocence, but can you be certain about Lord Henry? As a younger son, he must have very little money and may be seeking to feather his nest at my expense!"

Rory knew Kitty still harbored doubts about Lucas. Her stepmother had been shocked to learn that he'd been helping Rory search for the diamond necklace in pawn-shops. Lady Milford had convinced Kitty that because the letters had been written by his father, Lucas must have taken them. Now she seemed to have transferred the blame to his brother.

But she was wrong about Lord Henry. The young man might be guilty of courting Celeste on the sly, but that was the extent of his subterfuge. Rory had not been able to wrest the truth of their romance out of her sister. Celeste had coyly refused to admit that she and Lucas's brother were anything more than friends.

Clearly exasperated, Lucas took a step toward Kitty. "Good God, woman! A man would never think of poking through a lady's sewing basket. Another woman is far more likely to have done so. Your friend, Mrs. Edgerton. She is undoubtedly working with Stefano."

"Bah. I shall ask Nadine when I see her this evening. She is sitting with Celeste and me in the duke's box at the theater."

"You daren't ask her such a question outright," Rory cautioned. "What if she *is* the blackmailer? You'll have alerted her that she's under suspicion!"

"All of this is nonsense," Lucas said crisply. "Time is short and we should be devising a plan to entrap the villain. The next payment is due tomorrow evening. The letters must be found before then—unless you wish to give up a thousand pounds."

"Good heavens, no," Kitty said faintly, wilting into a chair and fanning her face with a lace handkerchief. "I haven't the means to come up with such an amount, anyway. Oh, what shall I do?"

Rory stared at her stepmother in shock. That thousand was supposed to be her reward for finding the blackmailer. "But you must have the funds!"

"Not after the expense of Celeste's come-out. And the

marriage, too! Whittingham's mama is demanding that I pay for the wedding breakfast—and there shall be more than three hundred guests!"

Anger surged in Rory. She felt betrayed, tricked by a false promise into helping her stepmother recover the stolen *billets-doux*. Now there might not even be any recompense for her efforts. What was she to do?

Too incensed to speak, she pivoted to stare fiercely into the darkness. She had been counting on that money. It was to be a nest egg for her and Aunt Bernice. She'd already been planning to purchase new furniture for the cottage, to refurbish her wardrobe, to provide her aunt with a few comforts in her old age . . .

Something moved in the gloom of the garden. Rory leaned closer to the window glass. A hooded figure slipped through the shadows and disappeared out the rear gate.

Foster!

Rory made a snap decision. If she failed at all else, she could at least discover for certain where the lady's maid went in the evenings.

She spun around. "Foster just left. I intend to follow her."

Ignoring the astonished look on Kitty's face and the glower on Lucas's, Rory snatched her shawl from the back of a chair and opened the door to head out into the chilly night. She didn't care what they thought. She needed to take action to clear her head and work off her fury.

Darting down the path, she reached the gate and pushed it open, the hinges squeaking. She had no sooner stepped into the murky darkness of the mews than Lucas appeared like a ghostly apparition at her side.

"You needn't accompany me," she snapped. "I know you won't consider anyone else but Stefano to be the culprit."

"No woman should be out alone at night."

"Foster is."

He said nothing to that, only kept pace with Rory as she headed toward the main street, where the occasional gas lamp glowed like a yellow moon against the deep purple twilight. Carriages rattled past, partially blocking her view of the few pedestrians who hurried along the foot pavement. Most appeared to be workmen heading home for the night.

After a moment, she spied Foster's slight, hooded figure a good distance away. Huddled in her cloak, the maidservant glided along the street, moving swiftly past a row of town houses. "There she is!"

By hurrying, they were able to close the distance and then maintain a pace half a block behind the woman. They crossed the busy traffic of Piccadilly and headed into a less prosperous area. As the night air cooled her temper, Rory found herself glad of Lucas's presence at her side, especially as they passed a number of dark alleys where thick shadows might hide any manner of criminal.

"I'm sorry I was short with you," she murmured, while keeping Foster in her sights. "I do hope this isn't a wild-goose chase."

"If nothing else, we'll benefit from a brisk walk."

"There *is* something odd going on between her and Grimshaw. I can feel it in my bones."

"We shall see, then, what it is."

"But you're still convinced the blackmailer is Stefano."

"Yes. He's proven himself to be unscrupulous. Any man who is corrupt enough to prey upon an innocent girl is more than capable of other crimes."

The conviction in Lucas's voice made her glance up at him. His jaw was set in an uncompromising line, his expression harsh in the gloom. She felt a thrill to know that he was firmly on her side when so many in society had turned against her. But she didn't want that to color his judgment in finding the blackmailer.

"She's going into that house," he said.

Rory looked ahead to see Foster mounting several steps to a row house. The neighborhood was dilapidated, rubbish piled in the street, the residences small and mean. There were no gaslights in this part of the city. Only a candlelit window here and there broke the darkness.

The maidservant disappeared inside the house. They made haste to follow, going up to the stoop, where Lucas knocked on a door with peeling paint of a color indiscernible in the darkness. Rory wrapped the shawl more tightly around herself. It was a blessing to have him with her, she thought again. She would not wish to be alone, unsure of what situation she might encounter in the house.

The door opened a crack. A hunchbacked woman wearing a white mobcap peered through the slit. "Who ye be?"

"We've brought an urgent message for Miss Foster," Rory invented. "May we see her?"

"Miss Foster, eh? Well, come along in, then!"

They stepped into a tiny foyer with a scuffed wood floor and a narrow staircase. The smell of cabbage soup hung in the air. The old dame held up an oil lamp, its amber light casting her round, wrinkled face into sharp relief.

"I'm Mrs. MacPherson, the proprietress here. Miss Foster's gone upstairs to say her good-nights. She won't be long. Ye kin wait fer her here."

Had the maid walked all this way merely to bid good night to her sick mother? If so, they'd followed her for nothing.

"If it isn't a bother," Rory said, "would it be possible

for us to go up and deliver the message immediately? It's quite important."

"Well, all righty, then. Don't suppose it can hurt none. Just ye, though. No menfolk allowed. 'Tis the first door on the left. Don't knock, lest ye wake the little uns."

Little ones? This must be a boardinghouse for women, then. Besides Foster's sick mother, there would be women with young children living here.

Dismayed, Rory exchanged a glance with Lucas. He clearly had come to the same conclusion, and she'd probably hear about this wasted visit on their way home. Or worse, he'd say nothing at all. He would let his silence speak volumes to make her feel guilty for accusing a blameless maidservant of nefarious deeds.

As Mrs. MacPherson ushered him into a small parlor, Rory proceeded up the steep stairs to a dark, dingy passageway with several closed doors on each side. She went to the first door on the left and opened it.

Stepping quietly into the room, she found herself in a dimly lit bedchamber with rows of cots along either side. Each one held a sleeping child.

Halfway down, Foster knelt at the bedside of a dark-haired boy. He looked to be about five years old. He was awake, but sleepy-eyed, and snuggled in the curve of her arm as she read to him from a book.

The sweet murmur of her voice held Rory in a spell. She stared, her mind in a whirl. There was only one explanation for the sight in front of her.

Foster had lied, after all. Because she had a son. A son she'd kept secret, quite likely because he'd been born out of wedlock. Of all the scenarios Rory had imagined, this one had not entered her mind.

Just then, Foster glanced up and her eyes widened in fright.

Chapter 21

*How like a man to use a woman without
benefit of wedlock!*

—MISS CELLANY

The maid started to arise, but Rory motioned her back
down. "You needn't rush," she whispered. "I'll wait right
here for you."

Foster nodded rather jerkily and returned her attention to the boy. His eyes were drooping as she finished
reading the story.

Rory retreated to a stool by the door. She felt like
an intruder peeking through a window at a private family
scene. It had been a mistake to come here. Although she'd
been correct to believe that the woman was hiding something, it had nothing to do with Kitty's stolen letters.

From the way Foster glanced up from time to time,
she clearly was terrified to have been discovered. For
that reason alone, Rory couldn't leave. She needed to re-
assure the maid that her secret was safe.

Foster tucked the coverlet around the little boy and
bent down to kiss his mop of dark curls. His eyes closed
the moment his head met the pillow. She picked up the
candle and came forward, her steps reluctant and her
plain features taut with apprehension.

Rising from the stool, Rory went out into the corridor. Foster cast one last backward glance at her child and

then quietly closed the door. Her pale blue eyes held a dull look of resignation to her fate.

"How did you find me, Miss Paxton?"

"Lord Dashell and I followed you."

"Oh! His lordship is here, too?"

The woman looked near to fainting, and Rory slid an arm around her. "Please, you mustn't worry. I won't tell a soul and neither will he. Now, do come downstairs where you can sit for a moment."

In a stunned state, Foster let herself be led down the steep flight of stairs. She was trembling, and Rory felt terrible for having caused her such alarm. The poor woman probably thought her world had come to an end. Any servant with a bastard child would be dismissed for immorality.

Reaching the foyer, Rory took her into the cramped parlor, where Lucas sat with Mrs. MacPherson by the light of a single lamp. He sprang to his feet, and she suspected by his knowing expression that the proprietress had already informed him about Foster's young son.

As Rory seated the maid beside her on a lumpy horsehair sofa, Lucas said, "Have you any spirits, Mrs. MacPherson? It appears Miss Foster is in need of a restorative."

"A wee tot of whisky should do the trick," the old woman said, bouncing up from her chair and going to a cabinet, which she unlocked with a key from the ring at her thick waist.

In short order, Foster was sipping on a glass, coughing a little from the strong drink. Rory patted the maid's back. "There now, you'll feel better in a moment."

Foster wore a look of quiet desperation. "Will you tell Mrs. Paxton? Please, you mustn't! I beg of you."

"Of course I won't tell. And neither will Lord Dashell. We've no wish to cause trouble for you."

"But . . . why did you follow me, then?"

Rory racked her mind for a plausible reason. She couldn't cite the stolen letters or the diamond necklace that had been paid to the blackmailer. Foster likely knew nothing of the matter.

"We were out for a stroll when we noticed you," Lucas said. "Miss Paxton was worried for your safety walking alone at night."

Rory sent him a grateful look, and Foster seemed to accept the lame excuse. She turned the glass around in her nervous hands. "Malcolm will have my head! He warned me not to come so often. But I had to see our little boy as often as I could. I miss him so dreadfully!"

"Malcolm?"

A blush spread over her plain features. "Mr. Grimshaw, I mean. Oh! I should not have called him that! Or said what I did!"

The revelation struck Rory like a thunderbolt. She exchanged a shocked glance with Lucas. "Miss Foster, pray excuse me for prying, but are you saying that Grimshaw is the father of your son?"

Lucas flagged down a hansom cab to drive the three of them back to Mrs. Paxton's town house. As the maid hopped out and scuttled into the mews, she cast a worried backward glance before disappearing through the garden gate. Then the cab proceeded around to the front of the house where Lucas's brougham waited to return them to Grosvenor Square.

Before entering the carriage, Rory stopped to glower at the painted green door and gleaming brass fittings of her stepmother's house. "I've a good mind to go straight inside and give that man a deafening lecture!"

"Foster will inform him that he has been found out," Lucas said. "Best to let Grimshaw stew for a time before you lay into him. He will be in an agony of conscience waiting to see what you will do with the information."

"Bah! The knave doesn't have a conscience."

Once Foster had admitted Grimshaw had fathered her son, the whole story came tumbling out. Six years ago, she had been governess for a family in Bath when Kitty had gone there to take the waters, bringing Grimshaw with her to direct the rented household. During that month, the butler had met Foster and seduced her. When she later realized her delicate condition, she was forced to leave her position. She'd thrown herself on his mercy and he had arranged for her to live with Mrs. MacPherson until the baby was born. Shortly thereafter, Grimshaw had recommended Foster to Kitty as a lady's maid.

"The fellow could have abandoned her," Lucas pointed out as the carriage traversed the short distance to his house. "You must give him some credit for lending her assistance."

"But he should have married her. How like a man to use a woman without benefit of wedlock!"

"I predict a new column in the works for Miss Conduct."

Rory blew out a breath. "It's Miss Cellany, and this is no joking matter. And why are you taking Grimshaw's side, anyway? I suppose all you men stick together."

"I'm not taking sides. I'm merely being logical. Servants are discouraged from marrying. So perhaps he did the best that he could manage in a difficult situation."

"That doesn't excuse him. And to think that ever since I returned to London, he has been sneering at *me* for being ruined when he himself is guilty of ruining Foster!"

Lucas's hand came down over hers, warm and reassuring. "Never mind Grimshaw. All that matters is that we have discovered the reason for his odd behavior. Which means that I can now focus my attention on Stefano."

The brougham came to a halt in front of his palatial house with its soaring columns and the tall, lamp-lit windows. Yanking her hand back, Rory frowned at him through the shadows. "*You?* May I remind you, we are partners in solving this mystery."

"I won't allow you to endanger yourself. You will stay here with my mother. Now, come inside and I'll tell you what *I* intend to do tonight."

Rory crouched in the bushes alongside an elegant rooming house near the Italian embassy. Lucas was hunkered down beside her, his attention focused on the window across the narrow alley. Clouds obscured the stars and rendered the night pitch-dark. Every now and then, a stray raindrop struck her face. The ground was cold, and she was glad for the warm cloak that Lucas had borrowed for her from his mother.

They had a clear view into Stefano's rented rooms. All of the windows were black except for one. There, the subject in question sat writing at a desk, the yellow light of a lamp illuminating his dark hair and olive skin. Every now and then, Stefano rose to refill his wine glass from a decanter on a nearby table or to walk around while puffing a cheroot. Then he would return to the desk to write some more.

"This is about as exciting as watching grass grow," she whispered.

"You shouldn't be here," Lucas muttered. "How I ever let you talk me into this has to be one of life's greatest mysteries."

"You can't do this alone, that's why."

"I can, indeed. And I should have."

"Oh? We have been watching here for well over an hour. It seems clear to me that Stefano is not going out tonight. In fact, I'm beginning to wonder if he's waiting for Mrs. Edgerton to call after the theater."

"Good God, you could be right." Lucas took out his pocket watch and flipped it open, angling it toward the light from a distant street lamp. "It's nearly eleven. If that is the case, she may arrive within the hour. And then I will lose my chance to search for the letters tonight."

"Not if we use *my* plan."

Despite the darkness, she could see his grimace. "Absolutely not," he growled. "It's far too risky."

"It's perfectly safe. I'll sit at a table in the café over there." She nodded toward the end of the alley, where lights shone in the windows of a small restaurant on the street across from the rooming house. "There will be plenty of people around. Especially once the theaters begin letting out."

She sensed his indecision and pressed her point harder. "Let's go to your carriage. I brought paper and pen to write a note. Your groom can deliver it to Stefano. I *know* he will come to meet me at the café. It's the only certain way to lure him out of his rooms so that you can search for the letters."

Lucas uttered a muffled curse under his breath. "All right, then. But you must promise me you'll take no chances. He's a dangerous man."

"Bah. He has already done his worst to me."

"I wouldn't be so certain of that."

He jumped up, then offered Rory his hand, drawing her to her feet. She was grateful for the chance to stretch her cramped legs. When she would have pulled her fingers free, Lucas held on tightly, hauling her flush against the solid wall of his body. His head swooped down to press a swift, hard kiss to her lips. With an answering moan, she kissed him back, heedless of the chilly raindrops that spattered her face.

She slipped her hands inside his coat to feel the broad muscles of his chest. Her fingers encountered a cold metal object tucked into his waistband.

Shocked, she angled back to stare at him. "You brought a pistol!"

"Of course. *You* may trust Stefano, but I certainly don't."

"I shall be completely safe in a crowd of people."

He hugged her close, his cheek rubbing against her hair as he said fiercely, "Don't underestimate him, my darling. Under no circumstances are you to let him talk you into leaving that café. Is that understood?"

She nodded, her face buried in his neck. *My darling!* Lucas had called her *my darling*. A heady joy made her spirits soar. She hoped it meant he'd forgiven her for putting his name in that essay. With every breath, she inhaled his pine scent and felt the beating of his heart against her bosom. She was sorely tempted to forget all about their mission and remain right here in the warm circle of his arms . . . forever.

But Lucas had other plans for his life. She had her own life mapped out, too, a life dedicated to her writing. She must not waste time wishing for things that could never be.

Better she should focus on recovering the stolen *billets-doux*. Then she would wrest that reward money out of Kitty by hook or by crook. Even if she had to hold the letters for ransom herself.

The first window that Lucas tried was locked. The sash refused to budge no matter how hard he pushed up on it.

Cursing, he descended the wobbly old ladder he'd found in the garden shed and moved it to the next window. Time was wasting. The note had been delivered, and the ploy had worked like a charm. Stefano had rushed into the bedroom to put something into a drawer, then to preen in front of a mirror, smoothing his abundant black hair and huffing into his hand to check his breath, before hurrying out the door.

That had been no more than five minutes ago. It seemed like five hours.

Lucas repositioned the ladder and climbed the rickety slats again. As he gave the sash of the second window a hard shove, the ladder swayed alarmingly. He grabbed at the sill to steady himself. If he failed to get in through a window, he'd have to try to jimmy the door lock with his pocket knife. Not that he knew such a skill.

It was damn lucky he'd been born to privilege, he thought with grim humor. Clearly, he wasn't cut out for a life of crime.

He tried again. This time, the sash moved slightly. Heartened, he gave another mighty push and the window opened with a raucous groan.

He hoisted himself through the narrow opening and landed on his feet in a darkened chamber. On the far wall, a pale rectangle of light revealed the outline of a door.

Heading in that direction, he made his way past black lumps of furniture. He could barely see his hand in front of his face. He bumped his shin on a bedpost and let loose another expletive.

Reaching the door, he wrested it open to find himself in a small parlor with a clutter of tables and chairs. The air smelled of smoke from the cheroot stub smoldering on a porcelain saucer. This was the room where Stefano had been writing. Thankfully, he had been in such a hurry to join Rory that he'd left the glass lamp burning on the desk.

Lucas stalked across the room and opened the drawers of the desk, searching through a mess of papers for the packet of letters. All the while, he wondered what that oily Romeo was doing with Rory. Had he tried to kiss her in greeting? Would he grope her beneath the table? Or attempt to entice her back here to his rooms?

Lucas itched to land his fist in the jaw of that too handsome face. The man was a slick operator who had bamboozled Rory once already. Though she was no longer that naïve girl, she might yet be fooled by his smooth charm. The bastard would use any trick to take advantage of her. She had far too much confidence in her ability to defend herself.

He prayed she would stick to the plan. All she had to do was to keep Stefano occupied for a short time. Then Lucas would fetch her once he'd found the letters. He only wished he knew what the devil she was telling him.

Rory hadn't gone into much detail, saying only that she would concoct a sob story to explain why she'd been compelled to reach out to Stefano so late in the evening. It was possible that Lucas himself figured into it. Maybe she would beg Stefano for protection because her employer was lusting after her.

God knew, that would be a true statement.

Hunger for her gnawed at him, a living beast clawing at his insides and tearing at his concentration. Life without her didn't bear contemplating. Yet it must be faced. He had a duty to his family, to his heritage, to the laborers on his four estates. Rory could write as many critical columns as she liked, but a man in his position couldn't marry merely for love.

He slammed the drawer shut, rattling the pens and inkpots. There was nothing in the desk except for papers written in Italian. Nevertheless, Lucas recognized the penmanship. The blackmail notes had used some of those same fancy curlicues. It only confirmed Stefano's guilt and made Lucas more determined in his search.

He looked around the parlor. Where would a sleazy diplomat hide a packet of letters? He glanced inside a large vase, checked behind the leather-bound volumes in a bookcase, and even looked beneath the cushions of the chaise and chairs. There were no other obvious places here in the parlor.

Picking up the lamp, he proceeded into the bedroom. The bureau was littered with a silver-backed comb and brush set, jars of hair products, and a collection of cheap stickpins. A wardrobe contained only clothing, but he shook out the boots and shoes just in case.

Stefano had rushed into this room before departing. He had shoved something into the bureau. Lucas opened the top drawer. Instead of the purloined letters, however, a lady's crumpled chemise lay on top of some folded cravats.

No doubt it belonged to Mrs. Edgerton.

The fact that Stefano had put it away before going to meet Rory made Lucas grit his teeth. It meant that the man hoped to lure her back here. The sneaky Casanova wouldn't want her to see an undergarment belonging to his mistress lying on the bed.

As Lucas trod across the room to check the bedside table, a floorboard squeaked beneath his foot. It felt loose and he squatted down to take a closer look. On a hunch, he used his pocketknife to pry up the board.

Something glittered inside the narrow space. He brought the lamp closer. A diamond necklace.

Beneath it lay a packet of letters tied with a length of pink ribbon.

Rory struggled not to grimace as Stefano rubbed his knee against hers underneath the table. Surreptitiously, she moved her legs away from him. She wanted to slap his face, but of course that would ruin the charade.

The café teemed with people, mainly bohemian types, men wearing colorful Gypsy scarves in place of cravats, women in flamboyant gowns with exotic jewelry. One of them had even used a slender paintbrush to anchor her auburn bun. Rory would have liked to have studied the crowd more closely had she not been busy inventing lies to hold Stefano's interest.

She had taken her time spinning a tale of woe, sniffling into her handkerchief, talking in detail about the long years of exile and then her return to London where she had been ill-treated by her mean, selfish stepmother.

"She sent you to the house of Lord Dashell," he said, his voice vibrating with anger. "You are too fine a lady to labor for a living. Especially for that cruel tyrant!"

Stefano clearly harbored resentment toward Lucas for interrupting his seduction of Rory in the garden the previous night. "Yes, Kitty did order me to work for him," she said, playing up to his assumption. "But that isn't the worst of it. You'll never believe what she has done now. Why, I don't know what to do or where to turn! I could think only of coming to you."

Stefano leaned closer. She had never before noticed just how large a Roman nose he had, or how he had carefully arranged a curly black lock to fall onto his brow. "What is it, *carissima*? I am at your command. Tell me so that I may help you."

When he made to grab her hand, she quickly lifted her half-empty glass. "It is such a terrible thing to admit. Please, may I first have a refill?"

"Perhaps you will feel more comfortable in my rooms across the street. I have brought the most excellent wine from my country."

"Oh, but that wouldn't be proper!" Rory lowered her

chin to gaze sorrowfully at him through the screen of her lashes. "However, if you are weary of listening to my troubles, pray do not let me keep you."

"Of course I shall stay. You have my undying love!"

Stefano flagged down a waiter, who delivered a carafe to the table. When the wine was poured, she lingered over a sip in order to draw out the moment.

"I am at my wit's end," she said tragically. "I don't even know how to put this into words. You will not believe me, I fear."

He clapped his hand to his lapel. "Trust me, *carissima*. I am your most loyal servant."

"All right, then. I suppose there is nothing to do but to say it." Rory paused for dramatic effect. "My stepmother is accusing me of blackmailing her!"

Stefano's reaction was almost comical. His brown eyes widened and he gave a jerk of surprise. He stared at her in slack-jawed consternation.

In that moment, all of her doubts vanished. She knew with absolute certainty that Stefano was the culprit. Otherwise, he would have laughed off such a ridiculous accusation.

"Blackmail?" He gulped and his voice sounded squeaky. "You?"

"Yes. She says that I've stolen something from her. And that I have been sending her notes demanding payments for its return."

"What . . . what is it that she thinks you have stolen?"

"It's silly, really. Just a packet of old love letters. I don't know why they are so valuable. But I swear I didn't take them." She affected a tremble in her lower lip. "You believe me, don't you?"

"Of course, *carissima*. But I do not know how *I* can help."

He reached out to clasp her hand, and this time, she

let him do it, even though his touch made her skin crawl.
She felt nothing for Stefano anymore but disgust, for his
handsomeness was merely superficial. How had she ever
fancied herself in love with such a shallow weasel?

Her heart ached with yearning for Lucas. If only he
was the one holding her hand. She glanced at the doorway of the café, hoping to see him. He was to come here
the moment he found the letters.

"Please," she begged, returning her attention to Stefano, "you must think of *something*. My stepmother is
threatening to take me to the magistrate. Tomorrow
morning, she is reporting the theft to the law to be investigated!"

His upper lip took on a sheen of sweat. "Investigated?"

"Yes. There will be officers from Bow Street Station
looking into the case. They will leave no stone unturned.
I hope they can find the true villain because otherwise
I will be locked in prison."

"I cannot think you will be imprisoned simply for letters. And without any proof of your guilt."

"It isn't just the letters. Kitty handed over a diamond
necklace to the blackmailer. Unless I return it, I will face
the full force of the law."

"But you were not even in London when the letters
disappeared."

"Why, how do you know that?" she asked in wide-
eyed innocence.

Stefano blinked rapidly. "It was a guess. You have
been back for only a few days."

"I will still be blamed. The police will take my stepmother's word over mine—especially since I am a ruined woman." She lifted the handkerchief as if to dab
away tears. "Oh, Stefano, whatever am I to do?"

Sitting back in his chair, he rubbed his square jaw and

stared glassy-eyed at her. Rory wondered what he was thinking. Would he allow her to take the fall for his crime? He was such a coward! If nothing else, she took perverse enjoyment in making him squirm.

He glanced back and forth as if to make certain no one was listening. Conversations buzzed all around them, along with laughter and the clinking of glasses. Then he leaned close to murmur, "I may know something of great interest to you, Aurora. But you must promise not to tell anyone."

"You have my word!"

"Your stepmother has a friend, Nadine . . . Mrs. Edgerton. Do you know her?"

"Why, yes, we've met. But if you think I should appeal to *her* for help . . ."

"No! You mistake me. Mrs. Edgerton has become . . . a friend of mine, too. She gave me a packet of old letters to hold for her. She said it was very important that I should conceal them."

Rory's heart thumped. The last thing she'd expected was for Stefano to admit any knowledge of the matter. But perhaps she'd scared him sufficiently with her talk of an investigation by the police. He must be hoping to shift all the blame onto his accomplice.

"Letters! Are you certain they're the ones stolen from my stepmother?"

"I did not examine them carefully, but I think they must be. That means Mrs. Edgerton took them. *She* is the guilty one, not you, *carissima*. Had I known, I would never have agreed to hide them for her."

"Hide them? Where are they?"

"In a very secret location in my rooms. Somewhere that no one would ever think to look."

His fear had been replaced by a superior smirk. The cocky man was proud of himself, she realized. So proud that he couldn't resist bragging. At the same time, his confidence alarmed her. What if the hiding place was so clever that Lucas wasn't able to locate it?

Over half an hour had passed since Stefano had joined her here in the café. All this time, Lucas would have been combing through obvious hiding spots like the desk and drawers. He must be having trouble because if the letters had been easy to find, he surely would have been here by now.

Rory gave Stefano a look of moon-eyed pleading. "Please, you must tell me where the letters are, for if I can return them to my stepmother, it will save me from being sent to prison."

"I shall do better than tell you, *carissima*." His dark eyes glittering, he held out his hand. "Come, I will take you to them."

Chapter 22

It is foolish, indeed, for a penniless lady to fall in love with a nobleman.

—MISS CELLANY

With quick steps, Lucas approached the café. He could see a throng of customers through the lighted windows. Despite the cold raindrops spattering his face, a sense of elation invigorated him. Both the packet of letters and the diamond necklace were tucked safely in an inner pocket of his coat.

Now, he had only to collect Rory from Stefano's greasy clutches.

The villain belonged behind bars, as did his accomplice, Mrs. Edgerton. Yet seeking a prison sentence would require revealing the sordid truth to the magistrate. The news would spread far and wide about the love letters Lucas's father had written to Mrs. Kitty Paxton. Lucas suspected that the contents must be extremely sensational.

It wasn't just for himself that he wanted to avoid a scandal. The letters also would cause great distress for his mother. Now that she finally had found the strength to rejoin society, publicizing another of her husband's affairs would reopen old wounds. She had suffered enough already.

For that reason, Lucas had devised a different punishment for Stefano and Mrs. Edgerton. He looked forward to putting it into effect.

He opened the door to the café. The hum of conversation and the clink of glasses enveloped him. He stopped to scan the crowded tables. From their colorful garb, the clientele appeared to be mostly artists and actors. He kept his eyes peeled for Rory. These were her kind of people, he realized with a pang. Bright, lively, avant-garde—and so different from himself. Perhaps because she blended in well with such folk, he didn't spot her at once.

A short man with a pencil-thin moustache bustled toward him. "Would you care to be seated, sir?"

"I'm looking for a black-haired woman in a dark green cloak. She'll be with an Italian fellow."

"Ah, you must mean Stefano." The proprietor nodded sagely. "I'm afraid you've just missed them."

"They've gone?"

"A few minutes ago, yes." The man peered closer at Lucas, apparently seeing the alarm on his face. "He's a bounder, that one. I do hope she isn't your wife—"

Lucas heard no more. He was already out the door, dashing across the street, his feet on fire. They had to have gone to Stefano's rooms. But why would Rory disregard her own safety? How could she let herself be fooled again by that scoundrel?

Stefano must have lured her there on a clever pretext. To seduce her . . . or worse.

Lucas ran into the alley to peer into the lamp-lit window. He spied the couple at once. Stefano was bending over the desk, scribbling something with a quill, while Rory stood nearby, a vision with her porcelain skin and inky-black hair against the green cloak. For a moment, Lucas couldn't breathe, so thankful was he that she had not come to harm.

She was glancing around the parlor, her expression alert. She edged over to peer into the darkened bedchamber. It struck him that she must believe he was still inside the flat and would come to her rescue if necessary.

Blast her! She should have obeyed him and stayed in the café. He had feared something like this might happen, that she might endanger herself on a whim. Now he needed to get her out of there. But he didn't dare climb through the window again since opening it would cause too much noise. It would have to be the door, then.

Drawing his pistol, he started toward the front of the rooming house.

While Stefano was busy dashing off a note at the desk, Rory strolled around the small parlor. It was clearly a bachelor's rented rooms with very few personal touches. She peeked into the shadowy bedchamber, and a jittery nervousness shook her. Lucas had to be in there. He couldn't have found the letters if they were concealed in a place that was impossible to detect.

For that reason, she had spoken loudly as they'd entered, to alert him to their arrival and to give him time to hide himself beneath the bed or behind the door.

No doubt he would rant at her for leaving the café. But she had seen no other solution. This might be her only opportunity to retrieve the *billets-doux* and earn that thousand-pound reward. She had to take the risk and play this game of pretense. And carefully, for if Stefano figured out that she had been scamming him, things might turn ugly.

"What are you writing?" she asked. "Can't you just show me where the letters are?"

He straightened with a square of white paper in his hand. "I must tack this note to the door first. To warn away any callers."

"Do you mean . . . Mrs. Edgerton?" Rory affected a pout. "Oh, dear. Have you invited her to come here to-night? Am I intruding?"

"Certainly not! She might stop for a glass of wine after the theater, that is all. But she mustn't find you here—or she will guess that I have betrayed her confidence."

"You needn't bother with the note, then. Just hand over the letters and I'll be gone."

"Oh, but you mustn't leave so quickly, *carissima*. It has been very long since we were alone together. I have missed you so much."

Before she could do more than blink, he sprang forward and yanked her close, his mouth aimed at hers. Rory managed to turn her head in time so that his lips merely grazed her cheek. His scent of pomade and wine sickened her and she wiggled against his wiry strength.

"Stefano, do stop! You'll make me think you're lying about the letters. That you lured me here only to have your wicked way with me."

"You will have your precious letters. But first, I wish to taste your delicious skin . . ."

As he nibbled at the side of her neck and made groaning sounds of delight, she tried not to cringe. She was in a pickle, for she didn't dare enrage him. Or likewise, Lucas. He was apt to come charging out of the bedchamber to confront Stefano before she had the letters safely in hand.

She took firm hold of his shoulders and gave him a little push backward. "You shall have your reward after you have shown me your secret hiding place. I promise, I shall be grateful. Very, *very* grateful." For good measure, she batted her lashes and fabricated an adoring smile.

He straightened, his brown eyes hot with desire. "Yes,

carissima. But first, let me pin this note to the door. Then we will have no interruptions."

Lucas would interrupt him, Rory knew. From his hiding spot in the bedchamber, he must be steaming with anger at her for coming here. She looked forward to placating him later with kisses and caresses. She only hoped he'd have the good sense to stay out of sight until Stefano retrieved the letters.

The Italian scurried away to the door. Just as he was reaching for the knob, however, a knock rattled the wood panel.

Stefano jerked his head around in a panic. "Nadine is here!" he hissed. "What shall I do?"

"Ignore her," Rory whispered. "She'll go away in a moment."

His finger to his lips, he retreated to where she stood near the desk. His eyes were wide, his manner nervous. Clearly, he didn't relish an encounter with the woman whom he had been painting as the blackmailer.

The doorknob jiggled slightly as if Mrs. Edgerton were testing it. But it was locked. Stefano had turned the key when they'd entered.

Silence filled the parlor. Rory felt a surge of impatience. She itched to hold those letters in her hands. Once Stefano showed her his secret hiding spot, she would quickly cool his ardor. Or Lucas would do it for her. Wouldn't Stefano be surprised to learn that his nemesis had been here all along?

The door flew open with a loud crash. A man came bursting into the parlor. He held a pistol trained at Stefano.

Rory's heart catapulted in her breast. She blinked in astonishment. "Lucas?" He was supposed to be concealed in the bedchamber.

Stefano uttered a squawk of surprise. He froze in

place, his rounded eyes focused on the pistol. Then in a flash he grabbed something from the desk. He caught Rory from behind and gripped her like a shield. To her shock, she felt the cold, sharp edge of a penknife pressing at her throat.

"You lily-livered coward," Lucas said in contempt. "Release her at once."

"Put down your gun," Stefano cried out. "On the floor, or I will kill her! I swear it!"

Rory could feel him trembling. Her own heart hammered. She held very still lest the blade inadvertently slice into her. Never had she dreamed Stefano was capable of violence. Or was he bluffing? She couldn't be certain.

Lucas stared at them for a moment. His face was a hard mask, revealing nothing of his thoughts. Then he bent down to place the pistol on the floor.

"Kick it toward me," Stefano ordered, his voice jittery.

Lucas complied, and the gun went skittering across the wood planks, coming to rest against Stefano's foot.

"Let her go," Lucas commanded. "You have diplomatic immunity for blackmail, though not for murder."

Rory didn't know if that was true or not, but she could feel Stefano's indecision. Hoping to catch him off guard, she played the weakling. "Please don't hurt me," she whimpered. "I thought you loved me. We're meant to be together."

"Of course we are, *carissima*. It is that tyrant you should fear."

She felt the penknife ease away from her throat. It was now or never. As he started to crouch down to grab the pistol, she stomped on his instep and wrenched herself free.

At the same instant, Lucas sprang forward. He grabbed

Stefano and landed a hard clout to his jaw. The loud crack sent the Italian diplomat staggering backward to hit the wall. He slumped to the floor in a daze, cradling his face and moaning like a baby.

Rory hurried toward the men. She grabbed Lucas's arm before he could haul Stefano to his feet for another blow. "For pity's sake, don't strike him again!"

"He deserves far worse." Rubbing his knuckles, Lucas cast an irritated glance at her. "Why are you protecting him, anyway? He intended to force himself on you!"

Her heart glowed in spite of his cross look. Everything in her liquefied into a soppy puddle to know that he would defend her honor. In a milder tone, she said, "I only meant that you mustn't knock him out. He can show us where the letters are hidden."

"Not anymore, he can't. They're in my pocket along with the diamond necklace."

"But . . . Stefano said he had a very clever hiding place that was impossible to find. That's the only reason I came here with him."

"They were tucked beneath a loose floorboard in the bedchamber. And why the devil would you be talking to him about the letters, anyway?"

"It was part of my ruse. I told him that Kitty accused *me* of blackmail. I coaxed him to admit that he had the letters. Of course, he tried to foist all the blame onto Mrs. Edgerton."

"You . . ." Stefano looked up at her, his bleary eyes revealing shock. "You tricked me, *carissima*!"

"She isn't your dearest, she's mine," Lucas snapped. "As for any trickery, it's poetic justice for what you did to her eight years ago."

The sparkle in Rory's heart kindled a river of fire that coursed downward to pool in the deepest, most private part of her. She reveled in the knowledge that Lucas would openly claim her as his own. She wanted to melt against him, but he stepped away to pick up his pistol.

The sound of a commotion came from the dimly lit corridor. Two people appeared through the open doorway, a stout older man hauling a woman. He was Lucas's coachman, Rory realized. He had a firm grip on Mrs. Edgerton's arm.

Her furious voice echoed in the passageway. "Unhand me, you varlet! Or I shall scream!"

The servant ignored her, bringing her through the doorway and straight to Lucas. "Here she is, milord. Just as ye asked."

"Thank you, John. Kindly stand guard right outside." Lucas handed his pistol to the man. "Feel free to shoot either of these two rats should they attempt to leave without my permission."

"Aye, milord." The coachman stepped out and closed the door.

Mrs. Edgerton sucked in an angry breath that made her bosom strain against her bodice. An elegant ruby gown edged in black lace adorned her curvy form, and a dyed red egret feather wagged in her black bonnet. "This is an outrage! Lord Dashell, what is the meaning of this? And you, Miss Paxton! What are you doing here?"

"Better I should ask *you* that," Rory said. "For it seems you are content to take my leavings." She looked pointedly at Stefano, who still sprawled on the floor, moaning.

Mrs. Edgerton's eyes widened as she spied him for the first time. She lifted a gloved hand to her mouth, then rushed to his side, looking down at him. "Oh, my poor darling. What have they done to you?"

"He has received his just deserts," Lucas said. "Or at least a portion, anyway."

She flashed him a calculating look, as if she were trying to figure out how much they knew. "What do you mean? Did he attempt to seduce Miss Paxton again?"

"Yes. And you'll not be surprised to know that he also had this in his possession." Reaching inside his coat, Lucas pulled out the packet of letters.

Rory stared. There were not very many of them, perhaps only five or so. They were neatly tied with a pink ribbon. So much fuss over a few scraps of paper!

Mrs. Edgerton stood very still. She gave an artificial laugh. "Letters? I can't imagine what they have to do with *me*."

Stefano stirred, a frown on his bruised face. "But Nadine—!"

A black shoe from beneath her skirt discreetly kicked him into silence.

"I also found something else hidden beneath the floorboard in the bedchamber." Lucas produced the diamond necklace. In the lamplight, it glittered in the palm of his hand. "I believe it belongs to Mrs. Paxton."

"It does, indeed," Rory confirmed. "My papa gave it to her on the occasion of their marriage. It is her finest piece of jewelry. But I'm sure you are well aware of that, Mrs. Edgerton."

"I've seen her wearing it, yes. Though not for the past week or so, come to think of it. Why, whatever is it doing here?"

"You *know* why—" Stefano began.

"Hush!" Mrs. Edgerton glared down at him. "*You* took the letters and the necklace from Kitty. I had nothing to do with this. Nothing whatsoever."

A string of rapid Italian phrases issued from him, and Rory could only assume they were curses. "That isn't what Stefano told me," she said. "He blamed it all on you."

"Me?" Her gloved hand fluttered to her bosom. "How absurd. Why would I blackmail a dear friend of mine?"

"Who mentioned blackmail?" Lucas asked, fixing her with a lordly stare.

Mrs. Edgerton's cheeks went pale. "I—I thought you said . . ."

"No, I did not. Nor did I ever say the letters belonged to Mrs. Paxton."

While her lips flapped wordlessly, Stefano struggled to rise. He leaned against the wall for support, his gaze sullen and a reddened welt on his jaw. "It was Nadine's plan," he babbled. "She found the letters in the sewing basket. I caught her stealing them during the ball. Then she forced me to write the blackmail notes!"

"Will you be silent?" she snapped. "*You* have diplomatic immunity. They can't do a thing to you."

"Quite the contrary," Lucas said, tucking the letters and the necklace back inside his coat. "As an influential member of the government, I can have a word with the Italian ambassador and ensure that Stefano loses his position, especially given his history of corrupt behavior. As for you, Mrs. Edgerton, blackmail is a serious criminal offense."

Her face appeared paper-white against the black and red of her bonnet. "You won't tell the magistrate. Why, the contents of those letters will create a scandal!"

"Perhaps. But it will be worth it to see you hang for all the trouble you've caused Miss Paxton—and her stepmother."

Mrs. Edgerton's hand went to her neck as if she were imagining a noose tightening around it. She swayed on her feet and then swung toward Stefano. "You cannot allow this to happen. Stop him!"

"How?" he whined, ceasing to cup his injured jaw

long enough to scowl at her. "I will lose my post because of you!"

Rory glanced at Lucas. Despite his impassive expression, she knew he was toying with them. He would never allow love letters written by his father to be made public in a court of law. What did he plan to do?

He paced in front of the couple, his hands on his hips. "There is another solution," he said. "One that will allow Mrs. Edgerton to save her pretty neck."

"What?" she squeaked, darting forward to clutch at his arm. "Pray tell me, my lord. I will do anything you ask."

He gave her such a withering look that she stepped back. "You and Stefano will depart England on the first available ship. And you will never return."

"Leave society? Forever?"

"Yes. And if I ever find you back on these shores, I shall bring the full force of the law down on both of you. Is that understood?"

"But, my lord—"

"This is not a negotiation. You may take my generous offer. Or you may hang. It makes no difference to me."

Rory gawked at him in admiration. It was the perfect solution. And far cleverer than anything she could have imagined. His powerful position and stellar reputation lent considerable weight to his decree. He looked forbidding and merciless, and they couldn't possibly know that he had a soft heart beneath that iron mask.

But *she* knew. He had defended her honor, protected Foster's secret, cared for his invalid mother. And he could kiss with toe-curling tenderness, making Rory feel as if she were the most important woman in the world.

She faced the truth in that moment. Foolish or not, she

had fallen head over heels in love with the Marquess of Dashell.

Walking up the steps to his front door, Lucas kept his hand at the base of Rory's back. A chilly breeze spattered them with raindrops. He was keenly aware that he had very little time left with her. Now that the letters had been found and the necklace recovered, she would be leaving his employ. There would no longer be any reason to continue the pretense that she was his mother's companion.

Both Stefano and Mrs. Edgerton had agreed to his plan. Lucas had given them a few days to tidy up their affairs here in London. Mrs. Edgerton, in particular, would need to arrange for an agent to handle the sale of her house and belongings. They were to tell anyone who asked that they were engaged and eager to go to Italy for the wedding.

Jarvis greeted them in the entrance hall. "Good evening, my lord, Miss Paxton."

Lucas handed over his hat and coat. "Is my mother asleep?"

"Yes, Mrs. Culpepper is staying with her tonight. They entertained quite a lot of visitors today. If I may say, her ladyship has never looked happier."

Lucas was glad of that, at least. "And my brother?"

"Lord Henry went out earlier and has not yet returned. Will you be requiring anything else this evening?"

"Tea and sandwiches in my study." Lucas looked at Rory. "We will continue our discussion, Miss Paxton, if that is agreeable to you."

"Absolutely!"

Her dark eyes danced with enjoyment, and he felt his gut tighten with excruciating desire. This might be his last opportunity to be alone with her. He didn't know how he could bear to see her walk out of his life. He wanted to slow the passage of time, to give him the chance to store up memories of her.

She removed her bonnet and cloak and handed them to the butler. The leaf-green gown was in the latest stare of fashion. She might have been a fine lady returning home from a party with her husband.

But he could never take her as his wife.

Weighed down by that reality, Lucas led her past the grand staircase and toward his study at the rear of the house. The echo of their footsteps sounded lonely in the long marble corridor. Tonight, his ancestral house seemed more like a mausoleum than a home. He ought to be elated at having recovered the letters. He had cleared the path for his marriage to Alice Kipling. Less than a week ago, he had thought his future was settled.

It was still settled, he reminded himself. Yet now more than ever, the course of his life seemed like a grinding duty.

They entered the study with its floor-to-ceiling book-cases and the large mahogany desk where he often sat to scrutinize the estate ledgers, valiantly checking and double-checking the numbers, hoping to find a way to pay off his father's crushing debts. They were his debts now. Only a vast infusion of wealth would save him from penury. He had an obligation to provide for his mother and brother, and to create a solvent legacy for future generations.

He had no right even to contemplate marrying for love.

"Will you return the letters to my stepmother?" Rory asked.

Lucas took out the packet and held its light weight in his palm. "I would be quite happy to burn them. Shall I light a fire?"

"No! They don't belong to us. Let me have a look at them, anyway."

She snatched the letters out of his hand and untied the pink ribbon, then took the topmost one to the desk to examine it by the light of the lamp. Frowning, she ran her fingertip over the writing. "The ink is quite faded."

Seeing her unfold the paper, he stepped to her side. "For God's sake, Rory. You can't read that. It's private."

"So? We went to an awful lot of trouble to find these letters. We ought to at least know what is in them."

Rory spoke absently without looking up at him. She was already scanning the first few lines. The last thing he wanted was for her to read lewd hyperbole composed by his father. "Give that to me."

He snatched it away, and she cried out, "Lucas, wait! Look at the date. Kitty implied that the affair took place shortly before my father's death seven years ago. But this letter was written nearly nineteen years ago."

He shook his head impatiently. "What difference does that make?"

"It makes a huge difference. It means that the affair must have occurred just *before* Kitty married Papa." Rory reached out, her fingers biting into his arm. Her dark eyes shone large and tragic in the pale oval of her face. "Oh, Lucas, you don't suppose . . ."

Her unspoken suspicion leaped wholly formed into his mind. His blood ran cold. It wasn't possible . . . was it?

Slowly, he said, "You're thinking she was already with child when she married your father. And that Celeste is . . ."

"*Your* half sister. Not mine."

Chapter 23

Polite society is savage toward ladies who fall from grace.
— MISS CELLANY

Grimshaw showed them up to the drawing room at her stepmother's house. Clinging to Lucas's arm, Rory noticed the butler's toadying manner only peripherally. Foster must have spoken to him. But Rory had no interest in berating him for his treatment of the maid and their bastard son. That would have to wait until another day.

At the moment, she was too consumed with trying to adjust her mind to the awful probability of Celeste's parentage. It pained her heart to think that Celeste wasn't truly her sister. They shared no blood relation at all.

Kitty had closely guarded that secret all these years.

Her stepmother paced back and forth in front of the fireplace. Still garbed in the gold gown she'd worn to the theater, she came scurrying forward. She was clutching a lace handkerchief, and her eyes were wet with tears.

"Aurora! How did you receive my message so quickly? I sent it only a few minutes ago."

"Message?"

"Oh, never mind. All that matters is that you're here! The most dreadful thing has happened."

"I see," Rory said tersely, thinking it likely had to do with a glitch in the wedding preparations. "Well, I didn't come here to listen to your petty problems."

"Petty? How can you be so cruel? And at such a time!" Kitty launched into a bout of noisy weeping. "Everything is ruined. Ruined!"

Lucas put an arm around her plump form and guided her to a chaise. He went to the sideboard and poured her a sherry, then returned to press it into her hand. "Drink this down and wipe your eyes," he ordered. "Then tell us what's wrong."

At his commanding tone, she gulped the wine and dabbed at her damp face with the handkerchief. "It's Celeste," she said brokenly. "Oh, dear heavens, she's gone!"

Her own anger forgotten, Rory rushed to her step-mother. "What do you mean, gone?"

"She pleaded a headache and stayed home tonight. When I returned from the theater a little while ago, I went to her bedchamber to check on her." Kitty drew a shuddery breath and pointed to a nearby table. "That . . . that note was on her pillow."

Rory snatched up the crumpled paper and read it aloud. " '*Dearest Mama, it pains me to inform you that I cannot marry Whittingham. I would be wretchedly un-happy as his duchess. Thusly, I have gone away with the man whom I love with all my heart. No doubt you shall be frantic with worry, but pray do not despair! He is a fine, honorable gentleman who adores me every bit as much as I adore him. By the time you see me again, we shall be husband and wife. Please do try to be happy for me. Your loving daughter, Celeste.'* "

Aghast, Rory lifted her gaze to Lucas. Every particle of her body turned to ice as dread caught her by the throat. Celeste had run off with another man. And only one name came to mind.

Lord Henry.

Lucas's face revealed his shock and alarm. She knew that he, too, was remembering seeing them together here in this room. Talking and laughing, their heads together, looking like the perfect young couple in love. There had been a conspiratorial air about them . . .

He grabbed Kitty by the arms. "Who? Who is this man?"

Shaking her head, she twisted the handkerchief in her fingers. "How am I to know, my lord? I thought she was happy with Whittingham."

"Of course she wasn't happy," Rory flared. "I warned you, but you just wouldn't listen."

Kitty's lower lip wobbled. "Oh, don't scold me, Aurora. I feel terrible enough already."

Lucas breathed deeply as if struggling to control his temper. "We found your letters tonight," he said tersely. "Mrs. Edgerton and Stefano admitted to blackmailing you."

He reached into his coat and brought out the ribbon-wrapped packet, tossing it down onto the table along with the diamond necklace. The jewels glinted in the light of the fire.

"None of that matters anymore," Kitty said woefully as she glanced at the items. "There will be a scandal anyway. Because Celeste has jilted the duke."

"It does indeed matter," he snapped. "I have every reason to believe that your daughter has eloped with my brother, Henry."

Rory stepped forward. "And I think you know the implications of that, don't you? They are half brother and sister."

Kitty stared, glassy-eyed, from her to Lucas. Her lips moved as if to deny it, but no words came out. She turned as pale as the handkerchief in her hand. Then she uttered a moan and crumpled into a swoon upon the chaise.

An hour later, Rory sat beside Lucas in an old curricle that had belonged to his father. It was past midnight, and darkness swallowed them as they left the gaslights of London behind. She had tossed a few essentials into a bandbox that was secured to the back. Lucas had done the same with a satchel on their swift return to his house to fetch a faster vehicle.

It was impossible to know how long it would take to find the runaways. They undoubtedly were heading for Gretna Green. Unlike England, Scotland had no waiting period for an underage couple to marry. She prayed they would catch up to the pair before they committed a tragic mistake.

"I'm surprised Henry didn't take this carriage," Lucas said, frowning at the darkened road. "The tilbury is faster, but it's far too dangerous to drive at night. Blast him, he should know better."

The tilbury had been the only other vehicle missing from the stables. They could only conclude that Henry had used it as the getaway vehicle.

Rory shivered, as much from worry as the night chill. She was grateful for the blanket draped over her lap. The curricle had a leather hood, but the open front allowed the wind to whip cold raindrops at their faces. A pair of glass lanterns fastened to the front provided the only illumination in the stygian gloom. She had to trust in Lucas's driving skills in handling the pair of horses that trotted into the night, hooves clopping and harness jingling.

"Celeste should have known better, too," Rory said. "Oh, I *wish* I had made her promise not to do anything rash!"

His gloved hand came down over hers in her lap. "It's as much my fault as yours for not keeping a tighter rein on Henry. But don't worry, we'll find them."

His gaze regarded her tenderly in the scanty light of the twin lanterns. His hand felt warm and heavy resting on hers, and an answering warmth leaped to life inside of her. If only they were the ones racing to the border to be married, she thought. But it was foolish to wish for something that could never be.

Her love for him was as doomed as the love between Celeste and Henry.

Lucas returned his attention to the road. Unwilling to distract him from the dangers of night driving, Rory said no more. Yet she leaned against him, wanting to savor every moment in his company, even under such dreadful circumstances. She prayed he was right about catching up to the runaways.

It broke her heart to think of the anguish in store for Celeste. She would have to be told of Kitty's affair and the identity of her true father. This marriage between her and Henry must never happen.

Once Kitty had been coaxed out of her swoon with a whiff of hartshorn, she had admitted everything, how she had tricked Rory's father into wedding her, and that eventually he had guessed the truth. How strange to realize that Kitty, too, had committed the grave error of being seduced by a married man. Although in Rory's case, she hadn't known Stefano had a wife back in Italy.

Cold droplets splattered them as their route to the north took them straight into a storm. Lightning flashed in the distance and thunder rumbled. The rain steadily increased to a torrent. The hood of the curricle protected them from the worst of the downpour, but Rory shivered from the icy trickles down her face and into the collar of her cloak.

Lucas had to slow the horses as the road turned into a muddy quagmire. The large wheels bumped and splashed through potholes. They passed no other vehicles. It was as if they were the only two people in the world. Or perhaps everyone else had had the good sense to weather the stormy night at home in their warm beds.

The howling wind buffeted the carriage. With every crash of thunder, the horses snorted and flinched. More than once, Lucas had to strain to guide the pair away from a ditch.

After one particularly loud strike, he bent his head close while keeping his gaze pinned to the road. "It's too hazardous to go on," he half shouted over the noise of the tempest. "We'll have to stop. Up there."

Blinking the raindrops from her lashes, Rory peered ahead and saw a glimmer of lights through the murky gloom. An inn. "Perhaps we can ask if anyone has seen Celeste and Henry."

He nodded. "Don't worry, we won't have lost any time. If my brother has a lick of sense, he'll have stopped somewhere, too."

As the carriage turned into the inn yard, a stable boy darted out to hold the horses in the pouring rain. Rory was thoroughly soaked by the time she stepped into the warmth of a common room. While she stood dripping by the door, Lucas went to speak to the proprietor. They had a few minutes' conversation during which she rubbed her chilled arms beneath the cloak.

Then he returned to her, his chocolate-brown hair damp and tousled, his face unsmiling. "Unfortunately, he hasn't seen them."

"Oh! I was so hoping . . ."

"Also, the inn is nearly full because of the storm. I'm afraid there's only one room left." His keen gray eyes fastened on her. "To protect your reputation, I had to tell him we were husband and wife."

Chapter 24

A noble bachelor is considered distinguished by age, whilst an unmarried lady is a spinster by one-and-twenty.

—MISS CELLANY

Rory sat on a stool by the small fire. Having unpinned her bun, she combed her fingers through the damp ends of her hair. It had stayed mostly dry thanks to the protection of her bonnet.

The tiny bedchamber was situated under the eaves. Rain sluiced down the dormer window, and every now and then, lightning illuminated the glass panes. It was long past midnight, and she ought to be weary after the volatile events of the day. Yet she felt alive with quivery anticipation.

Her gaze strayed to the double bed with its feather pillows and blue coverlet. In spite of all that had happened, in spite of the impossibility of their situation, she couldn't stop imagining herself lying there with Lucas. He had gone back out to fetch their cases and to check on the horses in the stable, leaving her alone with a riot of lascivious thoughts.

She wasn't a naïve young girl anymore. She knew exactly what would happen if she allowed it. The decision would be all hers because Lucas would never force himself on her. Yet she had made a mistake once before and had been sent into exile. Did she dare seize this one night of happiness?

A quiet knock sounded. She sprang to her feet just as the door clicked open and Lucas ducked his head to enter the cozy bedchamber. Her heart squeezed at the sight of him. His dark, wet hair was slicked back from his harshly handsome features. Rain dripped from his greatcoat and onto the wood planks of the floor.

Their eyes met. His gaze traversed over her loose black hair as it tumbled down the shoulders of her gown and curled around her bosom. He stared for a long, stirring moment before shutting the door, placing her bandbox and his satchel on top of a small dresser. He removed his wet coat and hung it from a wall hook.

As he turned back toward her, a jagged streak of lightning illuminated the grim tightness of his mouth. "You'd better get some rest," he growled. "I'll sleep on the floor."

He desired her. Oh, yes, he did. She could see it in the silvery gleam of his eyes and jerkiness of his movements as he untied his cravat. Their awareness of each other crackled in the air like the flashes of the storm outside.

He sat down on the stool by the fire to pull off his boots. The flames illuminated the quickened rise and fall of his chest. Shameless passion for him pulsed between her legs. She had been raised a lady and oughtn't be entertaining such carnal thoughts. Yet if she had to spend the rest of her life alone, she yearned to have this one bright memory of intimacy with the man she loved with all her heart and soul.

Rory whirled around, presenting her back to him. Over her shoulder, she said in a soft, throaty voice, "Will you unbutton my gown, please?"

Rain lashed the window for a moment before his heavy footsteps approached. She shifted the thick fall of her hair over her shoulder and out of his way. His fingers brushed the bare skin of her neck, sending sparks of longing sizzling through every part of her body. She loved his touch, so strong and capable yet gentle, as he worked his way down to her waist, unfastening the gown and exposing her undergarments to his view.

"It would be a great help," she murmured, "if you would loosen my corset strings, too."

His hands suddenly gripped hard around her waist from behind. "Good God, Rory! How can you ask me that? I'm trying to do the right thing here."

The torment in his voice pleased her mightily. She swiveled to face him, resting her hands on the solid wall of his chest, savoring the heat that he radiated. "You said we're to be husband and wife for this one night. So what could be more right than for us to share the bed?"

He stared down at her, his eyes glittering with hunger. He appeared to be wrestling with his conscience, and Rory knew that because of his father's depravity, Lucas had always exercised iron control over his own passions. She moved sinuously to entice him, letting her hips skate against his, relishing the sweet friction of their bodies.

To her joy, he made a harsh sound in his throat as his mouth swooped down to claim hers. She opened to him at once. The erotic slide of his tongue against hers pulled mewling sounds of pleasure from deep inside her throat. He kissed her long and hard, his lips ravenous and provocative. All the while, his hands skimmed up and down the open back of her gown. Then he brought one around to cup her breast, his thumb moving over the tip. She clung to him as her insides melted to liquid fire.

Lifting his head, he clasped her so tightly that she

could feel the heavy thumping of his heart against her bosom. His lips grazed her hair, nipped her ear, licked her throat as if he could not get enough of her. Then he sipped at her lower lip as if she were made of the sweetest nectar.

"God help me," he muttered. "I haven't the strength to resist you."

She ran her fingers inside his collar, absorbing the warmth of his skin. "I'll gladly play the scandalous flirt if I can tempt you into losing control."

He made a sound halfway between a laugh and a groan. "Must you remind me? I should never have called you that."

"It's the truth."

"No, Rory, you're far more than that. You're beautiful inside and out."

He gazed deeply into her eyes, his lips poised over hers. She could see the honesty in his gaze, for the stony mask was gone. His face was expressive with a yearning that arose from his heart. Though she knew it was wrong, a mad hope simmered in her. If only they could be together forever. Bracing her hands on his shoulders, she lifted herself on tiptoe to nestle her cheek against his, relishing the roughness of his whiskered skin.

"Oh, Lucas," she said on a sigh. "Make love to me."

He joined their mouths again in a drugging kiss that left her dizzy for more. Her need for him blossomed and grew until longing enveloped every part of her. Lucas was everything she wanted—and everything she could never have. At the edge of her mind she knew they only had this one night together, and that knowledge honed her desire for him to a keen sharpness.

When he drew back slightly to push the gown off her shoulders, she wriggled against him in her eagerness to disrobe, tugging on the tight sleeves until the garment slithered downward into a leaf-green pool at her feet. The same wild excitement seized hold of him as well. In between frantic kisses, they tore at each other's clothing, abandoning them to fall onto the floor in a scattered heap.

She craved to feel his skin against hers, to lie beneath him and accept the weight of his body. But when they were nude to the waist, Lucas didn't take her to the bed. He drew her flush against him and subjected her to another lingering kiss. The sculpted muscles of his chest against her bare breasts made her nipples tighten and ache. In a fever of impatience, she reached to the waistband of his pants.

He caught hold of her wrist. "Not yet," he said in a harsh whisper, his lips roving her face. "Or we'll be done too swiftly."

"Isn't it supposed to be swift?"

He cocked his head, and a smile quirked one corner of his mouth. "Not if you wish to reach the pinnacle of pleasure."

"But all of this is pleasurable."

His smile became a devilish grin. "It'll be better. Much better. Trust me."

With that, he bent his dark head and applied his attention to her bosom. He palmed one breast in his hand, playing with the tip before drawing it into his mouth to suckle her for long, delicious moments. Arching her head back, Rory closed her eyes and threaded her fingers into the rough silk of his hair. Rivulets of heat blazed downward to feed the fire in her privates. She had not known a man could kiss her in such a way, or that it could feel so heavenly.

Was this what he meant by better? Because she certainly wanted more of it . . . much more.

He hunkered down to unfasten her garters and peel

off her silk stockings. His touch stirred shivers over her skin. He kissed her knees and her thighs until she felt on the verge of swooning. With his face on level with the juncture of her thighs, she felt a hum of excitement sweep through her. He feathered his hand over the nest of fine hairs that protected her most private place. Yet he didn't quite touch the spot that wept for him.

"Lucas," she moaned in entreaty, bracing her hands on his broad shoulders to hold herself upright. "Please . . ."

At the first movement of his finger, she shuddered from an intense rush of delight. He fondled her lightly before venturing deeper into her sensitive folds. She ought to be embarrassed, yet she could not be. There was a fevered anticipation in her that she didn't quite understand. The sweet tension in her body pulled taut and compressed her lungs, making it difficult to breathe.

Then, in a shockingly intimate act, he slipped his finger inside and stroked her. That deep, soul-shattering caress wrested a cry from her lips. A burst of ecstasy radiated outward to convulse her body, and it was like nothing she had ever known, this tide of frenzied pleasure that held her enthralled and then gradually ebbed away, leaving her drained, dazed, and delighted.

She felt blissfully limp as Lucas swooped her up into his arms. "I want you in bed," he growled. "Now."

His guttural tone reminded her that this was far from over. He had not even joined their bodies yet. Floating in a sea of joy, she looped her arms around his neck and breathed deeply of his alluring masculine scent. "Mm."

He drew back the covers and laid her down against the pillows. Lightning flashed beyond the window, revealing the dark glitter of his eyes. Bending over her, he brushed a stirring kiss to her lips. "Happy?"

"Oh, Lucas. I didn't know such pleasure existed."

"There's more yet to come, darling."

Standing beside the bed, he shucked his trousers and kicked them away. She gloried at her first sight of a fully naked man. By the light of the fire, his member jutted long and thick, and her insides softened with readiness for him. He was flawlessly created, virile and masculine, the perfect complement to her womanhood.

The mattress dipped as he settled down beside her, molding her curves to the hot furnace of his body. She could feel the heaviness of his manhood burning against her thigh. Yet he didn't seek to satisfy his passions at once.

Instead, he held her in his arms and gently combed his fingers through the tangle of her hair. "Before we go any further, Rory, I want you to know something." His voice husky, he paused for the space of a heartbeat. "I want you to know that I love you."

She'd thought that the bodily pleasure he'd given her had been the ultimate bliss. Yet now, joy took wing inside her, showering her with feelings so powerful that tears sprang to her eyes. She reached out to cup his face in the palms of her hands. "Oh, Lucas. I love you, too. With all my heart."

A fierce sigh eddied from him. "Tonight, at least, you're mine. All mine."

"*Yes.*"

Their lips joined, his tongue stroking in and out, igniting that fiery river that channeled downward to the delta of her womanhood. This was true love's kiss, she realized hazily. This perfect paradise created by the two of them becoming one. It freed her to give herself to him with reckless abandon. She arched against Lucas, wanting desperately to absorb him into herself. He was too honorable a man to promise her more than he could give.

And since they couldn't have forever, she must wring every bit of happiness from this one night in his arms.

His big hand swept downward over her breasts and hips, following the shape of her curves, as if to imprint them on his memory. She relished the chance to explore him as well, the solid flesh of his chest, the corded muscles of his thighs and back. She pressed her lips to his throat where his pulse raced wildly. His skin tasted of salt and she inhaled the tempting scent that belonged to him alone. She knew that she would never again catch a whiff of pine or leather without yearning for him.

Or yearning for *this.*

He slid his hand between them to play with her again, teasing and stroking, encouraging a revival of that wonderfully enticing tension. With every particle of her being, she wanted to reach that pinnacle again, this time with Lucas there with her. When she moved her hips and moaned, he pressed her back against the linen sheets, his body descending over hers. She sighed at the sensation of his rougher skin gliding against her tender flesh. Everywhere he was hard, she was soft. They were made for each other, and she opened her legs in wanton invitation.

"Please, Lucas . . ." she whispered. "Love me."

"I do. For always."

On that fierce statement, he settled over her and she felt the exciting pressure of his thickness sliding inside her. A twinge of discomfort beset her, but only for a moment. When he was snugly sheathed in her depths, he went still, only his chest rising and falling with harsh breaths. He held tightly to her and gazed into her eyes. A distant flash of lightning revealed the tautness of wonder on his face.

"My God," he muttered, searching her face. "You were a virgin. I thought . . ."

"What everyone thought," she finished. "But you see, I never quite had the full enjoyment of being ruined until now." She moved her hips beneath him, relishing the sharp intake of his breath. "And I do enjoy it. Very much."

"Rory . . . I've dreamed of this. For so long."

He caught her mouth in a kiss that conveyed the force of his desire for her. His tongue stroked in and out, tightening the delicious coil of tension in her loins. *For so long.* She wondered hazily what he'd meant. They'd only become reacquainted this week, though at the moment she could not remember a time when she'd hadn't known him.

Then she was too enthralled to think about anything but the feel of him within her, linking their bodies into one being. As he kissed her, she felt him quiver as if he held his passions under strict control. But she didn't want restraint. She wanted the freedom of unbridled lust, the chance to follow these wild sensations wherever they might lead. Clinging to him, she undulated her hips to entice him along for the ride.

A groan rumbled from deep in his chest. He broke the contact of their lips to bury his face in her hair. She felt the touch of his tongue on the side of her neck as he began to drive inside her, moving in and out, in and out, creating a maddening friction that fed the gathering storm inside her.

Kissing and caressing, they rocked together in an ever more frantic rhythm. Her blood felt fevered, her heart beating with the same swift tempo as his. She tilted her head back against the pillows, arching up to meet his thrusts, her entire being focused on the place where their bodies were joined. His lunges became swifter, more frantic, and she felt on the verge of a precipice. Just as the tumult of their coupling became unbearable, the tempest within her broke, showering her with rapture.

Even before the bliss began to fade, Lucas gave one mighty thrust and then stiffened, groaning out her name in the throes of his own release. He melted on top of her while their breathing slowed and their pulses eased.

In the aftermath, Rory drifted in sleepy contentment. Her arms around him, she treasured the weight of his large body. The sound of the rain pattering against the windows underscored her happiness. If not for the storm, she wouldn't be nestled here in the warm cocoon of his arms.

So this was the joy of lovemaking, she thought hazily. This state of being in complete harmony with the man she loved. How was she ever going to live without him?

He didn't know how he would ever live without her.

As Lucas returned slowly to his senses, cold reality intruded on his lethargic contentment. He pushed the thought away. Tomorrow would be soon enough to face his duty. He was accustomed to taking charge, to solving problems, to making decisions. But this once, he would banish the outside world and savor the moment.

Soft and sated, Rory lay beneath him in all her naked glory. Inky strands of her hair spread across the pillows and clung to his sweat-dampened body. Her eyes were closed, her lips rosy from his kisses. His chest seized into an aching knot. He was the only one to have ever been inside her. It shouldn't matter, and yet it did. She was every man's dream of the perfect woman, beautiful, seductive, wanton.

And she loved him.

The fierce pleasure of hearing her say those words resonated in him. He felt shaken, as well. He hoped to God that she had been merely carried away by the moment, fancying herself in love in order to justify their lust. He himself had meant every word of his own declaration, yet the thought of subjecting her to heartache, too, caused a twist of pain in him.

Fearing to crush her, Lucas shifted position to lie on his side facing her. Rory made a mewling sound of protest and opened her lovely dark eyes. They were large and luminous, especially when she smiled, as she did now.

Lifting her hand to his face, she traced the outline of his lips. "So you're real," she murmured. "I was afraid this might all be just a marvelous dream."

He caught her finger and nipped lightly at it. "Then we're in it together."

"What did you mean when you said you'd dreamed of this for so long?"

He tenderly brushed back a lock of hair from her cheek. "Darling, I've loved you ever since the moment I first saw you, riding in Hyde Park. You were laughing, your eyes sparkling, the center of attention in a group of gentlemen. I was as besotted as them—perhaps even more so."

Her eyes widened. She pushed up against the pillows, propping herself on her elbow, her hair playing peek-a-boo with her bare breasts. "But . . . that was eight years ago."

He dragged his gaze from the allure of her bosom. A corner of his mouth lifted in a wry smile. "Indeed."

"I never imagined! You always glowered at me. And the one time you asked me to dance, you scarcely said a word—even though I *tried* to converse on everything from the weather to the crush of people in the ballroom."

He remembered her attempts to break him out of his shell. But he had been so keen on propriety that he hadn't allowed himself to pursue a girl who was so lively and vibrant. "I'm not an eloquent man."

"You seem to be doing quite well tonight." A wistful expression softened her face. " 'Beautiful inside and out.' Did you really mean that?"

"Absolutely."

She still looked doubtful . . . perhaps because of all she'd been through, tricked by Stefano, banished for eight years, treated as a pariah by her own family. Yet her remarkable spirit had remained unbroken.

"But I'm twenty-six and an old maid."

"I'm thirty-two. Does that make me ancient?"

"Men are considered distinguished as they grow older. But an unmarried woman is a spinster by one-and-twenty."

At the mention of marriage, their gazes met and held. The vulnerability in her eyes pierced Lucas in the chest. The future must not intrude for this one night. So he strove to distract her. "If you intend to write an essay on the matter, I believe you should change your *nom de plume*."

"Why do you dislike the name Miss Cellany?" she said in a huff.

"It's too tame. I much prefer Miss Behaving."

When she giggled at his jest, he tickled her belly for good measure. She squealed and squirmed, trying to get him back, and the conversation devolved into a gratifying tussle in the sheets for several minutes of breathless fun. He felt happier than he'd ever been in his life, especially when their shared teasing turned to carnal caresses.

Stroking the satiny skin of her bottom, he sealed their mouths with a warm kiss. Rory opened her lips on a sweet sigh, wrapping her arms around his neck. She tasted of heat and hedonism. Her breasts and hips writhed against him as if she could not get close enough to suit her. As he fondled her slim body, desire kindled in him again. It was too soon. She had already drained him dry. Nevertheless, he throbbed in a hot-blooded response.

As the rain diminished outside, he made love to her more slowly this time, honing her passions to a fever pitch. All that mattered was pleasure-seeking and fleshly indulgence. He found nothing in the least debauched about making love to the woman who owned his heart. With Rory, the act felt right and perfect. Their mutual love was a vow that bound them together.

He only wished it could be forever.

Chapter 25

A soft click lured Rory from a deep, dreamless sleep. She floated in a serene state midway between slumber and wakefulness. It was so very tempting to sink back down into heavenly oblivion. But a sensation of light tugged at her, drawing her upward into awareness.

She opened her eyes to the early morning sunshine streaming through the dormer window. Befuddled, she blinked at the low ceiling and the tiny, unfamiliar chamber. The bedclothes lay in disarray, the pillow beside hers bearing the impression of someone's head. The linens were still warm. Then the events of the previous night came surging back in a lovely rush.

Lucas caressing her, moving inside her, taking her to paradise. They had made love twice, the second time with beautiful and heartrending leisure. The last thing she remembered was him embracing her from behind, tucking her body into his as they'd fallen asleep together.

Where was he?

His satchel was missing from atop the dresser. Only her bandbox sat there, untouched. A soft click had awakened her. That must have been him closing the door.

She sat up in a panic. Had he left the inn without her?

Surely he wouldn't have done so after the spectacular night they'd shared. Or perhaps that was why he'd gone. Maybe he'd thought it best that they not see each other again.

Naked, she sprang out of bed, her toes curling against the cold floor. The chilly air restored her senses. She was panicking for nothing. He'd likely gone downstairs to see about the hitching of the horses. They would have to leave as soon as possible if they hoped to catch Celeste and Henry.

Dear God, how had her sister's plight slipped her mind so completely?

Feeling guilty, Rory quickly performed her ablutions, grateful for the pitcher of warm water on the washstand that Lucas must have fetched for her. As she ran the wet cloth between her legs, her skin felt tender and sensitive. Her scattered clothing on the floor brought a reminder of him undressing her. The tumbled linens on the bed made her yearn to lie there with him again.

But that was impossible.

A pang wrenched her heart. There was no time to linger dreamily, remembering all the ways he had loved her. They must hurry to get on the road and find Celeste before she made a terrible mistake.

Yet it seemed to take forever for Rory to dress, her hands straining behind her to fasten the buttons at the back of her gown. She brushed her tangled hair and secured it atop her head in a bun. Catching herself primping in front of the small mirror, she realized her own foolishness. She was trying to make herself beautiful for Lucas. But their one night together as husband and wife was over. They had both agreed to those terms.

Swallowing the lump in her throat, she jammed the straw bonnet onto her head and tied the green ribbons beneath her chin. She grabbed the bandbox and cloak and took one last look at the rumpled bed where she'd found such joy in Lucas's arms.

Then she stepped out and firmly closed the door. Going down the narrow staircase, she drew several deep breaths to compose herself. It wouldn't do to appear as woebegone as she felt inside. Or to fall at his feet in a puddle of weeping. She and Lucas were both adults, and she must make an effort to behave politely and pretend nothing had happened.

He was, after all, the Marquess of Dashell. He had a duty to marry well. A woman of her ruined reputation was only suitable for a dalliance.

She faltered to a stop at the base of the stairs. Lucas stepped out of an open doorway in the passageway, looking immaculate in his customary dark clothing. His eyes were a cool steel-gray, his features set in granite. Her heart died a little to see that mask back on his face. Against all reason, she had hoped for a smile at least.

Without speaking, he motioned her forward and stepped aside to allow her to enter. She found herself in a private parlor. An array of breakfast dishes held eggs and ham, toast and jam. It appeared several guests had eaten already. Just beyond the table, a young couple sat on a bench by the window. Rory's attention snapped to the blond girl.

Joyful shock energized her. Dropping her bandbox and cloak, she dashed across the small room. "Ce-Ce!"

Celeste jumped up, and the sisters came together in an exuberant embrace. Rory knew in that moment that she didn't care about bloodlines. Celeste would always be her dear sister. Tears blurred her eyes, and she squeezed them shut, her heart overflowing with happy relief. When she opened them again and drew back slightly, her gaze fell upon the young gentleman who sprang to his feet.

She blinked at his fair hair, the green eyes, the freckled features. "But . . . you're not Lord Henry. You're Perry Davenport."

He made a rather nervous bow. "Er . . . yes," he said, his voice squeaking a little. "Good morning, Miss Paxton."

Lucas strode forward to address Rory. "It seems your sister didn't run away with my brother, after all. Only a few minutes ago, I found these two rapscallions here eating breakfast."

Celeste slid her arm through Perry's. "Why would I run off with someone else when I love Perry? Lord Henry was only our messenger. He was very kind in helping us make our plans."

"You may be certain I shall have a talk with him about that," Lucas said darkly.

Rory stared at the young couple in befuddlement. Apparently, they too had spent the night at the inn. "But . . . I don't understand. The innkeeper said that no one fitting your description was here."

"He knew nothing of a brown-haired gentleman and a blond girl," Lucas explained. "Because, of course, Perry is sandy-haired, and Celeste was in disguise."

"I wore a black wig," Celeste said, pointing to the messy hairpiece lying on the bench. "It was Perry's idea. He found it in a costume trunk in his parents' attic. Wasn't it ever so clever of him?"

She gazed adoringly at the young man, and he gave her a soppily loving look in return. It was clear the two were mad about each other, and the sight tugged at Rory's heartstrings. Celeste looked so much happier than she'd been with the pompous old Duke of Whittingham.

"I trust you two secured separate chambers for the night," Lucas said.

The couple glanced guiltily at each other. Gulping,

Perry admitted, "I only had coin for one room. But nothing happened. I swear it on my life!"

"Perry slept on the floor by the hearth," Celeste asserted. "He was the perfect gentlemen."

Rory's gaze flew irresistibly to Lucas. *He* had not been the perfect gentleman, thank goodness. He was gazing intently at her, and heat flickered ever so briefly in his eyes. It told her that he, too, was remembering their wild tryst. A bone-deep pulse of longing assailed her. At least she would have that memory to cherish forever.

His gaze grew stern again as he looked at Perry. "Eloping is hardly the act of a gentleman. However honorably you behaved last night does not change that fact."

A blush made Perry's freckles stand out against his pale features. But he squared his shoulders. "Yes, my lord. I am aware of that. However, I believe it would have been *more* ungentlemanly of me to allow Ce-Ce to consign herself to a lifetime of misery."

His hands clasped behind his back, Lucas walked slowly back and forth in front of them. "And how do you mean to support her?"

"I've been studying the law at Oxford. I'll work after hours as a clerk in a barrister's office while I finish my schooling."

"And I will teach drawing lessons to young ladies," Celeste piped up. "Besides, there is my marriage portion of three thousand."

"Which your mother has every right to refuse to release," Lucas pointed out, "since you are underage and marrying without her consent."

Celeste turned her stricken gaze to Rory. "Do you truly think she'll do so?"

Rory doubted it. Kitty might threaten retribution, but

she would relent eventually, for she loved Celeste to pieces, the daughter of her torrid affair with Lucas's father. A pang resonated in Rory's heart. Celeste and Lucas were half siblings, though the girl didn't know it yet. And he was only doing what a good elder brother should do in making her see the ramifications of her actions.

"She was extremely distraught last night," Rory said. "Only imagine the worry you have put her through. I very much doubt she slept a wink."

Though Celeste's happy expression had dimmed, she stood firm. "I'm sorry to hurt her, but there was no other way. She'd never have allowed me to break the engagement. I would have been miserable married to the duke."

"Poverty can be miserable, too," Lucas said bluntly. "Especially when there are little ones to feed and clothe. You're both accustomed to luxury."

Perry put his arm around her. "I'm content to leave all that behind so long as Ce-Ce is my wife. I will come into a small legacy when I turn twenty-one next February. It isn't much, but it will tide us over until I become a solicitor."

Celeste snuggled against him, gazing adoringly into his eyes. "Dearest Perry, I shan't require fancy things so long as I have you."

Watching them coo at each other, Rory felt a melting softness. If only she and Lucas could be so happy.

His warm fingers closed around hers. She caught her breath and looked up to see him incline his head toward the doorway. Holding her hand, he drew her out into the corridor for a private conversation.

He bent closer to her, his gaze flitting to her lips. Rory hoped for one wild moment that he meant to kiss her. A wanton need for him flourished inside her even though guests could be seen at the end of the corridor, partaking of breakfast in the common room.

But he didn't draw her into his arms. He murmured for her ears alone, "What shall we tell them?"

His lordly mien reminded Rory that he valued duty above true love. "Tell them?" she whispered back. "Why, they must be allowed to marry. I forbid you to force Celeste to honor her betrothal to the duke!"

"You misunderstand me. I was inquiring about the secret of her birth. Is it wise even to mention it now, considering there is no longer any danger of brother and sister marrying?"

He was right. Everything had changed. They would have been obliged to reveal the sordid story to Celeste if she had run off with Henry.

"I don't suppose there is any pressing need for Ce-Ce to know just yet," Rory said slowly. "It might be best to return to London and discuss the matter with Kitty."

"That's what I was thinking, too."

He had not released her hand, and his thumb lightly rubbed her palm in a way that made her skin tingle and pulse leap. Their gazes clung, and his eyes were silvery hot with passion for a moment before he shuttered the look and dropped his hold on her.

He stepped back, once again the cool-faced marquess. "Perry's carriage damaged a wheel in the storm. It shall have to remain at the inn for repair. If it is agreeable to you, I'll drive the curricle back while you chaperone our young lovebirds on the mailcoach to London." He consulted his pocketwatch. "Can you be ready to depart in half an hour?"

"Certainly."

Her throat felt so taut she could barely utter that single word. So that was end of it. She wouldn't see him again, except perhaps in passing, for she could not possibly remain in his employ.

Not when he was marrying Alice Kipling.

Though her heart was breaking, Rory tried to summon a civil smile, but it wobbled on her lips. When she started to step past Lucas, he caught her by the waist and his fingers brushed a light caress over her cheek. "I'll call on you in London, Rory. If not later today, then tomorrow morning. I promise you that."

Releasing her, he strode away toward the common room. She watched until his tall figure vanished out the door. What was left for him to say to her?

The answer came in a dismaying flash.

He must mean to set aside his long-held scruples. He would marry his rich heiress and ask Rory to be his mistress.

Chapter 26

A spinster dons her cap as a badge of honor.
—MISS CELLANY

Late the next morning, Rory entered the drawing room to find Lady Milford seated on the rose-striped chaise. Rory had been in her bedchamber on the pretext of having a headache. It wasn't far from the truth. Despite the exhausting events of the prior two days and nights, she'd slept poorly. The last thing she wanted was to discuss the blackmail scheme with the dowager countess, which had to be the reason for the woman's unexpected visit.

Resplendent in a gown of lavender silk, Lady Milford patted the cushion beside her. "Good morning, Miss Paxton. Do have a seat here."

Rory stepped forward, though she declined to sit. "I'm afraid I'm not feeling well, my lady. I only came down to return these to you." She handed the woman the blue velvet bag containing the garnet dancing slippers. "I'll be returning to Norfolk very soon, so I won't be needing them anymore."

"Returning to Norfolk? Oh, please do sit down. I'm too old to crane my neck."

Rory reluctantly complied, arranging the skirt of her old blue gown. "I presume you've heard that Lord Dashell and I recovered the stolen letters. If you wish to know the details, you would do better to discuss the matter with my stepmother."

"I did learn that Mrs. Edgerton has become engaged to a certain foreign diplomat. Apparently, they will soon leave England to live in Italy."

"Yes. So you see, you were wrong to accuse Lucas— Lord Dashell—of the deed. He was entirely without fault in the matter."

"So it would seem."

"And you must cease spreading rumors that he lost his inheritance by making poor investments. His destitute state is entirely the fault of his father!"

Lady Milford gave her a keen stare. "Dashell has quite the fierce defender in you, Miss Paxton."

Heat sprang to Rory's cheeks. She realized she'd spoken sharply, her fists clenched in her lap. She had not meant to betray herself. "I don't like injustice," she explained rather lamely.

"I see. Will you remain in your post as Lady Dashell's companion?"

"Of course not. It was only temporary, for the sake of the investigation. Besides, my aunt is better suited to the role."

Rory's throat choked up a little at the thought of returning to Norfolk alone. The previous day, she had sent a note to Aunt Bernice at Dashell House, expressing a desire for them to go home to Halcyon Cottage. She had received a scribbled reply from her aunt, saying that she was having a marvelous time and wished to remain in London until the end of the season. She had even summoned Murdock to serve her there.

But Rory couldn't bear to stay. Not when she might read a notice of Lucas's betrothal in the newspapers soon. Possibly even by tomorrow.

She had returned here with Celeste and Perry the

previous day. Kitty had vacillated between hugging Celeste and scolding her. Perry had held up admirably before her reproaches. He had pleaded his case like an honorable gentleman, standing firm with Celeste until they'd convinced Kitty of the seriousness of their intent to marry.

Twenty-four hours had passed since then. Lucas had promised to call no later than this morning, and it was nearly noon already. Her insides ached with a hollow sense of loss. How pathetic of her to wait on pins and needles for him. He must be busy making up to Miss Kipling for neglecting her this week.

"I don't recall you wearing that spinster's cap the last time we met," Lady Milford observed.

Rory self-consciously touched the swath of lace draped over her upswept hair. She had occupied herself the previous evening by cutting and hemming the cap from an old fichu. The same fichu that Lucas had plucked from her bodice the day they'd gone to the pawnshop. "It's appropriate for a woman of six-and-twenty. After all, I am quite firmly on the shelf."

"Does Dashell agree with that?"

Her blush deepened until her whole face felt hot. Lady Milford's lips curved into a wise smile. As if she knew about the passionate night Rory and Lucas had shared at the inn. But that was impossible. The woman could not have heard about the elopement or even the broken betrothal, for the duke had not yet been told. The servants had been sworn to secrecy and the scandal kept under wraps until Whittingham arrived. Celeste had penned a note to the duke, begging him to call at his earliest convenience.

"Dashell? Why should *he* have any say in what I wear—"

Rory was interrupted by the sound of Grimshaw

clearing his throat in the doorway. She had been too dispirited to lecture him about his bastard son, yet his superior manner had given way to humility, nonetheless. "Lord Dashell to see you, Miss Paxton."

Lucas stepped into the doorway. Her lethargy vanished in a snap. Every fiber of her body sprang to life, and her heart slammed against her rib cage. She felt light-headed, unable to draw a breath into her beleaguered lungs.

His gaze went straight to Rory, and she drank him in as if he were a hot cup of tea on a cold day. He looked darkly handsome in a navy blue coat and charcoal-gray trousers, the white cravat at his throat complementing his masculine features. The granite hauteur was gone from his face today. He looked more approachable, especially with the faint smile that played at one corner of his mouth. It made her insides curl into an aching orb of desire.

Realizing she was gawking, Rory schooled her features into a polite mask. She had made up her mind to scorn the dishonorable offer that he'd come here to present.

He strolled into the drawing room. She sat tensely still as he came straight toward her. But instead of addressing Rory, he made his bow to Lady Milford. "My lady. I see that, as usual, you are spinning your web of intrigue."

Her violet eyes gleamed as she rose gracefully to her feet. "The question is, have you been caught, Dashell?"

"I certainly hope so!"

"Then I shall take my leave since my work here is done." Holding the blue velvet bag containing the garnet shoes, she smiled warmly at Rory. "Good day, Miss Paxton."

Rory watched in bemusement as the dowager countess glided away, pausing only to speak a word of greeting
to Kitty, who hovered behind Lucas. Rory hadn't even
noticed her stepmother's presence until that moment.

As Lady Milford disappeared out the door, Kitty
came bustling forward to give Lucas a toadying smile.
"I must thank you again, my lord. I can only imagine
how the tongues would have wagged without your help."

"It was nothing."

"Nothing! Why, you had to ride all the way to Newmarket! And then on to Wimbledon. And after you'd already been all night on the road during a storm! Celeste
and I owe you a tremendous debt."

"Newmarket?" Rory asked in confusion. "What do
you mean?"

"Never mind," Lucas said, looking distinctly uncom-
fortable. "There's no need to go into it now."

Kitty ignored him and addressed Rory. "Lord Dashell
offered to speak to Whittingham on Celeste's behalf. But
the duke went to the races yesterday and then to visit a
friend. Lord Dashell had to ride hither and yon just to
find the man. And he has convinced Whittingham to put
an announcement in the papers that the betrothal has
ended by mutual agreement. That means there will be
no scandal. Oh, perhaps a little talk, but at least no one
will know that Celeste threw him over to elope with another man."

"People will know when she marries him," Rory
pointed out.

"Not if a prudent amount of time has passed," Lucas
said. "Perry has agreed to wait until the autumn."

"Celeste will object to that!"

"Perry is speaking to her in the morning room at this
very moment," Kitty said, all aflutter. "Oh! I must go

chaperone them at once!" Looking remarkably cheerful despite having lost a ducal coronet for her daughter, she hastened out the door.

Rory's heart pounded as she found herself alone with Lucas. He was gazing at her with melting tenderness in his gray eyes. She wanted to despise him, yet he had gone out of his way to cover up the scandal. Why?

She threaded her fingers at her waist. "I suppose you felt compelled to help Ce-Ce since she's your half sister."

"You can't truly believe that was my primary purpose."

"What other reason could there be? By the by, Kitty has agreed to tell Ce-Ce about her true father. It's only fair that my sister should know she has two half brothers. You and Henry will wish to spend time with her."

He advanced on her. "I'm glad you still regard Celeste as your sister. Though I hope it will be true, anyway."

Rory retreated. The deviltry in his gaze distracted her so that she had trouble understanding him. "You're talking nonsense."

"Am I? I *did* tell you I was coming to speak to you today."

"Then you may save your breath. I shall not be your mistress!"

"I haven't asked you to be. Nor will I." He closed the distance between them in one long stride and took her into his arms. Then he eyed her quizzically. "By the way, why is that ugly doily on your head?"

"It's a cap. Dignified older ladies wear them."

"Spinsters, you mean." Pins went flying as he plucked off the square of lace and hurled it at the hearth, where the flames charred it. "You won't be needing it anymore."

"Lucas! I spent the better part of an hour hemming that last night!"

"My darling, for an intelligent woman, you're being remarkably obtuse. I came here today to ask you . . . to beg you to be my wife."

Her mouth dropped open. Her knees threatened to give way. Only the strength of his arms kept her from falling. Joy and incredulity swirled inside her heart. Through a cloud of burgeoning hope, she told herself he couldn't really intend to marry her. Yet the loving expression on his unguarded face spoke volumes.

He ran his fingertip over her lips. "It surely isn't possible that Miss Cellany is tongue-tied."

She found her voice. "You can't marry me. You need to marry Miss Kipling."

"I learned an important lesson from reading Miss Cellany's latest column. And again, yesterday, from my newfound half sister, who will soon be your sister-in-law. It's wrong to wed for anything less than true love. And I'd be miserable with such a peagoose as Alice. I much prefer a . . . how did you put it? A dignified older lady."

"But . . . the money . . . fifty thousand pounds . . ."

"I'll have to sell the London house and my two estates that aren't entailed. We'll cut back on luxuries and move to the country. Will you mind pinching pennies for a while, darling? Until my debts are paid off?"

"Oh, Lucas. I'm used to being poor. It's nothing new to me."

"Then will you kindly cease torturing me?" Reaching into his coat, he drew out a dainty diamond ring. "This is only an old family heirloom, but will you wear it, Rory? Will you be my wife?"

"Yes! Oh, yes!"

Blissful tears flooded her eyes as he slid the ring onto her finger. Then his mouth engulfed hers in an ardent kiss. As they clung to each other, a glow of happiness infused her. Melding her life with his was a dream come true, far better than anything she could ever have imagined.

She angled her head back. "But Lucas, are *you* sure? Lady Milford once told me that you wish to seek higher office. What if my secret identity comes out? I won't give up my radical writings!"

He nuzzled her cheek, his breath tickling her skin. "I would never ask you to do so. I love you as Miss Cellany. And as Jewel. And as Miss Rory Paxton. They're all part of who you are. There's only one thing I'd change."

"I *knew* there had to be a catch."

He chuckled. "It's only your surname that needs altering. Will you like being Rory Vale, the Marchioness of Dashell?"

Over his shoulder, she held out her hand to admire the ring that sparkled on her finger. "Oh, Lucas," she said on a happy sigh. "Of course. And the sooner the better. *We* will not wait until autumn!"

"Mm. A quiet ceremony can be arranged, perhaps in a few days . . ."

She took his face in her hands. "Wait, I nearly forgot. Kitty promised me a thousand pounds if I found the letters. It isn't much, but I will squeeze the money out of her somehow!"

"Why, you little scamp, not telling me there was a reward."

Grinning, he bent to kiss her, but their mouths had barely touched when the sound of voices emanated from the corridor. Rory drew back, though Lucas kept his arm around her waist as they turned to see the newcomers.

Aunt Bernice wheeled Lady Dashell into the drawing room. Murdock shuffled behind them with his usual half-drunken gait. The marchioness was complaining to Bernice, "That manservant of yours nearly stumbled while carrying me upstairs. I vow, the help these days is atrocious!"

Lucas walked Rory forward, then bent to peck his mother on the cheek. "Speaking of servants, Mama, you're about to lose one. Your companion is going to become your daughter-in-law."

Bernice gasped, rushing forward to envelop Rory in her cushioned embrace. "Well, fathom that! Are you truly in love, dear girl?"

"With all my heart, Auntie. I can't imagine loving any man more than I do Lucas." She smiled up at him, and he smiled back with such warmth that her heart skipped a beat.

"Blimey, that calls for a toast," Murdock declared. "I'll fetch us a jug o' rum." Turning, he lurched out of the drawing room.

"So you're to make me the dowager." Lady Dashell jammed the pince-nez onto her nose while peering up from her invalid's chair. There was actually a hint of fondness on her wrinkled features. "Well, better you than that namby-pamby heiress. Though I don't suppose you have a penny to your name. We'll all be moving into the poorhouse, no doubt."

"We shall manage, Mama," Lucas said firmly.

"You'll do more than manage," Bernice declared. "Was it not fifty thousand you were to have from that other chit? I shall be happy to match it."

Rory blinked at her aunt. "What?"

"During our travels on his merchant ship, my Ollie had a knack for making canny investments. Furs and lumber in Canada, gemstones in Brazil, gold mines in Africa. I put the proceeds in the Exchange all these years and it has paid off quite handsomely."

"Auntie, that can't be true! Why, you've lived as a pauper in that little stone cottage!"

Bernice shrugged. "I'm a woman of simple needs. I've been saving it for you, dearie. I'm sure I can provide something for Celeste, as well. I only wanted to be certain you were marrying for true love."

Rory could scarcely absorb the shock of it all. In a daze, she gave her skinflint aunt a big hug and then returned to Lucas's side to cling weakly to him for support. He looked as stunned as she felt. "It *is* true love," she said, smiling up at him. "I could not be more certain of that."

"Nor could I." Despite their audience, he pressed a heartfelt kiss to her lips. "There is no greater treasure in the world than love."